THE OBRENOVICH DYNASTY

OBREN MARTINOVICH and VISNJA

MILOSH OBRENOVICH
(1780–1860)
(Leader of 1815 uprising,
Supreme Prince of Serbia in
1817, recognized Hereditary
Prince of Serbia in 1830,
dethroned in 1838,
reinstated in 1859)

YOVAN
(1768–?)

YEVREM
(1790–?)

PRINCE MILAN
(?–1839)

PRINCE MICHAEL
(1823–1868)
(Elected Prince of
Serbia in 1858,
assassinated in
1868)

MILOSH

NATALIE KECHKO
(1859–?)
(Married in
1875,
divorced in
1888)

MILAN
(1854–1901)
(Prince of Serbia
from 1868,
King from 1882,
abdicated in 1889)

ALEXANDER, KING OF SERBIA
(1876–1903)
Married to
DRAGA LUNYEVITZA-MASHIN

Dance of the Assassins

M. FAGYAS

Dance
of the Assassins

G. P. Putnam's Sons, New York

SBN: 399-11118-2

Library of Congress Catalog Card Number: 72-97291

PRINTED IN THE UNITED STATES OF AMERICA

The author wishes to acknowledge her gratitude to Marcia Magill, her editor on four novels, who has given her unwavering encouragement and her manuscripts painstaking care.

Fagyas

FOR LACI

Dance of the Assassins

6 A.M.

HE stepped from the cavelike coolness of the station into the wide, sunlit square with its rippled sidewalk and cobblestoned roadbed torturous to feet and cartwheels, feeling bewildered and almost panicky as though he had got off the train at the wrong stop. It had been the same each time he returned after a long stay abroad, hoping always in vain to find the primitive drabness of the home scene if not attractive at least bearable. He knew that after a day or two his sight would become adjusted to the colors and dimensions of the town and his uneasiness give way to the simple contentment of belonging. With the family, especially the women, making a fuss over him, he would soon fit into the niche kept reserved for him during his long absences. The family, like a voluminous eiderdown smelling of lavender, slivovitz and sex, would eventually envelop him in its protective cocoon.

In Geneva the week before, the weather had been crisp and clear with just the hint of June in the air. In Vienna, where he had stopped over for a day, the sudden mildness brought swarms of people to the public parks. With hardly a bench left unoccupied, young and old, their faces turned to the sun as though taking part in a secret ceremony, sat in endless rows like migratory birds resting on telegraph wires.

Here in Belgrade, the rays beating down in the square seemed to come from a different celestial body, not Vienna's charitable sun, but a savage enemy bent on scorched-earth warfare.

9

Tilting back his head, he allowed the sun to hit his face full strength. His wintry pallor clearly marked him as a new arrival in town. Should the day end contrary to his expectations, he would make a ghastly corpse, he thought with a silent chuckle. People who had never laid eyes on him would have no trouble sorting him out from his tanned and swarthy comrades.

To keep his arrival a secret, he had written asking his father not to send a carriage. He expected the request to puzzle the old man. On the other hand, postcards bearing Lausanne and Vevey postmarks ought to have enlightened the family about his reasons for lingering in Geneva. He hoped that King Alexander's secret police were less adept in reading between the lines.

Up to now, he had been lucky, for there had been only strangers on the train. He had spotted a few familiar faces on the station platform, but by remaining a few minutes longer in his compartment, he had succeeded in avoiding them. Now glancing about the square, he recognized his former orderly, guarding a squad of prisoners assigned to roadwork. Some good-natured banter, colored with obscenities, was exchanged by the corporal and his charges, the jingle of the prisoners' fetters providing musical accompaniment. Fortunately, the guard wasn't looking Michael's way. It seemed unlikely, though, that he would have recognized Michael Vassilovich in his Swiss-made suit and green Tyrolean hat.

He had bought the hat in Vienna for the purpose of hiding his identity under it. He had hardly left the store when he realized his error. No headgear could have been more incongruous with his long-limbed leanness and sharply etched profile. Older women often told him that with his widow's peak and softly curling dark hair, he resembled Sir Henry Irving in *Hamlet*. His short and thickset fellow Belgraders mistook him for a Montenegrin, although as far as he knew, his ancestors had been Serbs from the province of Shumadiya. Michael was a maverick even in his own family. In the entire dark-eyed Vassilovich tribe, his eyes alone were the color of pale aquamarine.

As usual, a line of hacks awaited passengers in front of the station, the coachmen eyeing the thin trickle of arrivals with bored detachment. The contrast between the throbbing excitement of Western railroad stations and the Asian leisure of Bel-

grade's never failed to amaze him, for Serbian porters and cabbies acted as though they considered a call for their services a
humiliating intrusion upon their privacy.

Since his luggage consisted only of an overnight case, the rest
to be dispatched a few days later from Geneva, he pondered
whether to walk or take a cab. Until the day before, when he
had met a reporter from the *Neue Freie Presse* in the Meissl &
Schaden restaurant in Vienna, he had been convinced of the
absolute secrecy of his mission. Now there were doubts.

He had breakfasted with Milosh Nenadovich. The reporter
had stopped at their table and, despite Milosh's best efforts to
ward him off, lingered, expecting introductions.

"Captain Michael Vassilovich, Herr Max Schwarz" was all
Milosh said, yet the reporter's thick-lidded eyes focused with
searching intensity on Michael's face.

"Vacationing in Vienna, Captain?" he asked.

"Just passing through," Milosh answered for his guest.

"On your way home?"

Michael nodded.

The reporter forged on. "From Paris?"

"Geneva," Michael answered, automatically realizing his
blunder even before the reporter could flash a knowing grin at
him. "So it won't be long now?"

Michael threw a puzzled glance at Milosh and found him
staring noncommittally at Emperor Franz Josef's picture on
the wall.

"What won't be long now, Herr Schwarz?" Michael asked,
hoping to have misunderstood the reporter.

The young man moved his hand across his neck, in the un-
mistakable gesture of throat cutting. "For the king and queen,"
he said, chuckling.

"I don't know what you are talking about," Michael
snapped, feeling the beginnings of nervous perspiration trickle
from his armpits. Milosh still seemed miles away. The reporter
sniffed as though struck by the odor of Michael's sweat-soaked
shirt.

He lowered his voice. "You ought to know, coming from
Geneva. Frankly, everyone expected it to happen last Palm
Sunday." There was a pause. Finally realizing that no seat was

to be offered him, he executed a mock salute. "Glad to have met you, Captain. My best wishes to their majesties." Unceremoniously, he patted Milosh on the shoulder. "I expect to hear from you. Remember, you reap where you sow. And your man will need all the help he can get from us press boys." With this, he sauntered over to a table at the far end of the room occupied by a famous actor.

Michael turned to Nenadovich. "There must have been a leak."

The older man shrugged. "Don't pay any attention to him. He was merely fishing for information. That's how reporters operate."

"He knows."

"Not a damn thing. Of course, there have been rumors. It's no secret that the people at home are getting tired of Alexander and his old mare. But that's all Herr Schwarz knows."

"Is he a friend of yours?"

"Hell, no. But you've got to cater to the press here. You can get hurt if you don't. The papers, especially his, represent real power. That's what the lack of censorship does to a country. Freedom of the press. Damned nuisance."

It was an odd remark, Michael thought, coming from a man who was taking part in a conspiracy to unseat a monarch because of his unconstitutional rule.

"I shouldn't have mentioned Geneva," Michael admitted.

"True. But it can't be helped now. He'll put two and two together and try to find out who you are and what you were doing in Switzerland. By the time he does the whole thing will be over. So forget it. Anyway, it's too late to call it off." He glanced around and caught a waiter's eye. "Let's get out of here. It would be damned stupid if I let you miss your train."

Milosh Nenadovich's unconcern reassured Michael. He knew that the man had a great deal to lose, probably his whole livelihood, should the conspiracy fail. A few years before, Milosh, an aging and penniless émigré, had arrived in Vienna, then had suddenly become a popular member of the Balkan set with a seemingly inexhaustible bank account at his disposal. His enemies whispered that he had sold himself to the Asian Division of the Russian Secret Service, as well as the Austro-Hungarian monarchy's Ministry of Foreign Affairs. His lifestyle appeared much too lavish to be sustained by the espionage funds of only one country. The message he sent with Michael to Belgrade seemed to corroborate the rumor. According to his information, he had told Michael, neither Russia nor the monarchy would officially condone the *coup d'état*, yet both powers promised to abstain from interference should it really take place.

"I've had several conferences with the head of the Austrian State Security Bureau. Only yesterday he hinted that Foreign Minister Count Goluchowski has become exasperated with Alexander's antics. The ultimate offense, it seems, was Queen Draga's shameless request to be received by Emperor Franz Josef. They are a strange breed, these old Viennese aristocrats. Willing to overlook whoring, perfidy, and corruption, but not social climbing."

Another odd observation coming from a notorious social climber, Michael thought, expecting to detect a glimmer of self-mocking humor in the steel-gray eyes, but there was none.

On the station platform, a few minutes before the departure of the Belgrade train, a deliberately casual remark dropped by Nenadovich caused Michael to wish he had never become involved in the plot. They had been discussing France's refusal to grant another loan to Serbia, when Nenadovich, his fish-cold glance focused on Michael's face, stopped in the middle of a sentence.

"Incidentally, there's something I wanted to ask you. Is it true that you once had an affair with Queen Draga?"

Michael frowned. "I fail to see the connection," he said coldly.

"What connection?"

"I thought we were discussing the French loan."

Nenadovich's laugh was shrill. "Oh, but there *is* a connection. We wouldn't need the loan if we weren't bankrupt, and we wouldn't be bankrupt if Draga hadn't stashed away three million francs in her Swiss bank." No longer laughing, he glared at the young man. "Well, did you or didn't you?"

"Did I what?"

"Sleep with her?"

"You should've asked me that question before involving

me in this—this thing. What if I said yes? Would you shoot me dead here on the station platform? Or have someone else do it in Belgrade? Because how can you tell for certain that I haven't turned informer? I may have, right after our first meeting a year ago."

"You're not answering my question."

"No. And I never will. Because I consider it irrelevant and in bad taste. I might—"

He wanted to say that he might take the matter up with Milosh after the coup but was cut short by the conductor's whistle. Once again, Nenadovich was all bonhomie, patting him on the back. "Forget it, and good luck." Then, after a pause, which contrived a touch of solemnity, he added, "God bless you, my boy." His hand raised to Michael's face, his fingers traced the sign of the cross on his forehead. Then he embraced him, planting warm, brotherly kisses on both cheeks.

The hiring of the last free cab by an oily man, most likely a pig buyer from Hungary, left Michael no choice but to walk to the Officers' Club, a half mile away. For safety's sake, he chose to detour through a narrow alley lined with wooden huts, cow-sheds and the forbidding, faceless dwellings of the few Mussulmen who still lingered in Belgrade, twenty-five years after Serbia's liberation from Turkey.

At one point, the path ran past the backyard of the cottage where Draga Mashin had lived before moving to the elegant town house on Crown Street to be established as King Alexander's official mistress. Michael could not resist the temptation to peek over the fence at the weed-invested lawn and, beyond it, the rickety veranda, where on summer nights Draga and he had made love.

Reluctant to believe his eyes, he stared at the ruins of what six years before had represented paradise to him. Torn shutters, broken windowpanes and, behind them, the ransacked rooms testified to the work of busy looters. Even some of the tile had been carted off the roof, exposing the rooms to the whims of the elements. A valiant little acacia tree had sprouted, its rickety branches reaching skyward through the still-sturdy rafters, from between the decayed hardwood flooring of Draga's former boudoir.

The sight jolted him badly, bringing back the memory of the winter night when, furious at Draga's desertion, he had smashed the cottage's furniture, a rampage so alien to his nature that he had never ceased to be ashamed.

Disturbed by the resurrection of long-buried emotions, he marveled at the macabre quirk of fate that had chosen him to be the precursor of his ex-mistress' downfall.

Up to now the events of the past weeks had left him little time to think. Before joining the conspiracy, he had—after thorough soul-searching—resolved that the bitterness of a jilted lover failed to influence his decision. He wished Alexander and Draga dethroned because their reign had proven harmful for his country. He convinced himself that his mistress of six years before and the present queen were not one and the same person. His Draga had been sweet and gentle, while the queen had the reputation of being a greedy and reckless bitch. To save himself from a possibly painful reappraisal of his attitude toward her, he had come to Belgrade firmly resolved to avoid any personal contact with her.

As Michael turned into the street leading to the Officers' Club, at the spot where it skirted the grounds of Belgrade University, an infantry squad, led by a lieutenant, emerged from behind the dense shrubbery. Having the day before observed an Austrian regiment march down the Ring in Vienna, Michael was filled with a mixture of rage and shame at the sight of the Serbian soldiers, their ill-fitting tunics left unbuttoned over bare chests, their feet shod in red leather opankï with straps wound around their pantalooned legs. Once again he was deeply aware of the stark backwardness of his country. Stuffing a horde of fiercely independent guerrillas into blue serge trimmed with green, had evidently failed to turn them into an army. With their handmade footwear resembling children's booties, they looked hopelessly Balkan. Queen Draga's money in the Swiss bank could have bestowed a professional sheen on the standing force of eighteen thousand men: new boots, up-to-date arms and some financial security instead of the on-and-off trickle of pay they were forced to exist on.

As the squad passed him, Michael noticed the lieutenant's searching look. The possibility of the plot's having been detected or the conspirators betrayed crossed his mind. In Vienna, Nenadovich had shown him Colonel Mashin's reassuring letter, yet that had been written days before and much could have happened since. Even Mashin admitted that the command of the Morava Division, stationed in Nish, had remained steadfastly loyal to the king. He had described the chasm as a minor annoyance to be bridged over after the coup. Out of touch with the home scene, Michael had accepted Colonel Mashin's optimism as sound, but now he wondered if he weren't walking into a trap. He glanced at his heavy gold watch, his father's gift after his graduation from the War College, and saw that he was already ten minutes late for the rendezvous. Since any deviation from the tight schedule for the day could jeopardize the coup, he dismissed his apprehensions and quickened his pace.

He had not been inside the barnlike building of the club for three years and lost his bearings in the vaulted corridor with doors leading to wine cellars, kitchen, storage rooms and orderlies' quarters. When he asked a soldier for directions, the man gave him a long, suspicious look. To Michael his eyes resembled lenses snapping an indelible photograph of the stranger in the green Tyrolean hat.

He knocked on the door indicated. His entrance caused the eight officers, ranking from colonel to second lieutenants, and the one civilian to freeze into a *tableau vivant*. For a split second their faces reflected his own anxieties and doubts. The first to rise was Captain Dragutin Dimitriyevich, nicknamed Apis for his bull-like good looks.

"At last!" The big man greeted Michael with an exuberant hug. His hot breath, reeking of tobacco and schnapps, felt like the exhaust from a ship's engine on Michael's face.

The civilian with thinning salt-and-pepper hair, ferociously waxed mustache and short beard, Michael recognized as Colonel Alexander Mashin, Queen Draga's ex-brother-in-law, who, after Draga's marriage to King Alexander had suddenly been placed on the retirement list, forbidden even to wear a uniform. Michael knew him to be, no doubt because of his Czech descent, one of the few well-educated officers of the Serbian army, a European in the true sense of the word. His diabolic hatred for Draga, his brother Svetozar's widow, so inconsistent with his urbanity, was like an ugly crack in a marble monument to a hero.

The rest of the officers were strangers to Michael, at least so they seemed at first sight. Young or mature, they were of the same breed: stocky and muscular, with eyes like small, black pinheads, complexions like tanned cowhide and sharp, defiant noses. Most wore the dark blue trimmed with green infantry tunics of King Alexander's own Seventh Regiment, stationed in town; one lieutenant wore the light-blue uniform with the yellow braiding of the guards. Michael later learned that he was Peter Zivkovich, who would be on duty at the guardhouse of the Old Konak later that night. Despite their uniforms, the men failed to make a truly military impression on Michael, for he suspected underwear of questionable cleanliness and holes in their socks. There lingered a whiff of horse manure and perspiration mixed with the odor of patchouli about them. Descendants of peasants, small burghers and outlaws, they nevertheless formed the elite of a newborn country clamoring for admittance to Western civilization.

"What is the good word?" Colonel Mashin asked. "Is Prince Peter ready and willing?"

Michael took a deep breath. "He is. But he wants no bloodshed."

Mashin frowned. "That we understand. But will he ascend the throne even in the unforeseen case we have to resort to"— he hesitated for a moment—"to more drastic measures?"

Michael felt nine pairs of eyes watching him with fierce intensity. If he answered no, he knew the drama planned for nightfall would be postponed until another applicant for Serbia's shaky throne was found. Whether or not it was Nikita, ruling Prince of Montenegro, his son Danilo or some other princeling, descendant of a bona fide royal house, willing to swap his Protestant or Catholic faith for the Orthodox Church of Serbia, the rehearsal would continue with the same cast; only the opening night would be changed. The heart of the matter was not the question of who was to take over, but who had become disposable.

Finding the pause too long, Mashin exploded. "Damn it, Captain. We could've done it two weeks ago at the circus. The king and the woman decided to attend on the spur of the moment. They thought they were safe. We were notified they would be there. One sharpshooter could have finished them both. But we haven't heard from Prince Peter yet, and without a new king acceptable to the people an interregnum would have given the Austro-Hungarian monarchy a welcome excuse to occupy us. You have now discussed the matter with Prince Peter. What exactly is his attitude?"

"I've told you. He wants a peaceful transition. A coup d'état without violence. But in my opinion"—Michael repeated the phrase—"in my opinion—he will accept in any case. Only because he is aware of his responsibility. He knows that his refusal would plunge Serbia into a revolution."

There was complete silence; then one of the lieutenants emitted a scream, an ear-shattering animal cry that brought to Michael's mind the 1885 massacre of Bulgarian women and children by blood-crazed Serb guerrillas, a scene he had witnessed in horror. Now more voices joined in, men jumping to their feet, embracing and kissing one another in an orgy of comradely love. Their obstreperous outbreak caused Michael to wonder momentarily about the virtue of their cause. The king was a bastard and the queen a whore, but weren't they the rulers these savages deserved? He looked at Colonel Mashin, the only one to avoid the Laocoon group writhing in the coils of passionate patriotism, and found him watching the scene with the detachment of a researcher trying out the effect of a new drug on a cageful of rats. A few or perhaps all of the exuberant young men might be dead by daybreak, Michael thought, but Colonel Mashin would escape unscathed, no matter what. There was something solid and indestructible about the man which both reassured and antagonized Michael. Plots hatched by his breed had to be successful, regardless of the high cost to foe and friend.

At last, Mashin decided to put an end to the delirium. "Calm down, Damn it. Want to bring the security police down on us?" When the shouting subsided, he turned to Michael.

"What do you base your opinion on?"

Michael felt a sudden fatigue. The long voyage, the two sleepless nights, one spent in talks with Nenadovich's friends in a smoke-filled hotel room in Vienna, the second sitting up in the train, had drained him of his vitality. Despite his doctor's assurance that he had been completely cured, he now felt less fit, mentally or physically, than during his worst fever-plagued days. Existence in a sanatorium for tuberculars had resembled retirement in a Carthusian monastery, complete isolation, detachment, chastity and meditation, neither life nor death, but a long stretched-out transition between the two. Michael had often wondered how Lazarus had managed to adjust to the petty vexations of everyday existence after the dank but peaceful depths of the grave.

"I had several long talks with Prince Peter," he told Mashin, trying to put impressions that seemed even to him ambiguous into clear and decisive language, "and despite the difference in our ages, we understood each other. He accepted me for a friend, well, almost a friend. Some people find him cold and reserved, but that's not true. He is no average Serb—how could he be, not having set foot on Serbian soil since boyhood?—yet he has kept a close watch on the conditions here. When I asked him why he himself hadn't instigated an uprising against King Alexander, he said he hadn't thought it necessary. 'I knew that sooner or later Alexander Obrenovich would commit the final blunder that would finish him without my lifting a finger. I'd only have to wait.' These were his very words."

"Wait? How long was he planning to wait?" Apis burst out. "He is fifty-nine. If you ask me, I personally don't like a reluctant pretender. Sitting safely in Geneva, refusing to become involved."

Mashin threw him a reprimanding look. "He won't have to wait another day. So let's not digress. Go on, Captain."

"There isn't much to add," Michael told them. "Except that Prince Peter's insistence on a bloodless coup is also politically motivated. He feels that in this new century European civilization has reached the stage where wanton assassinations are unacceptable, what is more, revolting. Peter is willing to be king, but only if he can turn Serbia into a European country."

"What the devil does he think Serbia is?" Apis Dimitriyevich flared. "African?"

"No. Asian," Michael snapped. Fatigue was making him irritable. "If you ask a hundred Frenchmen what they know about Serbia, a few will tell you it is a Turkish province and the rest that they've never heard of it. The prince doesn't want his ascension to the throne preceded by regicide. He thinks it would be the wrong way to make the world aware of Serbia. And if—"

"Good God, Michael," Apis cut in. "Haven't there been assassinations in the West? Empress Elisabeth, Czar Alexander II, President Carnot of France? Even in America! Lincoln, McKinley, not to mention all the attempts that failed."

"Oh, but they were different. Perpetrated by anarchists, and lunatics, not members of the officers' corps. How will Prince Peter ever convince the world that there is no blood on his hands if you—"

"What the hell is he so squeamish about?" a lieutenant shouted. "Blood on their hands never bothered the princes of Serbia before. Certainly not his kind, the Karageorgeviches."

"Exactly. That's why he is different. And that's why you want him, or do you? You have a king now who is not a bit squeamish, who has the stomach and the conscience of an alligator. Why don't you keep him?"

Apis emitted an obscenity that came from his lips in intricate curlicues like smoke from a pipe. Silent resentment emanated from the rest of the men. Their iciness caused Michael's skin to tingle. Colonel Mashin alone seemed to preserve his friendly composure.

"We shall offer King Alexander the choice between a peaceful abdication and a bullet in the gut. It will be up to him to decide which. He is a smart boy. Once he sees that the cards are stacked against him, he'll get the hell out of the country, taking his whore with him. No, Prince Peter needn't worry. We'll make the coup as clean and respectable as a garden party at Windsor Castle."

Because the windows were closed, the air was beginning to feel unpleasantly heavy. No one commented on the colonel's little speech; the expressions on the men's faces merely darkened a few shades. Michael wondered if it wouldn't be advisable for him to drop the subject. Still, there was one thing he must discuss because it was part of the message from Geneva.

"Prince Peter is even more deeply concerned about the queen's fate than the king's," he began, but was rudely cut short by the lieutenant of the Guards.

"What queen? That cheap, ten-franc whore? Ten francs, that's what her fee was in Paris. Any bloke with a ten-franc note could fuck her. And now every ministry in Serbia is run by her pimps. The cabinet is nothing but a front without power. Laza Petrovich controls the military advancement list at the Ministry of Defense. Mata Boshkovich, though only a department head, decides about foreign policy and named his father minister to France, although the old man was hopelessly senile and wet his pants at President Loubet's New Year reception for the diplomatic corps. So Prince Peter is afraid to lose face if, God forbid, the damned bitch is harmed? Tell him that we have no face left to lose. Not since she became Queen of Serbia!"

An infantry lieutenant stepped up to Michael. "What about her brothers, the Lunyevitza bastards? The day after the new elections, that little shit Nikodiye went to the Kolaratz restaurant and demanded that the orchestra play the national anthem and everyone stand up, honoring him because the new Skupshtina was going to declare him heir to the throne. And this isn't mere gossip, because I was there. It is common knowledge that the elections were rigged so the new parliament would carry out the whore's orders. And if we fail tonight, she is going to make her brothers princes and that dog Nikodiye will be king one day. Yes, Captain, officers with long and honorable service records had to stand at attention because the little shit ordered them to. They did stand, but there was murder in their eyes. They were damn close to reaching for their swords and hacking him to pieces, and then going straight to the Konak and staging the bloodiest massacre this city has ever seen."

The officer had a shrill, unpleasant voice that grated on Michael's nerves. After a moment's silence, as though on second thought, the man turned to Colonel Mashin. "Sir," he said in a strange, solemn tone, "would you, in recognition of my services to the cause, appoint me executioner of the Lunyevitza brothers?"

Mashin, not at all shocked, a trifle pensive, looked at him as though the answer required serious consideration on his part. "Well, we'll see about that. Haven't reached that stage yet." For the first time during the meeting, he seemed uneasy.

"But you won't forget me, will you, sir? I mean when the time comes."

"If the time comes, Tankossich," the colonel corrected him, a touch of impatience in his tone. "If worse comes to worse."

Michael had listened to the exchange with growing concern. More and more, the men resembled a hunting party: spirits high, beaters hired, guns oiled, ammunition sorted. He feared that nothing short of an earthquake or forest fire would keep them from engaging in their favorite sport. How was he to impress upon them that Prince Peter was serious in his wish for a bloodless transition, that he was no conventional pretender, probably no pretender at all? An expatriate since his fifteenth year, the product of France's École Militaire de St-Cyr, a Geneva resident for nearly two decades, he had made a respectable living as a bookkeeper in a small hotel and later as a translator of legal documents. An intelligent and basically lonely man, frugal, not only because of poverty but by nature, he had long reconciled himself to the quiet existence of a Swiss bourgeois. During recent years, he received a modest appanage from the Russian Ministry of Foreign Affairs, the reason for this being Russia's intent to keep Alexander Obrenovich in line by holding Peter Karageorgevich as a threat over his head. At the same time, Peter's sons, George and Alexander, had been appointed pages to the czar's court. The prince accepted the Russian goodwill because it provided his children with a more comfortable life and a better education. When the news of the conspiracy reached him, his response had not been overly enthusiastic. Nevertheless, he recognized the historical inevitability of a coup. When Michael delivered to him the conspirators' offer of the throne, he had listened pensively, arching his eyebrows as if hearing a vaguely familiar melody the lyrics of which he was unable to remember.

"To become king at fifty-nine?" he mused. "At the age of completions and not of beginnings? Couldn't the young fool in the Konak have plied his trade a bit more cautiously, held on five or ten years longer, giving me time to grow too old for the job? I wish I could ignore the summons, yet evidently men born to the House of Karageorgevich aren't destined to be buried in Swiss cemeteries. God is my witness, I have for years hoped to be spared this adventure. My dear young man, don't your friends know that by the time I learn the king business I'll be too senile to practice it?"

"Anything else, Captain?" Mashin's sharp voice recalled Michael to the present.

"No, Colonel, that sums it up."

Mashin rose as did a few of the younger men. If they had

been officers in Franz Josef's army, Michael knew, they all
would be on their feet now. In a classless society, however,
respect was accorded only to age, not to rank.

"We'd better get moving," Mashin told them. "There's still a
great deal to be done."

"Is there anything you want me to do, sir?" Michael asked.

Mashin gave him a long look. "Keep your mouth shut in case
you are arrested. You just dropped in here on your way home
to see a few old comrades."

"Do you expect me to be arrested?"

Mashin turned on him one of the stares from ice-gray eyes
that had scared his young recruits out of their wits. "You've
been abroad, haven't you? In Geneva, too, of all places. Your
passport was checked at the border, wasn't it? Don't think your
arrival hasn't been reported to Secret Police Chief Marshityanin, and he is one of Draga's creations." He paused for a
second. "Be at the fortress at noon. The Sixth Infantry is having a Slava celebration. A number of our men will be there, a
few from country garrisons. We'll be able to discuss some last-
minute details. Provided we're still at liberty by then."

"I am sure we will be, sir."

Another stare from the ice-gray eyes. "Don't be so sure, Captain Vassilovich."

7 A.M.

ENTERING the home compound was like
taking a huge backward step from the twentieth century into
the eighteenth. Michael's first reaction was the same as at the
station: shock and disbelief.

The Vassilovich homestead, outside the southern city limits,
sprawled over several acres of sloping grounds and consisted of
a rambling main house and more than a dozen cottages, re-

mainders of the times when the clan, eighty-odd men, women and children, had formed a zadruga, a family community with Michael's late grandfather as its leader. The old man had died in 1878, a year also remembered for Serbia's obtaining full independence after five hundred years of Turkish rule. Following that, a desire for modernization began first to undermine, then to eliminate old institutions and customs. There had been desertions in the Vassilovich zadruga even during Michael's grandfather's declining years. Two sons and a first cousin had left, taking their families with them, but enough new babies were born and new sons- and daughters-in-law added to fill their places.

For children like Michael, his brothers, sisters and cousins, growing up within that closely knit community had been sheer paradise. Offspring of Western-European parents—no matter how well cared for—never enjoyed the security of zadruga children. When crossing the parks and playgrounds of Western cities, Michael couldn't help feeling pity for the clean-scrubbed, well-dressed little boys and girls who, like cattle put out to pasture, played their polite games under the watchful eyes of dutiful, but bored, mothers and nannies. Thinking back to the first years of his life, he often wondered at what age he had become aware of who of the many loving adults were his parents and which cottage was his house. Possessive pronouns like "mine" or "yours" or "ours" had no meaning to him; children curled up near the hearth, where sleep overtook them, and were fed by the woman who happened to be cook that day. Tears of baby hurts were kissed away, scratches and abrasions bandaged promptly and expertly, because there were always enough willing and eager hands to do it.

The property of the Vassilovich zadruga had consisted of several thousand acres: pastures, forests and fields cleared for planting or left to lie fallow after a few years' rich yield. Herds of cattle, swine and children would erupt from the buildings at daybreak, roam the country in Saturnalian freedom to return only when in need of food and shelter. Despite the seeming lack of restraint, life had its unbreakable rhythm with grandfather Ljubomir the *staresina*, the chief, and his word the law. It was the power of his personality that held the Vassilovich clan together years after the dissolution of most Serbian communes. In

1840, the year he had been elected to rule the clan, Belgrade had consisted of a few dozen European-style stone buildings, the rest wooden hovels, delapidated mosques, Turkish army barracks and, beyond them, a ring of ill-smelling marshes hiding both human and animal predators.

Young Michael had been the old man's favorite, frequently taken on patriotic pilgrimages to the sites of long-past skirmishes between Turks and freedom fighters that at times had ended in Serbian victories but more often in tragic defeats. In 1804 Grandfather Vassilovich as a boy had been witness to the slow and torturous execution of Christians impaled on stakes, infants thrown into boiling water in mock baptismal ceremonies, women violated while bleeding to death from horrible mutilations. The walls of Belgrade Fortress were adorned with the chopped-off heads of seventy-two Serbian patriots, and the entire population of Shumadiya Province was either killed or fled to the woods.

What amazed Michael in retrospect had been the dispassionate tone of his grandfather's remembrances, as though he had considered the atrocities, as gruesome as they had been, part of the normal law enforcement procedure of an occupying power.

If the Turks had been diabolic oppressors, the Serb freedom fighters who had risen against them were their equals in savagery. Legendary Black George, also known as Karageorge, leader of the first organized and—for a time—successful revolt against the Janizaries, a body of Turkish infantry that had subjected Serbia to a veritable reign of terror, had possessed the courage, as well as the bloodthirstiness, of a tiger. A giant of a man, he had punished the slightest transgression against his code of morals with death meted out, at least in one hundred and twenty-five cases, by his own hands. Not even members of his own family were safe from his murderous rages. Having found his brother guilty of rape, Black George hanged the boy from the eaves of the family home. When, following his initial successes against the Janizaries, he committed the error of attacking the sultan's regular army units, such a miscalculation leading ultimately to the rout of his own forces, he lovingly shot his old father between the eyes to spare him from falling into the hands of the pursuing enemy. Then, leaving his men to shift for themselves, he quickly fled to Austria.

The bloodcurdling reprisals inflicted upon Serbia by the vengeful Turks prompted one of Karageorgevich's rivals, the equally illiterate pig breeder Milosh Obrenovich, to rekindle in his countrymen the will to fight for their freedom. Just as fearless as Black George, but shrewder and more cautious, he restricted himself, while repeatedly declaring his loyalty to the Sublime Porte, to skirmishes with the irregular Turkish units that had harassed and pillaged the defenseless Serbian peasantry.

Milosh's tactics and shrewd diplomacy had paid off. On December 4, 1815, he was appointed Knez, hereditary Prince, of the Pashalik Serbia. In addition, his domain was granted a semblance of autonomy by Sultan Mahmud II.

Despite his Christian contempt for his Mussulman masters, Milosh Obrenovich was more an Eastern potentate than a European prince. Rebellion against his authority was punished by death on the wheel, common theft by the loss of the thief's right hand and minor misdemeanors by vicious canings, some of his drastic measures remaining in force long after his death.

Milosh had been the wise founder of modern Serbia, as well as its worst tyrant. When a rebellion staged by his long-suffering subjects forced him to abdicate, first his elder son, Milan, then his second son, Michael, acceded to the throne. Each reigned for a short spell, as the Skupshtina, the assembly of Serbian notables, having suddenly tired of the Obrenoviches, called upon Karageorge's son, Alexander, to replace Michael.

Fifteen years later, the Skupshtina, playing musical chairs, exiled Alexander and brought back Michael Obrenovich, who, during his second term, proved to be the most gifted and enlightened ruler ever to occupy Serbia's throne. His reign ended, in true Balkan manner, in his assassination by Karageorgevich partisans.

The assassins, however, failed to achieve their goal. Instead of the hoped-for Karageorgevich restoration, fifteen-year-old Milan Obrenovich, Prince Michael's nephew, was elected Prince of Serbia by acclamation.

During the eighty years of rivalry between the two houses, the Vassilovich family had steadfastly sided with the Obrenoviches. In 1808, in a purge staged by Black George, a Vassilovich great-uncle had paid with his head for the tribe's loyalty.

On the other hand, in 1817, when it was Black George's turn to lose his head in order for it to be sent as a peace offering to Sultan Mahmud II, the delivery of the unique gift was entrusted by Milosh to another Vassilovich, Michael's great-grandfather.

In politics, the Vassiloviches had faithfully followed the Obrenovich preferences, swinging, like the pendulum of a clockwork, from right to left and left to right, from radical to liberal, from Russophilism to Russophobism. Prior to 1900, their loyalty had never wavered; then, suddenly, they were confronted with the dilemma of having to choose between *two* Obrenoviches, the forty-seven-year-old ex-King Milan and the twenty-four-year-old reigning King Alexander. The young king's decision to marry his mistress, Draga Mashin, finally led to his irreparable break with his father.

Without doubt, Milan had proved to be the most fascinating personality ever to rule Serbia. The son of a Moldavian mother and the grandson of Milosh Obrenovich's brother, Yevrem, he had been reared in the Bucharest house of his mother's lover, the Rumanian Prince Cuza.

A wild, neglected little boy, he was plucked from anonymity after Prince Michael's assassination. With a three-man regency guiding the affairs of state, he was sent to France for an education befitting his new identity. There he grew into a brilliant, though somewhat willful and capricious young man. Coming of age, he took over the government of his fiercely independent and restive nation and married Natalie Kechko, the fabulously beautiful daughter of a rich Crimean boyar. After thirteen years of marital hell, their differences caused partly by Milan's morals and partly by his politics, the couple divorced in 1888, an act which failed to put an end to the hostilities between them. Natalie was passionately Russophile, while Milan had believed in a close association with the Austro-Hungarian monarchy. The intrigues of her Russian friends in high places remained—during his entire reign—a constant source of frustration and bitterness to him.

Michael Vassilovich had been more than a partisan to Milan. As his aide-de-camp and friend, he accompanied him on his travels abroad, later sharing his exile and finally keeping vigil at his lonely deathbed in a Johannesgasse apartment in Vienna.

His love for Milan had been the kind of masculine passion that—like a rare plant—was indigenous only to the rugged and long-tormented Balkans, where a deep and satisfying affection, free of the slightest taint of homosexuality, could easily develop between two men.

What caused Michael's affection to be more than a young man's admiration for his king was the gratitude he felt toward Milan for having saved his life.

When, in his mid-twenties, Michael had suddenly been stricken with tuberculosis, his loving father, one of the richest men in Serbia, had refused to recognize the seriousness of the illness. No son of his would ever languish in bed like a palsied old man because of a touch of fever, was Yovan Vassilovich's reaction. For a cure, he suggested a regimen of vigorous exercise, rich food and a liter of a certain red wine from Cyprus, known for its restorative powers, with every meal. When told about this, Milan exploded. Unable to convince Yovan that his son would be a corpse before his thirtieth year if he followed such primitive therapy, he simply dispatched Michael to a Swiss sanatorium and paid the bill from his own pocket.

Despite his devotion to King Milan, Michael had been fully aware of the man's faults. A steady visitor to the gambling casinos of the Côte d'Azur, the racetrack of Deauville and the exclusive bordellos of Paris, Milan loved cards, horses and women and had the embarrassing habit of buying his pleasures with the taxpayers' money. This, oddly enough, had been, for a long time, good-naturedly tolerated by his subjects. If he had not emptied the treasury, they reasoned, his ministers would have, spending the dinars just as fast as he, but without his grace and elegance.

Like all men who lived successfully by their wits, Milan knew how far to venture without running serious risks. On March 6, 1889, he abdicated in favor of his then thirteen-year-old son, Alexander. His decision took the country by surprise. His enemies rejoiced, but not his people. Virile and handsome, Milan looked like a king even after he had formally ceased to be one. He never completely lost the affection of his people, probably because he never wore a pince-nez like his son and never rewarded his mistress with the crown of Serbia.

While Milan was alive, it would have been unthinkable for

Michael to join the partisans of a Karageorgevich pretender. It was Milan himself, the next-to-last Obrenovich, who—a week before his death—entrusted Michael with the delicate mission of getting in touch with Prince Peter in Geneva and feeling him out about his reaction to a *coup d'état* aimed at the dethronement of Alexander.

Two and a half years had since passed, and what had been a vague notion then was reality now. The meeting at the Officer's Club, however, raised painful doubts in Michael's mind. Demented young army men, thirsting for blood, a country on the brink of revolution, regiments marching against one small woman shielded from their bullets solely by the whalebones of her corset. Was this what Milan had wanted?

Michael entered through the creaking gate and found the Vassilovich front yard empty, the sultry heat of the morning evidently having driven the household indoors. He knew the compound was far from deserted, though. The stables still held horses and cattle, not to mention the overstocked pigpens and the number of uncles, aunts and elderly cousins, some bed-ridden, others still sprightly, living out their allotted time in what had been their honeymoon *vayats*. No Vassilovich kin would go without food or shelter as long as the manor house remained standing or one sack of flour was left in the larder.

On entering the house, Michael was literally swept off his feet by an onslaught of love. Half a dozen females fell upon him like a troupe of savage maenads, showering kisses on his cheeks, shoulders and hands. The commotion brought his mother to the room, and the troupe deferentially stepped aside. She, too, pressed her lips first to his cheeks, then to his right shoulder and finally to his hand while a young niece knelt down before him to untie his shoelaces and exchange his boots for a pair of opanki.

In his grandfather's time the main house had been one of the most impressive buildings in Serbia. Now, after the palaces of the West, it appeared primitive and crude to Michael, though not without a certain robust charm. The front room consisted of whitewashed walls, heavy oak beams, a long table with two dozen chairs, a row of unmatched cupboards and—in one corner

—an enormous Hungarian-style tile stove with a bench built around it. The furniture was partly homemade, partly imported, bought in one of the Jewish-owned stores in Teraziya. The huge kitchen spread to the right; to the left lay a long porch used—weather permitting—for skinning rabbits, sewing clothes, delousing and bathing children and entertaining guests.

Smoking his long-stemmed meerschaum pipe and reading the latest issue of the *Odjek,* the radical daily, Michael's father was seated in an old leather armchair on the porch. The paper was held at a distance of two yards from his eyes by Ljubica, his youngest daughter-in-law. At seventy-seven, he still insisted on reading without glasses. The last three years had added a few lines to his already-furrowed face but had left his big frame as straight and solid as ever. With a wave of his hand, he dismissed Ljubica and, hoisting himself up from the soft depths of the broken-springed chair, enclosed his son in the bear hug of his embrace.

"When is it going to be?" was his first question.

Caught off guard, Michael stared at him, suddenly disturbed. His father knew he had been in Geneva, but nothing of his contact with Prince Peter Karageorgevich. Michael had considered it safer to restrict his correspondence with the family to reports on the weather or his own health since King Alexander's censors never slept.

The realization that his father, long retired from politics, knew that the coup was imminent, added to Michael's inner confusion.

"Who told you about it?" he asked.

"You don't have to be told. It's in the air. *They* know it, too; Alexander and the woman. What puzzles me is why they go on provoking the country. The last elections, for instance. Did he really think the people would accept such clumsily doctored returns? When two out of three voters are radicals, a conservative victory is inconceivable. Yet that's what the official results showed. Whom did he try to fool? Us or himself? As for the woman, she is sucking the country dry. The spoils, that's all she cares about. She is negotiating now with some Brussels bankers to open a gambling casino in Toptcider. There's talk about a diamond necklace wrapped in a check from a foreign entrepreneur for the concession to build new railroad lines. And to top it all: her madness in wanting her brother Nikodiye declared heir to the throne!"

Ljubica came from the house carrying a towel and a water pitcher. "Your mother has breakfast for you in the kitchen," she told Michael.

Descending the steps from porch to yard, Michael stopped at the crude gutter running downhill and held out his hands for Ljubica to pour water over them. His father had adamantly resisted indoor plumbing, considering it a foul invention that would allow adults to defecate in the house, thereby contaminating it with stench and poison. Even washing in a washbowl was considered unsanitary by him. The water lost its purity the moment one's dirty hands were dipped in it. Summer and winter, the men of the family bathed in the open in water, cold as it came from the well, poured on them from buckets. Women alone took their ablutions indoors, more for reasons of modesty than convenience.

An entire meal was laid out on the large kitchen table. The family, after an eyeopener of Turkish coffee and slivovitz at daybreak, had breakfasted at six, but his mother insisted that Michael eat a few bites to keep up his strength until the midday meal. She heaped an assortment of cheeses, heavily spiced pork sausage, bacon and smoked meat on his plate. His father joined him for a cup of strong Turkish coffee, brewed by Ljubica. Being the youngest daughter-in-law, the duty of waiting on the old man fell to her. He kept her busy all day and often at night, but her tasks were lighter than some of the other members'. Household help was against the principles of a man as conservative as old Vassilovich; besides, servants were a luxury, imported from Hungary or Austria. Michael always had difficulty explaining this aspect of Serbian life to his Western friends— namely, that Serbs weren't fit to be servants. Slaughtered, robbed, tortured, exploited by an alien race, during their five hundred years of occupation they had remained like wolves in a zoo, untrainable, forever refusing to be domesticated. No reward could ever turn them into house dogs. The periodic extermination of their upper class by the Turks had fused them, in good or bad luck, in defeat or victory, into one classless mass of equals. Serfdom, the common lot of the Continent's peasantry, was unknown to them. Conditioned to an existence of hardship and frugality, few Serbs felt inclined to exchange their independence for the security of regular wages.

The heavy food and glasses of his father's special *klekovacha*, a plum brandy distilled with juniper, made Michael sleepy. To keep himself awake, he decided to tour the grounds and visit the elderly Vassilovich relatives, who, like all peasants, dreaded hospitals and, bedded under heaps of eiderdown in their *vayats*, waited out their end in the bosom of their family. After seeing a great-aunt and an uncle in their dank hut where the air, heavy with the stench of death, made him nauseated, he postponed calling on the rest, fleeing, instead, to the plum orchard and dropping on a bench in front of the last *vayat*.

He had been sitting quietly for some time before it dawned upon him that this was the same *vayat* his father had once offered to Draga after the death of her first husband, the Czech engineer, Svetozar Mashin. Closing his eyes, he could remember her clearly outlined against the dark curtain of his eyelids as she had appeared to him on the day of their first meeting.

He had just arrived home for the Christmas holidays from the Military Academy and had eaten his breakfast in the kitchen warmed by the enormous wood-burning stove. The door to the yard had opened and a girl came in, dressed in mourning, the thin wool of her blouse threadbare at the elbows, her skirt bespattered with the mud she had had to wade through. The black dress made her look even skinnier than she really was. Because he was used to the solidly built Serbian women, as broad-beamed and muscular as the ugly and indefatigable little horses of their country, her slimness had seemed almost ethereal to young Michael. Shivering, she handed a small mug of milk to his mother, asking to have it heated for her cat. The *vayats* boasted neither stoves nor fireplaces, and people less hardy than the Serbs would have considered them uninhabitable during the cruel winter months. Invited by his mother, she settled down on the bench built around the stove. When his mother handed her the warmed milk, she forgot what she had said about the cat, lifted it to her lips, sipping it slowly and with relish as if it were nectar and not goat's milk. When offered a *pogacha*, she took the small round cake with the unself-conscious grace of a pigeon picking up breadcrumbs in the park and chatted with a cheerfulness unbefitting her black garb. Her gaiety seemed infectious, for even his usually stern mother responded to it with frequent laughter. It was during that long-ago meeting that he first became aware of her disarming warmth. She could look at the gruffest stranger with the soft, trusting eyes of a puppy that had never been kicked by a boot. Even after her short-lived marriage to Svetozar Mashin, an aging and vicious alcoholic, her smile had still radiated an infinite belief in the goodness of men.

Michael never learned what prompted his father to offer her, not even a distant relative, one of the *vayats*. She had stayed one whole winter, taking her meals three times a day at the long family table, invariably choosing a chair at the far end among the children, as if, despite her eighteen years and widowhood, she failed to consider herself a full-fledged adult. Otherwise neither shy nor humble, she could hold her own with any of the grown-ups, exchanging quick repartee even with Michael's not easily amused father. It was inevitable for Michael, on the threshold of manhood, to fall in love with her. She yielded to his advances with an eagerness that both delighted and disturbed him. She wasn't the first woman in his life; his brother Voyislav had arranged for his initiation in sex at the best brothel in Zimony when he reached thirteen, yet before meeting Draga, he had slept only with prostitutes or semiprofessionals, like the cashier at the Serbian Crown Café or the Levantine wife of a rug dealer, believing that for respectable women lovemaking was a joyless obligation to satisfy their husbands and conceive children. His affair with Draga had changed all that. With her, sex gained new dimensions, became elevated from a carnal act to a rite of love and mutual gratification. For a woman of eighteen, widowed after only a year of marriage, she proved to be an expert at giving and receiving pleasure, which, however, was not her sole attraction. Her mind was as different from the average Serb woman's as her delicate, small-boned body. She possessed an immense curiosity about the world that lay beyond Belgrade and an unfeminine thirst for knowledge. Her petit bourgeois father had been unable to give his four daughters and three sons a decent education, so she eagerly picked up bits of information wherever she could. During their quiet moments together, as they hud-

dled under the heavy eiderdown, their sole protection from the
damp chill of the unheated *vayat*, she amused Michael by con-
jugating irregular French verbs or memorizing the names of
foreign capitals. Her dreams were of travels abroad, leaving
Serbia and poverty behind. From what little she was willing to
reveal about her marriage, Michael gathered that it had been a
nightmare. She had married to flee the wretchedness of her
father's home and found more of the same with Svetozar
Mashin. After her husband's death, her brother-in-law Alexander—at that time Major Mashin—considered it his God-given
prerogative to take command of her life, forcing her to move
into his household, a servant without pay. When Draga tried to
rebel, he kept her in line with threats to report certain suspicious circumstances of her husband's death to the police. In
those days he had been King Milan's friend, influential enough
to cause her serious trouble. After he had asserted a claim to her
personal services as well, she had fled his house. At least, this
was what she told Michael. Between her departure from Major
Mashin's house and moving to the Vassilovich compound, there
had been a hiatus of several months which she refused to account for to Michael.

Toward the end of that winter, she disappeared at times for
days, driving Michael mad with jealousy. Allowed home from
the academy only on Sundays, he learned of her absences
after some thorough detective work since no one in the family
considered them worth mentioning. With twenty-odd people at
the dinner table each day, one missing person was hardly noticed. Then, one spring Sunday, he discovered her gone for
good. Her two sheets, two pillows, two changes of underwear,
one eiderdown, three dresses, several jars of face powder, one
comb, one brush and one tabby cat—all her earthly possessions
—had disappeared with her. When with tears in his eyes, unbecoming a cadet, he asked his mother for an explanation, she
merely shrugged. Draga had left without saying good-bye. He
had turned the *vayat* upside down, hoping for a message, but
there was none.

Weeks later the Vassiloviches learned that Draga had gone to
Shabats with a rich pig breeder. That summer Michael was
graduated from the academy and entered the army with the
rank of second lieutenant. A liaison with a Greek actress soon

faded Draga's face to a colorless blur in his memory, with only her lovely green eyes shining through the mist of time like two precious stones.

If there was any hurt left in Michael, he refused to admit it even to himself. One never brooded over women, was his philosophy, for they weren't worth it. He fought in the Serbo-Bulgarian War, was decorated for bravery by Milan and later, when peace returned, appointed his equerry. Around that time, Draga suddenly reappeared in Belgrade, of all places, at the Konak, as Queen Natalie's protégée. The queen, supposedly deeply attached to Draga, had surprised many with the liaison, though not Michael. If Draga had been able to charm his dour mother, anyone else, including the spoiled, fiery queen, had to be an easy conquest.

Belgrade was abuzz that spring with rumors of friction between Milan and Natalie. Belonging to two enemy camps at the Konak, Michael to Milan's and Draga to Natalie's, there was little chance for them to meet. Not yet officially appointed to the queen's court, Draga never appeared at state functions and kept to her patroness' private apartments to which Michael had no access.,

On one occasion, however, they happened to find themselves face to face in the palace vestibule. Taken by surprise, Draga flashed him a timid smile, which rapidly wilted under the heat of his angry, reproachful scowl. Analyzing his own reaction later, he had to admit to himself that as far as she was concerned, he still had a long way to go to reach the restful plateau of indifference.

Soon after the encounter, the revengeful Natalie left Serbia to engage in a campaign of defamation against her husband. Raised to the status of lady-in-waiting, Draga accompanied the queen in travels that took her through most of Europe to cities, the names of which Draga had so diligently memorized between flurries of lovemaking in the Vassilovich *vayat*. Later Michael also heard that she had become, most likely under the influence of the queen, the paragon of refinement and culture, favorite of old duchesses and countesses and pen pal to such distinguished men of letters as Pierre Loti and Paul Bourget.

After the royal divorce, the two women settled in a villa the queen had built in Biarritz. Michael, too, spent the ensuing years in Western Europe with the, by then, ex-King Milan, developing under his tutelage into a sophisticated cosmopolite. The combination of his good-natured wit and Slav handsomeness attracted the women to him in droves. If he ever thought of Draga, it was with the detachment of the mature man recalling the tender follies of his youth. She had been his first love, the heroine of an interlude which he had no reason to regret, but never intended to relive. At least not until the grim February day in 1897, when he ran into her in Paris, on the Rue de Poissy.

Thirteen years had passed since their nights on the hard, rustling straw sack of the *vayat*, and Michael was no longer a sex-starved adolescent, but a man in his early thirties, sophisticated and, as he prided himself, blasé. He had survived a severe attack of tuberculosis, coming to Paris after a six-month stay in Menton, to join the ex-King Milan. Despite the beastly weather, the change from a sleepy resort town where one's fever chart was the most important topic of the day to glorious Paris filled him with an elation that bordered on recklessness. With all promises of restraint made to the good Dr. Audoly of Menton forgotten, he drank, danced, stayed up late and took long walks in the rain. Even the reflection of city lights on the wet pavement—the streetlights having been parceled out with bold theatricality as though Paris were a vast stage set—exhilarated him. He was like a boy on vacation from boarding school. He had been in Paris before, but not with Milan Obrenovich. Asian potentate, *arbiter elegantiarum, bon vivant* and art connoisseur of faultless taste, Milan was the perfect guide to introduce a young man to the best of this special city: its women, art or food. Though tinged with a touch of regret over finding in another man's son the traits he had so sadly missed in his own, Milan's affection for Michael had over the years turned from the approval of a commandant into an almost paternal love.

Life was a series of happy adventures. In the mornings, Michael would accompany the ex-king to art dealers. His enemies saw in Milan's predilection for such black sheep of the art world as Paul Cézanne and Vincent Van Gogh, the same *épater les bourgeois* attitude as in his spectacular bets at racetracks and his friendships with high-priced courtesans. Michael knew him better than to accept the verdict. Milan was truly intrigued by the black sheep, found betting on outsiders more thrilling than on favorites and considered the witty girls of the demi-monde better company than prim duchesses.

On the afternoon Michael unexpectedly encountered Draga on the Rue de Poissy, he was on his way to an amusing young lady's where he would join Milan for five o'clock tea. The four o'clock lovemaking that preceded the tea the ex-king preferred to indulge in without his aide-de-camp.

Wearing a weather-beaten tweed coat, the leather of her shoes caked with mud and her hat looking as though it had borne the brunt of a typhoon, Draga Mashin seemed much too bedraggled to be the darling of French aristocracy and *dame d'honneur* to a queen, albeit a Balkan queen. The feather trim on her hat—two drooping, rain-soaked wings held together by the small glass-eyed head of a dove—suggested defeat. No woman with an ounce of pride would have appeared in public in that hat. What startled Michael most was the hunger to be seen on her face. Not emaciating hunger, but bloating hunger; the rings under the eyes and the pasty skin that a diet of potato dumplings might produce.

He had almost passed her when her half-pleading, half-demanding gaze, like a barrier lowered in his path, brought him to a sudden halt. He stared at her, his lips moving, but no sound leaving them. When he finally addressed her, it was in French as if, in his perplexity, he had forgotten that they possessed a language in common.

"Is that really you, Draga?" he asked, her self-mocking smile causing him to wish he had not.

"Hard to believe, isn't it?"

"Heavens, no—you look—you haven't changed a bit."

Amused, she shook her head. "Liar."

He felt that she was waiting for a word from him to bridge the years of their separation, but his mind went blank, producing, after a long wait, the lame: "What are you doing in Paris?"

The self-mocking smile reappeared. "Enjoying the climate. I'm on leave of absence from Queen Natalie's court. Permanent absence, to be exact."

"How long will you be staying?"

She shrugged. "It depends."

"Depends on what?"

"Among other things—" she began, then halted. "A long story. Much too complicated."

Despite her chatty tone, tinged with false gaiety, he knew she was depressed, probably desperate.

"What about you?" she went on. "You look marvelous. Where on earth did you acquire that deep tan?"

"Menton."

"Oh." Her expression intimated that she guessed the reason for his stay there. "Will you be going back?"

"Not if I can help it."

A brisk gust of wind blew the rain against their faces. "Must we stand here and get soaked to the skin?" she asked. "If you have five minutes, I'll let you invite me for a brandy. There is a nice little bar around the corner."

He pulled out his watch and glanced at it. "I'd love to, but I'm afraid I'm late for my—"

Her face reddened, and she cut him short. "Never mind. I just thought— But I understand." She turned to walk away, but he took hold of her arm and pulled her back.

"No, you don't understand," he shouted in a burst of sudden, unwarranted anger. He should have passed her without stopping, he told himself. The old, presumably well-healed wound began to sting like a fresh burn. "I happen to be on my way to the Quai d'Orléans to meet King Milan. You know he doesn't like to be kept waiting. But I want to see you. Where are you staying?"

She named a hotel he had never heard of on the Boulevard St.-Germain.

"I'll look you up as soon as I have a free moment. My days very much depend on the king's schedule."

She smiled, and for a moment, it seemed as though they were thirteen years younger. She proffered her hand. Taking it, he was surprised to find how icy cold it felt through the thin cotton glove.

He went to see her two days later. It took him half an hour to find the hotel, which was not on the Boulevard St.-Germain, but in one of the narrow side streets. Her room on the third floor, above a dark stairway, though not dark enough to hide its filth, was even more depressing than the rest of the building: a bed without the modesty of a spread, walls decorated with fingerprints, a small mirror over a pockmarked commode, a wardrobe with its unhinged doors at half-mast, a washstand and the inevitable bidet hidden by a tattered curtain. The air lay heavy with the smell of warmed-over food and the smoke from a potbellied stove.

She wore a Japanese kimono of rich red silk, beautifully hand-embroidered, with each medallion depicting a different landscape, and nothing, not even a chemise, under it. Red, Michael acknowledged, was her best color, emphasizing the ivory paleness of her skin and the green of her eyes. Her bare feet were stuck into a pair of frayed evening slippers. Her hair, in two loose braids, reached to her waist. She had answered Michael's knock with a cheerful *"Entrez,"* but stared at him in utter surprise when he entered.

"Oh, it is you." Her tone made him unsure of his welcome. Then immediately, her face brightened with the duty smile of the well-mannered hostess. "How kind of you to come."

She took his coat and cap and hung them on the large rusty nail in the wall which served as a rack.

Pointing to the single chair, she settled on the bed. "Please, sit down. Not very elegant, is it?"

"What happened? What made you leave Biarritz? Queen Natalie?"

She winced as though in pain. "I'd rather not talk about that. The queen has a very volatile temper, to put it mildly. I remained with her nine years, which, believe me, was an unparalleled achievement."

"But why come here? Why not go home?"

"Home?" Her eyes grew wide with anger. "Where to? To Colonel Mashin's house? He hates me like the plague. Tells every one that I poisoned his brother. To my father in the insane asylum? My sister Maria who is rearing not only her own children, but Voyka, Georgina, Nikodiye and Nicola? Up to now she's been able to make ends meet because I sent her seventy pounds sterling a year. I don't know what she will do now."

"But what about you?"

"I have a ninety-franc widow's pension. Monthly. Not much.

Each time the coffers of the Serbian State Treasury become deflated, which is quite often, widows' pensions aren't paid."

"But the queen! You spent nine years with her. She can't just—"

She cut him short. "I've told you, we won't talk about that."

He wondered how to offer her money without offending her. "What are your plans?"

She shrugged. "I never make plans. I just take what comes."

Exasperated with her apathy, he raised his voice. "But you can't possibly stay here!"

She looked about as though seeing the room for the first time. "Why? Is this so bad?"

There was a knock on the door. As though stung by an invisible whip, she leaped to the door and quickly turned the key in the lock. Only then did she ask, "Who is it?"

A hoarse male voice rasped in French, and the doorknob rattled. "It's me, Jurieux. What the hell did you lock the damn door for?"

She became strangely agitated. "Some other time, Monsieur Jurieux, I'm afraid I can't see you today."

"Why not?"

"I don't feel well—I—"

The caller refused to give up. "There's a man with you."

"I've told you I don't feel good. Please, go away."

Jurieux banged on the door. "Let me in, you bitch! Let me in, or I'll break your goddamn door down."

Michael, listening in petrified silence, now started for the door.

Draga barred his way. "Don't. The concierge will get rid of him."

As though on cue, someone came tramping up the stairway. After a loud exchange of insults and a scuffle, the intruder was dragged away by an evidently superior force. The noise of commotion descended like a bucket lowered on a clanking chain into a well.

"You'd better go now, too," Draga said when quiet returned.

"What did that man want?"

She turned away, indicating that the audience was terminated. "Never mind that. Just go."

The hollow desperation of her tone, more pathetic than a

flood of tears, caused him to step to her and cautiously, as if afraid that she would fall to pieces like a cracked vase, take her in his arms. "I cannot leave you in this hovel. Let me find a decent place for you."

She freed herself. "No, thank you. This isn't the Ritz, but it'll have to do for me. At least, for a while."

He reached for his wallet and pulled out two hundred-franc notes, dropping them on the commode.

She glared at him. "Take that back! I don't want King Milan to hear that I accepted charity from one of his flunkies."

Now he understood the hostility that, like last autumn's growth under a blanket of snow, had lain beneath her forced friendliness. For reasons not clear to him, a feud of many years had existed between King Milan and Draga Mashin. Court gossip had offered several explanations: he had made advances to her but was rebuffed, she had made advances and was rebuffed by him, Natalie's infatuation with her had caused the final breakup of the royal marriage. All theories that were elaborated on in penny dreadfuls about the court of Serbia.

Michael picked up the banknotes and stuffed them into his pocket. There was a limit to every good Samaritan's benevolence.

"I am not in the habit of discussing my private affairs with the king. Anyway, you seem to consider Monsieur Jurieux's money less distasteful than mine." Jerking his coat and cap from the nail, he started angrily for the door.

She barred his way. "Please, don't go. I know, you meant well. You're not like them—like Milan and Natalie. It's so dreadful what they've done to me. I always knew Milan was evil, but I trusted Natalie. Nine years—for nine years I was a slave to her— Had she asked for my life, I would have given it to her. Anything to please her. Though, God knows, that villa of hers was no Garden of Eden. There's more freedom and gaiety in a convent. At least, convents don't have tigresses going through menopause for mothers superior."

"What made you stay for nine years?"

"I don't know. Weakness, laziness or plain cowardice. I'd been through such difficult times after Svetozar Mashin's death. Besides, I loved her. Worshiped would be a better term. Pierre Loti once said: She is like a Greek goddess, like Hera, larger than life and twice as mean. Yet she could be adorable if she chose to be. Irresistible. And so beautiful. The most beautiful woman in the world."

"Why did you leave?"

"I was relieved of my duties. Given one hour to clear out. While my luggage was loaded on a hack, a certain Mademoiselle Mica Orshkovich was already moving into my room."

"But why? What made the queen do this to you?"

She took a deep breath as if wanting to answer, then changed her mind. "I've told you I don't want to talk about that."

He took her to dinner that night, choosing a restaurant where there would be no chance of running into King Milan. Before going out, she accepted one hundred francs, but only to redeem her pawned clothes so she wouldn't embarrass him by looking like a waif.

They had gone out together at least a dozen times when once again Michael realized he was in love with her.

It was not difficult to love Draga. If ever there was a dream companion for a man, Michael considered her just that. An afternoon with her was like a stroll on the first mild and windless spring day when the trees sprouted their first tender green.

She could be as still as a mouse for hours, yet willing to do whatever was expected of her: cook dinner, sew on buttons, run errands or make love. Sex with her left a man pleasantly enervated like a good game of tennis. Because ex-King Milan's plans were vague, Michael rented a furnished flat near the Étoile for her on a week-to-week basis. Since she never knew when to expect him, she remained at home, waiting for his two short knocks and one long knock on the door. She kept her high spirits throughout their stay in Paris. It amazed him to discover how well read and informed she had become. In 1884 she had had only the craving for knowledge, but thirteen years later she had acquired the taste and manners of an upper-class Frenchwoman without losing the compliance and gentleness of the Slav. She dressed with elegance, knowing that cheap clothes were no bargain. Taking care of the small flat required no great domestic skill; nevertheless, Michael sensed that in a proper milieu she could be a wizard homemaker. In addition to her womanly virtues, he concluded she was faithful beyond the shadow of a doubt.

Their Paris sojourn came to an end in May, when Milan moved to Vienna. After cautiously feeling out the ex-king about Draga Mashin and finding his antipathy as virulent as before, Michael saw to it that the two never met. Milan used his year-round suite at the Hotel Imperial, which included a room for his aide-de-camp, while Draga stayed at the Hotel zum Weissen Lamm in the Leopoldstadt section of the city.

"My son wants me to go home with him next time he passes through Vienna," Milan told Michael after their arrival from Paris. "I might take him up on his offer. This gypsy life is beginning to tire me. It happened while you were in Menton that I became a passionate horticulturist. When I go home, I won't settle in Belgrade, but in Topolnitsa where I've decided to found an institute for botany and horticulture. It'll be the first in Serbia. Yes, that's how I am going to spend the rest of my life. In quiet retirement, teaching young farmers to grow crops the modern way."

Despite his great affection for the ex-king, Michael's reaction was one of serious doubt. Besides, he knew that the decisions would not be left up to Milan. After the abdication, he had received a gift of two million francs from the Russian government in return for the promise that he would leave Serbia never to set foot on its soil again. Of course, Milan wasn't the man to feel bound by old promises; nevertheless, he had to know that the Russians wouldn't write off the two million as an uncollectible debt. His sudden passion for the bucolic life wouldn't fool them. They would assume that his real intent was to retake the throne from his son. Their entire Asian Division, assigned to espionage in the Balkans, would concentrate its efforts on forcing him to leave Serbia. His frequent conferences with Count Goluchowski, the Austrian minister of foreign affairs, and his frequent dinners with Franz Josef in Schönbrunn added fuel to the Russian animosity.

Old Franz Josef's affection for Milan was a phenomenon that constantly amazed Michael. Outsiders misinterpreted it for the sovereign's generosity to a faithful satellite for services rendered, yet that wasn't quite true. The emperor, paragon of bourgeois rectitude, felt a warm friendship for this man whose scandals and excesses were the talk of Europe.

With Austria's blessing and to the exasperation of Russia, ex-King Milan returned to Belgrade. By the time he reached the capital, Topolnitsa and the botanical institute were forgotten. Instead, he undertook the modernization of the Serbian army. King Alexander, who had never been able to establish rapport with the military, named his father commander in chief and assigned to him the taming and training of his five unruly divisions.

In Vienna, Michael had seen no reason for telling Milan about his liaison with Draga. However, Vienna was a metropolis and Belgrade a small town where everyone knew about everyone else's affairs, so he considered it advisable to disclose to Milan that the Widow Mashin was his mistress.

It took the ex-king some time to digest the information. Evidently, it was news to him.

"Are you in love with her?" he asked not unkindly.

It was a question he, Michael, often asked himself. "I am afraid so."

"That's a mistake, yet not irreparable unless you marry her. So don't. She is defective merchandise. Fuck her to your heart's content, but don't marry her. She is not fit to be an officer's wife."

Draga had never uttered the word "marriage," yet ever since their return to Belgrade, Michael felt the topic dangling above their heads like a honey-encrusted sword of Damocles. Buying the cottage behind the Officers' Club was already a move toward permanence, even though she refused to accept it as a gift. There were arguments about it, but for the first time in their relationship, she refused to yield.

The end came suddenly, but not, as he realized later, without warning. Returning from a two-week trip, he found the cottage dark and unheated, Draga's personal belongings gone. He looked for the maid. Judging by the empty wardrobes in her room, she, too, had moved out. Reluctant to ask the neighbors for information, he mounted his horse and rode to the house of Draga's married sister.

Maria, an older and plumper replica of his mistress, pretended to be surprised at Draga's disappearance, although he sensed a certain uneasiness in her. Like the rest of the Lunyevitza tribe, she was under obligation to him for gifts and favors. Nevertheless, she kept insisting that she had no idea where her sister had gone.

It was only later that evening at the Serbian Crown, where he had dropped in for supper, that Michael had learned from the chatty headwaiter of Draga's whereabouts. Unaware of the captain's connection with her, the man offered him a quick rundown on the events, among them the latest royal scandal, that had taken place in his absence.

The first rumors that the celibate king, reputedly a woman hater, had taken an interest in the opposite sex were set afloat when Alexander attended a gala performance at the National Theater in the company of his mother's former lady-in-waiting. The rumors were followed by the discovery that Madame Draga Mashin had established residence in an elegant town house on Crown Street as the official mistress of King Alexander.

It surprised Michael how little the news affected him at first hearing. He finished supper, even had a drink with a friend who had drifted in just before he was leaving. Out in the street, he stopped to think what to do next. He wished neither to sleep in the deserted cottage nor to arouse his family at this late hour, so he decided to take a room at the Crown. Feeling wide awake despite the long day, he chose to return to the cottage for the few things he would need in the morning.

Still perfectly calm, he entered through the front door, found matches and lit the petroleum lamps in the hallway. The bedroom he had shared with Draga revealed signs of a hasty departure. His usually neat mistress had left empty boxes, laddered stockings and clothes hangers scattered around, drawers pulled out and wardrobe doors ajar.

Feeling a bitter flush of anger slowly burn its way from the pit of his stomach to his head, Michael suddenly became aware of the fact he had refused to face up to now: that he had irrevocably lost her. The truth burst upon his mind's eye like a scene from an obscene Punch and Judy show with Draga and Alexander entwined in bed, mockingly sticking out their tongues at him, the cuckolded lover. Emitting a hoarse animal cry, he reached for the nearest chair and smashed the mirror of the dressing table, then attacked pillows and mattress with his drawn sword. Recalling his mad rampage later, he realized with a grim shudder that neither Draga nor the king would have escaped unharmed had they been in that bed. As though his sword were not effective enough, he used the ax from the kitchen to wreck the furniture. A chip of broken china hit his cheek, missing his eye by a scant centimeter. The realization that he had just hurled Draga's favorite aspidistra in its pretty Sèvres *cachepot* through the closed window of the sitting room brought him back to his senses. Pressing a towel to the profusely bleeding cut on his cheek, he sat down, ashamed and defeated. His anger gone, he discovered he no longer hated Draga, only himself. Theirs had been a unique relationship which he had destroyed.

All along, he had been aware of her desire for permanence and security, yet he had deliberately ignored it, what is more, cautiously avoided uttering a single word that she could interpret as a promise. No woman had ever satisfied his need for both sex and affection as completely as she, her mere presence in the house filling him with a sense of restful joy, yet instead of chaining her to himself, he had thoughtlessly set her adrift.

He had received enough warning signals. A few weeks before, when his youngest brother had become engaged to the daughter of a Cabinet minister, she had intimated to Michael that she would like to attend the wedding. He had brushed her off with the excuse that it was to be strictly a family affair, although he knew, and so did she, that invitations had gone out to the entire *haut monde* of Belgrade. Not once did he appear with her in public. If a show she wished to see was presented in town, he bought tickets for her and her sisters, but he never accompanied them. A man of his position at court must not be the object of gossip, was his explanation for keeping their affair a secret.

Neither her attitude nor her disposition had changed, still he sensed a new, strange element entering their liaison. At times she would sit, hands resting in her lap, head slightly turned to the side, like a traveler on a railroad station platform, waiting for the announcement of the train's departure.

Michael wondered later what really had kept him from uttering the magic words. Was it the memory of boisterous Monsieur Jurieux or the ghost of others who had had similarly easy access to her bed in Shabats and in Paris? Or was it King Milan's warning? After years spent in the sophisticated West,

Michael was still a Serb with deep disdain for any woman willing to sleep with a man without the blessing of the church. A woman was either a whore or the sainted mother of his future children. The same woman couldn't be both. Anyway, the most significant relationship for a Serb was not love for the opposite sex, but friendship for his own. Lovemaking lasted but a few moments, friendship a lifetime. Milan disapproved of Draga; thus, Michael was forced to choose between the two and, in true Serb fashion, chose not the woman, but the friend.

Had all the small but cruel humiliations to which he had subjected Draga come to her mind when she sat in the royal box of the National Theater? Michael wondered. Had the king's hand kiss for the whole world to see and the rides through Belgrade, in an equipage pulled by four thoroughbreds, reminded her of the times Michael Vassilovich had refused to join the afternoon *corso* on Teraziya with her?

Visualizing her in bed with Alexander, Michael felt a renewed flash of anger against the young clown masquerading as a man who had evidently blinded her with promises that he was in no position to keep. Sooner or later he would have to marry, and where would that leave Draga? Michael wondered.

If someone had told him on that miserable wintry night that three years hence Alexander would elevate Draga to the eminence of lawfully wedded wife and Queen of Serbia, he would have spit in the man's face. Or dashed to Crown Street, broken down her door, forced her to leave the king and married her himself.

8 A.M.

THE sound of light, running footsteps brought Michael back from the past. Her cheeks flushed, her eyes wide with fear, Ljubica came rushing from the main house.

"A guardsman from the Konak . . . has brought you an order to report to General Petrovich . . ." she told him in a breathless half-whisper.

Michael rose. So they had learned about his arrival. But why a guardsman and not the state police?

"I'll tell the man that I couldn't find you," she said. "Go to the old hen house—the roof's completely overgrown with shrubs—you can hide there till after dark and then—"

He patted Ljubica's cheek. "No. I'll see what they want. And don't worry. I haven't done anything wrong."

"That makes no difference. Not to the woman!" Her eyes flashed angrily. "You've been away too long. You don't know what's been happening around here."

"Come on. It can't be all that bad." He wondered if Ljubica had ever been told that the "woman" had once lived in the yellow *vayat*. "Why do you hate the Queen? She never harmed you."

"Because she's no good. Shameless. When she used to take rides in an open carriage with him, he would sit beside her and never take his eyes off her. Never pay any attention to the people along the road greeting him."

"That was his mistake, not hers."

"Oh, but she gloried in it. Isn't that shameless? To let a man, a king, make a fool of himself in front of the whole world."

The guardsman, in a spotless light-blue tunic trimmed with yellow braiding, was leaning against a porch post, pensively chewing on a blade of grass. On spotting Michael, he stiffened to attention, executing a faultless salute. Guardsmen were a select group, chosen for their above-average intelligence and loyalty to the king.

The order he handed Michael was enclosed in a sealed envelope and written on court stationery. "Captain Michael Vassilovich is requested to report to the office of General Laza Petrovich at the Old Konak."

Michael stared at the note, frowning. How naïve he had been to believe he could slip into the country unnoticed and unreported. General Petrovich was not only one of King Alexander's aides-de-camp, but the second most powerful man in Serbia. To be summoned to his office presaged a courteous interrogation to be followed by a more insistent one by the state police. After that, Michael feared, would come the cell in the fortress or worse.

Michael dismissed the guardsman, then showed his father the general's order.

"What will you do?" the old man asked.

"Report to the bastard. What else?"

Old Yovan Vassilovich looked worried. "They know you saw 'him' in Geneva. They have their informers everywhere, even Switzerland."

"I'm not so sure about that. Spies are an expensive commodity. I doubt that Alexander can afford a secret service organization abroad. Not when he is too broke to pay for train fare, let alone hotel bills and expense accounts. He may get tidbits of information and gossip from abroad, but no accurate reports."

"He isn't calling you to the Konak to break bread with you, that is certain."

"We'll see. I'd better change and hope my old gala uniform still fits me. I had a new one made in Vienna three years ago, but that's in the trunk on its way here."

Before reporting to the Konak, he had to get in touch with Colonel Mashin and tell him about the order. Going to his house meant taking chances; phoning him was not without danger either. There were few private telephones in Belgrade, none at the Vassilovich compound. Any stranger having the right to ring him up at will was an idea unacceptable to old Yovan.

Michael decided to make the call from the nearest police station. Even if Mashin's phone were tapped, the talk in the presence of the law should convince the listener of its harmlessness.

The police commissioner on duty had no objection to the captain's using the phone but kept his eyes on him like an eagle on a grazing lamb. As usual, the operator was agonizingly slow in making the connection. Luckily, the colonel was home and available.

"This is Captain Vassilovich," Michael said. "I want respectfully to thank the colonel for his invitation, but I'm afraid I won't be able to attend the *déjeuner*. I've been ordered to report to the Old Konak."

At first, there was a long silence. Then Mashin's voice came from the other end of the wire. "What the hell are you talking about? Is it really you, Vassilovich?"

"Of course, sir. I am to see General Laza."

"Is that so?" Mashin finally said. "I do appreciate your call." He still sounded flustered.

"You've been most kind, Colonel. Now I'd better hang up. The general expects me to report without any delay."

At last, Mashin managed to grasp the full meaning of the call. "Let me know how things turn out. Let's remain in contact by all means—"

"Thank you, sir." Michael hung up. He felt the touch of the commissioner's pudgy hand on his shoulder.

"Report to General Petrovich! Isn't that something! He is a great man, the general is." A wide grin spread over his face. "Only count your fingers after you've shaken hands with him. You might find one missing."

His cackle followed Michael out to the street, floating after him like gossamer in the summer air. The weather had turned hot and sultry. His gala uniform felt as warm as a quilt, probably because it was a bit too tight around his middle. He had evidently gained a few pounds since he had last worn it. Not knowing what to expect at the Konak, he hired a hack instead of using the family landau. Progress through the sun-baked streets was very slow amid the congestion of peasant carts. After turning the wide, chestnut-tree-lined Milan's Road, traffic moved a bit more freely. This section with the newly erected ministries, the British Legation, the Military Academy, the parliament and, farther up, the royal palaces, the New and the Old Konaks, was the very heart of the city. His eyes combed the street, looking for changes. On the sidewalks, Western suits and dresses mingled with men's baggy trousers and women's loose Zouave jackets of maroon velvet embroidered in gold. Children wrestled under the feet of strolling pedestrians; a group of gypsies was seated on the curb; here and there a woman stepped from a house to empty a pail of dishwater into the gutter. Once again, Michael felt a shock over the behind-the-times quality of the scene and—at the same time—an odd warmth which came from belonging. As much as he loved the West, he could never feel proprietary about its streets, parks, people. This motley crowd was his people; looking at each passerby, he could tell the man's or woman's background, present station in life and expectation for the future. It was during his endless days spent in a Menton nursing home and, more recently, in a Swiss sanatorium, hundreds of miles away from Belgrade, that he had learned to understand and love his compatriots. Even the city men in ill-fitting imitations of Savile Row suits, with starched collars and removable bib fronts hiding their frayed shirts, aroused his admiration for their valiant effort at survival with dignity. He often wondered which class had the harder lot: the city men, teetering on a tightrope strung out between nineteenth-century stagnation and twentieth-century élan, balancing gentlemanly prestige against beggars' humility, or the peasants with their abysmal poverty and endless labor.

It was his encounters with squinty-eyed French landladies, indifferent Swiss hotel men and greedy, yet obsequious Austrian clerks that had made him aware of the Serbs' unique qualities. Capable of saintly virtues and animal cruelty, they could mercilessly maim and slaughter the enemy, ravish his women, skewer his infants in their cribs, then turn gentle and tolerant in peace, allowing no orphan to grow up homeless and unloved, no old man to starve, no vagrant to die without shelter. Even the Vlachs, those strange and taciturn men Michael had come to know during maneuvers, reminded him of medieval saints. No African tribe lived under more primitive conditions than these shepherds with their huts dug into the ground and their mutton fur capes serving them not only as garments, but also as beds, wardrobes and—at the end—shrouds. Money never touched their hands; even if given any, they wouldn't have known what to use it for. It couldn't help them find water in the mountains, where they took their sheep to graze, stop the wind from chilling their bones or the snow from burying them. Yet even these dour and ferocious people were hurt if a stranger refused to share their meal of hard cheese, onion and corn bread. Serbia was a savage land, the Serbs were an untamed nation, yet spared by the two greatest killers of a man's spirit: hunger and loneliness.

In the large courtyard of the Old Konak, the king's own guardsmen, under the command of Captain Panayotovich, were relieving, amid drumbeats and bugle calls, the company that had been on duty during the night. Outside the gates, there was the usual crowd of children and out-of-towners, mostly peasants in their regional Sunday best, the women with their dowries, chains of gold and silver coins, hung around their necks. Some were in Belgrade for the first time in their lives, probably to attend, as freshly elected deputies, the opening session of the Skupshtina. They were spending the time unclaimed by politics inspecting such wonders of civilization as the railroad bridge across the Sava River, the shopwindows on Teraziya and the caryatids supporting the balconies of the New Konak. Though impressed with certain aspects of city life, they retained a touch of contempt for some of its absurdities, such as, the flower beds in public parks. What a waste of money, they commented, when God turned the countryside green every summer, dotting it with wild flowers. Why pay gardeners when nature offered its abundance and beauty to mankind free of charge?

After a cursory glance, the guard at the gate admitted the hack into the palace grounds. As Michael alighted, a second lieutenant came charging across the courtyard, catching him as he was about to enter the building.

"What the hell are you doing here?" the lieutenant asked in a low, breathless tone.

Michael recognized the man as one of the subalterns he had met at the Officers' Club but failed to recall his name. "I've been ordered to report to General Laza Petrovich."

"You must let Colonel Mashin know."

"Already have."

The lieutenant gave Michael a long, suspicious look. "Watch out for the bastards. They might trick you into talking."

"Not me." The young man's brashness irritated him. "What's your name, Lieutenant?"

"Peter Zivkovich. I introduced myself to the captain this morning," the lieutenant added reproachfully. "The general has ordered maximum security measures for today. He must have received some warning. So watch out."

"I know how to take care of myself, Lieutenant," Michael pointed out, slightly peeved.

"Let's hope you do." After a limp salute, Zivkovich turned to his squad.

It had been three years since Michael had last crossed the

entrance shielded by a glass and wrought-iron marquee and walked up the steps to the vestibule onto which the office of the adjutant on duty opened. This morning a pockmarked little lieutenant was enthroned behind a desk scattered with audience lists and guards reports. The man who had been on night duty was on his way out. Recognizing Michael, under whose command he had once served, he hurriedly shook his hand, then darted from the office as though running for his life.

"Poor Captain Miljkovich isn't himself today," the pockmarked lieutenant volunteered when he noticed Michael's puzzled reaction to the captain's lack of camaraderie. "His wife is in labor with their first child. I thought he'd bite my head off when I was a few minutes late relieving him."

"By the fourth he'll be more relaxed," Michael said. "I didn't know he was married."

"Shows how long you've been away. To the daughter of General Tzintzar-Markovich. That's why he didn't ask to be relieved of duty last night. Afraid people would say he's taking advantage of being the prime minister's son-in-law. Wish we had more men like him in this wretched army."

His tone, like Zivkovich's, revealed to Michael how conditions had deteriorated since ex-King Milan's time. Under his command, officers had never called the army wretched. They were proud of serving in it. Michael wondered if the pockmarked officer was one of the conspirators or—more likely—an *agent provocateur*. He chose not to react to whatever the man's intent was.

"I have orders to report to General Petrovich," he said to bar any further conversation.

'Yes—yes—I know," the other man mumbled surlily. "He is expecting you. Go right in. I assume you still know your way around."

Three shallow steps led from the vestibule to the entrance hall of the royal apartments, the reception rooms, as well as the aides-de-camp's office. The Old Konak had been built under Milosh, Serbia's first reigning prince, and except for a few minor improvements, little had been done to modernize it. Since the New Konak was used for state functions, the old served as residence for the royal family.

The entrance hall, with King Milan's hunting trophies

mounted on its walls, resurrected long-buried memories for
Michael. An enormous brown bear shot by the ex-king in the
woods of Valjevo, stood stuffed and erect in one corner, its
paws, with the respect-commanding claws, lifted for a lethal
strike. The passing of time had left no mark on the place, and it
wouldn't have surprised Michael if Milan, the top button of his
tunic open and an unruly lock of hair falling over his forehead,
had suddenly materialized from the shadows and approached
him, arms outstretched in greeting.

Of the three doors opening from the entrance hall he chose
the one that led to the aides-de-camp's office. Impeccable in his
white and gold uniform, made to order by the Viennese firm of
Haberstein (appointed to the court of His Majesty Emperor
Franz Josef) "Lepi" Laza, Handsome Laza as he was known in
the salons of Belgrade, sat at his desk, talking into the phone.
The instrument was a very sophisticated model, installed on a
panel with several push buttons and lights. No one could say
King Alexander's court failed to keep step with the progress of
the young century's technology.

General Laza acknowledged Michael's salute with a noncha-
lant wave of his manicured hand and continued talking. They
had last met in Vienna two years before, when Laza had called
on the dying Milan to bring greetings from his son, Alexander.
The encounter had failed to dispel the animosity that had existed between Michael and Laza ever since their entrance into
the service of the royal family, Laza as confidant of the about-to-
be-divorced Queen Natalie and Michael as Milan's man. Because of Laza's loyalty to the queen, King Milan fostered a
virulent dislike for him, a feeling shared by his entire staff.

The phone conversation lasted several minutes. Michael deliberately ignored the general's "at ease" gesture and remained
at attention. Having finished and hung up, Laza rose and extended his hand.

"Glad to see you, Mika. I understand you've managed to
outmaneuver the grim reaper."

"At least, for the time being." Michael didn't want to point
out that in Serbia a young man's premature death wasn't always
caused by TB.

"I have here your petition to the Ministry of Defense requesting your reassignment to active duty. Says here, beginning
August first. Yet you're already here, on the tenth of June."

"The eleventh, sir," Michael corrected him, then adding: "I wanted to give myself time for readjustment. I've been away too long."

"Only three years."

"Yes, sir. And for years before that. Now I want to settle down, but I have to be sure I can become acclimatized again. Get used to the way of life around here."

"Is it so different from life abroad?"

"You've been abroad, General. You know it is."

"Yet you want to return home for good. Why?"

"The explanation is in the word 'home.' I'm thirty-seven years old but I've never had a family of my own. No wife, children, not even a dog. My doctors assured me that tuberculosis is not a hereditary disease. Anyway, they've pronounced me cured."

Laza sat down and offered Michael a chair. His handsome face, now etched with the fine lines of his fifty years, was a rigid mask camouflaging his feelings, yet Michael knew that behind the empty stare of those dark eyes there was fervent mental activity.

"Well, Mika," he spoke at last, "the ministry chose to have you posted at the Konak. You'll replace one of the king's equerries returned to field service. That is, if you have no objection to the appointment."

Michael was nonplussed. Equerry to King Alexander. No matter how hard he tried, he couldn't hide his bafflement. "I'm deeply honored," he muttered, then halted, wondering what scheme lay behind the appointment and how Colonel Mashin would want him to react to it. He had no doubt that the decision to bring him to the Konak had been made right here, in the aides-de-camp's office.

"Frankly, I had hoped for field service, sir. That's what I requested in my petition."

"So you did. I can read, you know." A frown of annoyance darkened Laza's face. "Will you accept the appointment or won't you?" Michael was thinking. They counted on his yes, but what if he gave them a no? Would they arrest him, and if so, what effect would that have on the planned *coup d'état*? Would the officers go ahead without him or—assuming that he had betrayed them—abandon it? Under the circumstances he had no choice but to consent.

"I shall accept the appointment most gratefully." Despite his best efforts he failed to sound convincing.

Evidently ignoring the false note in Michael's answer, the general nodded with obvious satisfaction. "I'm glad to hear that. I assume you're surprised by the appointment. We all knew of your devotion to the late King Milan. However, he has been dead for two and a half years, and the time has come to exorcise his ghost. It is against the national interest to have an officers' corps with divided loyalties. We must let bygones be bygones and strengthen the bond between King Alexander and his army."

Was that the true reason behind the offer? Michael wondered. Was Lepi Laza really trying, much too late, to heal the breach between the throne and the army? Had he received a warning about a conspiracy brewing? Was he in such a rush to put forth feelers that he reached for the help of an enemy? Or did he choose bribery in order to use him for a go-between?

"When do you expect me to report for duty, General?" he asked.

"You have already. The king might want to see you, so don't leave. He hasn't come over from the apartments yet. He seems to need more rest than others his age."

The prospect of facing King Alexander disturbed Michael. He didn't consider himself a good enough actor to pay court to the man whom he despised and whose downfall he was preparing. Besides, he wanted at all costs to avoid a meeting with Queen Draga.

"Anything you want me to do while I wait?" he asked Laza.

The general thought for a long moment. Michael wondered why a simple question should call for such intense concentration.

"No—just stay around. You'll need some sort of reindoctrination. There have been changes here, as you know. As in every bachelor's household when a woman moves in." The chuckle with which he said it sounded almost like a snarl. "In your time we had a court à la Potsdam. Frederick the Great. At least, that was the idea. Now it is Versailles. Whether under King Louis the Fifteenth or Sixteenth, only time will tell."

Michael tried not to look puzzled. Although Laza was probably just his usual self, poseur and cynic, it disturbed Michael how close he had come to the truth. The most unlikely speculation flashed through his mind but was immediately discarded. Laza couldn't be one of the conspirators. He was much too closely identified with King Alexander's regime. As a matter of fact, he *was* the regime.

The general rose. "You may wait in the adjutants' office. I'll send word when the king is ready to see you. In the meanwhile, brush up on the new *modus operandi* from Lieutenant Bogdanovich there. He is the man on duty this morning. You met him when you came in. The short fellow with the pockmarked face."

Descending the steps to the vestibule, Michael couldn't rid himself of the feeling that despite the hail-fellow-well-met reception, he was being kept prisoner at the Konak. If he defied Laza's instruction and made his way to the gate, no doubt he would be ringed by a detachment of guards, their rifles pointed at him. Still more curious than alarmed, he resigned himself to spending the rest of the morning in the company of surly little Lieutenant Bogdanovich.

9 A.M.

THE queen awakened with a murderous headache. The night before she had had too much wine in order to ease the pressure that felt like a steel hoop upon her forehead. It was the same painful sensation she had endured at the Belgrade Cathedral three years before, when, wearing a gold tiara designed to resemble the crown of Byzantine queens and weighing what seemed like a ton, she had been married to the King of Serbia by the archimandrite. Throughout the wedding ceremony, the ride across town and the gala dinner at the Konak, she had borne the pain without a whimper, rebelling only later, when in the privacy of their bedroom Alexander, her Sasha, insisted that she make love to him wearing the crown and nothing else. Such caprices were typical of him, reminding her of the ten years' difference in their ages. At twenty-seven, he was, despite his self-conscious attempts at appearing mature, still a boy, unstable, reckless and impatient, while she accepted herself resignedly as a burned-out light bulb that no current could induce to glow again.

Without moving her head, she opened her eyes to glance at his face, half-buried in the ruffled sleeve of her nightgown. In sleep his features were relaxed, the mouth devoid of petulant pucker, the forehead unfurrowed and the eyelashes long and silky against the somewhat puffy cheeks. Without his pince-nez he resembled a slightly imperfect replica of his stunning mother, a portrait drawn by a master, but the details filled in by a dabbler.

Feeling a cramp in her leg, she shifted position. Without waking, his body adjusted itself to hers, flesh to flesh stuck together, she mused, never to be unglued. Years before, she had found his desperate need for physical and spiritual intimacy touching, especially as his dependence on her had given her the crown. Now, in their third year of marriage, lying night after night inseparably entwined, his closeness made her feel as though she were a sultan's fallen-from-grace concubine, sewn into a sack, weighted down with rocks to be dumped into the Bosporus. Alexander's capacity for deep, loglike sleep late in the morning set her, the insomniac's, teeth on edge. His body, growing soft and heavy with too much food and liquor, lay sprawled over her, hardly allowing her to breathe. Her twisting and turning never disturbed him; only her attempts to slip out of bed woke him with a jolt, making him grope for her with hands as eager and ineludible as the tentacles of an octopus. They never ceased to travel over her, exploring, petting, subduing. There was no choice for her but to submit to their caresses. Satisfying the carnal and spiritual hungers of this eternal adolescent who had never known another woman, was, after all, the essential part of her queenly duties. The thought of what would happen to her if he ceased to care made her shudder. Her enemies, she knew, would fall upon her and tear her apart.

Belgraders, early risers, used their crowing cocks as alarm clocks and the setting sun as their bedtimes. For their king to be sound asleep at nine in the morning, while stacks of state documents piled up on his desk and petitioners gathered in the anteroom to his study, was strictly un-Serbian. Draga understood this and also that she would be blamed for his dereliction of duty—this fault, as well as all the others.

She touched his shoulder gently. He came to with a start, his eyes wide with fright, reminding her of the twelve-year-old boy who had once crawled into her bed, seeking security and protection from horrors known only to him.

He had been a much too proper and serious child for his age, no doubt because his warring parents, Milan and Natalie, were too immature for theirs. During the second year of her much publicized separation from Milan, Alexander's mother had taken the child to Wiesbaden, Germany. Her hatred for her husband had already colored Serbia's political life a poisonous shade of bile green. The boy, pawn in a contention which was not only a marital battle, but a power struggle as well, was tossed back and forth between the two. His love was competed for as if he were a victory trophy.

In her role as *dame d'honneur* appointed to the queen's court, Draga had occupied a small room in her mistress' suite. During a storm one night she was awakened by whimpers from the corridor. She first thought it was the queen's Pekingese at her door, but when the sound grew louder and distinctly human, she jumped from bed and opened the door to the nightshirt-clad Alexander cowering on the threshold. He stared at her with his mother's velvety dark eyes, except that the queen's were seldom filled with such despair.

"Good God, child, you'll catch your death!" she gasped. By then the boy was in her room, his skinny body shaking with cold.

"Get into my bed!" she ordered.

He obeyed, curling up under the still-warm comforter, his frightened pleading eyes fixed on her face. Then he broke into wild sobs.

Chilled to the bone, she stood barefoot, helplessly watching the display of inexplicable misery. When no soothing words could check his sobs, she slipped into bed and took him in her arms. During their stay in Wiesbaden, they had at times exchanged a few words, she trying to cheer him up and he preserving his solemn, unchildlike countenance, yet nothing had occurred to warrant his present appearance at her door. Now he clung to her as though afraid of plummeting to his death if he let go.

"What's the matter, Sasha?" she asked, calling him by the Russian pet name his mother had given him. When he failed to answer, she pressed on. "Was it the storm? Did you have a nightmare?"

"A nightmare," he mumbled.

"Tell me about it."

Instead of answering, he pushed closer, burrowing his head into the soft valley between her neck and shoulder.

"But you should've called Mademoiselle or Dr. Dokich." Both his Swiss governess and his tutor had been appointed by King Milan.

"I hate them," the boy told her in a clear, sharp voice.

"Then your mother."

"I hate her, too." The cold fury of his tone, a sudden switch from his sobs, startled Draga.

"How can you say that when she loves you so much?"

"No, she doesn't. Nobody loves me."

"Nobody loves me"—as the years passed on, she often felt that these three words were the leitmotiv of Alexander's life. She had heard them from him again and again, in Biarritz, in Meran during their illegal honeymoon, in the royal coach rolling through the streets of Belgrade.

In Wiesbaden, she took his petulance for a passing mood. "Oh, but you're wrong, Sasha." She stroked his forehead, still moist with the cold sweat of the nightmare. "I can't tell about others, but I love you very much."

He lifted his head from the pillow and gave her a long look. "You—I believe."

During the fifteen years of their relationship, he, at times distrustful of his most loyal subjects, never doubted her affection, though—and this she knew—she had never really loved Alexander. Others? She wasn't certain whether her brief infatuations, some climaxing in satisfactory, others in disappointing sex, could be called love. It was Michael Vassilovich alone who had possessed her body and soul, the proof of which was that he alone could cause her to suffer. For Alexander, there was only pity, combined with the trained nurse's concern for a difficult patient. When people labeled her a whore, they weren't far from the truth, because that was what she really was, a competent practitioner of her profession, a woman catering to her lovers' needs with expert thoroughness. As well as knowing all the tricks of her trade, she was also endowed with an ample measure of professional pride. Satisfying the customer was almost as important to Draga Mashin as her own enjoyment.

General Laza Petrovich, another ex-lover, had once told her that there was a portion of mother in every good whore's makeup and that in hers, the mother often outranked the mistress. She was also fond of children and maintained a deep compassion for all creatures young, helpless and abused. Taking the boy into her bed that night had been a natural gesture for her. He was in need of comfort, and that was what she offered him.

They had lain entwined for minutes before she became aware that the shivers running through his lean body pressed against hers were no longer prompted by a child's panic, but by a young male's desire.

"Oh, you little bastard," she cried, pushing him away. Both amused and annoyed, she rose, put on a robe and settled for the night in an armchair. Before daybreak she woke him and sent him back to his room. The following night she locked her door and ignored his persistent knocking. Further attempts at entrance were frustrated when an unexpected action by his father put an end to his stay in Wiesbaden.

Milan had suddenly decided to snatch Alexander from his mother's custody. After having repeatedly demanded the return of the boy to Belgrade, he appealed to the German emperor to act as mediator. Kaiser Wilhelm II politely but emphatically advised Natalie to comply with her husband's wishes. When the queen refused to give up her son, the emperor placed the matter in the experienced hands of the Wiesbaden chief of police.

Herr Rheinhaben executed the task with proverbial Teutonic efficiency. He personally delivered the ultimatum to the queen, giving her twenty-four hours to put Sasha on the Belgrade train. Outraged, she ignored his request, unaware that neither tears nor threats could deter a German policeman from doing his duty. On the following morning, at the given hour, Herr Rheinhaben, accompanied by several gendarmes, entered the royal suite and simply abducted the boy.

The queen's reaction to the intrusion could be heard all over the hotel and was even reported later in such dignified publications as the *Times* and the *Frankfurter Zeitung*. Her Levantine hysterics proved infectious, producing in Alexander one of the mad rages that during his reign were to become the talk of Europe. He attacked the two-hundred-and-forty-pound Rheinhaben, flailing at him with his matchstick arms. Draga, present during the scene, had literally to peel him off the big man in order to save the Wiesbaden chief of police from being bitten in the thigh by the future King of Serbia.

At the railroad station, those present attributed Alexander's angry tears to a small boy's despondency over being torn from his heartbroken mother. Draga alone noticed that his parting glance fell upon her.

Alexander stretched with a yawn, then reached for his pince-nez on the pink-marble top of the night table. Fitting his glasses on the bridge of his nose, he threw back the comforter, his feet searching for his well-worn slippers. While he shuffled off to the adjoining bathroom, Draga rose and crossed to the dressing table.

The face that stared back at her from the mirror was beginning to show the wear and tear of its thirty-eight years. The striking green eyes were ringed by dark shadows, and their lids showed thick, unattractive folds. Before their marriage, the ten years' difference in their ages was—because of her fresh prettiness and his pince-nez and stern mien—hardly noticeable, but now she knew she looked more like his mother than his wife. Each time she entered a crowded room, she felt hostile glances searching her face for new signs of deterioration. All her faults and blunders could be forgiven, she was certain, as they had been Queen Natalie, if only she possessed her mother-in-law's disarming beauty. Even her own looks of ten years before would have sufficed. The Serbs, a primitive people, cared little about a royal consort's family tree as long as her image fitted their idea of what a queen should be: a living legend, inspiring poets and folk singers to immortalize her for the benefit of future generations.

Oddly enough, the years had failed to leave their mark on her body. Despite the additional weight, it remained beautifully proportioned with breasts as full and firm as a young girl's, a flat stomach, smooth thighs and a skin that had the sheen of perfect porcelain. What a pity, she thought with an inward grin, that the Queen of Serbia could not show herself in the nude to her subjects. If she did, they would certainly substitute the sobriquet "tired old mare" with a more flattering one.

While still in her bedroom, she was told by her personal maid, the Viennese Frau Weber, that the king's first aide-de-camp, General Laza Petrovich, wished to see her on a matter of great urgency. The request was not unusual; lately the members of the royal entourage and even the Cabinet preferred to discuss their problems with her rather than with Alexander. The informality of their approach made her wonder how, for instance, Czarina Alexandra or Queen Victoria would react to similar breaches of court etiquette. She resented the fact that the two-story Old Konak with its yellow walls badly in need of a fresh coat of paint was no more revered by the people of Serbia than some village kmet's residence. If it weren't for the guards at the gates, peasants with grievances and requests would simply barge into the royal apartments demanding to be received by the king. And sometimes they did, despite the guards.

During the three years of her reign she had done everything in her power to command respect, yet with little success. In the beginning, she had tried to win the people with kindness and applied stricter measures only when the friendly approach failed. Immediately, she was accused of being revengeful, ruthless, a Jezebel. In moments of despair, she toyed with the idea of leaving Serbia, a country of peasants where successful pig breeders passed for an upper class, highwaymen for national idols and illiterate village magistrates for politicians. It was really impossible to civilize such people, teach them manners, refinement, decorum. If only they would give her time, let her be there when the new generation came of age. She could be friend, educator, mother to them. The most she found she could achieve with the old was to keep them in check, a task that required the strength and quick reflexes of a lion tamer.

Although peeved with Laza Petrovich for sending a message by a servant, her curiosity superseded her annoyance. The matter was of great urgency, he had said to the maid, and "urgent" was a word seldom used by the lackadaisical Laza. She slipped on a robe and told Frau Weber that she would receive him in the boudoir.

A friendly, comfortable room, its walls were covered with paintings and photographs depicting Alexander, the child, the adolescent and the king. The only other portrait was of the late King Milan, showing him in the uniform of his Austrian regiment with the order of St. Stephen pinned to his tunic. All the bric-a-brac in the room consisted of souvenirs of her travels abroad, such as the tiny replica of Paris' fabulous Eiffel Tower, a miracle of French engineering, still standing, fourteen years after its erection, in its three-hundred-meter grandeur, defying all prophecies to the contrary. The picture she loved best was a likeness of the very young Alexander, resplendent in his coronation robes, led heavenward over a path of cumulus clouds. A group of men and women, representing the provinces of Serbia, knelt in prayer at the bottom of the canvas.

Lepi Laza was ten minutes late. Draga's love affair with him began before her appointment as the queen's lady-in-waiting and had lasted with interruptions until 1897. Despite the chasm which separated them now, the general's attitude retained, especially when alone with her, more than a touch of the old intimacy.

Insanely jealous of Laza, Alexander nevertheless retained him as his first aide-de-camp. Men of the general's loyalty were a species almost extinct in Serbia. Despite his dependence on Laza, he treated the general with a mixture of rudeness, petulance and suspicion. Once, when the general had drunk too much champagne and permitted himself a quip at Draga's expense, Alexander had knocked him down, given him two black eyes that became the talk of Belgrade. On another occasion, because of some minor laxity, he had struck Laza across the face with his riding crop. Laza submitted to all indignities without protest. His enemies maintained—some even reporting to Draga —that he was finding ample rewards for his martyrdom in the power bestowed on him and the graft that went with it. She knew the accusation to be based on fact, yet others in her entourage were no less corrupt than Laza, but lacked his doglike faithfulness and forbearance.

"Honestly, General," she greeted Laza, "first you send me a message by my maid, then keep me waiting for half an hour."

As usual, her pique failed to impress him. "Only ten minutes."

She extended her hand, but he merely gave it a lukewarm squeeze without kissing it. To indicate her annoyance, she remained standing, offering him no seat.

"What is it you wanted to tell me? I hope it is really important. I have a million things to do and am not even dressed yet."

"You should be. It's almost ten o'clock, you know. People will say you're slacking off on the job." He waxed serious. "I've come to tell you that I saw Michael Vassilovich this morning."

Under the hastily applied makeup, Draga paled, then clutched the back of a chair for support. Laza, along with most Belgraders, knew that Michael had been one of her lovers. And judging by her reaction to the mention of his name, not an entirely forgotten one, he concluded. Nevertheless, he pretended to be unaware of her sudden turmoil.

It took her quite some time to collect herself. "Did you really?" she asked, attempting to sound casual. "I didn't know he was back."

"Arrived this morning. I've appointed him equerry to Sasha."

She discarded her attempt at composure. "Appointed him what?" she cried. "That's the most idiotic—"

He cut her short. "I want you to get Sasha's approval."

"You're out of your mind. I can't possibly—"

"Will you, please, listen to me? The man was King Milan's intimate, member of a clique bitterly opposed to Sasha. If Sasha doesn't make peace with them and fast, there will be trouble. His hold on the people isn't firm enough without the support of the army. He must win over the officers' corps or give up the throne. This is the twenty-fourth hour, Draga. He cannot wait for them to hold out the olive branch; he must take the first step. We could have had Captain Vassilovich arrested and charged with treason. He's been in Geneva where he was one of

Peter Kara's inner circle. On his way home he stopped in Vienna to see Milosh Nenadovich. Men have been sent to prison for less. But what have all the harsh sentences gotten us? More trouble. In the end, the pressure of the domestic and foreign press forced us to give amnesty to the prisoners—that is, the ones who were still alive. No, Draga, we must turn over a new leaf."

"Next you'll suggest that Sasha recall Colonel Mashin to active service.

"An excellent idea. I'll make a note of it."

"You've certainly changed your tune, Laza."

"I'm a sensible man, my dear. If I see that one method fails, I switch to something else. The new password is 'rapprochement.' " He stepped closer. "Promise to obtain Sasha's consent to the Vassilovich appointment. Tell him, it is a *fait accompli*, so there isn't much he can do about it."

She shook her head. "No. You do what you think best, but don't involve me. Not in this. I've never as much as uttered his name in front of Sasha. And won't now. It would have the opposite reaction. Do what you want, but don't count on me." She started for the bedroom. "I'd better dress."

He reached out, holding her back by the arm. "That isn't all I wanted to see you about. I'd prefer it if for the next few days you and Sasha refrained from appearing in public. We might issue a communiqué that he has one of his attacks of gastric fever."

She gave him a startled look. "Why? Are things that bad?"

"Probably just rumors. You know this town. Not much happening. No theaters to speak of, no concerts, no art expositions, no social life. Nothing to talk about except the rising cost of living, the hog market and politics. And politics mean plots in Serbia. Besides, there is this sudden heat wave. The moment the sun sets, people spill from their sweltering houses into the streets. There's nothing for them to do but gossip. So rumors start and spread. If you ask me, the first big summer rain will wash them away. But until then, stay inside the Konak. It's safer. They won't be able to get at you there."

"They? Who the hell are they?" She raised her voice. "Don't attend the Palm Sunday celebration at the citadel or the services at the cathedral, because that's where *they* are going to get you. Don't go to the laying of the foundation stone for the Home of Arts, because *they* will be there. I've been hearing this for the past six months. You seem to know everything about *them* except who they are. What's the use of having a secret police force when all you do is repeat vague rumors?"

She dropped into an armchair and buried her face in her hands. The past three years she had tried to convince the world that she and the woman known in the past as Draga Mashin weren't one and the same person. That she was born the day King Alexander took her to be his lawful wedded queen. The walls of both Konaks were hung with paintings depicting her in her new incarnation, but not one as a girl or young widow. She expected the people who had known her before July, 1900, not to admit they remembered. Those unwilling to comply were simply banished from court or public life. Laza alone felt at liberty to ignore her whim, because he knew that she needed him more than he needed her.

"Just do as you're told," Laza said patiently. "Don't leave the Konak. Remember the sixth of March. And it was winter then."

Although it had happened months before, the investigators were still unable to detect whether the incident had been a planned riot or a spontaneous demonstration turned into a riot. Supported by students, a group of shop clerks had gathered on Teraziya to protest long working hours and low wages. The men decided to call the king's attention to their demands, but nearing the palace gates, they were ordered by the police to disperse. It was never established who fired the first shot, the demonstrators or the police, but seconds later dead and wounded littered the street.

"As usual, Sasha was blamed," Draga remembered. "Rather I was, his evil spirit. And we weren't even at the Konak that day, but at Smederevo. Yet next day there was an article in the Petersburg *Novoje Vremja* that I personally instructed Prefect Marshityanin to open fire on the demonstrators."

He placed a placating hand on her shoulder. "Don't let them upset you. You ought to know the Russians by now."

"They're trying to crucify me." Stinging tears flooded her eyes. To hide them from Laza, she turned and crossed to the window. "After what I've done for them. Without me, Serbia would've been turned into an Austrian province. They should be forever grateful to me."

Beyond the shrubs of the Konak park and the chestnut-tree-lined avenue, the building of the Russian Legation, the breeding place of all the venomous gossip that made her life miserable, was basking complacently in the morning sunshine. A maid was brushing a rug thrown over the upstairs balcony rail, and in the service yard, the dust was being beaten out of the huge Tabriz that usually covered the reception-room floor. The sight of it brought back memories of the countless times she had walked on that rug.

"Looks like spring cleaning at the Russian Legation," she remarked. "Wish they'd sweep out Minister Tcharikoff with the rest of the trash."

"He isn't the worst."

"Not the best either. I used to think he was my friend"

"Diplomats, they're all puppets. You ought to know that by now."

"I wouldn't mind him if his strings were manipulated by his Foreign Office, but he is the puppet of their secret service. We too have a few good agents, but theirs are incredible. The Asian Department knew that Sasha had a crush on me before I did. Remember that summer when he first came to visit his mother in Biarritz?"

Laza grinned at her. "How could I ever forget it?"

"That part you might as well," she snapped.

She had gone swimming with Alexander. When they had tired of the water and stretched out on the beach to rest in the sun, Alexander had suddenly turned to her to ask if she knew what the most beautiful memory of his life was. She guessed it to be his anointment, but he shook his head. It was the night he had spent in her bed in Wiesbaden, he told her. Startled by the intensity of his tone, yet careful not to hurt his feelings, well aware of his rages when crossed, she tried to laugh off the confession. He kept the glassy stare of his myopic eyes fixed on her and told her in a hoarse voice choked with passion that he would marry her one day.

He was king, but still a boy of seventeen, in some ways mature for his age, in others naïve, and she refused to take the incident seriously. There had been no witnesses since Natalie and her Russian friends had been sitting under a beach umbrella out of earshot. Nevertheless, from that day on, the entire Russian colony seemed to have fallen in love with her. She was surprised but for some time failed to see the connection. She did, however, the following year, when Alexander invited Natalie to visit him in Belgrade.

The queen's return to the city she had been banned from since her separation from Milan produced the exalted overtones of a coronation. Jubilant crowds lined the streets, carriage horses waded knee-deep in bouquets and children were raised above heads like religious offerings to a saint. Natalie, looking as beautiful as ever despite her forty years, accepted the adulation as due reward for her martyrdom.

Draga, too, had been in the festive cortege, modestly seated in one of the carriages of the retinue. At first, she believed that she alone suspected the real reason behind Alexander's sudden craving for his mother's company but soon realized that others, too, had ferreted out the secret. The same Russian expatriates without cause, travelers without destination, diplomats without portfolio who had frequented the Villa Sashino in Biarritz now descended upon her like ants on a piece of honeyed bread. After paying their respects to the queen mother, they invariably found time for a much longer chat with the lady-in-waiting. Their approach was tactful and discreet, their gifts never valuable enough to attract attention.

During the ensuing years, Alexander made it a habit to spend at least part of his vacations from royal duties in Biarritz. His attitude toward Draga was friendly, but aloof, with no repetition of the scene on the beach. Invariably accompanied by Laza Petrovich, he seemed to enjoy his stay, remaining blissfully unaware of the blazing love affair between Draga and his aide-de-camp.

Draga by that time was beginning to consider the Villa Sashino a mental institution where, owing to their long cohabitation, all distinction had disappeared between inmates and nursing staff. She was no longer a girl, but a woman reaching thirty, with her hopes for a rich marriage slowly fading. She was experiencing what the Germans referred to as *Torschlusspanik*, the terror of seeing all exit gates slammed shut. The hours when she sneaked from the villa to a nearby hotel for lovemaking with Laza were a much-needed, though momentary deliverance from the boredom of her existence.

In the summer of 1897, on the last night of his visit Alexander had broken into her room, determined to rape her. After a fifteen-minute wrestling match, he left, his mission uncompleted. His defeat was partly due to Draga's superior physical condition and partly to his inexperience in the technicalities of rape. Slouching from her room, he vowed never to speak to her again. For her, the incident held no more importance than the one on the beach. She felt reluctant to risk a secure and prestigious position for an affair with a moonstruck adolescent.

Nevertheless, the scandal erupted because one of Alexander's love letters filled with references to their "nights together" landed in Natalie's hands. With the fury of an avenging angel, she dashed to Draga's room and, in a clear voice that reverberated through the villa, ordered her to leave. She had recognized the political dangers of Alexander's infatuation before everyone else did, and her intuition told her that unless it were stemmed quickly it could threaten the survival of the Obrenovich dynasty.

Despite her determination, her shock tactics, instead of leading to victory, merely served as delaying actions, for a year later Alexander boldly drove to Draga's cottage, banged on its door and persuaded her to leave Michael Vassilovich. His promises were wealth and eternal love, commodities no other man had ever offered her.

Her first copulation with Alexander had been a nightmare. To her surprise, he was indeed a virgin. Impatient, awkward, insatiable and wretchedly self-conscious, he alternately sobbed and raved, clawing at her with carnivoral hunger, then collapsing in deathlike exhaustion. His ludicrous ardor subsided only at daybreak when she sent him back to the Konak.

Michael was due home from his trip to Vienna that afternoon. She began packing immediately, for she knew that the mere touch of his hands would cripple her determination and she would fall into his arms, happy to settle for crumbs instead of the whole loaf.

She had left their cottage hours before Michael's train pulled into the Belgrade station.

Earlier that fall Milan had been named commander in chief of the Serbian army, establishing residence at the Konak as the king's *éminence grise*. Despite his disapproval of Draga, he tolerated the affair for a while, evidently preferring a mistress to the rumors about the young king's impotence or homosexual tendencies.

The admirers who had vanished after Draga's expulsion from Biarritz returned to her now in droves, making her feel the brightest, most attractive, respectable woman in Serbia. Sensing the Russians' endeavor to win her goodwill, Belgrade's diplomatic set followed the trend. Her parties at the Crown Street house were attended by the most fashionable people in the city. Only Milan and the officers' corps kept a cool distance.

In the beginning, the bribe was social recognition, bouquets, boxes of bonbons. The first hint that there could be more was dropped by a new close friend, Madame Taube, wife of the Russian military attaché. Alexander had been a generous lover, but living up to her status as official mistress of the king was proving expensive. Her servants were imported from Hungary and Vienna and her *toilettes* designed by the *haute couture* House of Drecoll. At first, she refused to listen to Madame Taube's offer of a handsome appanage, but pressed by the accumulation of unpaid bills, she finally accepted it.

The Russians needed her even more than she needed them. Urged on by Milan, Alexander had retightened Serbia's allegiance to the Austro-Hungarian Monarchy which threatened Russia with a loss of influence over the Balkans. This was a hard blow for Czar Nicholas II's government. The Asian Department had to find a way to counteract Milan's influence. To enlist her services for their cause seemed like a very shrewd solution.

The entire Lunyevitza clan profited by her new status. Her younger brothers, Nicola and Nikodiye, were admitted to the Military Academy, her three sisters boosted to a life of comfort. Her glory even became reflected on her long-buried grandfather, the grain merchant and pig breeder Nicola Lunyevitza. Court genealogists now traced her family tree back to the twelfth century, crediting her ancestors with heroic deeds in Serbia's struggle against the Turks. Grandfather Lunyevitza became one of the great voivodes, freedom-fighter chieftains of the 1804 War of Liberation. That Nicola was only three years old at the time, disturbed no one. His official birthdate was set back seventeen years.

At the dawn of the new century, Alexander was twenty-three, an age when a king could no longer postpone begetting a lawful heir. The search for the mother of his unborn child had narrowed down to three women; Princess Xenia of Montenegro, the choice of Count Muraviev, Russia's minister of foreign affairs, and two German princesses favored by Count Goluchowski, his Austrian opposite number. There was also talk of a genuine Habsburg archduchess, provided Serbia proved itself worthy of the great honor.

On Wednesday, July 5, 1903, a meeting had taken place with Colonel Taube and Russian Chargé d'Affaires Paul Mansuroff present in the king's study. It lasted six hours. By sundown, when the three men parted, it had been decided that the king would wed neither Princess Xenia nor a German princess, not even a Habsburg archduchess, but the Widow Mashin, née Lunyevitza, a commoner and for the past three years Alexander's mistress.

The nationwide furor unleashed by the king's decision to marry Draga Mashin took her by complete surprise. Up to that moment she had considered herself well liked by most and disliked by only a few. That she, a simple and harmless woman, could be the object of such violent hatred seemed incredible to her.

The king reacted to the country's protest with wrathful indignation. During the days following the announcement, he looked at the world with the bloodshot eyes of a wounded animal. Politicians and friends calling on him to dissuade him from the marriage risked arrest, even death. Acting Premier Vukashin Petrovich braved the king's revenge by repeating the rumors circulated about Draga's shady past to his face. He and his entire Cabinet handed in their resignation and were emulated by several members of the king's retinue, among them his private secretary.

Draga waited out the storm behind carefully bolted doors, an unnecessary precaution as no demonstrators attacked the house. The sole unpleasantness she had to endure was the visit by

George Genchich, the newly abdicated home minister, who begged her to abandon her marriage plans.

She sent him away promising to comply with the will of the country, leave Serbia and break with the king. A few hours later, people passing Crown Street could see her luggage being loaded into carriages and she herself, wearing a traveling outfit, driven away in a fiacre. Her brothers and sisters and the staff stood at the curb, waving tearful good-byes.

Her exit preceded Alexander's usual afternoon visit by a few minutes. He arrived and, pulling rank on her brothers, ordered them to tell him where Draga had gone. He fetched her back from the friend's house where she had stopped before boarding the train. In the presence of her family, he slipped an enormous diamond ring on her finger, declaring himself officially engaged to her.

The news of his son's marriage plans reached Milan in Karlsbad, where he had gone to meet the family of the German princess chosen by him to become the future Queen of Serbia. His first reaction was to return home. To prevent a face-to-face confrontation, Alexander ordered the border guards to "shoot Milan and kill him like a mad dog" should he attempt to cross the frontier.

The country was on the verge of a revolution when an item printed in the *Official Gazette* brought about a sudden change of mood:

"Belgrade, July 13, 1900. Last evening, at the order of His Imperial Majesty Czar Nicholas II, the Imperial Charge d'Affaires, Monsieur Paul Mansuroff, called on His Majesty King Alexander to congratulate him in the name of his exalted Sovereign, on his engagement. The Chargé d'Affaires also paid a visit to the Serene Fiancée of the King, Madame Draga Mashin, to express his good wishes."

Across the street, at the Russian Legation, the big Tabriz was being pulled off the crossbar and carried into the house. Behind the open windows of the upstairs salon two footmen were climbing a ladder to clean the ornate crystal chandelier.

"Are the Russians planning some sort of affair?" she asked Laza. "Reception or dinner?"

"Not to my knowledge. Why?"

"They clean house twice a year, spring and fall, otherwise only if there is a change in the top echelon or someone important is expected from Petersburg. Funny. They had their big housecleaning only last month."

"I should have your worries, Draga."

"Oh, you can learn a great deal from such telltale signs. I remember when Czar Nicholas promised to be *koom* at our wedding. The first indication that he wasn't to be best man, that not even a grandduke would be sent to represent him was the business-as-usual doings at the legation. No housecleaning then. And by God, Monsieur Mansuroff was our best man."

"No doubt, it was a letdown."

"Nevertheless, I fulfilled my part of the deal. I had Sasha declare the secret pact with the monarchy null and void and give amnesty to the Radicals implicated in that stupid assassination attempt against King Milan. What's more, he put them in power. Then came the famous invitation from Nicholas and Alexandra to visit them in Livadiya the following summer—an invitation extended only to be canceled. What deceit! She was to be godmother to my first child!"

"Your big mistake was that damned pregnancy trick," Laza told her. "That's what's wrong with you women in politics. You never know how far you can go. What on earth made you think you could go through with the bloody fraud?"

She gave him one of her queenly reprimanding gazes. "It was no fraud. Let's change the subject, shall we?"

Laza, however, refused to be silenced. "To smuggle a child into this damned anthill where every second person is a spy. And every third a double agent."

She shrugged. "I think I'd better get dressed." She started for the door.

Laza stopped her. "There is more I want to tell you. Your little brothers misbehaved again last night."

She halted in her tracks. "That's not true. They had dinner with us, then went home."

"They went to the Serbian Crown, smashed a few mirrors and hit an infantry captain over the head with a wine bottle." Now that she hadn't exploded, he moved closer. "And that's no story invented by your enemies because the gash on the captain's head required eleven stitches. I saw the hospital report."

She sighed resignedly.

"All right, I'll talk to them. I'll have to dispense with a few audiences this morning, but I'll see them as soon as you can get hold of them. Send them a note and let them know it is serious. Oh, yes, and leave word with the Chancery that we won't attend the closing of the song festival this afternoon. In case other public appearances are scheduled, have them canceled." She forced a grateful smile. "Just to comply with your wish."

She dismissed Laza, then dressed and went to see the king in his study. Colonel Michael Naumovich, a corpulent, flabby-fleshed man, was equerry on duty in the small anteroom. At her entrance, he struggled to his feet, holding onto the edge of his desk for support. His face was pasty-white and in bad need of a shave.

"What's the matter with you, Colonel?" she asked, startled. "Are you sick?" He must have been on a drunken spree again, she thought, and probably gambling. And losing, too, when only a few days earlier, Sasha had gifted him with eight hundred pounds sterling to settle his shady debts. She could have used the money herself, but Sasha had felt it would reflect badly on him if his closest friend became involved in a scandal. Loyalty to one's sovereign was a shining virtue, also a large drain on the royal pocketbook.

Naumovich stared at her with bloodshot eyes. His breath, reeking sulfurously like a fairy-tale dragon's, came in hot spurts from his thick-lipped mouth. She noticed the neck of a bottle sticking out of a half-closed desk drawer.

"I feel simply terrible, madame," he stuttered. "It must be the grippe or something."

"Why don't you go home? You won't be of much use to the king in this condition."

Bowing low as if he wanted to fall on his knees before her, he ignored the barb. "Oh, no, madame, I couldn't. There's so much to do. His majesty has a full schedule. The Austro-Hungarian military attaché, the minister of home affairs, and Paul Marinkovich, our envoy to Bulgaria. His majesty has specially ordered him home for an interview." His voice trailed off as if the speech had sapped all his strength.

"I still don't see why you can't ask to be relieved?"

Naumovich protested much too heatedly. "No, no, madame— I'll be all right. And please, don't say anything to his majesty. I don't want to have his attention called to my—my condition. That I am not quite myself today."

"In that case get that two-day beard off your face!" she snapped, and turning her back on him, she entered the king's study.

With a groan, Naumovich dropped into his chair.

"God, dear God, please, help me live through this horrible day," he mumbled, crossing himself.

10 A.M.

COLONEL Mika Naumovich was a drunk, a gambler, an errant husband and an unprincipled patriot; however, all his vices were successfully camouflaged by his resemblance to a cuddly but lovable teddy bear. While looking at his ageless baby face with the big, blue, innocent eyes, even the victims of his petty larcenies were inclined to attribute them to his Slav laziness and insouciance. His name was a dubious asset: All Naumovich men had been loyal to the House of Karageorgevich in the past. Colonel Mika, however, was the first of his tribe to defy tradition and opt for the Obrenoviches.

Never a champion of lost causes, he felt no compunction in transferring his devotion from the vanquished Kara clan, deprived of power for half a century, to the victors, first to Milan and then to Alexander. Appreciated by both father and son as converts usually are, he advanced rapidly to the rank of colonel, although he was an average field officer. Appointment as equerry to King Milan was the crowning glory of his career. At the time of the final clash between Milan and Alexander, he once again displayed his special talent for choosing the right side when he crossed to the son's camp with the cheerful detachment of a Sunday-afternoon stroller.

He lived not far from the Konak in one of the Hungarian-style white-walled houses, built around the turn of the century, that dotted the hillside below the citadel. No officer of his rank, unless born rich, could afford the luxury of a residence in such an expensive neighborhood: six spacious rooms, indoor plumbing, grounds with flower garden, orchard and stables.

The contractor who had built the house was soon afterward awarded a well-paying royal appointment to erect a number of elementary schools in the provinces, and the antique dealer who furnished it was by accident the man decorating Queen Draga's private suite at the Old Konak. Mika's wine cellar was stocked with the same brands and vintages as the king's, and whenever a large quantity of food supplies was ordered from one of the city's importers, the store's delivery cart invariably made a stop at the Naumovich house. To remarks dropped about his greased palms, Mika reacted with a good-natured shrug.

"No sparrow nesting near a granary has ever died of malnutrition," was his disarmingly frank answer.

Far from being the most respected man in Alexander's entourage, still he was the least disliked by friend and foe.

Naumovich had been on duty since eight in the morning, much too early an hour for someone who'd spent the previous night playing twenty-one and losing almost half the money King Alexander had given him. The loss failed to disturb him, as the services expected from him later in the day promised an ample reward.

The night was to bring enormous changes, erase the past and mark the beginning of a new epoch. Nevertheless, he was unable to shake off a sick despondency that physically hampered his every move as if he wore fetters.

He glanced at the clock on the wall. It showed five minutes past ten. He had last talked to Colonel Mashin the night before. Since then, he had had no contact with anyone in the group, although a lot could have changed in the meanwhile. He'd told his wife to phone him in case of a message from Mashin. She might have tried and failed, especially if something had gone wrong with the plans.

The queen's unusual harshness also worried him. Did it mean that she'd learned of his involvement in the conspiracy? Her reprimand for his unshaved look gave him an excuse to leave his post if only for a short time. The tension was maddening and at a time when serenity and clear thinking were essential. He told the duty officer to take over in the anteroom and rode home in one of the royal carriages.

Reaching his house, he dismissed the coachman, telling him that he would walk back to the Konak. He went around the building to enter through the back door, as was his habit, when he noticed a cavalry horse tied to a post in the corral. The sight caused him to accelerate his steps; someone of the group had come to his house with a message.

The back door, kept open day and night, was now, to his surprise, locked. He pounded on it, then on the kitchen window, but there was no response. He shouted for the cook and concluded that she must have gone shopping. The orderly had to be absent, too; otherwise, his voice would've summoned him, even waked him from a stolen siesta. The heat of the day, his repeated nips from the bottle and the shock of finding the house oddly deserted produced a dizzy spell. Retracing his steps to the front door, he cursed himself for having forgotten his key. He rang the bell, keeping his finger on the button till he heard steps descending the stairway.

Her hair mussed, his wife, wearing a bathrobe, cool and collected as usual, opened the door. "What's the matter?" she asked, a strange edge to her tone.

"Why the hell is the back door locked?" he bellowed.

She remained standing on the threshold, erect and motionless, as though barring his way to the house. "Why shouldn't it be locked? How was I to know that you were coming home?"

"Where are the servants?"

"Shopping."

"Both?"

"I decided to lay in some supplies in case there are riots. Who can tell what's going to happen after tonight. We might all be dead by this time tomorrow."

"The dead don't need supplies," he pointed out.

She still refused to budge from the entrance. Anyone passing the narrow front yard could have seen them from the street, him with one foot over the threshold like a door-to-door salesman and her in the long white bathrobe resembling a cherub posted at the gates to forbidden Eden. She was long past her first bloom and not really beautiful; nevertheless, her dark-skinned face with the high cheekbones and the bold, almost masculine nose reminded him of the legendary Serbian heroines who were as adept at making love as brandishing a sword on the battle-field. Long-legged and almost lean, except for her firm, round breasts, she moved with the grace and insolence of a gypsy. In his rare moments of contrition, he sought relief in the thought that it was her castrating haughtiness that had turned him into a gambler and lecher.

"Whose horse is that chestnut in the corral?"

She looked him straight in the eye. "Dragutin's."

"Apis? Is he here?"

"Must you always ask the goddamnedest questions?"

He winced at the profanity, but she ignored him. "Of course, he is here. You thought the horse tied himself to the post? Apis came to remind you of something you're supposed to do to-night."

She stepped aside, letting him enter.

Dragutin Dimitriyevich stood under the arch of the staircase, his thick black hair tousled, the three top buttons of his tunic open. Naumovich realized with absolute certainty that had he entered the house a few minutes earlier, he would have found Apis upstairs, sprawled on the wide connubial bed, making love to his wife. He had never before suspected them, yet now, looking at them, he knew them to be lovers. There was an indefinable aura of rapport about them, of that unity that sets a man and a woman in love apart from the rest of humanity, surrounding them with an impenetrable wall of their passion for each other. The discovery rendered him speechless. His code of honor decreed that he reach for his gun and shoot them dead; instead, he stared at them with an idiot grin on his face.

He, at last, managed to address Dimitriyevich. "What's new, Apis?"

"Nothing." The other man's tone indicated that he was aware of the colonel's train of thoughts, even of the likelihood of a shooting climax. When it failed to occur, his facial muscles relaxed, and he emitted what sounded like a sigh of relief. His gun was probably still in the upstairs bedroom, where he had dropped it while undressing, and for Apis to be unarmed was like finding his right hand amputated. In the third year of the new century, he was still a nineteenth-century Serb, courageous, ruthless and incorruptible.

After achieving their country's complete independence, most Serbs had lost their fiercely patriotic zeal, settling back to enjoy the rewards of their victory. Most Serbs, but not Dragutin Dimitriyevich. Half highwayman and half visionary, he was capable of putting friend and foe to the sword in the pursuit of his bold dream, the unification of all Southern Slavs in one powerful empire, Yugoslavia, to extend from the Tisza River to the Black Sea. At twenty-seven—the same age as the king he wished dethroned—he was feared and respected by men twice his age, mainly because they all had minor or major imperfections while he possessed none, none, that is, of the kind that counted as such in their eyes. One of the most highly qualified graduates of the War College, he considered a well-aimed bullet more effective than the most inspired political oratory. No devotee of the democratic system, he had watched the activities the Skupshtina with jaundiced eyes, hoping to see one day the entire parliamentary institution replaced by a military dictatorship, in his opinion the only effective form of government. Immensely popular among the younger officers of the army, he had powerful opponents in the older set, which fact, however, failed to disturb him. At the peak of his mental and physical strength, he considered himself untouchable and immortal and them—anyone over forty—impotent and doomed. With time on his side he was sure of victory, provided he managed to stay alive.

Mika Naumovich, too, was over forty. One of the expendables. Human surplus, a drone to be used if necessary, but never to be trusted.

"I dropped by to leave word for you that we shall definitely go through with the plan tonight," he told Mika. "And to remind you that we are counting on you."

"I wasn't going to forget it."

"All I can say is don't. We shall win, and as for you, siding with us is your sole chance to save your skin. There will be a thorough housecleaning after the coup, and better men than you will be summarily dealt with."

Naumovich's face turned red. "I've told you I'll do my bit. You don't have to resort to threats or blackmail."

"What exactly will you do?"

They were standing in the long brick-paved hallway. Feeling suddenly weak in the knees—cognac on an empty stomach hadn't been a wise choice—Naumovich dropped to the bottom step of the stairs.

"Almighty God, how many times must I go over that? I'll unlock the damned door for you. I'll be there waiting for you at one sharp. Just remember to keep the men under control. Don't let them talk or make any noise. I'll hear you coming because I'll be behind the window overlooking the entrance. Incidentally, who is going to deal with Captain Panayotovich? You promised he wouldn't be harmed."

"Not unless something unforeseen happens."

Naumovich gave him a startled look. "You promised."

"Of course, I did. I don't want any bloody massacre either. Panayotovich is a good man; we need officers like him. Give Lieutenant Zivkovich a few bottles of wine from the Konak cellar. Have the wine drugged. Once Panayotovich is asleep, Zivkovich can get the keys to the southern gate from him. By the time Pana awakens the whole thing will be over."

"Or we all will be dead."

Apis shrugged. "That, too, is possible."

"Has Michael Vassilovich arrived?"

"This morning."

"Have you talked to him? Has Prince Peter given his consent?"

"We would've called off the affair if he hadn't."

"King Peter!" Naumovich muttered. He grimaced as if he had bitten into a lemon. "King Peter," he repeated. "I'll be damned. To choose a man of fifty-nine."

"He'll do for a while," Apis told him.

"Till you find someone better. Then you'll kill him, too."

Apis gave him a long look. "Probably. It seems to me, Mika, that you disapprove of our methods. However, there's no way out for you now. Not anymore. Don't ever forget that."

Anka Naumovich listened in tense silence, turning her head from one to the other like a spectator watching the flight of a ball at a tennis match. Suddenly, she stepped between them.

"Must you discuss all this in the hallway? Let's go inside, shall we?"

Reaching down, she pulled her husband to his feet, giving

him a playful shove. "Your ass will freeze on that stone. Why did I have the parlor sofa upholstered if you prefer to sit on the steps like an old peasant?"

Naumovich recognized the subterfuge. She wanted him out of the hallway, so she could rush upstairs and straighten the bedroom, removing all telltale signs of lovemaking. The thought filled him with impotent rage, but obediently he shuffled to the parlor door and opened it for the man who'd just cuckolded him. Pulling the door closed, he could hear the wooden heels of Anka's slippers clitter-clatter upstairs.

"Everything's been arranged," Apis told him. "At midnight sharp, Colonel Mashin will go to the Palilula Barracks and order the entire regiment under arms. He'll lead the first battalion to the palace grounds to surround them on three sides. At the same time Colonel Mishich and the first battalion of the Sixth Infantry will descend from the citadel and occupy the street between the Russian Legation and the Old Konak. None of the soldiers and very few of the field officers will be informed about the true purpose of the move. If necessary, they will be told that the king intends to expel Draga from the country and wants them to stand by in case of riots. The officers involved in the coup will meet at different cafés. I'll be at the Officers' Club, another group at the Serbian Crown, a few at the Kolaratz. With Lieutenant Zivkovich opening the gates to the palace grounds and you unlocking the door to the royal apartments, there should be no unnecessary bloodshed. Once the king has been dealt with, not even his closest friends will be insane enough to rise against us."

Naumovich slumped down on Anka's newly upholstered sofa, his hands sweating so profusely that dark spots appeared on the imported French damask where they rested.

"The king and queen . . ." he muttered. "Who else is on your list?"

"Never mind that," Apis said. "I might tell you, however, that your name was on it before you agreed to cooperate with us. So don't turn informer now. There are people in this thing you don't even suspect. They'll settle with you in case something goes wrong. The king might have me arrested, or Mashin or Zivkovich, but the coup will be carried out regardless."

"I am with you. How many times must I repeat it?" Naumovich groaned. "True, I used to be rather fond of Sasha, but not anymore."

"He's been very good to you, hasn't he?" Apis asked.

His cool, calculating tone infuriated the colonel. "So he has! So what? He had reason to be. I've given him more than I've got. My time, my nerves, my health. And to the woman, too. You should've heard her talking to me this morning. Just because I hadn't shaved. I wonder if in her whoring days she turned down a customer just because he wasn't freshly shaved."

He stopped as Anka entered the room. He had heard her descending the stairs, crossing to the coatrack in the hallway and hanging up something.

"I'll have to leave you now," Apis said, suddenly in a hurry. "Pull yourself together, for God's sake. For once, Draga Mashin was right. You look ghastly. No king's equerry ought to look like you. Not even a Serbian king's. Tomorrow you can grow a beard like Rumpelstiltskin, but today be your dapper self, dear old Mika, so they don't become suspicious."

They crossed to the hallway. Apis' sword and gun belt with his service revolver hung from the coatrack. Naumovich clearly remembered that they hadn't been there before.

"Is Nicola Pashich with you in this thing?" he asked while Apis girded himself.

Apis laughed mirthlessly. "In spirit. His body, meanwhile, is in Abbazia, enjoying the tepid waters of the Adriatic. He's given us his unequivocal approval, though. Verbal approval, nothing in writing. Day after tomorrow, provided everything has gone well, he'll be back to claim his dues. Perhaps as early as tomorrow. But I'm afraid he's in for a surprise. He won't be included in the new Cabinet. By then it will have been formed by men who've stayed here and risked their skins."

"According to a secret police report that has reached the king," Naumovich said, "the Radicals have decided on Stoyan Protich for prime minister. How is that going to work out with Prince Peter? Stoyan favors a republican government."

"He favors any government that lets him have the spoils. Politicians! Ought to be stood against the wall and shot. Every one of them. Whatever party. But rest assured, Stoyan Protich isn't going to be Prime Minister. Not as long as I have a say. He'll be in the new Cabinet, so the Radicals won't kick. The rest will be Liberals with Yovan Avakumovich the prime minister."

"Why Avakumovich?"

"Why not? Someone's got to fill the job. He's had experience in government. Besides, his wife has steadfastly refused all social invitations to the Konak, saying she was not going to curtsy to a whore."

"Is that sufficient qualification?"

"As good as any. A wife with grit can be a handicap sometimes. In this case she'll be an asset." He threw a mocking glance at Anka. "That should be a lesson to you. You've been much too eager to kiss Madame Draga's hand. Now your husband won't be prime minister."

"I couldn't afford not to kiss it," she answered, looking at her husband as if he were a heap of ordure. "That was the hand that paid my husband's gambling debts."

Naumovich let Apis out through the back door to avoid any secret police agent loitering around the house, a possibility he couldn't discount. During the past months he had watched an epidemic of hysterical suspicion spread over the entire Konak, a malaise affecting everyone from the king to the kitchen help, with the most loyal subjects no longer trusted and the disloyal ones even less. Spying and being spied on had become the order of the day, Russian, Austrian, even French and British agents masquerading as cooks, footmen or ladies-in-waiting, friends denouncing friends and wives betraying husbands. Playing royal court in the shabby Old Konak that any bona fide king would have refused to stable his horses in and addressing Draga Mashin as "Her Majesty" had long become a flat joke even to Naumovich. Whenever he passed a group of young army officers strolling on Teraziya—spurs jingling and caps jauntily cocked—he saw them as God's revenging angels sent to Sodom to announce its impending doom. It was his fear of them that condoned—at least in his own eyes—the eagerness with which he responded to their halfhearted invitation to join the conspiracy. His wife had also helped him reach a final decision. Anka who had never before shown any interest in politics suddenly became wildly Russophile and a Peter Karageorgevich partisan.

Despite their long marriage she had in many ways remained a stranger to him, someone who might have turned out worth knowing if only he could have spared the time. When this stranger, whom he secretly feared, respected, perhaps even loved, came to the same conclusion as he—namely, that the time had come for him to leave the sinking Obrenovich ship—he began to consider himself not a traitor, but a man drifting with the currents of history. But now his finding Anka in league with Apis had changed the picture. He had sold out for money and she for sex. No longer a visionary or crystal gazer, she was now simply an adulterous wife, inducing her cuckolded husband to further her lover's case.

"How long has this been going on between you and Apis?" he asked her after he'd seen Apis gallop out the gate.

"How long has what been going on?"

"Has he been here before?"

"But of course. Night before last. You let him in yourself. Were you so drunk that you don't remember?"

"I mean in my absence."

Turning her back on him, she started upstairs.

"Get cleaned up," she told him. "You look a mess. Take a bath. I had the boy light the fire under the heater. The water must be hot by now."

"I asked you a question."

She was halfway up the stairs. "Go to hell," she muttered without turning back.

A moment later she was out of his sight, the sound of her footsteps dying away on the hall's Persian rugs. He heaved a sigh, then headed for the bathroom to shave and soak off the grime and perspiration of the previous night's dissipations.

11 A.M.

MILICA PETRONOVICH, *mademoiselle d'honneur* on duty, was deeply engrossed in a romantic German novel entitled *Das Schloss am Meer* when the door flew open and Captain Nikodiye Lunyevitza burst into the room.

"What the hell does she want from us now?" he asked, ignoring preliminaries. "We saw her last night and parted the best of friends."

The girl had risen to drop a quick curtsy. Though Nikodiye's succession to the throne had not yet been officially confirmed, it was clear that the queen expected the court to treat him as if he were already the heir presumptive.

"I don't really know, sir," she told him. "Her majesty seemed rather piqued when she sent for you and your brother. Perhaps if you think hard, you'll remember what you did last night rather than what you shouldn't have done."

The two young people were the same age, and an easy camaraderie existed between them. Milica's plain looks and sharp tongue, however, had saved her from the advances Nikodiye often made to the prettier females of his sister's court.

"It wasn't me who hit the captain and smashed the mirror at the Serbian Crown. It was my brother. But I won't tell her that. She might forgive me, but not him."

"Aren't you lucky to be her favorite?" Her glance held a touch of irony.

He frowned and said wistfully, "I wonder."

At that moment a large black bird, more than likely a crow, flew past the window, its shadow falling for a split second on the captain's handsome face. For some odd reason, the picture remained indelibly imprinted upon Milica's memory.

"You'd better go see what she wants. She doesn't like to be kept waiting. You'll find her in the salon."

To reach the salon, he had to cross the Serbian room, its walls decorated with homespun rugs and the portraits of Obrenovich predecessors. The enlarged photograph of Draga's grandfather, the grain dealer Lunyevitza, stared down in oxlike stupor from its heavy gold frame hung between portraits of two dead princes.

As was usual for the time of day, about half a dozen women waiting to be received by the queen were seated on the low divans upholstered in peasant needlework. Recognizing the captain, they scrambled to their feet to greet him, each in her own way: a plump lady in a Paris-style dress with a curtsy, others with deep bows and an old woman, her head wrapped in an assortment of shawls, with a kiss on the hand. Any other time, such reverence would have pleased and flattered him. The days when he had lived on beans and cornmeal and attended school barefoot were still very alive in his memory. He had been the laughingstock of his classmates, the wretched little Lunyevitza, the youngest son of the town drunk, destined for no better future than his father. Even later, when he wore shoes and ate a full meal at least once a day, the mockery continued because people knew that the family's sudden affluence was due to a whoring sister. The stigma followed him into the army as well. Although promoted out of turn because by then his sister wasn't just a whore, but the king's whore, he could never feel at ease in the barracks. The contempt he had seen on his classmates' faces was mirrored now in the eyes of his fellow officers. They looked at him as though he were an impostor. He was ready to quit the army when his sister's enthronement had changed his mind. Now firmly ensconced in the cozy shelter of her queenly power, he hoped for the first time in his life to be secure from the derision of his contemporaries.

Much too soon he learned that he had been an optimist. Once again, there were the sneers, the tauntings, the rebuffs. It was as though he and his brother Nicola were back at the Shabats elementary school. With one difference, however. Now the Lunyevitzas were armed. They could hit back and did: send a recalcitrant comrade to the guardhouse, have him demoted, even cashiered. Whenever they entered the Officers' Club or a public place, they could order the gypsies to strike up the national anthem and generals to stand at attention.

With a brief nod to the plump lady, Nikodiye shoved the old woman out of his way. Her lips, moist and cold on the back of his hand, disgusted him. To be ordered to an audience annoyed him, he was in no princely mood and had had other plans for the morning.

He found his sister standing in front of the window. The squeak of the door, an irreparable malaise of all doors in the Old Konak, caused her to wheel about. The frown that had been on her face furrowed a bit deeper as she caught sight of him.

"What's the matter with you?" she asked him shrilly. "Haven't I ordered you to keep out of trouble? Just for a week or two—until the Skupshtina passes the damned law."

Nikodiye Lunyevitza was well aware that by the "damned

law" she meant the bill having him declared heir presumptive
to the royal throne of Serbia. Ever since her sterility had become common knowledge, his sister had worked feverishly on
the project. But now, just as she came close to achieving the
impossible, the foolish boy seemed to be willfully thwarting her
plans.

He looked at her with the expression of wide-eyed innocence
that, he knew, never failed to appease her.

"What have I done *now*?" he asked.

"Last night you promised to go home and straight to bed.
Did you?"

"Oh, is that what's bothering you. I should've known. Let
this be a lesson to you. Don't ever make me promise something
that you know I won't keep."

"Don't be impertinent."

"For God's sake, Draga, isn't it enough that I've come home
from Paris? I wouldn't have done it for anyone else but you. I
hate this place. I always have. Belgrade, Shabats, the whole
damn country. How many times do I have to tell you I don't
want to be cooped up here for the rest of my life. At least, not
while I am young. Let me go back. Paris is the only place to be.
I am free there, nobody gives a damn about me. I want to get
something out of my life now, while I am young, not in thirty
years!"

In utter desperation Draga stared at him. Her plans were to
make him king, and the little idiot insisted on throwing away
the most magnificent chance ever offered a young Serb. No
doubt, she decided, he had left some pretty slut behind in Paris
and was in a hurry to return to her.

Because she had no children, this chit of a boy with the
reddish chestnut hair and puckishly freckled face was the person she loved most in the world. From the moment of his birth
—the youngest child of the Lunyevitzas, two hopeless alcoholics,
unfit to be parents—she felt it her duty to care for him as
though she alone were responsible for his existence. Even as a
young girl she loved him not as a sister, but with the passion
and anxiety of a mother, and tried—in the fat as well as the lean
years—to shield him from the curse of poverty. The third oldest
of the seven Lunyevitza offspring, she gave her siblings all the
care and money she could afford, and often what she could not,

but to him she had given her heart. At times she wondered if her family allegiance would have remained as strong had she been able to bear children. One thing was certain: She could never have loved her own son more fiercely and possessively than she loved Nikodiye.

"You certainly make life hard for me," she told him. "I get very little pleasure out of my role as Queen of Serbia. Sleepless nights, yes; humiliations, yes; slaps in the face, yes. To have you proclaimed heir would make all my sacrifices worthwhile. We'll find a fine girl for you. I've been looking at photos of eligible princesses. There are some real beauties."

"Don't waste your time. They're not for me."

"For heaven's sake, what's wrong with a girl coming from a royal house? Having manners and education? Doesn't she possess the same equipment as your bitches in Paris? Except that you'll never get the clap from her."

He answered her angry outbreak with a burst of laughter. In her gray-and-white silk dress with its boned and tightly laced bodice, her breast pushed up almost to her chin, her little feet tripping about nervously, she reminded him of an aroused pouter pigeon.

He gave her a tight hug, partly because he loved her and partly because he felt it advisable to pin her arms down. Her unexpected little slaps could sting.

Still holding her, he asked, "Why do you insist on making me king?"

"Because I want to keep you. Or maybe because I don't want the country and everything else to go to some Karageorgevich bastard."

"Is Sasha so happy?"

"Much happier than if he were clerking for some storekeeper in Geneva."

"That he'd never do. He's smarter than old Peter Kara. I'm sure Sasha has a cool million francs stashed away in some Swiss bank. Perhaps two. And so do you." His eyes lit up with a mischievous glint. "Now here's an idea! Let's take all the money we can lay our hands on, empty the treasury to the last dinar, then get out of here."

"That's not funny."

"I am not trying to be funny. I am serious. You've raided the treasury before." She tried to push him away, but he kept a tight hold. "They don't want us here. So what have we got to lose? Look at it this way: We'd be rich and they'd be bankrupt. Wouldn't that be something?"

She laughed, despite herself, as he kissed the tip of her nose.

"You're out of your mind," she told him. "Besides, raiding the treasury wouldn't make us rich. I doubt there's a hundred thousand dinars left there. Eighty thousand is more likely."

"All right. Let's take that. Beggars can't be choosers."

"Don't ever utter such a foolish thing in front of Sasha. He may be my husband, but he is still king."

"Who says we have to tell him? We'd be better off without him anyway. And he without us. Let's go. Just us, the Lunyevitzas. And soon. Because we might be kicked out anyway. The city is full of rumors. You've heard them, haven't you?"

"Of course, there are rumors. And more than just rumors. That's because Sasha has been much too lenient. Now, at long last, he's awakened. There are several bills ready to be presented to the new Skupshtina. Once they're passed, we'll be able to use stronger measures."

"What makes you so sure the Skupshtina will pass the bills? It hasn't before."

"This Skupshtina will."

"Just because you've rigged the elections? Don't be so sure. They are Serbs. Even your handpicked deputies might surprise you and vote against you. I still don't understand why you needed the whole travesty, this pretension to democracy? Why not give all parties a kick in the pants? Send both the senate and the parliament packing and take over. *L'état, c'est moi!* If Louis the Fourteenth could do it, why can't Sasha? He's been called a tyrant anyway. Why not be one?"

"No. Not that openly. Not in Serbia where every village kmet is a Balkan Gladstone. No, we need a parliament. It's an illusion, but it puts people's minds at ease. In a week or two it will be harvesttime. Members of both houses will have to go back to the fields or their families won't eat next winter. If they can go in the belief that the constitution has been saved, we might have peace at last."

"But what about the cities?"

"They don't count. Except Belgrade. But we have the list of

the chief rabblerousers and know how to deal with them. If there's no other way, we'll hit them with treason charges. That'll gag them. Don't think we have our heads buried in the sand. We know what's happening and are prepared to deal with it."

He gave her a look of exasperation. "You're hopeless, but I have a suspicion you like being queen."

There was a light knock on the door, and with unqueenly swiftness Draga turned around. Lately she had been unable to control her nervous reactions to sudden noises, no matter how faint.

When Nicola Lunyevitza entered, her frown softened to a smile. She even forgot that she was supposed to be angry with him.

Of all her kin, Nicola bore the most striking resemblance to her. Slightly taller than his brother, he was darkly handsome with a smooth, olive complexion, the hint of a mustache and his sister's green eyes.

"If Nikodiye told you that he broke the mirror, don't believe him. It was me!" Nicola insisted. "He always tries to be so damn noble."

Dismayed, Nikodiye shook his head. "The mirror hasn't even been mentioned yet. She may not know about it."

Draga turned on him. "I certainly do. And I am disgusted with both of you. You're the elder, Nicola; you ought to have some sense even if your little brother hasn't. You can't go on like this."

Nicola plumped down into the delicate Louis XV sofa, resting his feet on the lilac-colored upholstery. "That's what I've been telling you," he said moodily. "But you refuse to listen. However, my mind's made up. I am quitting."

"Take your feet off that sofa," she scolded. "That's imported French brocade." Now that she'd given voice to her house-wifely concern and scored a minor victory—for he'd moved his feet—she waxed regal. "What do you mean, you're quitting?"

"Just that. As a matter of fact, I've already resigned my commission and—"

"When?"

"I handed in my resignation to General Petrovich, in writing, too, when he came to see me in Brussels about a month ago. He promised that he would clear the matter with you and Sasha. I asked him yesterday why he hasn't done it yet, and he answered that he was waiting to find you in a more mellow mood."

Incensed, she stared at him. "Is that what he said?" and crossing to the bell cord hanging at the door, she gave it an energetic tug. When a footman entered, she ordered him to summon General Petrovich.

"Tell him to bring whatever paper Captain Nicola gave him," she called after the man.

Nicola jumped to his feet. "Be sensible, Draga. I want to settle in Brussels."

"With your Nanette?" The name was uttered as though it were a curse.

"Yes, with Nanette. I've lived with her on and off for four years now and still love her. We want to get married. I'm not ungrateful to you, but it's high time I made a life for myself."

"Is being my brother and an officer of the Serbian army no life?"

"Not the kind I want."

She was dismayed to find tears in her eyes. "After all I've done for you two. One wants to go to Paris, the other to Brussels. Neither cares about me. Hasn't it ever occurred to you that *I* might need you? That I am surrounded by a sea of hatred and need a few souls I can trust?"

Nicola shrugged resignedly. He was usually able to cope with her fury, but not her tears. He knew that she was not exaggerating when she spoke of the sea of hatred. He, too, had sensed the presence of hostility, even at court, undetectable to the naked eye, but as lethal as carbon monoxide. Even his two younger sisters, Voyka and Georgina, both gentle and friendly girls, blessed with Draga's beauty of earlier years, complained about it.

Nikodiye spoke up in support of his brother. "He doesn't want to leave you, Draga. Not for good. You can always count on him. On me, on all of us. He's just not cut out to be a prince. You cannot become a prince overnight. You feel like an actor or, worse, an impostor. How can you make people believe that you are a prince if you yourself don't believe it? Not everyone is like you. You don't ever seem to doubt that you're the queen. Just like Eleonora Duse when she plays Mary of Scotland. They say it takes her hours after each performance to revert to her own self because the moment she sets foot on the stage, she really becomes the character she is portraying. You're like that."

"In other words, I am an actress." She rose and walked nervously to the window as though the view held an irresistible attraction. "If you both prefer to remain commoners, why do you act like two demented Borgias? Hitting an officer over the head with a wine bottle."

"Because we were provoked. Because the fellow officer chose to drop a few unflattering remarks about our sister who thinks she is the Queen of Serbia."

"We have laws to deal with such offenses. Wine bottles aren't the proper instruments of punishment."

Without bothering to have himself announced, Laza Petrovich strolled in.

"You sent for me," he said to Draga in a slightly reproachful tone.

She looked at him coldly. "Since when do you take it upon yourself to encourage by brothers to defect?"

"They don't need my encouragement, madame."

Nicola reached for her hand. "Please, leave Laza out of it. He never advised me one way or the other. I handed him my resignation to forward it to you. He was kind enough to say that he would try. That's all."

"Where is it?" Draga asked the general.

Laza reached into the inside pocket of his tunic and handed the envelope to her. Without opening it, she tore it into a handful of scraps, flinging them angrily into his face.

"That takes care of that!"

Laza, his hands nonchalantly flicking off the bits of paper clinging to his tunic, endured the affront with the calmness of a father waiting for a child's tantrum to play itself out.

"What a shame," he said quietly. "It was such a well-written piece of work. I'm sure the captain spent days on it."

Nicola grinned. "It wasn't all wasted. I've kept a copy."

"You've been taking too many liberties, General," Draga pointed out petulantly. "You're only the king's aide-de-camp. Don't fancy yourself his *éminence grise*."

Laza shook his head with quiet aggravation. "You certainly make life hard for the people who love you, madame." He started for the door, but when he reached for the handle, was stopped by Draga's voice.

"May I remind you, General, that I haven't dismissed you?"

Turning, he remained at the door.

"Let's quit playing games, Draga," he said, annoyed. "At least when we're among ourselves. You may be queen to all people, but not to me. The day I accept you for my queen will be a very sad day for you. Because I could never be loyal to you as a queen or to any queen for that matter. I am no medieval knight to break lance with my lady's detractors. But I can prove to be damn loyal to a friend. I hope I don't have to remind you of that."

He walked off, irreverently slamming the door. Nikodiye began collecting the shreds of the torn letter from the carpet, rolling them into a ball, which he handed to Nicola.

"Here. You don't want your resignation picked from the wastebasket by mysterious hands. It might reach the newspapers before it reaches Sasha. You know how funny he is about such things."

There was a knock on the door.

"Now what?" Draga sighed. "Entrez."

It was Milica. She curtsied. "Forgive the disturbance, madame, but there are ladies waiting in the anteroom who have been ordered for nine o'clock. And six more in the Serbian room. It's eleven thirty now. Shall I tell them to come back another day?"

"No," the queen said. "I'll receive them." She turned to her brothers. "You may go. Leave through my bedroom, so you don't bump into Sasha and have to tell him what you came to see me about."

They reacted like schoolboys to the "Class dismissed" bell. Dashing through the boudoir and the bedroom, they slammed the doors shut with loud bangs, causing the windowpanes to rattle.

"Keep out of trouble, will you?" the queen called after them without hoping for an answer. She heard them, spurs jingling and heels beating a joyous tattoo on the stone floor, storm through the laundry room and the entrance hall to the front exit.

With admiration and a touch of envy, Draga shook her head and murmured, "So spirited, so full of life." Then reaching for the audience list in Milica's hand, she said aloud, "Let's see what the punishment is for today."

Wearily she studied the list. All women scheduled to be received had come to her expecting help, in the form of miracles: a son freed from military service, a widow granted an old age pension, a nephew enrolled in the Military Academy or helped to a government job. Young men with high school diplomas considered it beneath their station to follow in their father's footsteps, to be peasants or pig breeders or artisans. All of them wanted to work for the government, yet there were just so many positions to be filled in the ministries and just so many posts for prefects or subprefects in local administrations. No one, not even the queen, could conjure up new career opportunities. Even Alexander's bold stroke of simply closing ten high schools throughout the country had failed to remedy the situation. Classics education still produced a greater number of graduates unwilling to go back to the land than Serbia's bureaucracy could absorb. Each petitioner sent home empty-handed joined the ever-growing crowd of malcontents. In other countries, the key to progress lay in the education of the masses; in bizarre, ungovernable Serbia it merely added to the initial chaos. Why was it, Draga wondered, that familiarity with the declension of Latin nouns, Newton's law of gravity or the history of the Thirty Years' War invariably turned docile young Serbs into militant radicals?

In countries west of the Danube, banks, factories, import and export agencies, department stores and utility companies employed millions of clerks, tellers, bookkeepers, salesmen, managers, yet the sole use to which a graduate of a Serbian Gymnasium could put his hard-earned education was either to work for the government or to take a walk in the Kalemegdan Gardens and recite Schiller's "Der Ring des Polycrates" to the starlings perched on their shady oak trees.

"Let's begin, Milica," Draga said with a sigh. "I wonder what impossible requests I'll have to deny today."

Noon

"**W**HAT seems to be the trouble now, Mika?" the general asked. It had been a day full of vexations.

"General Tzintzar-Markovich," Naumovich reported, choking on the words. "He wants to see the king immediately."

"Jesus Christ, you make it sound as if the Turkish army were storming the palace. Do you know what he wants?"

"He didn't say."

On a day when the king rose late, the arrival of the prime minister threatened to upset an already-tight schedule.

"Where is the general?"

"I made him wait in my office," Naumovich said. Despite the shave and the freshly pressed uniform, he still looked as though he hadn't been to bed or changed his clothes for two days. Laza wondered what could possibly contribute to making a man age so rapidly overnight.,

"Why the hell didn't you announce the prime minister to the king? Why run to me?"

"Because the king won't see him. I have orders from his majesty to turn the prime minister down in case he asks for an audience." Naumovich looked miserable. "I really don't know how to handle the situation."

"What's there to handle? Tell the prime minister to go home."

"He says he'll hand in his resignation if he isn't received immediately."

"He might do it even if he is received. Then the king will appoint a new Cabinet. Happens every few months."

Nevertheless, Laza rose and, emitting a deep sigh of frustration, left the office, with Naumovich following him like a man on his way to be flogged.

As though he were his own statue, Prime Minister-General Tzintzar-Markovich was seated—stiff and immobile—in the chair where Naumovich had left him. A tall, impressive-looking man, he resembled in many ways the late King Milan, yet without Milan's disarming charm. Since he outranked the other man in seniority, he accepted Laza's greeting with a nod, indicating his displeasure by the nervous twitching of his mustache.

After some polite small talk to which the premier responded with icy yesses and nos, Laza said, "Paul Marinkovich, our minister to Bulgaria, is presently with the king. But I'll see what I can do."

"I know who Marinkovich is," the premier snapped. "I appointed him. Listen here, General"—he pulled out his watch and glanced at it—"I'll give you one minute to announce me to the king or I'll go in without being announced."

He was mistaken if he hoped to disconcert Laza.

"That wouldn't do much good, General. You must know by now that his majesty is very keen on observing the rules of court etiquette."

"This is not the court of Queen Victoria."

"How true, sir. Because in that case you'd be the Earl of Balfour and not General Tzintzar-Markovich."

Without waiting for the prime minister's reaction, Laza entered the adjoining conference room, used primarily for Cabinet meetings and small, informal receptions. Blaho Bukovacz's paintings depicting scenes of Serbia's heroic past decorated its walls. A ray of sun found its way through the partition of the lace curtains to Queen Draga's marble bust in a corner. Laza couldn't help comparing the smile around the soft, young lips to the deep lines revealed on the queen's face that morning.

The double-winged door to the audience room, decorated in Arabian style with silk-upholstered divans and mother-of-pearl-inlaid taborets, stood wide open. Talking in a tone much too loud and shrill for the intimacy of the milieu, the young king was pacing the floor. Paul Marinkovich, a dapper man in his thirties, pivoted politely on his heels in order to keep his face turned to the royal presence. Seeing Laza approaching Alexander halted in midsentence. The aide-de-camp bowed, advanced a few steps and bowed again.

"I am sorry to disturb your majesty, but the prime minister is humbly requesting an audience."

The king frowned, then nervously removed his pince-nez and cleaned it with his handkerchief. Looking at his young face left naked without the by now characteristic glasses, Laza once again became aware of his strange resemblance to his beautiful mother. With his pallid complexion, premature puffiness under the eyes and an expression of discontent covering his entire face like a mask, Alexander wasn't—even by his most devoted subjects—called handsome, whereas his mother had been considered the greatest beauty ever to grace a throne. The late Empress Elisabeth of Austria, Eugénie de Montijo, Princess Alexandra of England all were lovely ladies, but none had possessed the striking, sensuous perfection of Alexander's mother, Natalie Kechko.

It was on a summer day in 1874, that Natalie had first set foot on Serbian soil. The previous May the news that its reigning prince—Serbia had become a kingdom as recently as 1882—had chosen a Russian commoner instead of a princess for his future wife shocked and disappointed the country. All resentment evaporated completely, however, the moment Natalie, seated beside her handsome fiancé, rode in an open carriage through the streets of Belgrade.

She and her aunt had been on their way to board a Danube steamboat to the Kechkos' Crimean estates and had stopped over for a day in Belgrade. Freshly out of the Military Academy, Lieutenant Laza Petrovich and his company formed part of the honor guard lined up along the pier. Natalie wore a pink-and-white batiste dress crisp as a freshly opened rose and on top of her coal-black hair a tiny hat of pink net. Though only eighteen and so slim that she seemed practically weightless, she radiated the unadulterated sexuality of a pasha's favorite concubine.

She submitted herself with the easy grace of the invulnerably rich to the inspection of dignitaries and gaping mob and her never-fading smile and ready response to the most asinine speeches captured and overwhelmed her former detractors.

Her family of mixed Russian and Bessarabian blood, with an ample dose of the Levantine, had immense holdings in the south of Russia which assured her a life of far greater luxury and freedom than that of most royal princesses. Spoiled by her doting parents, she had never had a wish denied, her beauty turning every member, male or female, of her social circle into an admiring slave. After her presentation at the czar's court, she moved in the glamorous world of international society, as several young Kechko men and women had married into the aristocracy, replating many a historical name with commoners' gold.

Laza had stared at her just as bewitched as any unsophisticated housewife or common soldier in the crowd. Her beauty left him dazed. His infatuation with her had remained always in some strange way, the leitmotiv of his life.

Every man, Laza realized, even a Don Juan as cynical as he, thirsted at times for the wonder of a worshipful emotion untouched by carnal desire. What he felt for Natalie was a young monk's adoration of the Virgin, an art *aficionado*'s appreciation of the "Winged Victory." It failed to keep him from affairs with other women, including Draga, or from marrying his wife and begetting four children. Even Natalie's own imperfections of character could never dampen his devotion, the strongest proof of which was his unfaltering loyalty to her son.

The resemblance between mother and son had never seemed more striking to Laza than during the ceremony which followed Milan's abdication. The thirteen-year-old Alexander was being proclaimed King of Serbia. Staged by Milan, the great "director *manqué*," in the White Hall of the New Konak, it was a highly dramatic event, culminating in Milan's sinking to his knees before the boy to pronounce his allegiance to him, his new sovereign. It was a touching moment, and no eye remained dry in the packed hall, none except the young king's. He stood with an expression of triumph on his face, his hand failing to reach out for the father kneeling at his feet. He continued to retain his uncanny poise later, as well, when the state dignitaries and high-ranking officers of the army paid homage to him. Watching his performance, Laza had been filled with a mixture of awe and aversion.

The by then divorced and exiled Natalie must have been aware of Laza's devotion, for she chose him to be liaison between herself and the son from whom she was now separated. To be equerry to a thirteen-year-old boy was not the most glorious appointment, but a loyal Laza had remained at his post waiting for the boy to grow up and become king in the true sense of the word.

This happened sooner than anyone, even Laza, had foreseen. He had been on duty on the night which later became known as Alexander's first *coup d'état*.

The seventeen-year-old king had extended dinner invitations to the two regents, Yovan Ristich and General Yotsa Belimarkovich, who were to head the government until his coming of age. He had also invited the principal members of the Cabinet.

Only Lieutenant Colonel Tyirich, his first aide-de-camp, had been in on the plans; the rest of his entourage merely suspected that some important event was about to take place. During the meal of Serbian peasant dishes—the regents, in their patriotic fervor, had banned Milan's French chef from the royal kitchen —Laza detected a certain absentmindedness in the usually very proper and self-possessed Alexander. The young king kept glancing at his watch, which wasn't in character either.

The entrance of Lieutenant Colonel Tyirich, who had been conspicuously absent during the dinner, seemed to be the signal he had been awaiting. After listening to the colonel's whispered report, he rose and in a perfectly calm voice informed the regents and the Cabinet members that he no longer needed their services, for he considered himself of age and consequently was ready to assume the prerogatives of the crown.

After a moment of stunned silence, the regents reacted with outraged protests. Alexander, still perfectly cool and in control, called their attention to the troops ringing the palace grounds. The coup had been prepared with the approval of the army; consequently, all resistance was futile. He invited the dignitaries to spend the night at the palace as his guests; should they refuse, he added, he would be compelled to consider them his prisoners.

General Belimarkovich, a rather simple man, still too bewildered to grasp the gravity of the moment, muttered an obscenity and, turning his back on the king, headed for the exit. At a gesture from the king Colonel Tyirich barred the way, sword drawn. Perplexed, the old man halted. With his back arched, his bushy head lowered, he reminded Laza of a bull ready to charge the toreador's cape. It was a tense moment with the threat of violence in the air. Then the starch of defiance left Belimarkovich's heavy body. He slumped as though stung by an invisible whip and trotted back to the dismayed group around Yovan Ristich.

The scene, a seventeen-year-old boy imposing his will on men twice, three times his age, had touches, Laza thought, of the grotesque and the diabolical. Of course, there had been advisers and strategists available; nevertheless, the decisive act, the final confrontation had been left to the king. It called not only for impudence, but for courage. Serbs, even when asked to a royal dinner party, seldom went unarmed. By the time the palace guards dashed in, Alexander could have been shot dead or hacked to pieces by his guests. It was his incredible sangfroid that prevented the deposed regents and Cabinet members from putting up any resistance. They spent the night—just as he had ordered them to—in the New Konak. By dawn his royal proclamation had been posted on every available wall in the country, and all army units had pledged their allegiance to him.

Since the dismissal of the regents and a Cabinet composed of Liberals, Alexander had caused the three parties—Liberal, Radical and Progressive—to play musical chairs. The Radical Cabinet of Dr. Lazar Dokich, Alexander's onetime tutor, was followed by a Liberal one, then a coalition of Liberals and Progressives, only to bounce back to the Russophile Radicals after the king's marriage to Draga. Once again the Radicals were dismissed to be replaced by a group without party affiliations. The king, believing in the theory of the new broom, still discarded his old ones too swiftly, allowing them no time to sweep the dirt left by their predecessors under the rug.

Demeter Tzintzar-Markovich, distinguished veteran of wars with Turkey and Bulgaria and ex-commander in chief of the active army, represented the last of the brooms. Complying with the king's wishes, he had conjured up election results that completely eliminated the troublesome Radicals from the new parliament. Perturbed by the hostile reaction of the country, Alexander had decided to save face by making his premier the scapegoat. For days, he had been conducting secret interviews with politicians to find a successor to the general, yet without much success.

"What does the premier want?" he asked Laza.

"I don't know, sire."

"Haven't you asked?"

"No, sire."

"I won't see him," the king retorted.

"Very well, your majesty. I'll tell him that." Laza bowed and began backing from the room. Just as he expected, the king stopped him before he could reach the door.

"Wait!" He turned to Paul Marinkovich. "I'd better see the old buzzard. Don't leave town, though. Come back tonight at eight. We won't be disturbed then."

Laza waited for the envoy to leave the room, then said sternly to the king. "I wouldn't call my prime minister names if I were you. At least not before you found a replacement."

If Alexander resented the tone of the remark, he failed to show it. Appearing suddenly weary and at least ten years older, he slumped down onto a soft divan.

"Call him in," he sighed.

Ramrod-stiff and wearing the expression of a scornful Olympian, General Tzintzar-Markovich strode in, halted at the proper distance from his sovereign, clicked his heels and bowed low.

"General of the Army Demeter Tzintzar-Markovich, president of your majesty's Cabinet, is respectfully reporting," he rattled off in the correct military manner.

To be at hand in case nerves became frayed, Laza had followed the general.

"What seems to be the trouble, Mito?" the king asked. His addressing the premier by his diminutive indicated to Laza that his warning had made an impression.

"I've come, sire, to respectfully tender my and my Cabinet's resignation." The voice was loud, but hollow as though coming from behind a wall.

Scowling his surprise, the king shook his head. "You can't do that to me!" he cried petulantly. "No, I won't accept your resignation!"

"You have no choice, sire," the general told him, looking not at the king, but through the open doorway at the entwined bodies of Turk and Serb warriors in the picture representing the Battle of Kosovo. "I've reached the point, sire, where I am no longer able to carry on. I must seek relief from my responsibilities as they've become too heavy a burden for me."

With a suddenness that made the general recoil, Alexander jumped to his feet.

"You can't do that to me!" he repeated. "Not now! Not before the reaction to your goddamn elections has quieted down."

Tzintzar-Markovich's mouth fell open, and his eyes turned glassy, reminding Laza of a stuffed shark he had once seen mounted on the wall of the Maritime Museum in Trieste.

"*My* elections?" he asked. "May I remind you, sire, that the elections were conducted in the very manner you yourself delineated to me. And may I remind you, sire, that I did predict they wouldn't work. That neither at home nor abroad would the results be accepted. That the idea of Captain Lunyevitza's succession to the throne would be rejected by both the army and the population. That the only way out of the muddle would be to drop the whole scheme for the time being. Last night Captain Nikodiye and his brother created another incident at the Serbian Crown. The sole condition under which I and my Cabinet are willing to carry on is the Lunyevitza brothers' demotion. Prove to the people, sire, that you consider the dignity and prestige of the army more important than a woman's whim."

Alexander removed his pince-nez, rubbing it pensively against the cloth of his trousers, a boyhood habit he had often been scolded for by his mother.

"You've always hated the queen, haven't you?" he asked in an oddly muffled tone.

"No, your majesty." The premier shook his head. "I have great admiration for her as a person, even as a wife. But as a queen? That is an entirely different matter."

"You've always hated her." The king repeated it with the stubbornness of an intractable child. "Don't think I have forgotten how you sided with Papa against her."

"Why bring that up now? That's past history." Laza spoke from the far end of the room.

"You and Milovan Pavlovich!" the king went on. "Some Cabinet! I'm certainly blessed. Both my premier and my minister of defense are my sworn enemies!"

"I respectfully resent that accusation, sire, in my as well as Milovan's name. We have served you faithfully and to the best of our abilities."

The king's pasty cheeks turned red as he worked himself into a rage. "I know you, I know you all. You don't give a damn about me, the dynasty or the country. You'd sell your souls to the devil for a few lousy dinars. You don't care whom you are working for, just so you can stay near the fleshpots!"

The general had been standing at stiff attention, but now became literally petrified.

"Sire, you've insulted not only me, but also the uniform I am wearing. If you weren't my sovereign, I'd kill you for it. But you *are* my sovereign, so I merely demand that you apologize."

"Your uniform," the king scoffed. "There isn't one officer in this whole goddamn army who can't be bought. Of the corps, eighteen hundred are illiterate peasants and the rest drunks, gamblers, social climbers, pimps, embezzlers. Just remember the scandals we've been through. Regimental funds evaporating, frauds, criminal negligence. . . ."

"When a man has a wife and children and must exist for months without getting paid—" the general began, but was cut off.

"We're a joke of a country with an army that's nothing but the sad imitation of the Western military. So don't pretend you are knights in shining armor—"

His anger approaching boiling point, the premier raised his voice to a loud, disrespectful bellow. "Let me warn you, sire, the country is at the end of its rope. If you were smart you'd put good relations with the army above everything else, because the moment you lose us, you've lost the throne. Stop persecuting able officers for political reasons, pay them regularly, listen to their grievances and see to it that they're promoted according to seniority. Allow me to give you one more bit of advice. Whoever my successor will be, treat him with more consideration than you've treated me, because whether you accept my resignation or not makes very little difference. I consider myself as having resigned." Clicking his heels, he executed a military about-face and marched from the room.

"You don't have my permission to leave!" the king shouted after him as the door fell shut. "I'll have Tzintzar-Markovich arrested!" he screamed to Laza.

Dismayed, Laza shook his head. "You'll do no such thing. I don't understand you. Why didn't you accept his resignation? You wanted him out anyway."

"It's up to me to say when."

Laza's look was one of reprimand. "Good God, Sasha, won't you ever grow up?"

It wasn't often that he permitted himself reversion to the intimacy of Alexander's boyhood. Right now he felt the avuncular approach was badly needed. That the young king was becoming increasingly difficult to handle, though failing to surprise Laza, troubled him deeply. No one could expect a person born to the throne and brought up by parents as impossible as Milan and Natalie to mature as a normal human being.

"I'll call on the general this afternoon," Laza said, "and see if I can make him reconsider. In the meanwhile, if I were you, I wouldn't have the bill about the succession of Nikodiye—or even about the inviolability of the queen's family—submitted to the parliament. At least, not for a while."

"I'll have to ask the queen about that." Alexander pulled out his watch and glanced at it. "It's twelve forty, almost time for *déjeuner*. I won't receive anyone else this morning. How about a game of billiards?" As he started for the billiard room off the study, Laza barred his way.

"There's someone I want you to see first. And, please, don't bristle when I tell you who it is."

Alexander screwed up his eyes. "Tell me."

"Michael Vassilovich."

The king's face turned purple. "That bastard? What the devil should I see him for? And who gave him permission to set foot in the Konak?"

"I did. What's more, I ordered him to report to me. And I want you to approve his appointment to equerry."

"To what?" Alexander screeched, then burst out laughing, a shrill, feline laughter. "You're out of your mind! What are you trying to do? Demolish the Konak from within? You don't even put the enemy in a wooden horse, just invite him to move in. *Qu'est-ce que vous faîtes de moi? La risée du monde?*"

"Make peace with your father's clique, Sasha. You can't

afford to have the whole world against you. This man has never been involved in politics, not even while in your father's service. Despite his unquestionable devotion to King Milan, he's never uttered a bad word against you or Draga, although he had enough reason."

"That's what I mean. We can't have him here. The queen wouldn't stand for it."

"She would. I've asked her."

The flicker of jealous suspicion behind the thick lenses of the royal pince-nez warned Laza to tread with caution.

"She wasn't pleased, but I talked her into leaving the decision to you. Understand, Sasha, you must become reconciled with the army. Of course, not overnight. You can't, for instance, recall Colonel Mashin to active service, because that would be too abrupt. This man, Vassilovich, has many things in his favor. He stayed abroad, not as an exile, but for reasons of health, was never a controversial figure, is well liked by both the younger and the older members of the officers' corps. Use him now and discard him later. I wouldn't want him here forever, either."

The king reflected for a long moment, then sighed resignedly. "All right, I'll see him." Watching Laza start for the door, he called after him, "Later this afternoon."

"No," Laza said, as he left the room. "Now."

For the better part of the morning, Michael had been sitting on a hard, straight chair in the adjutants' room waiting to be admitted to the king's presence.

The most conspicuous change he had noticed in the Old Konak, at least in the rooms he had seen, was the abundance of portraits of Draga Mashin—paintings and photographs—covering every inch of available wall space. In some instances, old pictures had been removed to make room for her as though the building were a museum dedicated to the memory of a much revered and dead martyr.

The staff consisted of mostly new men except for a few old hands like Laza, who at one time or another had belonged to Alexander's entourage, yet not during Milan's tenure as king. Watching them scurrying about, Michael noticed a strange restlessness in them, the kind migratory birds display before starting out for warmer regions. It might have been his imagination playing tricks on him, for he knew of a tomorrow they did not. Or did they?

Merely to while away the tedium of waiting, he tried to engage Lieutenant Bogdanovich in conversation but gave up after receiving only noncommittal grunts in return. There was constant traffic through the office: people arriving for audiences, petitioners leaving written requests, members of the staff reporting for duty or being relieved. Bits of information kept falling on the room like loose feathers from a flight of birds. Michael learned that the king had gone straight from the queen's bedroom to his study to confer with the minister to Bulgaria who had been ordered up in great secrecy and haste from Sofia the day before. Shortly after noon the stormy arrival of Premier Tzintzar-Markovich caused considerable commotion. His sonorous basso from Colonel Naumovich's office reverberated throughout the upper and lower floors, then, after a period of quiet, boomed from the king's audience room. Intermittently a younger and more strident tenor, which Michael recognized to be Alexander's, cut through his deep voice like a lighthouse beacon through a foggy night. The next sound Michael heard was the prime minister's angry footsteps thumping to the exit.

"No great harmony between king and government," Michael remarked to Bogdanovich.

Without looking up from the heap of documents he was sorting, the lieutenant mumbled, "No. The saying 'thick as thieves' doesn't apply to them."

It was surprising irreverence coming from the officer of the day at the Old Konak. Under Milan, Michael thought, Bogdanovich wouldn't have lasted an hour at his post.

"You don't seem to approve of the general," Michael went on.

He never received an answer, for at that moment he was summoned to General Laza's office. The king had consented to receive him.

1 A.M.

MICHAEL halted in the doorway, saluted, took a few steps forward, then saluted again.

"Captain Michael Vassilovich respectfully reporting for duty, your majesty," he said, feeling grateful for the military code that allowed him to cover his discomfort with a set phrase.

The king nodded. "Thank you, Captain." There was an uneasy silence. "So you've returned home, after all. Well, what's new in—wherever you've been."

Alexander seemed nervous, yet in perfect control of himself. Michael knew that there was a sharp and absorbent brain enclosed in the oddly shaped cranium, but also harmful and uncontrollable passions in the body with the narrow shoulders, long, thin limbs and protruding embonpoint. The strange, jerky walk revealed a certain lack of coordination, and the prison pallor of the face and the flabbiness of the flesh an unrestrained regimen. Although having spent years in close contact with another king, Michael was still puzzled, though certainly not awed, by the very nature of royalty, of a sovereign's unshakable belief in his own superiority and infallibility. If Alexander had ever had doubts about the wisdom of his actions, he failed to show it. Milan could occasionally say, "I am sorry," or "I was wrong," but one had yet to hear those words from the son. Alexander, the grandnephew of swineherds and highwaymen, only three generations removed from Milosh Obrenovich, who had considered an enemy's head the most suitable gift to consolidate a friendship, judged himself to be the sole person fit to rule over his two and a half million fellow citizens.

"I was in Switzerland, sire, and nothing new ever happens there. Same old lakes, same old mountains, same old people."

"Did Peter Karageorgevich impress you as old?" Alexander asked sharply.

Involuntarily, Michael glanced at Laza to see whether the king's question was the beginning of a planned inquisition or merely boyish braggadocio, yet could detect only an expression of bored annoyance on the general's face. He decided to play it straightforwardly.

"No, sire, I think he looks fairly well for his age."

"Ah, you saw him."

"Yes, your majesty. At church. For a free thinker, he attends services quite regularly."

His answer must have taken the wind out of the king's sail, for he dropped the subject of Peter.

"So you were in Geneva."

"Yes, sire, Geneva, Lugano, Davos, Zurich."

"You seem to like Switzerland." Alexander steered away from dangerous grounds.

"I have every reason to. Switzerland restored my health."

They were sparring, both aware of the other's thoughts. Michael: *So this is what she's been sleeping with for six years.* And Alexander: *Would she sleep with him again if he wanted her to?* The woman's specter hovered over them, and each envisioned, in the secret recesses of his mind, the other one in bed with her.

"I am glad to hear that," the king went on. "I mean that your health has been restored. Lucky for you that you didn't stay in Serbia. I'm afraid our medical facilities are still in a primitive state. We have to depend on foreigners or physicians educated abroad. Usually factory rejects. Doctors who can make a good living in the West don't come here. One of my most urgent tasks is to establish a medical school. *Mon Dieu,* there is so much to do. If only one could be allowed to concentrate on the needs of the country instead of wasting one's time and energy on placating ruffled political egos. *Eh bien,* one tries to do one's best for the people, and, with God's help, *on va réussir.*" He halted for a second, looking put upon. "Thank heaven, I am young enough. That's my advantage over men like Peter Karageorgevich. The difference of thirty years. Just think what I'll have achieved by the time I am his age."

He kept pacing the floor, throwing out his legs from the hip joint, stiff-kneed and pigeon-toed, as if he were a tabetic old man. The silence dragged on, with Michael waiting tensely for a word of dismissal. He knew that his summons to the Konak would keep Colonel Mashin and his men in suspense, and at the present time, any added pressure might cause a premature explosion. Also, he lacked the born conspirator's cunning and nonchalance, and the king's ignorance of the danger lurking around the corner unnerved him. Up to now the *coup d'état* had had a fictitious quality, but the face-to-face encounter with its victim suddenly turned it into sobering reality.

Meeting Colonel Mashin's group in the morning had been the first disturbing shock, and now the sight of the man who might be a corpse by midnight was the second. It made him physically ill with a nauseating headache, illuminating a long-forgotten picture in his memory.

Michael had been six years old when a traveling circus came to Belgrade, setting up its big tent on the parade grounds. One of its attractions was a scantily clad lady performing with a boa constrictor. After the show, he had sneaked into the enclosure where the wagons were parked. It happened to be feeding time for the animals, and he watched in wide-eyed terror a small white rabbit being placed in the snake's glass-fronted cage. As a cheery afterthought, someone pushed a lettuce leaf through the slats on the top of the cage. Unaware of the coiled reptile, the rabbit began to chew greedily on the lettuce and was half finished when the snake stirred and—its mouth opening wide— pounced upon the rabbit, seizing it—lettuce and all—with the swiftness of lightning. Michael clearly remembered the mortal terror that had made him scream, also his mother's slaps that had brought him back to his senses. What was so incredibly cruel about the scene was not the moment of the kill, but the rabbit's innocent enjoyment of the lettuce leaf seconds before its death.

God knows, Michael reasoned, Alexander was no white rabbit, yet his untroubled feasting on the lettuce leaf of royal power repulsed and, at the same time, perturbed him.

A magazine lying on the desk seemed to have caught the king's attention. Without picking it up, he leaned over to leaf through its pages. There was a long, awkward silence, the kind that settles on a party after all topics have been exhausted, except the one foremost on everyone's mind.

"I understand, you remained with Papa till the very end." Alexander's tone was deliberately chatty.

Absorbed in his thoughts, Michael was slow to realize he had been addressed. When he finally answered, his words erupted in nervous spurts. "Yes, yes, sire—till the very end."

"His death was rather abrupt, wasn't it? I mean, completely unexpected."

The king's eyes were still on the magazine. Behind his back, Laza flashed a signal to Michael, warning him to watch his answer. Michael chose to disregard the warning.

"No, sire, it wasn't at all unexpected. He had been ailing for some time. Losing his strength, his vitality." He observed with secret satisfaction the fake unconcern fade from the king's face. The bastard was mistaken if he expected to hear an absolving word, Michael thought. "When I took the liberty of wiring your majesty about his illness, he was already critically ill."

"If he were alive today, he'd be only forty-eight," the king mused. "He seemed so strong. I expected him to live forever. The day I became anointed, there was a ninety-year-old peasant in one of the deputations. I asked about him the other day. He is still alive, yet Papa is dead. I think, forty-eight is terribly young to die." He suddenly wheeled about to face Michael. "We had our disagreements; nevertheless, I miss him. *Il me manque beaucoup.*" He turned to the general. "I'm afraid we won't have time for our billiard game, Laza. The queen has invited a French couple to *déjeuner,* people she met in Biarritz. I promised her not to be late."

He started for the entrance hall. Passing Michael, he stopped, proffering his hand. *"Adieu,* Captain. I hope you won't find it difficult to get used to our barbaric ways again. This isn't Switzerland, you know, and I am not Peter Karageorgevich."

Although he knew Alexander expected him to kiss it, Michael took hold of the hand, giving it a firm shake.

The encounter with the king had stirred Michael more deeply than he had thought possible. He had joined the conspirators in the strong belief that his motives were strictly patriotic, with his personal grudge against Alexander playing no part in it. The king was a misfit and had to be removed from the throne for the good of the country. Fully independent for only twenty-five years, Serbia was still going through the trauma of a painful birth, and its survival depended on the man who was to lead it during its next crucial years. To justify —mainly to himself—his participation in the *coup d'état,* Michael considered Prince Peter this man.

Milosh Nenadovich's message informed him that preparations for the *coup d'état* were completed, thus the time had come to ask Prince Peter for his final consent, and Michael found himself going through a period of painful self-appraisal. He had reached his mid-thirties without any meaningful or praiseworthy achievement to his credit, the realization of which caused him to see himself as a failure and a drone. There were moments when he wished he were back in the Swiss sanatorium where survival had been considered a brave accomplishment. Gaining a kilo a week or reducing one's temperature by a tenth of a grade elicited envy and admiration from one's fellow patients. The man with enough willpower to follow conscientiously his doctor's orders, abstaining from cigarettes, drink and women, was the winner over the patient in the next room, who had succumbed to the temptations of the flesh. Unfortunately, in the outside world, as Michael was learning, no one became a hero by merely staying alive.

When the gates of the sanatorium had slammed shut behind him, he felt as though he had entered a vast amusement park. Like a small boy wondering whether to ride the roller coaster or the merry-go-round first, he approached its exhibits with breathless haste. Then, suddenly, his euphoria evaporated. The barkers' spiels grated on his nerves, and none of the promised thrills attracted him. An inheritance from his grandfather offered him financial security, service in the peacetime army a daily schedule, his friends relief from loneliness, but none of these a *raison d'être,* a justification for his existence. Politics would have been the answer, if he had not detested Serbian politicians and their *modus operandi.* Supporting the *coup d'état* was not politics but an act of patriotism; he even made it a condition for his participation that he be left out of the new government. His role would be to keep his independence and act as watchdog each time the new set appeared to be repeating the old one's mistakes.

What alone disturbed him was his still much too virulent loathing for Alexander. He feared it would—in his own conscience—degrade his patriotic mission to a personal vendetta against the rival who had stolen his mistress.

As God was his witness, there was a strong enough case against King Alexander. As Milan's constant companion and closest friend, Michael had had an unique opportunity to observe the son's transformation from a cuddly, restive small boy into a treacherous, vengeful adult. None of the royal entourage possessed the kind of insight into the young man's character that he did, for he alone had witnessed incidents affecting not only the relationship between father and son, but the destiny of Serbia and, in the long run, of the entire continent as well.

As he recalled the events leading to the estrangement between father and son, it never ceased to amaze Michael how such a seemingly trivial matter had led to the most fateful tragedy in Serbian history.

In the spring of 1899, Michael had accompanied the two kings, Milan and Alexander, on a tour of western Serbia which, as it turned out, became the high point of Alexander's reign. It was hard to tell whether the population's enthusiasm was artificially fostered or genuine; all Michael remembered was a sea of beaming faces and waving hands and the roar of *Zhiveo Kralj Alexander* mixed with *Zhiveo Kralj Milan,* ebbing and flowing like the sound of waves.

Russian-sponsored articles in the foreign press labeled Milan's return to Serbia a disgrace; nevertheless, it seemed to have the sincere approval of the common people. His presence promising—if not *panem*—certainly *circenses,* Milan, with his warm smile and firm handshake, could mellow his severest critics and turn them into partisans.

Michael had marveled often at the perfect smoothness with which the double-headed kingship had functioned in all respects except matters concerning the Draga Mashin affair, which at that time didn't appear to be of vital importance, however. The ease and cooperation between the two men seated on the same throne were truly remarkable. The *modus operandi* had invariably been determined by Milan; Alexander simply followed directions. In public, Milan went out of his way to treat Alexander with the loyal subject's reverence, yet none of their intimates had any doubt that all governmental decisions depended on the father's approval. If, at times, Alexander seemed uncomfortable in his role, it was only because he lacked his father's great histrionic talents. He was a poor actor, and his performance became strained occasionally, while his father breezed through his with the self-assurance of the born professional.

The reason for the tour to be indelibly etched in Michael's memory had been a strange encounter in Valjevo, the first town visited by the two kings.

While taking a late-afternoon stroll, Michael happened to glance into an alley, where he caught sight of Draga Mashin hurriedly entering the basement door of a house. Though unable to recognize her with any degree of certainty—she wore a long duster—his instinct told him that it was indeed she. Later that night, after Milan and son had retired to their suites at the prefecture, Michael left for another walk, this time stopping in a dark doorway opposite the basement entrance through which he had seen Draga disappear. It had not taken long to have his suspicions confirmed. Unescorted and wearing an officer's greatcoat without insignia, his cap pulled down over his eyes, King Alexander came rushing down the alley to be admitted, without having to knock, by someone who had obviously been awaiting his arrival.

Draga had to have a firm hold on her little king, Michael reasoned with a touch of bitterness, if Alexander was willing to brave his father's displeasure by taking her along on the royal tour.

When Alexander's liaison with her had first become the talk of Belgrade, Milan, no doubt feeling it wouldn't last, chose to ignore it. Within a few months' time, however, his patience worn thin, he embarked on a campaign against this woman he had always viewed with a jaundiced eye.

The first clash between father and son occurred over Draga's presence at a gala dinner held at the New Konak. The argument ended in a promise from Alexander that he would never again permit her to attend an official function. Of course, he couldn't prevent other people from inviting her to their homes, he added apologetically. After all, whether his father agreed or not, she happened to be a very attractive young woman, admired by Belgrade's society, as well as by the diplomatic corps.

During the ensuing months, Michael was often present when Milan's annoyance with his son's infatuation exploded in tiffs of increasing sharpness. On the rare occasions when he found her invited to the same social affair, Milan would retire to the host's study and remain there, sulking, until it was time to leave. On another occasion, as Alexander and his father were on their way to the house of the German minister, Baron Waecker-Gotter, Michael, escorting them on horseback, overheard Milan ask his son: "By the way, will your mistress be at the soiree tonight?"

"*Mon Dieu*, Papa," Alexander answered, peeved, "the baron isn't my subject. I can't prescribe whom he should invite."

"Which means that you know she'll be there. Well, *mon garçon*, that's just fine. You can't tell the baron whom to invite; neither can you tell me whom to associate with. So let's stop the carriage, because I am getting out." He called to the coachman. "Pull to the curb, Yovan!"

Before the coachman could execute the order, it was rescinded by Alexander, who placed the poor fellow on the horns of a dilemma about whom to obey.

The squabble continued with Alexander's high-pitched voice nervously overshouting his father's grumbling. They must not have a scandal, he insisted. His father's getting out in the middle of the avenue would start tongues wagging, and the foreign press would have a field day.

Milan finally gave in. "All right. I'll go with you to that damn party, but only if you give me your word of honor that I shall never again run into that woman."

Michael missed Alexander's answer. Evidently he gave his word, for Milan rode on.

In both Lazarevats and Obrenovats, the second and third towns on the royal itinerary, Michael succeeded, though not without some discreet detective work, in locating Draga's hiding places. Since he had never intended to inform on the pair to Milan or to anyone else, by the time they reached Shabats, the last stop on the tour, he had regained control over his obsession to spy on them and had stopped playing Sherlock Holmes.

The enthusiasm with which the Shabatsers received the two

kings dwarfed all previous demonstrations of loyalty. The crowds were denser here than elsewhere, the torches brighter, the parades more colorful. Of all present, only Zivko Andjelich, the newly appointed prefect of the city, failed to take part in the general rejoicing.

Michael knew him to be a man of easily dispensable conscience who, during his long and shady career, had rendered certain invaluable services to politicians, including King Milan. By the spring of 1899 he had achieved a semblance of respectability; hence his elevation to the prefecture of his city.

When earlier in the afternoon, a veritable rain of medals had fallen on Shabats dignitaries, Andjelich had expected to receive the Order of Milosh the Great, the highest Serbian decoration. Instead, the White Eagle Fourth Class was pinned to his chest.

Alexander had been informed of Andjelich's aspirations, yet when he mentioned them to Milan, the ex-king exploded.

"You must be out of your mind, *mon garçon*, to give the Order of Milosh to that scoundrel!"

The debate had taken place in the father's bedroom. Of the entourage, Michael alone was present.

"But, Papa," Alexander had argued, "Andjelich has rendered invaluable services to the dynasty. You were pretty generous with the Order of Milosh in your time, even giving it to Karageorgevich partisans."

"To honorable men, despite their party affiliations. Andjelich is a criminal. True, I used him for actions I was reluctant to dirty my hands with. He performed faultlessly, just as a hired gunman should. Give him the Order of the White Eagle. *Cela suffit.*"

"He's had that already. Fifth Class."

"Then give him Fourth Class. Much too good for him."

Alexander's face clouded over. For a moment it seemed as though he would press his case; then, as always, he acquiesced in his father's verdict and slunk from the room like a chastised puppy.

The Andjelich incident was overshadowed, at least temporarily, by the excitement of the two kings' departure for Belgrade. They were to sail on the royal steamer, *Nicholas II*, trailed by four small excursion boats rented from the Austrian Donau Schiffahrtsgesellschaft by the more affluent citizens of the region who wished to prove their loyalty to the crown by escorting their sovereign to the capital. Thousands of cheering Shabatsers lined the shores of the Sava River. The strains of the national anthem played by the military band mingled with the salvos of ancient cannons as Milan and Alexander boarded the *Nicholas II*.

The tempest that Michael had anticipated throughout the tour exploded a few minutes after the royal embarkation. Milan in search of a toilet happened to open a cabin door with the lettering PRIVATE affixed to it and found himself face to face with Draga Mashin, who had been smuggled onboard some time before the arrival of the official party.

For what seemed to be an interminable minute, Milan stared in stunned silence at the woman, then, emitting a wild bellow, ordered Michael—close by as always—to summon Alexander to the spot, a very embarrassing errand even for a courtier as experienced in soothing ruffled royal nerves as Michael.

He found Alexander in the ship's salon, basking in the adulation of loyal Shabatsers who had come to bid their final farewells. The expression on Michael's face revealed to the young king the reason for the paternal message. His first reaction was a grimace of defiance, which immediately gave way to that of surly resignation. Dismissing the deputation with a curtness that caused raised eyebrows, he strode briskly from the salon.

The confrontation took place on the narrow companionway leading to the cabin.

"You get her off this ship," Milan shouted at his son, "or we won't sail."

The cabin door was closed, but Michael entertained no doubts about Draga's being able to hear every word. He tried to sneak away, but Milan's peremptory gesture commanded him to remain.

As though caught playing a practical joke on his *cher Papa*, Alexander approached his father with a pained grin. "What have I done now?" he asked, trying to sound lighthearted, while his eyes blinked nervously behind the thick lenses of his pince-nez. When they met his father's furious glare, he involuntarily pulled himself to stiff attention as though Milan, not he, were the ruling king.

"You heard me! Get her off this goddamn crate!"

Alexander relaxed his stance. His grin fading, two deep lines of truculence appeared at the corners of his mouth. He uttered a word that up to then had seemed to be missing from his vocabulary: "No!"

Milan reacted with the expression of a man who had been hit by a rotten egg. "Don't be a damn fool, Sasha!" he roared. "This hasn't been a pleasure trip for you. By visiting your people, you've discharged a royal obligation. You've accepted their homage and devotion, but unless you remain the shining symbol of probity they expect their king to be, you are going to lose them. Every city you honored with your royal presence reacted to it as if it had been the Second Coming. It would be a sobering shock to your people if they learned that their chaste Galahad had spent every night of his tour in the bed of a camp-following whore."

His eyes fixed on Milan's highly polished boots, Alexander gave no indication of having heard his father's words. The master of the steamer appeared at the far end of the companionway to ask how long he was to hold up the departure.

"His majesty is not ready to sail," Milan snapped at him. "You'll be told when he is. Now get the hell back to your bridge."

The man executed a shaky salute, then, tripping over his own feet, beat a hasty retreat.

Milan turned back to his son. "Well, what about it?"

Carefully avoiding his father's eyes, Alexander raised his gaze from boots to ceiling. "*De qui s'agit-il, Papa?*"

"Is she or isn't she getting off? The anthem has been played, the cannons fired, people must be wondering what in the devil's name is holding us up."

The change in the mood of the masses lining both shores and on board the escorting vessels could be sensed even here below-deck. The *zhiveos* had faded away, replaced by a nervous cacophony repeatedly punctuated by gunshots. Serbian peasants never failed to attend festive occasions armed with their rifles, as integral a part of their Sunday attires as their embroidered vests and white linen shirts. Shots taken at crows flying overhead or at hats tossed into the air by overenthusiastic buffoons was part of their fun.

"Why is it, Papa, that you always set different standards for me from those for yourself?" Alexander asked petulantly. "I still remember some of *your* camp followers. And the heartache they used to cause *chère Maman.*"

"I am setting different standards for you because I am trying to keep you from repeating my mistakes. If I'd had a father as concerned about me as you have, I'd still be king today."

For the first time during their dispute, Alexander looked his father straight in the eye. "Am I king?"

Milan exploded. "You sure as hell are! And I want you to remain king. Now will you tell that woman to get off or do you want me to?" With this, he stepped to the cabin door, but it flew open before he could reach for the knob. Draga, dressed in her voluminous duster, the veil of her wide-brimmed hat thrown back to free her face, stood on the threshold. Her incredibly beautiful green eyes blazing with indignation, she confronted Milan as though ready to lunge at him. Waiting for her to strike first, he braced himself for prompt retaliation, when she suddenly changed her mind and turned to Alexander, executing a deep curtsy.

"With your majesty's permission, I wish to go ashore immediately."

His lips twitching nervously, Alexander whipped off his pince-nez and fumbled in his pocket for a handkerchief. Not finding one, he replaced the glasses unpolished.

"If that's what you want, madame," he stuttered. "I think—"

She cut him short. "That *is* what I want, sire." She dropped her veil over her burning face. "Always what is best for my king. Permit me to wish you a pleasant boat ride to Belgrade." Dropping a second curtsy to Alexander and ignoring Milan, she started up the companionway.

Michael took a step back to let her pass. Her duster brushed against his tunic, and his nostrils became filled with the strong, hyacinth fragrance she had worn during their love affair and evidently remained faithful to even in the days of her new affluence. As their glances met briefly, he longed to tell her how he regretted having witnessed the scene of her embarrassment and humiliation. He thought he detected a shimmer of tears in her eyes which caused an inexplicable surge of tenderness to well up in him. Startled by this new proof of his vulnerability, he angrily told himself to sort out, once and for all, his feelings about Draga Mashin, to choose between love or hate or—what would be most desirable—complete indifference. He had to purge her out of his system, or she would always remain, like the head of a broken arrow, painfully embedded in his flesh.

Milan waited for the pitter-patter of Draga's footsteps to become swallowed up by the growing racket on the decks above, then motioned to Michael. "Tell the captain that his majesty has given permission for the steamer to shove off."

Unable to restrain his curiosity, Michael cast a furtive glance at Alexander. His lips pressed into one narrow line, he looked like a small boy ordered to eat his spinach. His pale skin a sickly gray, he seemed on the verge of throwing up.

From the bridge where he delivered the royal order Michael caught sight of Draga as she descended the gangplank. Though hiding her face behind the double thickness of her veil, she was—judging by the snickers and leers that followed her—recognized nevertheless by the better informed in the crowd. For the first time during his tenure as aide-de-camp to Milan, Michael felt a strong resentment against the ex-king for subjecting this woman to such unnecessarily cruel humiliation.

During the entire boat trip down the Sava, Alexander preserved a mien of sullen aloofness. While his father held court in the salon, he planted himself, feet apart, face to the wind, at the prow of the vessel, his coldly forbidding expression discouraging anyone from keeping him company. Only hours later, when the steamer was approaching Belgrade, did he deign to heed his father's suggestion, delivered by an equerry, to join him on the bridge.

As the royal party was ready to disembark, Milan came up with a sudden brainstorm.

"Look, *mon garçon*, before you leave the ship, it would be a good idea to express your thanks to the good people for escorting you to Belgrade. After all, it cost them a lot of money."

Alexander threw a slyly acrimonious glance at his father. "*Plaisanterie à part*, Papa, you don't think I could outshout this god-awful racket."

"Oh, I didn't want you to make a speech. Heavens, no. Just order the four ships to defile past you. *Prends la revue de la flotte*."

"*Tiens, cette une bonne idée,*" Alexander muttered, his sour expression in crass contrast with his words.

Michael delivered the royal order to the captain, and a few minutes later, to the cheers of the multitude, the steamers *Delingrad, Ferdinand Max, Matchva* and *Belgrade* sailed past the *Nicholas II* with the eagerness of four goslings demonstrating their skill in navigation to the mother goose. Standing tall and erect on the bridge, the young king received their salute with grimly tight lips.

He appeared to be frozen in a pose of royal dignity with only his right hand moving stiffly up and down like a marionette's. Behind the thick lenses of his pince-nez, his eyes had turned glassy. The last of the steamers was already churning away in the distance and the *Nicholas II* was ready to dock, yet he still seemed too deeply engrossed in thought to move. It was the touch of King Milan's hand on his shoulder that finally stirred him from his detachment, and he came to with a jolt, throwing a strangely hostile glance at his father. A footman appeared with the two kings' swords and gloves, and the business of disembarkation diverted Milan's attention. Alexander's changed mood went unnoticed by everyone, save Michael.

It was about six weeks later that the episode of Zivko Andjelich and the denied Order of Milosh gained sudden significance. On the late afternoon of a pleasant end-of-June day, a would-be assassin fired four revolver shots at ex-King Milan as he, in the company of an equerry, rode in an open carriage past the corner of Prince Michael Street and the Kalemegdan Gardens. One bullet merely grazed Milan; another wounded the equerry in the shoulder, while two others went astray. The culprit, a Bosnian Serb named Knezevich, a former member of the Belgrade fire brigade, was caught and handed over to the police by the crowd assembled at the scene.

Michael happened to be off duty that day, and the news of the assassination attempt reached him at the Officers' Club. As was usual in such cases, the first reports were wild exaggerations, claiming that both Alexander and Milan were dead. Michael immediately rushed to the Old Konak to find, to his indescribable relief, Milan not only alive, but in high spirits. The would-be assassin Knezevich had already admitted his guilt to the Belgrade chief of police. When questioned about his motives, he readily acknowledged having received a killer's fee of five hundred napoleons, with another five hundred promised after a successful completion of the assignment, by a group of gentlemen in Bucharest. He named Zivko Andjelich, prefect of Shabats, as the go-between who had arranged the meeting and provided him with a permit to cross and recross the Serbian-Rumanian border.

What Michael found strange from the very beginning was Knezevich's great readiness to cooperate with the police, revealing in minute detail all secrets of the conspiracy. At least, they seemed to be all the secrets. He told them that the deal between him and the gentlemen in Bucharest had been discussed in Serbian, which the men spoke with a Russian accent. When shown a picture of the house owned by a certain Russian colonel named Grabov, the head of the Asian Department's Balkan Division, he recognized it as the place where the meeting had taken place. He also incriminated a dozen or so Serbian politicians, members of the opposition Radical Party and others with anti-Obrenovich leanings. All the police had to do was mention a name and Knezevich branded the man as part of the conspiracy. He rarely said no and often contradicted himself. When caught lying, he merely snickered. He wanted to please the police, so he wouldn't be beaten, he told them.

Milan felt gratified by the results of the investigation. At last, he was able to prove to the nation that it was not the common people of Serbia who objected to his presence at his son's side, but the cruel ringmaster Russia and its trained monkey, the Serbian Radical Party.

Michael watched the developments with growing concern. Milan, in the belief that he was at last in possession of enough incriminating evidence against his enemies, wanted martial law declared, a swift trial and the firing squad for the party leaders. The Cabinet appeared reluctant to comply. The ministers found it difficult to sort out the truth from assassin Knezevich's five or six conflicting confessions. Prefect Andjelich, on the other hand, refused to talk. Locked up in a special security cell in the fortress, he was reported to be calm and cheerful, an unusual frame of mind for a man expecting to be hanged.

With every passing day, the mystery surrounding the case

grew more perplexing. A special commissioner, answerable only to King Alexander, was appointed to conduct the investigation. This move barred the Cabinet from access to whatever evidence the investigation brought to light. Alexander, to please his father, insisted on the enforcement of martial law and, when the Cabinet refused to comply, had an army colonel point his loaded gun at the premier's head, threatening to shoot him. Unable to resist so convincing an argument, the premier and his Cabinet signed the decree.

The proclamation of martial law was followed by mass arrests. The underground cells of the fortress were crowded with a wild assortment of prisoners: informers, double agents and some of the most reputable men in Serbian politics. During these hectic days, Michael took frequent boat trips across the Sava to the Hungarian city of Zimony, where he could read the foreign press banned from Serbia. If only one-tenth of what it reported was true, a veritable reign of terror existed in Belgrade. Some papers put the number of arrests at thirty thousand, wrote of torture, garrotings, men with broken limbs left to die of gangrene or starvation, women raped and thrown into the dried-out well in the fortress yard. Although he knew that the stories were Russian-inspired exaggerations to discredit ex-King Milan, he couldn't in all conscience absolve the investigators of the special commissioner from having engaged in a little torture when other methods failed.

Risking Milan's displeasure, Michael frequently warned him about the Western press reactions, yet without convincing the ex-king of their importance. What he didn't confide was his own suspicion about certain disturbing aspects of the case. A few personal letters criticizing the two kings and their manner of conducting the affairs of state were found by the search parties in the houses of Radicals, yet never any proof of their participation in the conspiracy. No doubt, the assassination plan had been concocted by the Russian secret police, yet the question "To what purpose?" remained unanswered.

On the eve of the court-martial, Prefect Andjelich hanged himself in his cell.

The news of his death reached the court in Nish shortly before a state dinner to celebrate the opening of the Skupshtina in that city. It was a warm summer evening and, as usual, guests and retinue had assembled at the fountain in the garden of the royal residence to wait for the two kings' appearance. Suddenly, Alexander emerged from the downstairs telephone room and, in a cheerful tone, related the news he had just received from Belgrade.

"Prefect Andjelich had asked the guard to leave his cell door open. The man complied but kept pacing the corridor. When after a while he wanted to shut the door, he found Andjelich hanging from a big nail hammered into its inside panel. The guard immediately notified the prison commandant who, in turn, contacted the special investigator and the premier. They both rushed to the fortress. In their opinion, which later was confirmed by the medical examiner, Prefect Andjelich undoubtedly had died by his own hand." The king, unaware of the group's startled reaction, then continued briskly. "Let's go in, gentlemen. I've just seen Papa come downstairs. I hope you are as hungry as I."

The party found ex-King Milan in the salon. Michael watched his face as Alexander repeated the Andjelich suicide story to him. Milan reacted with an expression of utter consternation.

"What on earth made him do it?" he asked in a strangely tremulous tone.

His son smiled indulgently. *"Mon Dieu,* Papa, tomorrow is the court-martial. He was a bright fellow, knew he had no chance. Perhaps he wanted to save his family from the disgrace of being hanged as a common criminal. Well, shall we eat?"

Milan, however, refused to drop the subject.

"Yes, but wasn't it reported that he had been amazingly cheerful? Telling his guards that he was looking forward to the court-martial?"

For the first time that evening, the smile faded from Alexander's face. "Who told you that?"

Milan ignored the question. "Incidentally, why is everyone so positive that Andjelich committed suicide?"

"He left a note to his wife."

"Could've been forged."

"No, Papa. People who knew his handwriting confirmed that it was his."

The answer failed to satisfy Milan. Others in the party

seemed equally puzzled. A peasant member of parliament asked the question that had been on everyone's mind.

"Is it customary, your majesty, to give prisoners paper, pen and ink?"

The king took off his pince-nez and rubbed it against the sleeve of his tunic.

"Well"—there was a pause—"well"— he replaced the glasses —"he wrote the note on a slip of paper with the help of a match dipped into his own blood." When he realized that everyone was staring at him in disbelief, he added: "The man suffered from hemorrhoids, so it was no problem for him to draw blood."

Monsieur Perrault was Milan's French chef, whose position in the royal kitchen had for years depended on Milan's momentary status at the Old Konak. After Milan's abdication he had followed his master abroad, easing the heartbreaks of life in exile with his perfect *milles feuilles* and *soufflés au fromage.* A faithful Leporello to Milan's Don Juan, he shared his master's passions and weaknesses, frequenting—on his off-duty days—the same racetracks, gambling casinos and music halls as his employer, but keeping a respectful distance from the table, betting window or bed his master was trying his luck at. Now, after years of roaming, they were once again in power, his master behind the throne and he behind the stoves of the royal kitchen.

On that night in Nish he had served a magnificent *potage aux champignons*, then *fogas,* the unique Lake Balaton fish *en gelée,* to be followed by *poulet mornay* and *aubergines farcies,* then *salle d'agneau rôti provençale,* ending the feast with a *charlotte russe* and fresh grapes from Belgium. That the Skupshtina representatives, used to *djuvech* and *kebabes,* left most of the food on their plates untouched was not surprising, yet so did the more sophisticated guests. Alexander alone ate heartily, untroubled by Prefect Andjelich's ghost lingering about the table.

Following the Nish episode, King Milan seemed to remain in a rather pensive mood. Michael knew that he was troubled by the discrepancies of the investigation, yet reluctant to undertake any detective work on his own. Why was the story of the guard who discovered the suicide accepted unquestioned, although it contained improbable details? Where was the rest of the blanket Andjelich had allegedly torn a strip from to use in lieu of a rope? Where did the big nail hammered into the cell door come from, and when had it been put there?

The consideration that kept Milan from asking the questions failed to restrict Michael. On his first free afternoon in Belgrade, he went to the fortress to do a little scouting on his own. He chose the day his friend Apis, at that time First Lieutenant Dragutin Dimitriyevich, was on duty at the prison.

The weather was beastly hot, and Michael felt the shirt sticking to his back as he crossed the cobblestoned yard of the prison compound. He passed the well dating back to the times of the Romans, the water level of which was supposed to be many meters below the river bottom of the Danube. From time to time, there were recurrent rumors about accidental drownings of prisoners who, when leaning over its stone parapet, suffered sudden attacks of vertigo and plummeted to their deaths. Since the commandant's office was just a few yards behind it, the stories were believed by only those lucky Serbs who had never been inside the prison walls. Looking at the well, Michael felt his throat constrict. In Belgrade there were many places that brought the memory of similar incidents to his mind.

He found Dimitriyevich in the guardroom. Although they hadn't seen each other for weeks, Apis didn't appear surprised at the visit.

"I was expecting you," he told Michael, adding, "Or someone from the Milan set."

The presence of a sergeant in the room restrained Michael from asking the questions that were foremost in his mind. Nevertheless, Lieutenant Dimitriyevich guessed them. Rising, he selected a key from the row hanging on the wall.

"Let's go. He might be taking a nap, but we'll wake him."

His reference to the prisoner simply as "he" was to indicate to the sergeant that Michael's visit had been prearranged.

As they climbed the stairway out of earshot, he turned to Michael. "I am taking you to Knezevich."

"I thought so."

On the second floor the largest and airiest cells were located, so-called honor cells, reserved for important or distinguished captives such as officers accused of killing a fellow gentleman in a duel. Ordinary prisoners were taken to the casemates. As did the well in the yard, these subterranean cubicles figured in many a tale of murder and slow, torturous death. Very few prisoners survived more than a year in them. The fact that Knezevich had been assigned such elite quarters was contrary to the usual procedure in capital cases with political overtones.

Knezevich had indeed been sleeping and woke with a start when he heard the heavy cell door open. About twenty-four years of age, darkly handsome and apparently relaxed, he scrambled slowly to his feet and executed a halfhearted salute. Having suffered a few superficial cuts and bruises when attacked by the crowd at the scene of the assassination attempt, he still wore his left arm in a sling, and his forehead was bandaged. Michael studied his eyes for some semblance of the panic he remembered seeing on the faces of other political prisoners—even the bravest and most defiant—but found none. As though considering the two officers' visit a pleasant interruption in the dull prison routine, Knezevich smiled at them in friendly expectation. He was a man of limited intelligence, close to being mentally retarded; still his calmness seemed inexplicable.

Michael's questions regarding the assassination attempt he answered with the well-known story: He had been sent by Prefect Andjelich to Bucharest, where he was given five hundred napoleons as an advance payment by the Russian gentlemen. After recrossing the border, he headed straight for Belgrade, stopping at the Hotel Macedonia.

"How did you know that King Milan would be passing the corner of the Kalemegdan Gardens that afternoon?"

"That was the usual route he took from the fortress to the Konak."

"Yes, but as a rule, he seldom went to his office in the afternoons. He made an exception that day."

Knezevich shrugged. "A message was delivered to my hotel that he'd be passing through there."

"A message from whom?"

"I don't know. It was pushed in under my door."

This was a new detail.

"And you didn't wonder where the message came from?"

"No, sir. Prefect Andjelich told me to follow orders without asking questions."

On their way upstairs, Apis had warned Michael not to mention Andjelich's suicide to the prisoner as the special investigator had given orders that it be kept a secret from him.

"Did Prefect Andjelich ever tell you who wanted ex-King Milan assassinated?" Michael asked.

"He said there were some people who thought that it was bad for the country to have King Milan in charge of the government when the Russians wanted him out. Then also, the prefect was mad at him because of the Order of Milosh the Great. You see, sir, the young king wanted to give it to him in Nish, but his father wouldn't let him."

The information jolted Michael. He alone had been present when father and son discussed the order.

"Have you seen Prefect Andjelich since your arrest?" he asked the prisoner.

"Yes, sir. About a week ago. Just for a second on the stairway. I was being taken down to the exercise yard as he was brought up. He told me not to worry, everything would be all right."

"Aren't you worried?"

Knezevich grinned. "No, sir. Prefect Andjelich told me what I'd done—rather tried to do—had been for the good of Serbia."

"And for five hundred napoleons."

"That was just so I wouldn't break my promise." Noticing Michael's perplexity, he hastened to explain. "Like a marriage vow. You make it to God, but you always give a few coins to the pope who performs the ceremony."

The logic seemed somewhat twisted to Michael. He exchanged a half-amused, half-disconcerted glance with Apis.

"To make it binding, is that it?"

"Yes, sir."

"You incriminated a number of people, Knezevich, then retracted part of your confession. Why?"

"I made my first confession at police headquarters. I just told them whatever they wanted to hear so they'd release me to the special investigator. Suspects can be given an awful rough time by the police if they refuse to cooperate."

"But you weren't afraid of the special investigator?"

Shaking his head, Knezevich answered with a soundless no through pursed lips.

"Why not?"

"Because he was appointed by King Alexander."

"And that made you feel safe? Why?"

"King Alexander is a just man. He knows I am a good Serb although I was born in Bosnia. And he'll see to it that I get a fair trial."

Michael threw a questioning glance at Apis, who answered with a puzzled shrug.

"So you admit that the men you first incriminated were innocent?" Michael continued.

The prisoner responded with a nervous grimace. Not understanding what Michael was driving at, he began to lose some of his self-confidence.

"How would I know that, sir? I've told you I only discussed the matter with Prefect Andjelich and those Russians in Bucharest. How would I know who else was involved?"

Michael wondered if the man was really an idiot or just extremely shrewd. Whichever, he certainly lacked the menacing power of great criminals. A small scoundrel chosen for a crime much too big for him. Michael had one more question to ask.

"What was your connection with Prefect Andjelich? I mean before he sent you to Bucharest."

Rather unwillingly, Knezevich answered, "I'd done a few small favors for him."

Knowing Andjelich's past, Michael could well imagine what kinds of favors they'd been.

"He also knew that I was one of the best shots in my regiment," the prisoner added proudly. "I served my two years with the Morava Division in Nish."

Michael had no more questions, and they left. The guard on duty was still pacing the corridor. Reaching its far end, a distance of about thirty meters, he halted, then, after a mechanical about-face, stamped to the landing and back again.

"Where was Andjelich's cell?" Michael asked Apis.

"Here on this floor. The fourth to the left."

Michael's eyes followed the moving guard. He concluded that it would have been humanly impossible for a man to hang himself while the guard walked from his cell to the end of the corridor and back. Especially if the cell door were open. When his glance met Apis, he knew that his friend shared his opinion.

"I go off duty in an hour," Apis told him. "It's been too hot today. Let's get out of this sweltering city and have dinner at the garden restaurant at Topcider."

They met for coffee on the veranda of the Serbian Crown,

then took the tram to Topcider. It was a beautiful, starlit evening, with the gold sickle of the new moon shining like a brooch pinned on a blue silk dress. To the south, the inverted cone of the Avala lay outlined in purple ink against the sky. The temperature was at least five degrees cooler than that in the city, and a light breeze wafted the fragrance of freshly mown grass and rich forest humus from nearby Deer Park. The two officers chose a table in a quiet corner of the garden, away from the other diners.

"You have something to tell me," Michael said after they'd ordered their meal.

"I do. It won't surprise you too much. At least not after what you heard this afternoon."

"Prefect Andjelich didn't kill himself. Is that what you mean?"

"Exactly. He had no reason to kill himself because he had been promised freedom, immunity and a lot of money by the men who hired him. I spoke to him several times during his stay in prison, and while he refused to talk about the assassination attempt, he acted like a man who'd just won a million on a lottery ticket."

"Oh—"

"Another thing. Andjelich had never been—well—tortured. I've seen many a political prisoner delivered to the fortress half dead after a police interrogation, then taken in chains to the dungeons and kept there on bread and water. Andjelich didn't have a scratch on him, and his food was sent in from the Serbian Crown. I was off duty at the time of his alleged suicide, but the next morning I conducted a little investigation of my own. The captain who had been in charge that night was immediately relieved of duty; so was the guard who'd discovered the suicide. Later that day I went to their homes and found that both the captain and the private had vanished with their families. I remembered that Andjelich had a brother who'd come to see him once in prison, of course, in the commandant's presence. It took me several days to find him, a man in deathly fear for his life, hiding at a friend's house. He was planning to flee the country, and I have reason to believe that by now he is somewhere in Austria."

What surprised Michael was that he was not at all surprised.

Apis went on with his story. "This brother, his name is Svetozar, has an orchard with a summer cottage in the outskirts of Belgrade. One day Andjelich asked him for the use of the place. It was for one night only and for a very important secret meeting. Unbeknown to his brother, Svetozar watched from the orchard as the participants arrived. They were: the prefect, Colonel Taube, military attaché to the Russian Legation, King Alexander and a man he didn't know. Realizing that the less he learned about the meeting, the safer it would be for him, he went home quickly, keeping silent about the whole thing."

"I gather you believe that the assassination plan was the subject of that meeting," Michael said.

"I don't know. It's a goddamn bloody mess. I only hope the truth won't come to light. It would reflect badly on Serbia's prestige."

"You're right," Michael agreed. "During my stay in France, I was shocked to find that the word 'Balkan' had become a pejorative in the West. When I refused to let a landlady cheat me on a bill or a bully push ahead of me on the tram, that's what they shouted: 'Balkan, Balkan.' And Serbia has the worst reputation of all the Balkan countries. Our constant government crises, each party in power wreaking bloody vengeance on members of the defeated party, laws and constitutions changed like sheets on a whore's bed and politicians ready to deliver the country either to Austria or Russia, whichever pays better."

"Oh, hell." Apis groaned. "If it were up to me, I'd kick Alexander and all political parties out, put an end to this thieves' democracy and set up a military dictatorship, I'd probably keep Milan, though in his youth he was a disgraceful off-and-on king. He's changed, however, become a man of conscience and integrity and produced miracles in modernizing the army. The troops are devoted to him, because he's made them what Serbs basically are: great and proud warriors. This country isn't ready for the institutions of the West. Ever hear the story of Colonel Dragomir Vutskovich's trip to Zurich? In his youth he'd been an ardent republican, with Switzerland his conception of modern Utopia. After years of pinching and scrimping, he managed to scrape the train fare together and set out for his Land of the Free. On the day of his arrival, he was arrested in Zurich for exercising his human prerogatives by relieving himself in the middle of Bahnhofstrasse. That's our present minister of defense, and that was his idea of a citizen's rights in a free democracy. Luckily, we still have regions where people have never heard of democracy, where gold coins are no medium of exchange, but ornaments to hang around women's necks, where villagers live to old age without ever having touched a banknote, where they eat what they grow and build what they live in and wear what they weave. And if they can't manage alone, they always find a neighbor ready to help. This is what we'll have to go back to, not only in the backwoods, but everywhere. The old simplicity and brotherly love."

Michael had heard the same words many times before but never uttered with such apostolic sincerity and visionary zeal. There was something about Apis that both moved and disturbed him. His ideas were absurd and impractical, yet Michael didn't have the slightest doubt that he would spend years, if not his whole life, trying to turn them into reality.

"That's all very well, but how will you pay for this dinner without touching money?" he teased Apis. "Go out to the kitchen, roll up your sleeves and wash dishes?"

Apis shrugged, laughing. "Oh, Belgrade is beyond redemption. I think, I'd just burn it down like Milosh the Great, when he wanted to clear the slums. Only I wouldn't rebuild it."

There was another long silence. At last, Michael broke it.

"What about Svetozar's story? Shall I tell it to King Milan? But how do you tell a loving father that his son wanted him murdered? Anyway, we have no proof."

"No, you can't tell him. The plan has misfired, and the repercussions have been embarrassing enough to keep Alexander from staging a repeat performance. He's gone out of his way to allay his father's suspicions, if any, willing even to decimate the Radical Party to please his *cher Papa.*"

"You're right. Let's wait and hope that Alexander has learned his lesson and will behave from now on."

On the first day of the court-martial, Knezevich retracted all his previous testimonies, once again absolving the men he had incriminated before and surprising the world by declaring that he alone had been responsible for the assassination attempt.

His twenty-six fellow defendants all pleaded not guilty, some admitting that, at times, they had criticized the government, yet as members of a democratic society considered free speech their inalienable right.

The trial was watched with nervous interest by the Western powers. Rumors of impending death sentences moved both Russia and Austria to undertake secret diplomatic maneuvers on behalf of leading Radicals like Nicola Pashich and Stoyan Protich, trying to save them from the firing squad. The monitors *Körös* and *Szamos* and two torpedo boats of the Austro-Hungarian Danube fleet were dispatched to Belgrade to be in readiness should the execution of Radical leaders trigger a revolution in Serbia. In the end, it turned out that all forebodings were unfounded. Only Knezevich was condemned to die, while the accused politicians received either prison sentences of various durations or were acquitted.

On September 13, 1899, the would-be assassin, Stoyan Knezevich, was taken to the parade grounds, a field outside the city limits used for artillery maneuvers, horseshows and executions.

Since his dinner with Apis, Michael had been waiting for an earth-shaking scandal to explode in the scandal-prone Old Konak, yet nothing happened. The relationship between father and son remained unchanged and, if possible, grew warmer. Alexander showed more regard than ever before for paternal sensibilities by keeping Draga Mashin out of his father's sight. As far as Michael could tell, Milan was blissfully unaware of his son's part in the assassination attempt, and Michael loved him too much to rob him of his illusions.

September 13 was an unusually sultry day for that time of year. The road to the parade grounds led past small farms and orchards. The plum crop was exceptionally rich that fall, and the dark purple fruit hung in heavy clusters from the branches or lay, like a thick, fly-infested carpet, under the trees, emitting the sweet smell of decay. In most yards, the making of *pekmez*, plum marmalade, was in progress. It was cooked in large caldrons over slow-burning open fires, young girls or children stirring it with flat wooden spoons as it thickened, adding its fragrance to the mixed odors of dunghills, fallen leaves and smoke curling from the earthen ovens where the rest of the plum crop was dried.

Michael was much too intrigued by the case to miss the last act. When he reached the parade grounds, the closed carriage bringing Knezevich had already arrived, and the condemned man was being led to the stand erected for the officials. A stake had been driven into the ground at a distance of about thirty meters, and an infantry company, under the command of a lieutenant, formed a square around the spot where the drama was to take place.

Knezevich, escorted by two gendarmes with bayonets fixed and followed by a bearded pope, halted at the stand. Calm and erect, he looked as though he expected a medal to be pinned to his chest and not a volley of bullets fired into his body. He listened with bored politeness to the sentence read by the president of the court-martial, his eyes fixed on the road to Belgrade. Was he waiting for the vision of a cavalry officer approaching the parade grounds at a wild gallop, with a white handkerchief signaling the king's clemency, fluttering from his drawn sword?

Michael was close enough to see the condemned man's face. As the president finished his lecture, Knezevich's calm slowly yielded to an expression of panic. Screwing up his eyes, holding his breath, he stared at the still-empty stretch of the Belgrade road. Pearls of perspiration appeared on his forehead; his mouth dropped open, saliva oozing from its corners. As if suddenly hit by the full realization of his hopelessness, he tried to tear himself from the grip of the gendarmes, causing them to tighten their hold. As they turned him around to lead him to the stake, his knees buckled and his head dropped; then, emitting an animal cry, he slumped to the ground. The gendarmes, aided by two infantry men, began dragging him. In their obvious haste to have the execution carried out, they deprived Knezevich of a chance to die with human dignity and tied him to the stake like a sacrificial offering to some pagan deity.

It was not the first execution Michael had witnessed. He had seen deserters shot and enemy guerrillas hanged during Serbia's unfortunate war against Bulgaria, in each case the feeling of guilt and shame making him physically ill. He was unable to conjure up any hatred even for the cheap scoundrel who had been within a hairsbreadth of killing Milan Obrenovich. He wondered whether others in the crowd around him also felt the painful nausea that troubled him.

At last, the man was securely tied to the post, and the pope pressed the cross to his still-babbling lips. The closeness of death suddenly cleared Knezevich's mind of its panic-caused befuddlement, and he shouted in a loud, ringing voice that was wafted by the afternoon breeze to the outer limits of the parade grounds.

"I am not guilty! I am innocent! I was ordered to shoot King Milan by—"

The commanding lieutenant's sword slashed through the air, and the volley outthundered Knezevich's last words. In the rush to execute him, no time had been taken for the customary blindfolding. The pope escaped the bullets by the skin of his teeth and stood, panting, a mere two meters from the stake, staring at the slumped form on it. The crowd of spectators, earlier so silent, stirred amid shouts of protest mixed with *zhiveos* hailing the dynasty. Here and there, a woman sobbed hysterically. A disturbing episode in Serbia's history had drawn to its conclusion, planting the seeds of doubt in many a judicious mind.

At the dawn of the new century, Alexander's marriage became the main topic of discussion in Belgrade's cafés, as well as at the parties given by the diplomatic corps. Michael witnessed several debates between father and son on the matter and even heard Alexander swear that he'd be married by the end of the summer.

A surprising number of people were engaged in the game of royal matchmaking: Queen Natalie, ex-King Milan, Czar Nicholas II, Kaiser Wilhelm, the Austrian minister of foreign affairs, the Russian minister of foreign affairs, even old Franz Josef himself. Perhaps the latter's involvement wasn't out of character. As a Habsburg, he knew the importance of an advantageous marriage.

The more optimistic Obrenovich partisans dreamed of a union with a Habsburg archduchess, possibly one of Archduke Friedrich's seven daughters. It mattered little which one, as each boasted the same prominent Habsburg nose, thick lips and big-hipped, strong-boned build of a good broodmare. Princess Xenia of Montenegro was the czar's choice. She would have meant a rapprochement between the two countries, both inhabited by Serbs, but separated by the bitter feud of their reigning dynasties. Marriage to her would have had a touch of piquancy, making Alexander a Karageorgevich brother-in-law as another one of Nikita's daughters, the late Princess Zorka, had been the wife of exiled Prince Peter.

Wily old Prince Nikita of Montenegro had certainly known how to turn the misfortune of siring a flock of girl children into a blessing. He married off two to Russian granddukes, Anna to a Prince Battenberg of Germany and Elena to the Crown Prince of Italy. Of course, neither could boast a Habsburg nose or the build of a broodmare, though statuesque Elena towered over Victor Emmanuel like a Lippizaner stallion over a Shetland pony.

There was wild speculation on how the royal marriage would affect Draga Mashin's position. Would it ban her from Belgrade or bestow upon her the status of a Madame Du Barry? To all eyes, Alexander seemed more devoted to her than ever; either spending the nights in her house or—on occasions when she for some reason refused to receive him—standing, in the company of Colonel Marko, one of his equerries, under her window, pleading with her to change her mind. These nightly excursions caused Rista Bademlich, police chief of Belgrade, to develop an acute case of ulcers. No matter how many plainclothesmen were planted in the vicinity, nor what a crack shot Colonel Marko was, there remained the possibility of an assassin hiding behind a doorway or a window. Aside from those dangers, Alexander could also catch pneumonia on a rainy night.

"I can well understand why Bademlich is worried," Milan had confided to Michael after having listened to the chief's laments, "but what can I do? The boy is crazy about the woman. I'd be more worried if she kept their relationship platonic. But she's been sleeping with him for almost three years, and that should sooner or later satiate him. Some people are shocked, but, *mon Dieu*, he is a young, healthy man and can't be expected to live like a monk. Hell, what would they say if he followed old Milosh's example and had any female, wife or virgin, he'd taken a fancy to ordered to the Konak? He could do it, you know. Perhaps not as peremptorily and blatantly as his great-uncle; he wouldn't have to because even in our twentieth century there is something about a king that makes him irresistible to women." He grinned. "And that God knows, is the truth. So let's just consider Madame Draga Mashin a temporary lightning rod safely grounding a young man's sexual desires."

No doubt, Michael concluded, Milan was whistling in the dark. In three years this was the first time Milan had spoken of her to Michael, which served to reveal the perturbed state of his mind.

"I wonder what the hell Sasha sees in her," Milan went on. "I think—" He halted, giving Michael a long look as though he had only now recalled the young man's past connection with Draga. "I wonder what *you* saw in her?"

The question was unexpected. Michael felt the blood rush to his face, a rather disturbing sensation for a man of thirty-four, wearing the uniform of a captain. "That is hard to explain," he began somewhat hesitantly.

"If you prefer not to—"

"No, no, sir—I really don't mind talking about her. Not anymore. She, she was very easy to be with. How shall I describe it? Always soothing and considerate, like a good nurse."

Milan groaned. "Some nurse."

"She was like one's favorite armchair after a tiring journey. Or a dose of opiate against pain or—" He stopped, wondering if he weren't sounding poetic and emotional. "She had no vanity, no social ambitions, no possessiveness, no greed."

"That's hard to believe."

"I know. Yet I found her quiet and uncomplicated, certainly not the *femme fatale* she is supposed to be in many people's opinion."

"If she was that perfect, why didn't you marry her?" Milan asked, a rough edge to his voice, evidently forgetting that *he* had advised Michael against the marriage.

This was, Michael realized, his cue to tell his sovereign about Monsieur Jurieux. Later he wondered if he had made a mistake by keeping the incident a secret. Perhaps Milan would have used it to destroy his son's illusions about his mistress, provided those illusions could have been destroyed at all.

"I wasn't ready to marry her or anyone else at that time, sir." After a pause he offered an explanation that he felt to be true. "Neither am I now, for that matter."

"I hope the problem with Draga will solve itself," Milan confided. "My good friend Kaiser Wilhelm has finally come up with the name of a princess who seems to fulfill most of our requirements. She might not be as rich as I would wish, but of a great house, closely related to several reigning monarchs and pleasant to look at." He chuckled. "I mean, for a princess. Hell, I married the greatest beauty ever, and where am I? No, the boy will be better off with someone plain and simple. After all, what rich luscious, smart princess could possibly want to marry the King of Serbia, who wears a pince-nez and is in love with a woman ten years his senior?"

On June 7, 1900, ex-King Milan, accompanied by Michael and a valet, left in all secrecy for Vienna to discuss the subject of his son's marriage with the interested parties. On the day of his departure, Alexander summoned Premier Dr. Vladan Georgevich to the Konak, asking him to take his summer vacation earlier than planned and be back by the time ex-King Milan returned with the final draft of the marriage contract, because after that he, Alexander, would have to leave for Germany in order to meet his fiancée. The premier, elated over the good news, congratulated his sovereign and went home to pack.

Michael would always remember the months preceding the catastrophe as the most pleasant time he'd ever had in the service of ex-King Milan. The restlessness in the past that had seemed to drive Milan from card table to card table, from woman to woman, appeared to have deserted him. In the forty-sixth year of his life, he had found his place in the world—that of architect of a new twentieth-century Serbia.

Having built up a strong army, he could now count on a long period of peace during which he—the *éminence grise* behind the throne—would bring prosperity and progress to two and a half million people. Since all the troublemakers and leaders of the Russophile Radical Party had been put safely behind bars, he could give his country the kind of democracy it was emotionally ready for: protection for the poor, control of the rich and prevention of graft and party patronage in the ranks of the bureaucracy. Milan had never believed in the blessings of freedom à la Great Britain or the United States; didn't think his people were ready for it, nor would they be in another fifty years. But he also was well aware that Serbs were wild and fiercely proud, so their leadership had to be the kind that satisfied their yearning for the ethical as well as the heroic.

His great friend Emperor Franz Josef gave a dinner for him, at which the place for the meeting with the princess' family, Karlsbad, and the time, June 25, were decided. Karlsbad seemed an ideal choice: A look at the future father-in-law silhouette was enough to convince any inquisitive reporter that it wasn't the prospect of marrying off his daughter, but the Czech town's miracle-producing springs that had brought him there. As for Milan, he had always believed in the beneficial effects of Karlsbad's water cure, mainly because he'd been luckier at the racetrack there than at any other in Europe.

The princely family arrived first, staying—as was the custom of lesser royalty—in the villa of a relative. It saved expenses, yet preserved decorum. Milan, of course, took the royal suite at Karlsbad's most elegant hotel, devoting his mornings to the cure, his afternoons to breaking his pledge of abstinence at the races and his evenings to cards and women.

It was the height of the season, with the famous and affluent of Mitteleuropa purging their systems of the poison and excess fat of a year's rich living at the fountains of the pump room. Glass in hand, taking small, measured sips of the alkaline-saline water, these corpulent, self-assured men closed many a million-dollar deal to build railroads and factories, launch freighters or bore tunnels under Alpine mountains as they took their constitutionals on the sheltered promenade. The great of the entertainment world also made their yearly pilgrimage to Karlsbad. Famous tenors, operetta composers and playwrights from Vienna and Budapest considered strolling through its hilly streets in the company of theatrical producers and music publishers a highly restorative cure. Even if the Karlsbad waters failed to improve their health, the contracts cajoled out of their walking partners made the sojourn worth while. There was always a sprinkling of *Kurgäste* from Eastern Europe, as well as Turkey, Egypt and India, to add a touch of the exotic to the scene. As a whole, the Hebrew race was most prominently represented, probably because tennis, riding and hunting helped the gentile rich to remain trim, while the Jews, mostly self-made men, had yet to acquire a taste for such strenuous outdoor exercises. For those who after three or four weeks realized sadly that Karlsbad had failed them, the face-saving solution was to buy a shirt at least two sizes too large and wear it on the homeward journey. It failed to fool the scales, but that was of minor importance. Karlsbad was not only a city, but a state of mind. One had at all costs to protect its prestige.

The historic session took place in the resplendent vacation house of a rich Jewish banker from Vienna, a man deeply interested in Serbia's welfare, mainly because he was one of its biggest creditors. As agreed, the host kept discreetly out of sight. When the carriage bringing the prince, his wife and daughter rolled up to the entrance, the trio were greeted by Aide-de-camp Michael Vassilovich, who then escorted the guests to the small downstairs salon where King Milan was to receive them.

If Michael had met the family at the pump room of the spa, he would have taken the father for a mason who had worked himself up to contractor and was now enjoying the fruits of his labors by treating himself and his women to a vacation in the Karlsbad of the rich men. Tall and bony, with a worried expression on her prematurely lined face, the wife wore the dehydrated look of an overworked charwoman. The daughter, twenty and quite attractive in a wholesome, bucolic way, seemed to have a twinkle in her eyes as though she were participating in a practical joke.

From the beginning of the meeting, it was ex-King Milan who held the upper hand. Michael was awed by the ease and proud of the grace of the man, this great-nephew of swineherds, so much more royal than the self-conscious princely couple, descendants of centuries-old ruling houses.

While being served tea by the banker's French majordomo and footmen, Milan entertained the family with anecdotes of life in rural Serbia, each one not only amusing, but also informative, hinting at the differences between Eastern and Western Europe. After the tea table had been cleared and the staff dismissed, he got down to business. Michael was told to escort the young princess to the library so the more prosaic details of the marriage contract could be discussed in her absence. Leaving her there, he remembered that their host was known to own the greatest collection of pornography in all Austria and secretly hoped that, in her boredom, the princess would pick out and thumb through one of the richly illustrated leather-bound volumes. She certainly needed a great deal of information on the subject of sex if she were to make her marriage to Alexander of Serbia a success.

The meeting ended in complete agreement between both parties.

"Their highnesses would have preferred an early winter wedding," Milan told Michael later as they rode back to the hotel. "But I—being *a tout prix* against dragging out things— persuaded them to accept September. Now everything depends on *les jeunes gens*. But I have hopes. The girl is really much better than I expected. Nice fresh skin, good firm body. She seems also to have a sense of humor, which is most important in a woman. I've told you, Karlsbad is my lucky place. The water. *Ça fait des merveilles*—even if one doesn't drink it."

The bomb exploded on July 9.

The prince and his family had left for home shortly after the encounter to begin the preparations for the wedding, while Milan remained to conduct negotiations with the Skoda factory in Pilsen for the purchase of their newest quick-firing cannon and repeating firearms. This business concluded, he returned to Karlsbad. The wire from the Serbian premier *pro tem*, calling him home, reached him there. Shortly afterward another wire, sent by Premier Dr. Georgevich, who was vacationing in Luzern, Switzerland, arrived: "THE DEPUTY PREMIER HAS HANDED IN HIS RESIGNATION STOP URGES ME TO RETURN HOME STOP PLEASE ADVISE STOP."

Perplexed and worried, King Milan ordered Michael to send a coded wire to the prime minister. The answer was a straight telegram, explaining that Dr. Georgevich was unable to establish contact with his deputy since the codebook he had taken along on his journey contained the wrong system. After a delay of twenty-four hours, the mystery was solved.

The deputy premier's telegram read: "King Alexander has decided to marry Draga Mashin. Unable to prevent the catastrophe, the government has handed in its resignation." The date was July 21, 1900.

Serbs, probably the hardiest and most enduring of the human species, had during their cruel past died of the most perverted tortures, been broken on wheels, impaled on stakes, chopped to death piecemeal without emitting a single moan or shedding a single tear. Tears, they philosophized, were for women, who could shriek their grief and pain to split the sky, but men were to remain tight-lipped and silent no matter how cruel the pain or the loss. The sight of a Milan prostrate on his hotel bed, convulsed in agony, filled Michael with embarrassment. But later the realization of the depth of the man's bitter suffering changed Michael's irritation to compassion. By then the first attack of hysteria had passed, and Milan was almost himself again. He asked for a cigarette, and Michael lighted it for him, then one for himself.

"It's all my fault," Milan confessed. "Mine and his mother's. We turned him into the sly, scheming monster he is. We used him as a pawn in our warfare and taught him to take advantage of it. He learned to cajole anything he wanted from either of us by betraying one to the other. He snitched on his mother to me and snitched on me to her. Divide and conquer was his way of keeping us in line. After it worked so well with us, he used it on the men around him, the politicians and the parties. Besides, I made him king at thirteen, when other boys were still being kept in line by their fathers' razor straps or their teachers' canes. At seventeen, he had the Regent Yovan Ristich, the most honorable man in Serbia, dismissed like a thieving servant. I applauded. He threw statesmen into prison, only to pardon them later and entrust cabinet posts to them, and still I applauded. Now he has sent me and the prime minister on a wild-goose chase so we wouldn't be around to prevent him from marrying his whore. You know, I still can't believe this is true!" He stopped, staring at Michael as though hoping to hear from his young aide that the wire had been a practical joke. "How am I to face Emperor Franz Josef? And the Germans? Good God! What humiliation! What shame!" Suddenly, his face turned deathly pale. His hands, their fingers contracting like the claws of a bird, moved to his left shoulder, and his head slumped back on the pillows.

Leaping frantically to his aid, Michael loosened his tunic, then pressed a wet, cold towel to his forehead. After a few

interminable seconds, Milan opened his eyes, grinning sheepishly.

"*Ce n'est rien. Merci, Michel, mais ne vous inquiétez pas.
C'est une petite défaillance.* Lately I've learned that I do have a
heart. Up to a few months ago, I thought it was made of steel,
but this last shock has proved too much. Don't worry. I'll be all
right. I think I'll just go to bed and sleep."

"Let me call a doctor, sir."

"No. I've been to doctors. It's really nothing. And don't stay
in on my account tonight. Go out! Have a good time. You are
young. I'll see you in the morning."

The news proved even more shocking during the following
five days. On July 24, Deputy Premier Vukashin Petrovich's
private secretary arrived in Karlsbad to inform King Milan of
new developments. It seemed that all the desperate efforts of
Cabinet ministers and high-ranking army officers shattered on
Alexander's stubborn determination to marry his mistress.

"Monsieur Vukashin was having an excruciating time, your
majesty," the secretary, a slight, bespectacled man with a huge
mustache and the reputation of being a minor poet, reported to
Milan. "First, King Alexander subjected him to the most humiliating treatment; then, when Monsieur Vukashin resigned,
his majesty simply tore up his resignation and ordered him to
remain at his post. The premier stuck to his guns, so the king
changed his tenor, appealing to monsieur's better feelings. He
talked of his lonely childhood, his fighting parents—" The secretary halted, looking apologetic. "Forgive my audacity, sire,
but Monsieur Vukashin gave me his diary to read and I am
quoting him verbatim." He produced a small leather-bound
book filled with the premier's convoluted longhand.

"Go on, don't spare me," Milan said. "I can take it, no matter what Captain Vassilovich has told you." He threw a mocking glance at Michael, seated at his bedside. "You see, the captain thinks that he is my nanny and not my aide-de-camp."

"The deputy premier has done everything humanly possible," the secretary went on. "At times he had reason to fear for
his life. Not of death by a firing squad, but of sheer exhaustion
—a stroke or a heart attack. His majesty is twenty-four and
monsieur sixty-five. Night after night the king kept him up till
four in the morning, repeating over and over that Madame

Draga was a most virtuous lady. He told monsieur that it had taken him years to possess her carnally."

"It certainly had," King Milan murmured, "because she's a damn tease, the bitch. She knew how to get him."

"It was only in Belgrade, when she saw that King Alexander couldn't live without her that she yielded to him." The secretary pointed to a page in the diary. "Monsieur V. is quoting the king verbatim. And now"—he blushed—"your majesty will forgive me if I touch upon a rather delicate matter. Well, as a last argument, King Alexander confessed to the premier that he was unable to—to function as a man with any other woman. Only with Madame Draga. At which point the premier suggested that he, I mean King Alexander, postpone the marriage for a month and let Monsieur V. take him abroad, for instance, to Paris, and introduce him to a few young ladies whose expertise Monsieur V. had personally tested in the past. And if after a week or two of consorting with the ladies, his majesty still had doubts about his virility, Monsieur V. will be ready to eat his hat."

"I could've told Vukashin to save his breath," King Milan retorted. "I tried the same cure on my dear son the last time we were together in Paris. Haven't had the nerve to face the girls since."

Uncertain whether the remark was meant as a joke or as a lament, the poet reacted with a half snicker.

"Aside from Madame Draga's reputation, there were also rumors about her sterility that caused great concern. When Monsieur V. dared touch upon the subject, his majesty replied that the reason she hadn't become pregnant by him was her reluctance to bear a bastard. He was willing to guarantee that within a year she would give birth to a son or at least a daughter. Upon which the premier offered to walk with the royal infant in his arms through the main boulevards of Belgrade wearing not a stitch of clothing—that is, he would be stark naked, not the infant—which would certainly result in his being committed to an insane asylum. When this, too, failed to make an impression on his majesty, Monsieur V. advised him to forgo marriage for the moment, but live with Madame Draga and marry her the instant she produced an offspring. I don't want to bore your majesty with all the arguments the premier used in trying to dissuade King Alexander from marrying Madame Draga, only that Monsieur V. suffered a complete physical collapse at the end of the five-day battle with the king and was carried on a stretcher from the Konak. Of course, he wasn't alone in this struggle. For instance, Colonel Solarovich, King Alexander's adjutant, offered his assistance in placing King Alexander under house arrest and having madame deported from Serbia. Politicians, regardless of party affiliations, heartily supported him; not one sided with the king. After the resignation of the Cabinet, no one was willing to form a new government. King Alexander's decision had taken the country by surprise, and the result was utter confusion."

"That's how he planned it," Milan cried. "Sending me and the prime minister abroad. God, what fools we were!"

The secretary tried to comfort Milan.

"Believe me, sire, all sorts of possibilities were discussed. An army revolt, a *coup d'état* with a regency taking over, expelling King Alexander and recalling your majesty, yet no decision was reached. In the meanwhile, King Alexander refused to receive the deputations, both civilian and military, that flocked to the Konak. He also turned down all requests for audiences from foreign diplomats. Only one person, Colonel Taube, the Russian military attaché, was allowed to see him. In the meanwhile, King Alexander was concentrating his efforts on finding a new prime minister and—I am sorry to say—went to extremes in his search. For instance, he invited a well-known politician to dinner and served him doped wine in the hope the man would, in a befuddled condition, consent to form a Cabinet. Another time his majesty went down on his knees in front of another politician and begged him to fill the post. He had a most disgraceful fight with Home Minister Genchich after he'd found out that the minister had been to Madame Draga's trying to persuade her to leave the country. The whole Konak could hear them arguing. His majesty locked himself into the toilet, shouting from there that he would commit suicide if Madame Draga left him, with the home minister shouting back to go ahead as that would be the best solution for the country. Another most unfortunate incident took place in the front yard of the Konak. His majesty attacked two generals—using the vilest language—because of their opposition to his engagement. After that he made a speech from the balcony, accusing your majesty of every conceivable wrongdoing, including the appropriation of public funds."

Milan rose. *"Ça c'est trop fort,"* he said. "Please, don't go on. I have the full picture now."

On July 25 Alexander had, as in previous times, to scrape the bottom of the political barrel and succeeded in appointing a Cabinet.

On the same day King Milan sent two letters to his son. In the first, he resigned his commission as commander in chief of the Serbian army, and in the second, he wrote:

MY DEAR SON!

In all conscience, I am unable to give you my consent to the impossible marriage into which you are about to enter. You must certainly know, that your decision shall be the ruination of Serbia. Our dynasty has survived many a tragedy, but will never recover from a disaster of this magnitude. You still have time to reconsider. Should you, however, adhere to your fateful decision, there would be nothing left for me, but to beseech God to have mercy on our fatherland. I shall be the first to hail the government that will expel you because of your unforgivably frivolous act.

Your father
MILAN

It was upon receipt of the second letter that King Alexander ordered the army units guarding the frontier to prevent his father from returning to Serbia. "Should the ex-king insist on crossing the border, I hereby order you to shoot him like a mad dog," was the exact phrasing of the ukase sent to their commander.

The news of his son's cruelty was conveyed to Milan by well-meaning friends who tried to goad him into action against Alexander, but Milan felt that when a man was mortally wounded, one more blow could make little difference.

"No," Milan told his visitors. "When I abdicated, it was forever. Besides, it would be morally wrong for a father to turn on his own son. It is sad enough that the son has turned on the father. I'm afraid it won't bring Sasha much glory. He is a weak and dishonest man and he won't last long on the throne.

Ce n'est que le premier acte qui se joue. This isn't a political crisis; this is the death of the dynasty. In a few months the drama will be over. If he is lucky, it may take longer. A year or two—*tout au plus.*"

The event that was to extend Alexander's reign by three years was Russian Chargé d'Affaires Mansuroff's call on Madame Draga Mashin, bringing her the imperial congratulations.

The proof that the Emperor of all the Russians, King of Poland, Grandduke of Finland and husband of Alexandra Fedorovna, née Alice of Hessen, had approved the young king's marriage to his jaded mistress calmed the country as though by magic. Basically, the Serbs had always been Russophile, with the czar a distant father figure, as incorporeal as God. If he gave his blessing to Draga as Queen of Serbia, perhaps God, standing only one rung above him, would give it, too.

The elation over the czar's approval was somewhat deflated, however, when Paul Mansuroff represented him at the wedding ceremony held in the Metropolitan Cathedral on August 4. Foreign press reports about the event were also less than flattering, describing the bride as a fading beauty with the hint of a double chin, her hair not black, but nondescript chestnut, her pale skin marred by thin lines around her large green eyes, her sole extraordinary feature. The Russian papers alone labeled her the embodiment of Slav womanhood. The same edition reported the amnesty granted by the happy bridegroom to all Radical Party members sentenced to prison terms for participation in the conspiracy against King Milan's life in 1899.

The news of the wedding reached King Milan in his suite at the Hotel Imperial in Vienna. Dreading to face people after the disgrace inflicted upon him by his own son, he kept to his quarters with Michael, now more nanny than aide-de-camp, as his sole companion.

Reading the reports on the amnesty, Milan suddenly lowered the paper.

"She is a Russian agent," he cried out. "How perfectly stupid of me never to have realized it." When Michael remained silent, he gave him a searching look. "Don't you understand? She's been in their pay ever since she started sleeping with Sasha. Perhaps even before that. And wait a second! Let's go back to the attempt on my life. Knezevich was shown the picture of Colonel Grabov's house and recognized it as the place where he'd received the five hundred napoleons. And Colonel Grabov is the head of the Balkan Division."

Michael was determined to prevent the sick man from learning the ugly truth. "She's never been to Bucharest."

"But was friendly with the Russian Legation in Belgrade."

"That doesn't mean much. I don't think a career diplomat like Mansuroff would be permitted to become involved in an assassination plot."

"Then someone else at the legation was the go-between. I'll tell you who: Colonel Taube and his wife. Incidentally Michael, what made you go up to the fortress and snoop around after Prefect Andjelich's alleged suicide?"

The unexpected question found Michael at a loss for an answer. He wasn't aware that Milan had known of his trip.

"Well, I was merely wondering—"

"Whether Andjelich really committed suicide. Is that it?"

"Yes, sire," Michael admitted.

"Well, then, my dear boy, it wasn't the woman alone who planned my assassination. It was someone powerful enough to order Prefect Andjelich garroted in his cell. Don't ask me who that powerful person was. You see, my son is not only a crook and a liar, but also a murderer. A patricidal murderer. And a coward. He was the king, and it would have been simple for him to order me to get the hell out of his country, as long as he wanted to rule it alone. No, he couldn't do that. He couldn't face me like a man. I would've become angry and shouted at him, and that would've made him shit in his pants. He decided to have me killed, so I would never shout at him again."

To reduce his expenses, Milan moved from the hotel to an apartment in Johannesgasse. In no time, Michael learned that Russian secret agents had rented a flat in the house across the street from which they could observe Milan, his visitors and his household. To spare the ailing man the agitation, he never told him of his Russian neighbors.

Early in the year 1901, rumors of Queen Draga's pregnancy appeared in the international press.

"The woman knows no shame," Milan told Michael. "She can't be pregnant; she's been altered like a stray cat. You'll see,

Michael, when she's found out, it'll be a scandal to rock Serbia to its foundations."

Late in January Milan caught a stubborn cold that a week later developed into pneumonia. When his condition was declared critical by the physicians, Michael sent a wire to King Alexander, informing him of his father's condition. He knew what Westerners would never understand, that Milan still loved his son with a brooding, inextinguishable paternal passion and that a reconciliation was probably the sole remedy that could save his life. For three days, they both, Milan hopefully and Michael with growing anger, awaited Alexander's response, their vigil ending with General Lepi Laza Petrovich's arrival in Vienna. Laza—as he admitted cynically to Michael—had been sent to see if the old boy was really ill or simply malingering.

At first, Milan refused to receive Laza, then changed his mind when he realized that the meeting was his last chance to communicate with his son. Michael remained in the salon during the general's visit at the dying man's bedside but heard nothing of what was taking place behind the closed door except a few agonizing outcries: "He is still my son!" "Doesn't he fear God?" "Won't he ever tire of that whore?" Red-faced and visibly shaken, Laza soon left to catch the first train for Belgrade.

"Michael," Milan said after General Laza's departure, "I'm going to tell you something that will probably shock you. If I ever recover, I shall contact Peter Karageorgevich and ask him to do everything in his power to take the crown from my son. For years now, I've been aware of the sad truth that Prince Peter would make a better king than Sasha, although Sasha is my flesh and blood and Peter Kara isn't. It's neither a sudden decision nor one to spite my son. I've been watching Peter, his life, his actions, his circle of friends. That man has the kind of wisdom and integrity that we Obrenoviches never had. True, Peter is fifty-seven but perhaps that's what Serbia really needs, an older man. It is too young a country to be ruled by the young. In the likely event that I won't recover, I want you to go to Geneva and tell Prince Peter all this, as my parting message. And when it comes to a showdown between him and my son, do everything in your power to help the Karageorgeviches to win."

Milan seemed to rally for a few days; then on a sunny, but freezing morning, after he had been helped from his bed to an armchair, he suddenly collapsed, dropping his tired head on Michael's shoulder. A panicky Michael held him in his arms, watching the color drain from his face. At that moment a cloud floated across the sky, cutting off the sun's brightness. The dark shadow falling on the room seemed to Michael cast by the physical presence of death. But just as Milan seemed to be gasping away his life, the ex-king opened his eyes and gave him a half-smile.

"Let's place one thousand francs on number three horse in the last race at Longchamps," he said in a surprisingly vigorous voice. Noticing Michael's startled reaction, he added with a faint chuckle, "I'm only joking. I know we're not in Paris. We're in Vienna. *Quel dommage.*"

There was a last, futile effort to sit up, and then he slumped back in Michael's embrace.

Entering the adjutants' office, Michael found a sullen Lieutenant Bogdanovich picking his nose and smearing the retrieved bits of snot on the underside of his desk drawer. Deeply absorbed, he looked up only when Michael was well inside the room.

"Must have been some audience," he commented, still sprawled in the chair. In Milan's time, no first lieutenant would have remained seated in the presence of a captain unless given permission to do so. "Lasted more than twenty minutes."

The long hours of waiting he had spent in the company of the lieutenant had left Michael with an intense dislike of him. "Get off your ass when addressing a superior officer, dammit," he barked.

Bogdanovich grinned, without budging. "Now hold your horses. You weren't this high and mighty before the audience." Nevertheless, he slowly, and laboriously hoisted himself up from the chair. "You'd better contact the colonel," he said, lowering his voice to a whisper. "He must be pretty curious about the outcome of the audience, you know. And worried. And I wouldn't let him worry too long if I were you."

"Colonel who?" Michael asked hoarsely. "What the hell are you talking about?" Trying to read the man's ugly face, he wondered if the smirk around the chafed lips could be interpreted as a trap or a threat. Was he delivering a message or firing a shot in the dark? Was he a conspirator or an *agent provocateur?* Or was he both?

Through the open door, the lieutenant threw a look into the anteroom. Finding it deserted, he turned back to Michael.

"Will it put your mind at ease, if I tell you to go out and ask Captain Ljuba Kostich of the Royal Guards? You met him this morning at the Officers' Club. He can tell you about me. He's just seen Colonel Mashin at the fortress. The Sixth Infantry Regiment is having its Slava today. That's where you'll find Colonel Mashin. Better hurry because I don't know how long he'll be there."

"I don't know who gave you that message, Lieutenant, but it's all Greek to me. You must have started drinking too early this morning."

The lieutenant chuckled. "Well done, Captain. Never let your guard down. But hurry now. I've told you, they're expecting you."

Confused and annoyed, Michael started for the door, then remembering that he hadn't been dismissed by Laza, halted. "In case General Petrovich is asking for me, I've gone out to have a bite and will be back in an hour at the latest."

"Eat at the Serbian Crown. Then you can tell Lepi Laza that you ran into friends who took you with them to the fortress, which is next door. You've got to play it safe. Especially with old Laza. When it comes to Alexander and his whore, he's like a watchdog. Ready to maul his own brother to protect them."

"Thank you for the advice," Michael said sarcastically, heading for the door. "Now you may make yourself comfortable again."

"I already have," the man replied from the depth of his desk chair.

2 P.M.

"WELL, here you are at last," Colonel Mashin grunted as he caught sight of Michael. "What's kept you? Now you'll have to wait till tonight to have a piece of the Slava cake."

They were in the yard of the Sixth Infantry barracks, Mashin in mufti as before. His last words were for the benefit of the people around them, civilians and military, invited to the Slava, the name-day celebration of the regimental patron saint.

Mashin took Michael by the arm, leading him away from the crowd. "What happened?" He kept smiling, but his voice was raucous with impatience and distrust.

"I've been appointed equerry to King Alexander," Michael answered matter-of-factly.

The smile faded from Mashin's face, and his eyes narrowed to slits through which lethal suspicion pointed at Michael like guns from behind a duck hunter's blind. "You? Equerry? How come?"

Michael felt a sudden touch of dizziness. His shirt under the heavy fabric of his gala uniform was becoming soaked with perspiration. "You'd better ask General Petrovich about that, sir. He talked of reconciliation between crown and army."

"Did he know you'd been to Geneva?"

"The king did."

The colonel scowled. "You met him, too? What did he say?"

"Asked me if I'd seen Prince Peter. I told him I had."

"That was careless."

"Not really. I told him I'd seen the prince in church. And that was the end of it."

"Was that all he discussed with you?"

"No."

"What else?"

"He told me the country needed a medical school."

The colonel's scowl darkened. "What the hell brought that up?"

"I mentioned that I'd been in Switzerland for health reasons. It was the cue for a soliloquy on the country's urgent need for home-trained physicians. You know, sir, how he likes to sermonize."

"You mean to tell me you were ordered to the Konak for that? It was eight fifteen in the morning when you called me, and it is now ten past two."

Michael shrugged. "I saw Laza Petrovich after I'd called you, but had to wait till one thirty to be received by the king."

"Did you ask for an audience?"

The cross-examination was beginning to grate on Michael's nerves. "No, it was the general's idea."

"You waited five hours to be received by the king. How much time did you spend with him?"

Michael finally asked irritably, "What is this, Colonel, an inquisition?"

"How much time did you spend with Alexander?" Mashin insisted.

"Ten to fifteen minutes."

"You arrived at the Konak at half past eight and left it at two, so—"

Michael cut him short. "I phoned you at eight fifteen, reached the Konak at nine, maybe a few minutes before and left around two."

"Where did you go from there?"

"I had a cup of coffee on the veranda of the Serbian Crown just as Lieutenant Bogdanovich suggested. Frankly, I was disturbed when he told me that I should meet you here at Colonel Mishich's command post. I thought you and the colonel didn't want to be seen together today."

"I am attending the Slava. If you look around, you'll see quite a number of retired officers. That's why we chose this day for the coup. The Slava was a good excuse for some of our men to come to Belgrade from their respective command posts. Incidentally, the word is good from everywhere, except Nish."

"The Morava Division?"

"First we had only the Drina, then the Shumadiya. Soon the Timok joined up. Now with the Danube here in Belgrade, we have the cooperation of four divisions out of five. It wouldn't make sense to wait for the Morava to come in. When faced with the imminence of a successful coup, they'll have no choice but to fall into line."

They were standing apart from the crowd that had taken refuge from the burning sun under the oak-branch-covered arbors set up for the occasion. At the far end of the yard, a group of soldiers, accompanied by a three-man gusla band, intoned a lusty folk song. Behind the open door of the dining hall, a private was guarding the leftover half of the Slava cake, swishing away the hungry flies that swarmed around it. In the morning, the cake had been blessed by the regimental chaplain, one-half ceremoniously sliced by a trio consisting of the regimental commander, the senior noncom and the senior private, then portioned out to and eaten by the early guests. The rest was saved for the evening.

Soldiers were serving food, wine and schnapps to people already seated at the long tables under the arbors. The air was filled with the sound of happy voices, its volume growing in proportion to the alcohol consumed. Among the sea of faces Michael caught sight of Colonel Mishich and several of the subaltern officers he had met that morning. Mishich was chatting with a civilian in a shiny-with-age cutaway, a comical old party resembling a weather-beaten crow. He was evidently telling a joke, and the colonel responded to it with a carefree laughter. Michael felt a mixture of resentment and admiration for the colonel displaying such easy joviality on a day that he knew could end for him and his comrades in the darkness of hell.

"Your friend Mishich seems to be having a good time," Michael remarked to Mashin.

"Why shouldn't he? He has nothing to lose. Not like you."

For the second time during their talk, Michael felt the blood rush to his face. "Just what do you mean, Colonel?"

"He wasn't appointed equerry to the king. Although, had he been, he would've declined the honor."

"I haven't declined the honor, Colonel," Michael said, mustering his self-control, "because it would've betrayed my true feelings toward Alexander. I let him and General Laza believe that they'd succeeded in bribing me and that I was going to stay bribed. After all, it was for twenty-four hours only. Hell, now not even twenty-four, only twelve. And let me tell you something else, Colonel. If offered a similar honor by the next king, I shall turn it down flat. I was a king's aide-de-camp once. It was a great honor, but never again. Because there won't ever be another king like Milan Obrenovich."

Mashin placed a placating hand on Michael's shoulder. "Come, come, easy now. I didn't mean to offend you. It's only— you don't know because you were abroad—that we've been living with this thing for months now and right under the noses of the secret police. I personally became involved shortly after my return from Russia last fall. At that time we were fewer than a dozen men, but now we have a nationwide organization of more than one hundred and fifty, most of them officers and a few cadets of the Military Academy. If a single one turns informer, we are lost. So you cannot blame me for being nervous, even suspicious."

"But not of me, for God's sake!"

Mashin ignored the protest. "Ours isn't an *après moi le déluge* conspiracy. We don't want to trigger off a chaotic revolution. Our aim is a peaceful change from a lawless system to a lawful one."

"The same as mine," Michael agreed. "Only I wouldn't call it a peaceful change if people get slaughtered in the process."

Colonel Mashin's whiskers twitched nervously. "We've been over that before. I've told you, we shall avoid all unnecessary bloodshed. Yet there is one basic truth that seems to elude you. The final victory over a political rival is to survive him. Just remember King Milan. He abdicated, left the country, what's more, collected two million francs from the Russians for a promise never to return, then five years later was back in Belgrade and three months after that reinstated as king."

"Only commander in chief of the army."

"That's a matter of semantics. He *was* king." Mashin glanced about. "We'd better separate now. I don't think it is wise for the king's equerry to be seen with a marked man. You said you'd accepted the appointment so you wouldn't be suspected of dissension. Talking to me amounts to that, you know."

"I can always plead ignorance. I've been away three years. How should I know who is or who isn't in favor?"

A group of riders entered the yard in slow canter.

"That blond captain just dismounting is Premier Tzintzar-Markovich's son-in-law. Yovan Miljkovich. A decent chap. We thought of approaching him about joining us, then dropped the idea. Too risky, because of his father-in-law."

"I met him this morning at the Konak. He was just relieved of duty when I arrived. I was told his wife was expecting their first child today."

"Is that so? She is a pretty young thing. I hope everything goes well with her. It's supposed to be a very happy marriage. I'd better leave you now. We'll have a last meeting here tonight. At the quartermaster sergeant's office. It opens from the alley in the back of the building. Come if you can. But watch out. Not everyone at the fortress is with us."

He moved away, and Michael crossed over to the group that had just arrived with Captain Miljkovich. Three of the men looked familiar, and he remembered they had been at the Officers' Club that morning. Gaunt, swarthy Lieutenant Milutin Lazarevich wore the engineers' dark-blue tunic with cherry facing; a thickset little man, Voja Tankossich, the infantry's dark blue with green; and the elegant Captain Ljuba Kostich the Royal Guards' light blue with yellow braiding.

"You left the card game last night with the excuse that your wife was in labor," Tankossich reminded Captain Miljkovich, who with his long legs, blond hair and pale complexion resembled an Afghan hound surrounded by short-legged and coarse-coated mongrels. "You made that up, didn't you, so you could take your winnings home?"

"I didn't say she was in labor, only that she was due," Miljkovich protested. "And I wasn't really winning. A few dinars at the most."

"How about a return game?" Lieutenant Lazarevich asked. "We can play right here in the ordnance room."

"Sorry, not now. I'll have a quick bite, then go home."

"Let him go, his wife needs him." Captain Kostich laughed.

"What for?" Lazarevich cackled. "He's done his part. It's her turn now."

On the wake of further banter, Miljkovich left the group. Michael felt oddly disturbed by the cheerfulness of the three conspirators. They displayed the exuberance of schoolboys on a class excursion. Observing them, he wondered which would be corpses, which killers by midnight. Somehow the fortress, its original chalk-white stones now mole-gray with age, was a fitting background for their buffoonery. These men were the descendants of the luckless warriors whose heads, severed by the Turks, had once adorned, like candied cherries on a Viennese torte, the parapets of the fort. Michael could never look at the ramparts without recalling his grandfather's remembrances of bloodshed and torture. The exploits of national heroes such as Karageorge, Milosh Obrenovich, even the *hajduks*, the sadistic Robin Hoods of the Shumadiya Mountains, were the favorite bedtime stories of the Serb children of his generation. As a small boy, Michael had dreams of following in his idols' footsteps, but his years in Western Europe had helped him outgrow his fascination for them. Looking at the young officers who had probably never been farther away from Serbia than the Hungarian Zimony across the Sava River, had never spent endless months in the hushed silences of a Swiss sanatorium or a French nursing home, he could sense the potential cutthroats and highwaymen under their freshly pressed officers' uniforms.

The bells of the cathedral struck half past two as he spotted Apis coming from the commander's office. One glance told Michael that the man wasn't his usual self. It was the unevenness of his steps, the quickness of his breath, the nervous look in his eyes. His gaze sorted out Colonel Mishich, who, although facing away from him, became mysteriously aware of the silent summons and crossed to him. Curiosity propelled Michael toward them. Apis nodded to them and then, in silence, headed back for the office. Colonel Mishich followed, as did Michael.

He led them down the corridor to a room usually occupied by regimental secretaries. This time, because of the Slava, the secretaries were off duty. Five officers, wineglasses in hand, stood around a captain seated in the chair behind the desk. On a small table was a half-filled carafe of wine, a platter heaped with bread, cold meat and sausage and dirty plates with leftover food on them. The scene had the appearance of a small, private party of friends who'd sneaked away from the crowd of outsiders to celebrate among themselves. The sole disturbing note was the captain behind the desk, who sat propped against the back of the chair, his head hanging sideways at an odd angle with a small trickle of blood coloring his right cheek. More blood was splashed on the whitewashed wall behind him. On the floor below lay some grayish-purple matter, resembling vomit. At a second glance Michael, stunned, saw that it was part of a blown-off skull and brain.

Michael remembered having seen the captain at the Konak earlier that morning. He had burst into Lieutenant Bogdanovich's office to give some instructions to the lieutenant. Michael couldn't recall his words, only the man's brisk, officious manner. Now he was neither brisk nor officious, only irrevocably dead.

Colonel Mishich stared at the corpse in silence, then shifted his glance to Apis. "Did he commit suicide or—" He halted when his unfinished question was answered with a nod.

A young lieutenant picked up the sheet of paper with a scribbled note on it that lay on the desk.

"Captain Dimitriyevich made him write this," he said in a voice choked with the excitement of a small boy allowed to join the grown-ups in a parlor game. No doubt, it was his first conspiracy, Michael guessed, while the rest, he knew, were seasoned veterans. The lieutenant handed the paper to Colonel Mishich. "At first, he refused, but Captain Dimitriyevich convinced him that he had no choice. That he'd be taken to the dungeons and given a bad time if he didn't. So he wrote the farewell note, then picked up his gun and shot himself."

"He was a gambler. Had been all his life," Apis informed them. "A good one, too. Used to take the worst losses in his stride." His eyes, filled with an odd tenderness, rested on what was left of the dead man's face. "He blew out his brains with as little fuss as if he were target shooting."

"Did he say why he'd turned informer?" Mishich asked.

"He said he'd sworn allegiance to Alexander and his conscience refused to let him go all the way with us. My feeling is he'd been playing a double game from the very beginning. I don't know why he considered this the right moment to act. Probably because by now he had enough evidence against us to get a good price from Alexander. A list with thirty-two names, including yours, mine and Colonel Mashin's. Yet he made a mistake; he didn't take the list to Alexander, but gave it, instead, to one of our friends to give to Draga. He probably thought Alexander might not believe him and stand him against the wall alongside us. That's our great advantage over the men still loyal to Alexander. They can never be sure of *his* loyalty to them."

The go-between who'd betrayed the dead captain to the conspirators was no doubt someone very close to the royal couple; otherwise, the captain, himself a member of the palace staff, wouldn't have turned to him for mediation, Michael thought.

"Who was the go-between?" he asked Apis.

As though they had discovered only now that he was present in the room, all eyes turned to stare at him. He read not only suspicion, but judgment there. For a moment he wondered if he would be the next man ordered to write a suicide note.

"I'd rather not tell you," Apis said, his face the only friendly one in the group. It reflected the same sympathy he'd shown for the dead captain. "The less you know, the better it is for you."

Colonel Mishich pointed at the corpse. "We'll have to get him out of here. I hope no one heard the shot. At least I didn't. There's been too much loud noise in the yard. It always makes me wonder when I see Belgraders celebrate what the hell there is to be so damn happy about."

"With your permission, Colonel," Apis said, "we'll just leave the captain here. Lock the doors and take the keys."

"It's not likely that anyone would want to get in here before tomorrow morning when the secretaries report for work. So you're right. It's best to leave him here."

Wasn't it lucky for the conspirators, Michael thought, smiling inwardly, that the commandant of the Sixth Infantry had been antagonized by Alexander?

"By tomorrow morning we'll either have a lot more to worry about or nothing at all," the eager young lieutenant observed.

The men trooped from the room. Someone had the presence of mind to grab the meat platter, and a captain took along the wine carafe. Apis locked the two doors, the one leading to the commandant's anteroom, the other to the corridor. The dead captain stared after them with wide-open eyes, the blue of which was slowly clouding over like the surface of a lake on an early winter evening.

To his surprise, Michael felt thoroughly shaken. After having spent years in the communities of tuberculars, he should have been able to view the extinction of a life with detachment, he told himself, even indifference.

The world of sanatoria was an environment where one learned to take death in one's stride. Normal, meaning good or bad, relationships between inmates existed up to the moment when a patient became "terminal." Nurses and doctors were careful never to discuss the hopelessness of the person's condition, yet the news floated through the air like morning mist, seeping through the keyholes and wall cracks of the sickrooms. From that moment on, the dying man was no longer a member of the community, becoming almost an inanimate object, suddenly exiled from the reach of human emotions, neither loved nor hated, neither admired nor mourned. Mourning, if any, came later. While still alive, the patient became his own tomb, to which—as though following some ancient pagan ritual—one brought not only flowers and gifts, but food and beverages, although one knew that he could no longer consume them or derive any pleasure from them. Michael now wished he could feel no more perturbed about the suicide of the captain than he had about the death of the fellow patients he had watched drifting toward the inevitable end. He began to think of himself as a weakling unable to accept violence, at least not with the equanimity of his comrades. And there was a germinating doubt that he might not ever again settle down in his native country.

3 P.M.

THE page was first to spot the two women, the slim, stately queen and the graying, dimpled princess, as they turned the corner walking briskly up the Rue des Reservoirs toward the hotel entrance and followed, as usual, by curious glances. Few passersby were aware of their identity, and ogled them merely because of Natalie's striking presence, which usually parted the densest crowd deferentially—like the Red Sea for Moses—to allow her free passage.

"Here they are," the page whispered to the doorman.

"Go tell the concierge. And the prince. He is in the writing room."

White-haired and tall, with the commanding manners and bronzed complexion of an admiral, the concierge of the Hôtel des Reservoirs in Versailles acknowledged the page's report with a curt nod, then moved from behind the stronghold of his desk to the wide expanse of the lobby, halting expectantly in the middle of it.

The two women entered not through the revolving door, but the glass one on the right side, held open for them by the doorman. Once inside, safe from the brutal stares and whispered remarks of sightseers and families on excursion, who overran Versailles on balmy June days like the present one, they visibly relaxed. The princess unbuttoned her jacket and fanned herself with a lace handkerchief.

The concierge took a step forward and bowed deep, keeping his silence, for in the thirty years of his rise from houseboy to a position that to all practical considerations outranked the manager's, he had learned how to deal with exiled royalty, a much more exacting task than dealing with those currently on the throne.

The ex-queen stopped to bestow a gracious half-smile on him. "What is new, Boulanger?"

"This gentleman is asking to be received by your majesty," he answered, handing her a visiting card.

The thick dark eyebrows shot up into two indignant triangles. "I thought it was understood, Boulanger, that I am staying here incognito," she told him without as much as glancing at the card, holding it away from her as if it were a foul-smelling object, capable of contamination by touch.

"Oh, but we never told the gentleman that your majesty was staying here. He knew. And was most insistent on being received by your majesty. He said it was a matter of life and death."

Natalie lifted the lorgnette dangling on a thin gold chain from her neck to her eyes to read the name on the card. Then emitted a low gasp that sounded as if she were choking.

"What's the matter, Natalia? Who is it?" Princess Ghika

reached for the card, but her grasping hands were pushed away with unsisterly brusqueness.

Natalie turned her angry gaze at the concierge. "I won't see him. Go, tell him that."

The man responded with a polite shrug indicating that the decision mattered little to him. "As you wish, madame," and, bowing again, stepped back to yield the way.

"For God's sake, who is it, Natalia?" her sister, an older and less regal version of the queen, asked shrilly. During the early afternoon only a few people frequented the lobby, well mannered enough not to embarrass a fellow guest with inquisitive stares, yet now the princess' voice caused them to pop up from the depths of their overstuffed fauteuils and turn their eyes in her direction.

"One of the Karageorgeviches. Bozhidar. Prince Bozhidar!" The word "prince" was uttered with the sharpness of a pebble hitting glass.

"Oh, but he must have some important reason to come here." Princess Ghika threw a questioning glance at the concierge, still waiting politely for the sisters to move on. "Didn't he say it was a matter of life and death?"

"Yes, your grace. That was exactly what the prince said."

Now that the queen had used the visitor's title he no longer had to refer to him as "the gentleman," pretending not to have read the name on the card. "I quoted him verbatim."

"Oh, Natalia, you must receive him, you simply must!"

"I've never had anything to do with them and don't see why I should now."

"But he's come to you, Natalia, after all these years. You can't turn him down. Can't humiliate a man like that."

"Not a man. A Karageorgevich," Natalie said under her breath.

"Where is your Christian charity, Natalia?"

Natalie wondered where the prince was keeping himself while they argued. Was he watching from one of the recesses of the lobby, furnished with club fauteuils and settees grouped around tables, some already set for the five o'clock tea, or from behind a pillar, smirking over their indecision? He had been repeatedly pointed out to her at balls and the Opéra in Paris, yet she always refused to look at him, and now couldn't tell which of the middle-aged men scattered about the lobby he might be. Secretly, she agreed with her sister that no Karageorgevich would ever call on an Obrenovich unless the matter were to their mutual interest, as he would know better than to expect a favor that would benefit him alone. Although to follow advice was a sign of weakness in her book, she decided to listen to the voice of common sense, even though it came from the mouth of her flighty sister.

"All right, Boulanger," she told the concierge. "I shall receive the prince." She pulled her thin gold watch from the pocket set inside the waistband of her skirt and glanced at it. "We had quite a brisk walk with the princess. I need time to catch my breath. In twenty minutes you may escort the prince to my suite."

She kept Bozhidar Karageorgevich waiting ten additional minutes in the secret hope that he might feel hurt and leave.

When, accompanied by her sister who would act as witness and moral support, she finally made her entrance into the salon, she found the prince to be a man of medium height, slim and dapper, with thinning gray-blond hair, a small pointed beard and un-Slavic blue eyes that betrayed no animosity, merely gallantry and polite concern. If she hadn't known who he was, she would have taken him for a prosperous society doctor making a house call. Having moved in the same circles, although carefully avoiding contact, she had often heard him being discussed with the kind of excessive approbation that people save for the accomplishments of retarded children and wealthy dilettantes. A man of varied interests and curiosities, he filled his days with hard work, mental as well as physical, everything from writing elegant little essays on the racial landscape of northern India to designing and handcrafting furniture and *objets d'art*, all executed with infinite taste and to no practical purpose whatsoever. He had a box at the Opéra, appeared at the more important *vernissages*, wore Savile Row suits, drove a phaeton with two thoroughbreds at the Sunday *corso* at the Bois des Boulogne and maintained a family residence there as well. A Parisian of prominence, but no importance, he and his brother belonged to the rich branch of the Karageorgeviches; Peter, the pretender, and Arzon, the bohemian, however, were the poor relations.

He was standing at the window. Upon hearing the women enter, he turned and bowed.

"Prince Karageorgevich!" Natalie's exclamation was more a question than a greeting, spiced with a touch of astonishment. She had never suspected that the descendant of the terrible Black George could appear so thoroughly civilized.

He took her extended hand as though it were a fragile object and breathed a kiss on it. "I am deeply honored, madame," he said in elegant accent-free French. When he was introduced to Princess Ghika, the manner in which they greeted each other betrayed that they had met before, an act of treason for which a queen's sister would have paid with her life a few centuries earlier; the punishment now was merely a reprimanding glance.

Natalie was still dressed in the tailored suit she had worn for her walk to indicate that the prince's invasion of her privacy had taken her by surprise and was not to be construed as a social visit. "What can I do for you?" she asked in the tone of a French postal clerk, by worldwide consensus the most disagreeable female of the species.

"I've come to you, madame, as you are the sole person capable of preventing the most deplorable political crime in Serbian history."

"In that case you've come to the wrong person, I have no influence on—or any interest in—Serbian politics."

"It concerns your son, madame."

"You mean, the king?" The postal clerk now reprimanded the customer for placing insufficient postage on a letter.

He took the hint. "Yes, his majesty the king." Although he knew it would annoy her, he couldn't refrain from adding with pretended innocence, "And her majesty Queen Draga."

The name produced the expected effect. "I repeat, I am not interested in Serbian politics, consequently see no sense in continuing this conversation." Her tone, so icy, practically seared him.

He stared bedazzled at her pale Levantine face and told himself that now he knew what the Medusa must have looked like. Every line in that face expressed cruelty and hatred, which, oddly enough, failing to rob it of its beauty, enhanced it with the kind of magic attraction that Grand Guignol reserved for a few otherwise gentle and softhearted souls. He had seen Natalie many times before, yet always from a distance, a regal, bejeweled appearance, much too striking to seem human.

Her life story was no secret to him, though lately, since Alexander's marriage and Milan's death, he seldom read her name in the papers or heard her discussed at parties. The feud between her and Draga was common knowledge, but news too stale to repeat. He often wondered what she really was like, for newspaper reports and gossip gave a distorted picture of her, depicting her as either a long-suffering victim or an evil, destructive force.

The mature woman in the severe gray suit, the boned neck of her blouse brushing against the soft roundness that was the beginning of a double chin, brought to his memory the ravishing apparition that had alighted from a carriage trimmed with white roses in front of the Viennese Hotel zum Weissen Lamm some twenty-eight years before.

As a boy of thirteen, passing through Vienna with his family at the time of Milan's courtship of Natalie, he had joined the gaping crowd in front of the hotel where the couple's engagement party was to be held. Milan arrived with his mother, the mistress of Prince Cuza, a woman with the body of a fattened hog and the face of an angel. She had been summoned to Vienna by her son to have at least one member of the Obrenovich family present to counterbalance, if only by weight, the throng of Kechko relatives. For that day Milan pretended to have forgotten the neglect and loneliness of his childhood and sat beside his mother in the carriage as if it weren't the first time in their lives they had ridden together in public. Bozhidar was always to remember Milan the way he looked on that day, a beautiful young man resplendent in a white-and-gold gala uniform, his square face with the slanting eyes and the spruce little whiskers reminding one of a well-fed house cat, a glamorous puss-in-boots on his way to marry a five-million-franc dowry.

The bride was accompanied by her father, an average-looking little man, who gazed at her with admiration and wonderment as though doubting that this divine creature could be the issue of his loins. A flock of Kechkos followed them into the hotel, the women's *haute couture* splendor eliciting gasps of delight from the crowd that as yet failed to react—unlike their

Parisian or Berlin counterparts—with revolutionary anger to such a public flaunting of wealth. The Viennese, craning their necks in front of the White Lamb, were docile and peaceful, *Kaisertreu* to the very core of their hearts.

"Madame," he began, determined to shock her into listening before she could reach for the bell and have a servant usher him out. "Madame, your son might be dead by tonight unless you warn him to leave Serbia."

To his surprise, the disclosure made no impression on Natalie. She continued to gaze at him in cold silence. The only sound in the room was a schoolgirlish squeak from the princess.

At long last the queen deigned to ask, "How was that again?"

"You heard me, Madame. King Alexander might be dead by midnight unless he flees the country—and without a moment's delay."

Evidently, she was shockproof. The death threat to her son made no more impression on her than if she'd been told that he'd caught a cold.

"What do you mean, dead? Shot, poisoned, garroted? And just what do you base your information on? Or shall I call it wishful thinking?"

He ignored the barb. "I have it from a very reliable source, madame."

"Besides, what can I do here, in Versailles, at three in the afternoon to prevent something from happening in Belgrade at midnight?"

"Madame, I've received word that a *coup d'état* is being planned for tonight. A military group is determined to force the king's abdication. I understand the conspirators might resort to extreme measures should he refuse to comply."

She gave him a long, suspicious look. "A *coup d'état*? In whose favor?"

"That I don't know for certain. Rather, it's beside the point."

"You don't know. In that case let me enlighten you. Whenever there has been a conspiracy against an Obrenovich, it was always in favor of a Karageorgevich."

"Not always. I happen to remember one assassination at-

tempt against an Obrenovich masterminded by another Obrenovich."

"That ugly gossip has never been proved true. Besides, right
now, there are no more Obrenoviches left."

"That, too, is debatable, madame."

Nervously, she turned her back on him. "I don't count bastards," she told him in a tone that made him wish he hadn't
permitted himself the quip.

He had opened an old wound, causing it to bleed again. The
world's most beautiful woman—an appellation bestowed upon
her by news hacks—had been constantly and indiscriminately
humiliated in her femininity by the man who alone had carnal
knowledge of her.

A week after their return from the honeymoon castle Ivanka
near Pressburg, Milan had revived his interrupted love affair
with a certain Ila Marinkovich, the very ordinary daughter of a
minor magistrate. A long line of females from all walks of life
had followed Ila, actresses, ladies-in-waiting, wives of Cabinet
ministers, foreigners. Owing to Milan's insouciance, all his affairs became promptly known to his wife. The royal carriage was
much too frequently seen in front of some cottage, with
Milan, in the matters of the heart a great romantic, entering the
lady's residence with his favorite flowers, a bouquet of
white roses. Carriage, coachman, footman and a bored equerry
remained on the spot waiting for the master to complete whatever business took him across the threshold.

For friends, who attempted to reform him, he had one excuse: Natalie's frigidity. When repeated to her, she refused to
admit or deny the charge. Decorum prohibited her from discussing her sex life, although the accusation was true. Yet the
fault lay not in her. She would have become as warm and yielding as any bride in love if it had not been for an ugly scene on
the eve of her wedding.

Milan had come to their hotel to sign the marriage contract.
Her room adjoined the salon where her father and her fiancé
ironed out the last details, and she had overheard the stormy
discussion regarding the financial conditions of the contract.

Like all the fabulously rich, she considered preoccupation
with money degrading and vulgar. Her kind spent it the way

they breathed, never afraid that a deep breath would thin the air around them. She was shocked to learn that a man—a prince —could spend the better part of his life chasing after money as if it were some mythical beast, an elusive unicorn.

The way Milan haggled over the dowry made it obvious to her that he was more in love with her money than her person.. He would have married her had she been cross-eyed and hunch-backed, because her much-admired beauty was for him merely the extra bonus of a profitable deal. When her father tried to insert a clause into the marriage contract that would have at-tached strings to her five million francs, Milan threatened to cancel the wedding. Chilled to the bone by the cold-blooded haggling, Natalie found her passion turned to ice. On their wedding night, she lay cold and insensible in his arms. Neither his ardor nor his expertise as a lover ever succeeded in awaken-ing the woman in her.

Next to money, politics seemed to be the second curse of their existence. Following her engagement to Milan, she had been received, with honors reserved for royal personages, in an hour long private audience by Czar Alexander II.

"Even though you will be the wife of Serbia's ruler," he had told her with great solemnity, "never forget that you were born a Russian. Unfortunately, your fiancé's foreign policy has been influenced by the Austro-Hungarian monarchy. This must change. It is not only my and every Russian's wish, but evi-dently God's will as well, that the link between our Slav coun-tries be made strong and everlasting. Otherwise He wouldn't have directed Prince Milan to fall in love with you. He has entrusted you with a historical mission. You must never let Him—or us—down."

Milan's obstinacy prevented her from proving to Alexander II that his trust in her had been justified.

The meter-and-one-half-thick walls of the royal apartments weren't soundproof enough to keep the racket of their argu-ments from reverberating throughout the Konak. Hers was the temper of a tiger, and whenever Milan tried to play the *domp-teur*, she aimed, with the fury of a rabid cat, straight for his jugular vein, and no whip could ward her off.

She also become expert and resourceful in the disposition of Milan's favorites. She had powerful allies in the minister of home affairs, the chief of police and, at times, even the Cabinet, men who, unlike her own husband, became mesmerized by her beauty. Having a foreign actress expelled or a Belgrade resident of indefinite social status banned to some godforsaken village on the Macedonian border was no problem with such confederates. There were also other, more subtle methods, such as marrying the woman off to an ambitious army officer or a rich pig breeder yearning to head a Serbian legation in the West. If the lady in question was court society, passing her over at the Easter Sunday reception, when all women present were honored with the queen's traditional Easter kiss, could automatically make her an outcast.

His wife's maneuvers failed to disturb Milan; what's more, he often welcomed them because they helped him extricate himself from liaisons that he no longer enjoyed. She had, of course, no control over his adventures abroad, reported in detail by the foreign press. These she was forced to endure in tortured silence, the final disgrace being Milan's affair with Artemisia Johannidi, the daughter of a Levantine architect, whom he met during a state visit to the sultan's court and who a year later bore him a son.

He had humiliated, practically destroyed her as a woman, Natalie felt. Then, instead of allowing her to regain her peace of mind after the divorce, he continued his attacks against her as both mother and queen.

Some time after his abdication he extracted a promise from the regents that his ex-wife would be barred forever from returning to Serbia and exercising influence on the young king's education. To make certain the regents adhered to his wish, Milan gave his consent to a law which sent both parents into exile, leaving their son's upbringing exclusively in the regents' hands.

Natalie was at her family's estate at Yalta when the news of Milan's stroke reached her. Her first reaction was a crying fit; the second to board a train for Belgrade.

Even now, thirteen years later, she derived a secret satisfaction from the panic her unexpected arrival caused in governmental circles. The startled regents barred her from the Konak, even prevented her from meeting Alexander elsewhere. To spite them, as well as Milan, she rented a house on Teraziya, the boulevard through which her son was driven every day to attend to his royal duties in the city. Standing in an open window, she waited for him to whiz by, usually in a brougham. Never sure whether he saw her or not from the speeding vehicle, she varied her routine at times by going to the grilled gates of the Konak courtyard—though certain of a refusal—to plead with the guards to let her enter. The scene never failed to attract an impassioned crowd of spectators, as well as reporters from the foreign press, who wrote heartbreaking stories about the tragic mother prevented from seeing her only son. Although Milan had settled abroad by then, the blame for her torment was nevertheless placed upon his head, just as she had intended.

It was an exciting game, this psychological warfare against Milan. It gave her life both meaning and direction. Every printed report sympathizing with her and denouncing Milan was counted a major victory. It cost her time and energy, but was worth even more.

After a few embarrassing weeks, the regents realized that they were mistaken in hoping Natalie would tire of the *Mater Dolorosa* act, pack up and leave Belgrade. Since the scandal was beginning to undermine their already-shaky popularity and threatening to turn sympathy demonstrations into riots, they were forced to employ drastic measures, always their way of dealing with touchy problems.

On a sunny May noon, Natalie was handed her expulsion orders, allowing her two hours to board the vessel *Delingrad* which was to ferry her across the Sava to Zimony.

This order had been preceded by repeated offers of a more dignified exit: a festive banquet at the New Konak, followed by a ride to the river and farewell ceremonies at the pier attended by her son, the regents and the entire government. All these, she promptly refused, insisting instead on being removed by force.

"I want your gendarmes to drag me handcuffed and in chains to the ship," she wrote to the regents. "I want the entire civilized world to see how the Queen Mother of Serbia is treated."

When the two hours passed with the front door of her house still bolted, the embarrassed police prefect, accompanied by two aides, had no choice but to scale the garden wall.

Their sudden appearance in her boudoir took her by complete surprise. She had never really believed that the regents would subject her to a treatment usually meted out to foreign prostitutes and pickpockets.

At first, she was at a loss for countermeasures; then the realization that the three husky men were more bewildered than she restored her energy and cunning. Tears were always good for a delaying action, so she cried. The next move was to object to the good ship *Delingrad*, an old tub, considered unsafe by all. The debate on the ship's condition was followed by a protest against a ride in a hack with the prefect beside her and the gendarmes seated on the box. To save precious minutes, the prefect made a concession permitting her to take the short trip in her own landau closely followed by him and the aides in a hack. Having cleared that delicate point, she asked for time to change into traveling clothes, and—as she was without ready cash—to send a servant to the bank for money. Both requests appeared fairly reasonable to the prefect. The servant left for the bank, but not without a detour to one of Natalie's friends, who, in turn, alerted other friends. By the time she declared herself ready to depart for the pier the boulevard in front of her house was swarming with an excited crowd: men, women and children, plus the student body of the nearby Teachers' Training College. The people's passion grew more and more heated, the arrival of a hastily summoned squad of gendarmes bringing it close to the boiling point.

By then a detachment of mounted palace guards had been ordered to clear the boulevard of demonstrators. In the ensuing melee, several of the guardsmen were wounded by slingshots and rocks. The first revolver shot was fired when a missile hit the captain of the Guards on the forehead, causing him to tumble from his horse. This was followed by three volleys that scattered the crowd. Minutes later seven dead and twenty wounded lay on the cobblestones.

The tragedy had a sobering effect on all participants. Natalie feared the people might blame her obstinacy for the bloodshed and this time accepted the prefect's suggestion that she board a special train to Zimony at four thirty in the morning when all Belgraders were fast asleep. From the Hungarian border town she was to take a steamer down the Danube and across the Black Sea to her home in the Crimea.

Her foreboding about the change in the people's sentiments

proved unfounded. Her departure was turned into a ritual close to canonization by the more than three thousand Belgraders, who the next morning crossed the Sava to throng the streets of Zimony around the Europa Hotel, where she had stopped.

While the crowds of the previous day had been full of indignation and fury, the ones at Zimony resembled pilgrims visiting the shrine of a martyred saint. They were awed, somber and secretly hoping for a miracle. There was singing and flowers and lighted candles and people sinking to their knees on the waterfront as she, dressed in deep mourning for the victims of the battle on Teraziya, alighted from a carriage to board the steamer.

Hands reached out for her; lips touched the hem of her black silk dress; tears fell on the marabou trim of her short wool cape. The sound of sobbing, mixed with outcries of "God bless you, Mother of Serbia," accompanied her to the red-carpeted bridge of the *Kasan*, where Captain Gruich, resplendent in tailcoat and white tie, was waiting to greet her.

Standing at the rail and waving at the tear-streaked faces below, she suddenly realized that she had just forfeited the greatest victory of her life over Milan by failing to utilize the love of the Serbians for a coup in her own favor. A spark would have sufficed to explode a revolution, placing her on the throne not as a regent, but as reigning queen. In addition to humiliating Milan, she would have, at long last, fulfilled Czar Alexander II's expectations and made his dream come true. Now it was too late.

Two years later, when her son visited her in Biarritz, she asked him what impact the Belgrade incident had had on him. As always, he gave the answer expected of him. He had been outraged at her maltreatment by the regents, exhilarated by her triumph over them. Later, with his father, on his way home from Biarritz, Natalie had no doubt but that he told him the exact opposite, Alexander's problem being that he never remained permanently loyal to either parent. Like a fortress taken and retaken by two equally strong and determined forces, he pledged allegiance to whichever held him prisoner at the moment.

Had Alexander ever loved her? she wondered. Perhaps when

he was a little boy, mischievous, sly and affectionate like a house cat. Until his involvement with Draga Mashin, she had at times even suspected him of being incapable of loving anyone, especially a woman.

After having missed her first great chance in Belgrade, her second fatal mistake was Draga. She had used her as bait to cajole her son away from Milan until the bait swallowed the fish. That the marriage proved an even harsher blow to Milan than to her failed to make up for her losses.

For nine years, Draga had served her as slave, wailing wall, even friend, filling the terrible emptiness of her life after she had ceased to be Queen of Serbia. Draga she thought of as her private property, very much like the serfs on her father's land, legally emancipated, yet bound to her for life. By bewitching Sasha, the younger woman in turn found a way to escape from her dominance. She was no longer the chattel as close to her mistress as the cord leading from the push button on Natalie's nightstand to the bell in her room, no longer ready for service, a rubdown after Natalie's bath or lulling her to sleep with the recital of Serbian folk ballads or kissing away the tears shed over Milan's latest peccadillo. The realization that Draga could leave her at any time first alarmed, then infuriated her. She felt betrayed and cheated. Had this woman been sleeping around while she believed her to be almost virginal? Suddenly she recalled Laza Petrovich's evident interest in Draga, then the young French captain who'd followed them from hotel to hotel while they toured Italy. Once she had caught Prince Ghika, her own cousin, leaving Draga's room at four in the morning. Without batting an eye, the prince had informed her that he had lost his way to the bathroom, which, in her blind trust in Draga, she chose to believe.

She had dismissed Draga Mashin in a fit of jealous rage, then was sorry, but pride prevented her from making amends. She had completely lost track of her ex-lady-in-waiting when she received the shocking news that she had become established as Sasha's official mistress in Belgrade. She learned then also of the enmity existing between Draga and Milan. It pained her to find herself in the same camp with her ex-husband.

Nevertheless, her hatred for Milan survived, though somewhat diminished in virulence. Sasha's marriage turned her hated husband, her wily and elusive prey, into an ailing beast whose mangy hide was not worth a bullet. His death half a year later was like a knife thrust letting the heated air out of the balloon of her passion, a balloon already badly mauled by ill winds. It left her depleted, empty, useless, a heap of tattered rags. What energy she had left she wasted on futile attacks on Draga—ineffectual pinpricks compared with the bloody forays she had undertaken against her husband. On a postcard mailed to Belgrade friends, she had labeled Draga a ten franc street-walker who had used her professional skill to make a man out of her impotent son. Her methods in undermining her daughter-in-law's already-questionable prestige were certainly beneath her. This she understood all too well; nevertheless she was unable to control herself.

In the past, her hatreds contained the force of conflagrations, now they were merely the small fires lighted in ash cans by tramps to warm their chilled hands.

After fifteen years of marital warfare, divorce, reconciliation, annulment, amicable separation and finally Milan's death, the wound was still bloody and sore under the thin graft of skin. By some mysterious conspiracy, everyone she met sooner or later touched upon the sore spot, just as Prince Bozhidar had done now. Could the world never forget, she asked in silent anguish, would the disgrace never end? She had a hard time keeping herself from venting her bitterness on the prince by wishing him to leave. Somehow, she regained control of herself and continued the conversation without betraying her resentment.

"If there really is a coup planned, why do you want to prevent it?" she asked. "Of all the pretenders to Serbia's throne, your cousin Peter alone has some chance. If my son is eliminated, Prince Peter will be king. Don't tell me, you'd rather see my son on the throne than your cousin."

"Of course not, especially as it was on King Alexander's orders that I was sentenced to death *in contumaciam*, simply because my name happens to be Karageorgevich. If I set foot on Serbian soil today, he'd have me shot. Besides, I have great admiration for my cousin, which I don't have—"

"For my son," the queen cut in.

"I didn't say that; you did, madame. But don't let's digress.

There is a *coup d'état* planned. It might turn into an ugly mess.
And that's what I am trying to prevent."

"Oh, please, stop telling me fairy tales."

"My cousin is a strange man, madame. He might refuse the
throne if offered by regicidal hands. Yet the number of his
partisans keeps growing as if they multiplied by division like
amoebae. The conspiracy has become a web covering half Europe. That's why even I know about it."

"You've been talking in generalities. I cannot take you seriously unless you give me particulars. The name of your source."

"It's not one name, madame. It is a group." He paused. "I
don't think you've ever met my cousin Arzen, Prince Peter's
younger brother."

"Certainly not," she said indignantly.

"But you've heard of him?"

"Who hasn't?"

"I 'know what you mean. He's quite a flamboyant character,
to put it mildly. A man who attracts hangers-on, especially
around every quarter day when the check for his appanage is
due. Since he is a great deal more accessible than his brother,
Peter, a number of opportunists cluster around him. Basically,
he isn't a bad sort, just careless in choosing his circle of friends.
That includes female company as well. His favorite lady owns a
bar in Rue de Helder. I come from there. A previctory celebration is taking place at this very moment, although without my
cousin Arzen, who is waiting for news from Belgrade in his Rue
Cambon flat. I talked to him before going to the bar, and he
showed me letters and coded wires from people committed to
the Karageorgevich cause. So you see, madame, I have reason to
believe that my information is accurate."

They remained standing, the queen having refrained from
offering him a seat or taking one herself. Shortly after their
entrance, the princess had dropped into a fauteuil at the far
end of the room, where she sat fanning herself with a theater
program.

"Your concern for my son's safety is really touching, my dear
prince," Natalie told him with a slow, ironic smile, "if only I
could discard the suspicion that your maneuver is a clever move
to bring about my son's abdication. You think if I scared him
sufficiently, he would pack up and run."

"Oh, Natalia!" Her sister jumped to her feet. "The prince wouldn't do such a thing. You say that only because you don't know him."

"Do *you?*" the queen asked archly.

"The fact is, I do." The princess faced her sister defiantly. "Yes, I've had the pleasure of meeting him before. We also have mutual friends. You musn't judge a man by the name he bears. He was born a Karageorgevich. As much of an accident as if he'd been born a Jew or an Indian."

Bowing, the prince tried to suppress a smile. "Thank you very much, Princess."

The queen glared at her sister. "I am surprised at you. Although I ought to know by now that I cannot expect loyalty, even from my own family."

Unimpressed by the queen's reproach, the princess continued. "It is hard for a person to figure you out, Natalia. All one hears from you is how you've been crucified by the Obrenoviches, yet you turn on everyone who criticizes them. It doesn't make sense, at least not to me."

"I won't ever confide in you, Elena. I did discuss certain private matters with you, never expecting you to shout them from the rooftops."

The princess answered with a petulant shrug of her well-padded shoulders.

"May I tell you, madame," Bozhidar said, "that my cousin Peter had repeatedly expressed his indignation over the treatment accorded to you by your late husband's ministers?"

"I don't wish to discuss my late husband or his ministers."

The prince ignored her hostility.

"My cousin considered you not only a noble and dutiful queen, but also a highly intelligent lady whose political acumen could have righted some of the wrongs committed by King Milan's various governments. He was outraged when he'd heard of your expulsion in 1890. He was also aware of the indignation it had stirred up among the Serbians. The people loved you, madame. They still do."

Despite herself, she began to warm to the man. Instinct told her that, somewhat naïve and *precieux*, he was sincere.

"Won't you sit down?" Unintentionally the words slipped out. She lowered herself onto the sofa. His manner of taking the proffered seat, his smoothing down his redingote over his knees as though it were a skirt caused her to wonder momentarily if he were a homosexual.

"We are running out of time, madame," Prince Bozhidar said. "You must act now, or you won't save your son."

Nervously, she rose to pace the floor. The prince, too, stood up, his gaze captured by the ferocious beauty of her movements. She halted before him.

"You say my son's life is in danger. Let's suppose I believe you. What in God's name can I do to save him? You should have come to me days ago, so I could have taken the train and gone to him. Yes, the Serbs still love me and my appearance at his side would have protected him. Unless he had me arrested. I've been indicted for antidynastic activities by his government and would be tried for treason the moment I crossed into Serbia. I insulted his queen, which in his book calls for the firing squad."

"What you can do is send him a coded wire. Persuade him to cross to Zimony and wait out the storm there. The Austrians are under obligation to protect him after all he's done for them. He is not stupid; he'll realize that you must have serious reasons for contacting him after an estrangement of three years. Besides, I am sure he's aware of trouble brewing. Putting two and two together, he'll know the time has come for him to leave."

The princess left her observation post at the far end of the room to cross to her sister. "Yes, you must telegraph him, Natalia. Imagine how you'll feel if something terrible happens to him and you haven't made an effort to warn him. You must do it not for him, but for yourself."

The princess' voice shook with emotion, and two tears, large as pearls, rolled down her cheeks. Annoyed, the queen pulled out the lace handkerchief she kept tucked into her coatsleeve and handed it to her. It was an instinctive gesture, taking her back to her childhood, when she had been constantly aggravated by Elena's emotionalism manifested in a running nose. At this moment, however, she found herself resenting her sister's meddling. The problem at hand was hers alone.

She turned to Bozhidar. "Thank you for the information." Her tone indicated that the audience was over. "I appreciate your concern and shall in time inform my son of your visit, a unique gesture in view of the long-standing discord between our families."

"Not so unique, madame. After all, we are all Serbs, aren't we?"

"He said you should send a coded wire," the princess reminded her after Prince Bozhidar had been seen to his carriage by the concierge. "Do you know the ciphers by heart? If not and you don't have the book with you, I'd better phone the desk to have the carriage ready." She turned to waddle to the house phone mounted on the opposite wall when her sister's strident voice stopped her.

"For heaven's sake, don't press me, Elena! Let me think first, will you?"

"What is there to think about? You heard him. Every minute counts."

The queen dropped wearily into an armchair. "I still don't believe the man. His clan wants Sasha out of the way. What difference does it make to them how he goes? They want him out; that's all they care about. Suppose there *is* a coup planned. How can they be sure it will succeed? It may fail. So they try to trick me into persuading Sasha to flee, clearing the deck for a Karageorgevich take-over."

The princess stared at her in wide-eyed alarm. "You mean you won't send the telegram?"

"I haven't said that. I've told you not to press me."

"You yourself repeated time and again that Sasha's situation was untenable. That he'd come to a bad end because of the woman. The prince isn't the first one to bring you reports on trouble in Serbia. Sasha is still your son; you don't want to lose him, no matter how you hate his wife."

"His whore," Natalie murmured.

"All right, Natalia, so he married his whore. He isn't the first man to do it, or the first king for that matter. If only he'd acted a bit more wisely during the past three years. Remember, how Czar Nicholas couldn't wait to send them his blessing? And a diamond brooch for her and an invitation to Livadiya? If Sasha hadn't gone astray politically, she would've been received with open arms by Alexandra and after that by Franz Josef and by

Wilhelm and perhaps even by old Victoria, and in no time everyone would've forgotten that she'd been Sasha's mistress." She waited for her sister's reaction and, when none was forthcoming, added defiantly, "I personally always liked her and found her to be a good soul. No woman willing to put up with you for nine years can be all bad, Natalia."

The moment the words slipped out, she knew she should never have uttered them. Her sister's face turned a fiery red, then a sickly grayish white.

"I don't fell well," the queen told her, struggling laboriously to her feet. The princess, alarmed now by her sister's look, rushed to her but was pushed brusquely away.

"Will you, please, leave me alone?"

"Where are you going?" the princess asked unhappily.

"To my room. To rest for a spell. And I don't want to be disturbed."

"Am I to understand that you have decided against the telegram?"

The queen had already reached the heavy plush draperies which closed off the passage to the bedroom. Without turning back, she threw a curt "yes" at her sister, then angrily parted the drapes with both hands and disappeared into the darkness beyond.

The princess stared after her, deeply saddened, her fingers nervously rolling the lace handkerchief into a small ball. Her eyes overflowed with tears, and two glistening mucous pearls appeared on the tip of her upturned nose.

4 P.M.

THE *déjeuner* was a success, despite the absence of Lieutenant Colonel Jankowski, the Austrian military attaché, and Russian Minister Tcharikoff. Their regrets were delivered at the very last moment, just as everyone was ready to be seated. Having their place cards removed in the guests' presence caused the queen to blush with embarrassment. She had invited the two men because they belonged to that rather select group of intellectuals in Belgrade who spoke perfect French and kept themselves well informed on the literary scene abroad. Her intent was to impress upon her guests of honor, the French professor of contemporary poetry at the Sorbonne and his essayist wife, that Serbia was not a barbaric country, despite the rough treatment they had been subjected to at the Belgrade railroad station the day before. Having arrived on the train from Vienna, they were arrested by the border police when two books by authors whose works were banned in Serbia were found in their luggage. The charge took them by surprise. It had never occurred to them that the two harmless novels could be considered subversive. They were released only after the wife produced Queen Draga's letter of invitation from under layers of lingerie in her suitcase which indicated that they had come to Serbia to eat at the Konak and not to blow it up.

The couple were gracious enough to dismiss the incident or, at least, to pretend to have forgotten it. Since they were amusing and witty, their presence turned the *déjeuner* into a pleasantly sophisticated affair, quite different from the usual meals at the palace attended by rich merchants and Skupshtina members, some in baggy Turkish pants under their English-style jackets, who soaked up the meat gravy with pieces of bread and wiped their mouths on the tablecloth, their conversation consisting of discussions of Austrian import tariffs and the dangers of hog cholera.

The flow of limpid French in her dining room caused Draga to feel as though she were back in Biarritz, where the talk had centered on the latest Anatole France novel or the influence of the brothers Goncourt on Émile Zola's naturalism. Lately she had frequently longed for Biarritz. There she had been part of an elegant and dignified world, growing constantly in stature, instead of crumbling to dust like a marker on an untended grave, as she was here. The French couple, with their blessed ignorance of Serbia's political jungle, were like a fresh breeze from the West, blowing away, if only for an hour, the polluted air that made breathing so difficult at the Konak.

After bidding them adieu, she returned to her apartments in an almost happy mood, feeling like a true queen again, not the worn-out old mare she was called so openly in the cafés of Belgrade. Then the thoughtlessness of a servant brought her back to reality.

Actually, the girl was more than a servant, having been given the title "Mistress of the Robes," an honorary post bestowed at other courts upon ladies of the high aristocracy. Here at the Old Konak she performed as lady's companion, personal maid and secretary. Unmarried and in her early twenties, Yelisaveta Kostich, nicknamed Savka, was the niece of Captain Ljuba Kostich, commander of the Royal Guards. The queen liked her because she was pretty and vivacious, a bright streak of light across a somber landscape.

She had been summoned by Draga to help her change from the corseted dress she'd worn at the *déjeuner* to a negligee. Lately the queen had made it a rule to take a nap in the afternoons, hoping it would erase the drawn look from her face and provide her with more energy in the evenings.

She had rung three times before the girl made an appearance.

"What kept you so long?" Draga asked.

"I was busy." There was a jarring note in Savka's voice, the kind an engine gives off when foreign matter becomes lodged between its rotating wheels.

"I had to ring three times."

"I know."

In the past, Savka had occasionally allowed herself some small transgressions, but never the nervous, petulant tone she was using now.

Amazed, Draga stared at her. "What's the matter with you?"

The girl shrugged off the question. "What do you want to put on? Will the blue robe be all right?" Without waiting for an answer, she stepped to the wardrobe to lift the blue negligee off its hanger.

"Put it back," Draga said. "I'll wear the red one with the Turkish embroidery." Annoyed with the girl, she intended to let her know it.

Savka made a face. "Why didn't you say so in the first place?" and flinging the blue robe on the bed, she retreated a few steps, putting a safe distance between herself and the queen. She was familiar with Draga's temper. She took a deep breath and blurted it out. "I've decided to quit your service."

For a moment, Draga was too stunned to react. "Are you giving me notice?"

"That's right."

Her instinct told Draga that it would be senseless to argue. "You'll be relieved of your duties as soon as I find someone to take your place. Now, unhook me and get the red negligee."

The girl watched her without moving. "I wish to be relieved as of now."

"As of now? But why?"

Savka's words were brusque and impatient. "Because I want out now, that's why."

The picture of the Etna volcano, spitting stones and lava against the sky, came to Draga's mind. The more determined the girl sounded, the more Draga's anger subsided, turning slowly to a cold and numbing alarm. It was as though they had changed parts, the girl becoming the exacting mistress and she the servant anxious to please. "But who is going to dress me tonight?"

"You can dress yourself. You've done it before," Savka said. There was, Draga noticed, no "madame," no "majesty."

The urgency of the girl's tone revealed that there lay more behind her decision than plain discontent. "And what if I don't let you go?" Draga asked. "What if I give orders not to let you pass the gates?"

The girl paled, her eyes growing wide with panic. "Please, madame, don't." Now, it was "please" and "madame." "I have to meet someone. A young man. He's leaving Belgrade. Going abroad. It might be a long time before I see him again. I am sure your majesty understands. You, too, were young once." Recognizing the *faux pas*, she quickly corrected herself. "Of course, you're still young, but not eighteen."

"Neither are you," Draga retorted, her anger returning. She began to hate the girl, wondering if there *was* a friend. "Does your friend have a name?"

"I'd rather not tell your majesty. We have sort of a secret understanding. We haven't told our families yet."

Draga busied herself with unclasping her diamond brooch

and bracelets and placing them in the velvet-lined jewel box on her dressing table. The silence stretched uncomfortably long. Savka seemed to be at a loss for more excuses. Then, finding one, her face lit up. "If your majesty wishes, I'll come back tomorrow. First thing in the morning. As early as you want me. I'll be back, I promise. And I most humbly apologize for my rudeness, I didn't mean to hurt your majesty's feelings." She paused for a second. "May I ask your majesty to let me go now? May I? Please, please. . . ."

The sight of Savka, her young face a grotesque mask of obsequiousness, filled Draga with perverse resistance.

"No, you may not. And don't try to sneak out, because I'll have you brought back in handcuffs."

The girl's pleading smile changed to a grimace of anger. Draga crossed to the bell cord and pulled it twice quickly, then once slowly, the signal to summon her *mademoiselle d'honneur.* Seconds later Milica entered dropping a deep curtsy.

"Your majesty wishes?"

"Savka has given me notice." Draga informed her coldly. "She wants to leave immediately. She's been very rude and refuses to tell me why she wants to go."

"I've told you why," the girl whimpered.

"Not the truth, my dear. I know when you're lying." She turned to Milica. "Go to the guardhouse and tell Captain Panayotovich that Savka is not to leave the Konak grounds. Not until I revoke the order."

Milica's face revealed no emotion. "Very well, madame." She turned to go without glancing at the bewildered Savka. The girl watched the ramrod-straight figure, flat as an ironing board, approach the door, then rushed forward, grabbing Milica by the arm.

"Don't go, Milica! You know why I want to leave. I am scared."

As she tried to shake off the restraining hands, Milica's stare bore with the intensity of a searchlight into the girl's eyes. "Take your hands off me, Savka, and come to your senses. You heard her majesty. She wants you to stay, so you shall stay. Don't act like a spoiled brat."

"No!" the girl shrieked, her grip on Milica's arm tightening. There was a ripping sound as the sleeve tore. "No! And don't you tell me to stay when you'll be out of here the moment you're off duty tonight. You won't even take time to pack."

Draga listened in startled silence as the two at the door seemed frozen into a *tableau vivant*: Savka the picture of misery and Milica aloof and erect like an avenging angel.

"What is this all about?" Draga asked. "Why should Milica leave?"

The girl threw back her head. "Ask her, madame. Ask her about the message Captain Gagovich left with her this morning. Ask her why she never gave you that message."

"What message, and who is Captain Gagovich?"

"One of the officers assigned to temporary duty at the Konak," Milica said evenly. "He asked me this morning to arrange an audience for him with your majesty. I had to refuse in view of madame's crowded schedule. He seemed disappointed, yet I told him nothing could be done before tomorrow. So he left."

"Did you ask him why he wanted to see me?"

Savka answered, "He told her. To warn you about tonight."

"Tonight? What about tonight?"

"There will be a *coup d'état*. Or whatever they call it. Captain Gagovich was one of the men involved, but he felt sorry for you and the king and decided to warn you."

Milica stood calmly at the door. "She is out of her mind," she told Draga. "Madame, I've been in your service for three years now. Have I ever given you reason to question my loyalty?" When the queen failed to answer, she pressed on. "Have I?"

Draga looked from one to the other, her head swimming. "This Captain Gagovich. I don't recall having seen him. What does he look like?"

"Tall and very handsome," Savka told her. "Dark hair, blue eyes. He was recently transferred from Shabats."

"How do you know what he told Milica?"

"He is the man I mentioned before, madame. The one I have an understanding with."

"You said he was leaving the country."

"He might have to if things go wrong."

"She is mad," Milica said to no one in particular. "Stark, staring mad." Then she asked, "May I be excused, madame?"

"You may not," Draga snapped. She rang, this time for a lackey. When the man entered, she ordered him to fetch General Petrovich. Then she turned to Savka. "You might as well unhook me now. This corset is killing me."

"*Mais avec plaisir, madame.*" The girl curtsied eagerly, and her fingers began working on the hooks. While peeling the dress off the queen's soft, ivory-skinned body, she asked, "Shall I bring the red robe?"

"Never mind. The blue will do."

The queen had finished buttoning the negligee when Laza entered. Without knocking, as usual, Draga noticed, and there was a nervous flicker in his eyes that she hadn't noted earlier.

"What is it you wish?" he asked gruffly, sounding much too harsh and impatient for a courtier. "Make it short, because I have a lot to do."

"I'm sorry to inconvenience you, but there's something that couldn't wait. Savka just told me that she wants to leave my service. Not next month, not tomorrow, but right now."

"So let her go and get someone else. For Christ's sake, Draga, I am no employment agency."

He had never before used either her first name or this impatient, censorious tone in the presence of others.

"That's not what I really called you for. There is a Captain Gagovich on your staff, is there not?"

Laza reacted as though stung by a bee. "What about him?"

"Savka says he sent me a message with Milica about a *coup d'état* to take place tonight, which—"

She wasn't allowed to continue, for Laza turned on Milica with the swiftness of a tiger going for its victim's jugular vein. "Did he really?"

The girl shrank back, her spine pressed against the doorpost. "No—no—he didn't. Savka is lying."

"He did, too!" Savka shouted.

"For God's sake, have the man brought in and ask him," Draga said to Laza.

After heaving a deep sigh, Laza seemed calm and collected once more. Much too calm, it seemed to Draga.

"Don't let this shock you, madame, but the captain is no longer available for questioning. He's dead. By all appearances, a suicide."

"That's not true! It can't be!" Savka shrieked. "I talked to him shortly before noon."

"That's possible. About an hour ago he was found locked in an office at the Sixth Infantry Regimental Headquarters. Dead as a doorpost."

"Good God!" Savka whispered. "He did tell me he was going to the fortress." She addressed the queen. "The Sixth Infantry are having their Slava today. They were saving a piece of the Slava cake for him. He should never have gone." She began to sob. "He didn't commit suicide. They killed him. The conspirators did. They lured him to the fortress so they could kill him. They found out that he'd tried to warn the queen." She whirled about, pointing at Milica. "You betrayed him. You did! Because you are one of them!"

Milica laughed. "Don't be ridiculous. I was here all day. With madame. All through the audiences and the *déjeuner*. When could I have gone to the fortress?"

"You didn't have to. You sent the message with someone."

"Get them out of here," Draga ordered Laza. Turning her back on them, she crossed to the window facing the park and beyond it the narrow street which housed the Russian Legation. Gazing at it now, she suddenly became aware of how many hours she'd spent with her eyes fixed on that building as though hoping to catch some signal that could answer the questions perturbing her mind.

"May I leave, madame?" Behind her she heard Savka's pleading voice. "I'd like to go home. To my father's house."

"Why?" Draga asked without moving. "Are you afraid to stay here?"

"Yes, madame."

"What exactly did Captain Gagovich tell you would happen tonight?"

"That it might come to a battle between the conspirators and the Palace Guards."

"And he told you to go home, because you'd be safer at home."

"Yes, madame."

"Go then."

No one stirred. The girl, not quite sure that she'd heard correctly, stood rooted to the floor. The queen raised her voice.

"Go, damn you! Get the hell out of here before I change my mind!"

Savka whirled about and dashed out as if the room had burst into flames behind her.

"May I, too, be excused?" Milica asked calmly, seemingly unaffected by the scene that had just unfolded.

"I want her under house arrest," the queen told Laza. "For the time being, that is. Then we'll see."

Milica, pressing her lips into a thin, colorless line that resembled a badly healed scar, glared at Draga with unconcealed contempt. In one second, the gold coin of their three-year friendship turned into a counterfeit banknote.

It wasn't the first time in Draga's life that she had felt the scorn of an underling, the most searing of all insults. She had found it in the eyes of her drunken father's clerks, on the faces of maids and waiters in the inns where she'd stopped with a lover, on the features of the haughty majordomo at the Villa Sashino, of the clergy officiating at her wedding, Cabinet ministers she herself had appointed to their lucrative positions. She had hoped that the crown placed on her head by Sasha's gentle hands would have the power to change the derision that surrounded her into respect. For three years she had been friend and benefactress to Milica, promoting her from a simple schoolteacher to lady-in-waiting to a queen, showering her with gifts, bestowing privileges on her, only to have her side with a gang of would-be regicides. And Milica wasn't her first disappointment. Come to think of it, the rest of her protégées had showed no more gratitude either. Having been elevated to positions they weren't fit for, they evidently despised her for having chosen them.

Laza left to have Milica placed under house arrest. He returned shortly, looking a great deal less disheartened than before. It appeared that having a suspect apprehended and locked up always buoyed up Laza's spirits, producing in him the same kind of lift as tidying up a long-neglected cupboard gave to a housewife. A step in the right direction to make the establishment under his command function more efficiently.

"Good old Milica," he said with an angry grin. "So outspoken, straightforward and loyal. The bitch!"

"Did you question her?"

"Just briefly. Of course, she stuck to her story. Captain Gago-vich asked for an audience with you, and she promised it for tomorrow. Don't worry. I'll make her talk. But first things first."

"Are you sure the captain committed suicide?"

"Certainly not. However, I talked to Colonel Mishich, and he is convinced he did. He said Gagovich left a bona fide sui-cide note addressed to his parents. I've also sent Police Chief Marshityanin to the fortress to investigate. He doesn't agree with Mishich because it seems he's found certain suspicious circumstances. For instance, the door to the room where the captain was found had been locked on the outside and the key taken. The regimental secretary whose office it is went there accidentally today. He was off duty because of the Slava celebra-tion but had forgotten his wallet in the desk drawer the day before. He called a locksmith to open the door. The captain's body was still warm, and there were wineglasses and plates with food left around, indicating that several people had been in the room before or at the time the captain blew out his brains. Might have been the same people who locked the door."

"Did Marshityanin see the suicide note?"

Laza shrugged. "It looked genuine to him, but there are ways to obtain one from a doomed man." Laza's tone indicated he was familiar with the ways.

"What kind of man was the captain?"

"Bachelor. Good comrade. Excellent service record. Be-longed to the clique of Dragutin Dimitriyevich, the big fellow nicknamed Apis. Though lately, they haven't been seen to-gether very much."

"You seem worried."

"Frankly, I am. In the meantime I learned that the captain had also tried to see me when I was with Sasha. I wonder what made him attend the Slava. And if there were witnesses to his suicide, which seems quite certain, why didn't they report it? They knew his body would be found tomorrow morning by the secretaries who worked in that room."

"Because they thought it would no longer matter tomor-row."

"Seems likely."

"So Savka was right. Tonight is the night for the storming of the Bastille. What infuriates me," she said raising her voice, "is that I have to learn about it from Savka and not Marshityanin."

"Marshityanin is doing a good job."

"Not good enough. We've been warned to stay away from the cathedral, the citadel, the gala performances at the circus, and never to drive in an open carriage past the Foreign Office because the pigeonholes of its balcony are like duck blinds. That's all we hear from your Marshityanin. But who are the people we are hiding from? Don't they have faces, identities, names? Must we sit and wait for them to shoot us point-blank? No, Laza, not me. I am tired of waiting." She placed both her hands on the elegantly padded shoulders of his uniform. "Now listen. Go over to the Russian Legation and tell Minister Tcharikoff that at six o'clock sharp I shall call on him in person. And he'd better be home and ready to receive me, because if he isn't, I shall order a battery of field guns to level his legation to the ground."

"What do you want to see Tcharikoff for? What has he got to do with the death of Captain Gagovich?"

"Everything. He is behind this whole nightmare. He is the puppeteer manipulating the strings."

"You can't just go and hold him accountable. Besides, you must not leave the Konak. You are safe here, but don't tempt Providence."

"Don't you see? I can't bear this horrible insecurity. If their bullets don't get me, the insane asylum will."

"You've got to be patient. Just a few more days. Till the first session of the new Skupshtina. Once we're granted special powers, we'll swoop down on them. We already have an idea who they are. I could make a few arrests today, but I want the leaders, as well as the rank and file. And we need evidence to present to the nation. Good God, Draga, we've been over this before. Patience, patience, must I keep repeating it to you?"

"No use, Laza. I've run out of patience. We've got to clear the air. Once and for all."

"The moment I was told about Gagovich, I gave orders to Captain Panayotovich of the Palace Guards to reinforce all sentries and place his men on the alert. I also instructed Colonel Mishich to have the Sixth Infantry Regiment in readiness to move into town and surround the Konak at the slightest sign of a disturbance."

"We've had that too. Special alerts and troops around the Konak. I am going to talk to Tcharikoff today."

"You're insane."

"The bastards are too deeply in my debt. I have a few cards up my sleeve that might shake Czar Nicholas' throne to its very foundation."

"Let Tcharikoff come here."

"He won't; he is sick in bed. That's what his note said when he excused himself from my *déjeuner*. Wild horses couldn't drag him over here today. So if Mohammed won't go to the mountain. . . ."

"Ask Sasha what he thinks about it."

"No. And don't you ask him. We'll leave him out of this. And don't tell him about Captain Gagovich either. He won't admit it, but any talk of death—anyone's death—makes him literally sick. It's not fear, but a kind of phobia with him. He's always had it, but it seems to be getting more painful lately. He's no coward; it's just that the poor boy's nerves are badly frayed. People of his age rarely give much thought to death. But he seems obsessed with it. Such a preoccupation would be normal for old men, but not for someone twenty-seven. Death is part of life. Every passing day is a step closer to death. I know it now, but when I was twenty-seven, I felt immortal."

"That's just it. You're not immortal, so don't call on friend Tcharikoff. The moment you order your carriage from the stables there will be a sharpshooter dispatched to some convenient spot along your route."

"Oh, but I won't take the carriage. I'll just walk through the park, cross the street and ring his doorbell. I'll be perfectly safe at the legation, because they cannot afford a murder on their premises. They may plot it, support it, pay for it, but only behind the shelter of diplomatic secrecy. So go and tell the bastard that I'll be there at six sharp."

The general started for the door then halted halfway. "Look, Draga, if you're really bent on bearding the lion in his own den, do it unannounced. I agree you'd be safe at the legation, but there are so many ways unfortunate accidents can happen. A team of runaway horses knocking down a pedestrian, boys shooting at sparrows and missing their aim, a flowerpot dropped from a balcony by a careless maid. . . ."

The queen nodded. "You might have a point there. You seem to have heard the German saying: *Wie der Schelm denkt.*"

"I know what you mean. 'As the rascal thinks.'" Laza grinned. "I'll see you before you go."

"If Sasha comes looking for me, tell him I am taking a nap. Of course, I won't now. Even if I look like the devil's grandmother at supper tonight."

5 P.M.

HE pulled out his watch on the thin gold chain that girthed his middle still surprisingly flat and firm for a man his age. The time was five o'clock. If everything had gone according to schedule, he should have had word hours before. Delay could mean postponement or abandonment of the plan. A flicker of hope flashed through the back of his mind. He looked about, his eyes gliding like a caressing hand over the blue satin-covered walls of his drawing room, the grand piano in the corner, the modest desk in the bay window, the time-yellowed photos on the mantel and the marble and bronze clock, a wedding gift from Czar Alexander III. The clock was as disdainful of Greenwich mean time as its donor had been, yet he wound it religiously every Saturday, for its ticking was one of the sounds that made a home of a rented house—a home which he was desperately reluctant to leave.

Even in his youth, he had been only moderately eager to assume the burdens of kingship. Never a fully dedicated pretender to the throne, he filled the role with the secret misgivings of a tradesman's son who, after the death of his father, is forced by tradition to take over the family firm, despite a loathing for commerce.

His memories of Serbia, the memories of a fourteen-year-old boy, were a mixed bag. The rolling hills and green forests of

Shumadiya which he had roamed while hunting deer, the grammar school he had attended with peasant boys and the royal stallions he had ridden competing with the grooms were the good memories. The bad one was the Old Konak with its sepulchral silences occasionally disrupted by the bellows of his father's rebellious subjects storming through its musty rooms like stampeding cattle. The last stampede had caused his father to pack up and hastily seek asylum for himself and his family in the fortress still garrisoned by Turkish troops. Later his deposed prince-father had retired, a petulant exile, to the Karageorgevich estates in the south of Hungary. The years that followed were punctuated for young Peter by his enrollment in a Geneva boarding school, his graduation from France's École Militaire St.-Cyr and his studies at the University of Zurich, and they had changed him from a wild, untamed Serb into a solid Western citizen, an identity which of all the identities he had assumed during a long and turbulent life best suited him. Though he was probably the least war-loving graduate of St.-Cyr, his loyalty to France caused him to fight the Germans in the 1870–71 Franco-Prussian War and later, at the head of a *komitadji* band, the Turks in Bosnia.

His seven years as husband to Zorka, the eldest and most ambitious daughter of wily old Nikita, Prince of Montenegro, were like a chapter in someone else's biography.

Zorka's portrait, done by some obscure itinerant painter, hung in his bedroom and her photo, a much better likeness, in a silver frame above the drawing room mantel among half a dozen dedicated pictures of royalty. Hers bore no dedication; such urbane gestures would have been alien to her cháracter. Taken at the time of their engagement, the photo showed a young woman of brooding Slavic beauty. Despite her violent temper, he loved her more than he had ever thought himself capable of loving any woman.

They had met in 1882 in St. Petersburg, at the coronation of Czar Alexander III of Russia. Incensed over Milan Obrenovich's flirtation with Austria, the czar had decreed that Peter Karageorgevich be invited to the festivities to represent Serbia instead of its reigning king. For the czar, Balkan princes and pretenders were like chessmen on the board of international politics to be moved by him at will, and he often displayed a complete disregard for the most elemental rules of the game.

The idea of a possible alliance between the Montenegrin ruling dynasty and the exiled Karageorgeviches had come to him while watching the quadrille at the coronation ball. His eyes happened to alight on Zorka, dancing in the sedate crowd with the exuberance of a colt not yet broken to the saddle. Dressed in the national costume of her country and wearing as her only jewelry a chain of gold coins around her neck, she seemed a rather incongruous touch of rusticity among the throng of princes and court ladies ablaze with diamonds. The czar found her simplicity oddly appealing. At the reception the day before, he had talked at some length with Peter, admiring his intelligence and maturity. By the time the dancers returned to their seats after the quadrille, Peter's and Zorka's marriage was a foregone conclusion in the czar's mind.

Peter had been thirty-eight at the time, his hair already graying and his joints aching with insidious little pains, reminders of his youthful exploits, such as swimming the icy Loire after his escape from a German prisoner of war camp or the long nights spent on the bare and inhospitable rocks of Bosnia. The czar's wish, disguised as a friendly hint, came at the moment when he was beginning to feel that there had to be more to life than clerking for Swiss businessmen or translating John Stuart Mill's essays into Serbian. Had Zorka been Western European, her youth would have caused him to shy away from the marriage, yet he knew—at least he believed he knew—that girls from the Balkans were brought up to be malleable and accommodating, ready to love and obey any man chosen for them by their parents, so, after some reflection, he agreed to comply with the czar's wish. Alexander III took his acquiescence for a sign of loyalty, although in Zorka's strange, sensuous beauty lay the real motive behind Peter's decision.

The seven years that followed were the happiest, as well as the most disquieting period of his life. To please Zorka, he had settled in Cetinje, a stone's throw from her father's residence. Prodded by the old man, she pressed Peter to retake the throne of Serbia from the Obrenoviches. His reluctance to stir up a revolution in his favor both embittered and infuriated her. A rather painful memory of his marriage was a wrestling match she had staged, of all places, in their wide connubial bed, where only a few minutes before they had made love.

With her black tresses swinging wildly and her claws aimed at his eyes, she had lunged at him, calling him a spineless coward. For the first and last time in his life, he had lost his self-control and retaliated with an angry shove, which had sent her tumbling over the foot of the bed, where she fell with a loud thud to the floor.

The court physician, hastily summoned from his nightly tarot game, declared, after a whispered conference with her father, that she had broken her back. Her health, already weakened by recurrent attacks of tuberculosis and five pregnancies, with only three of her children surviving, began to deteriorate after the incident. In vain Peter tried to plead with Nikita to allow them to go abroad to the milder climate of the Côte d'Azur or the Crimea, but the prince refused to issue them passports. It seemed as though it suited the old fox's schemes to place the blame for his daughter's illness and, finally, her death on the grizzled head of her husband.

Although Peter knew that her back hadn't been broken and that the fight had no bearing upon her illness, its memory remained like a shadow over his life. Why was it, he often wondered, that there couldn't be grief without guilt, that one's loss was made even more unbearable by the recognition that at one time or another one had failed the deceased? Death had cleansed Eurydice of all her faults and weaknesses, while Orpheus, the survivor, became an ogre in his own eyes. It was probably the assumption of his own unworthiness, Peter rationalized, that caused the Thracian poet to fail when offered a chance to rescue her from Hades and take her back to the world of the living.

This chance was never offered to Peter, or was it? If he had been more determined to defy his father-in-law, bundled her up and whisked her in all secrecy across the Montenegrin frontier, he might have saved her life. It was a thought that was to plague him for the rest of his days.

After Zorka's death, he had defied his father-in-law, left Montenegro and settled in Geneva. He worked hard to make ends meet and reared his children with an equal ratio of sternness and affection, but he never ceased grieving for Zorka.

At times he wished he had remained among his own kind where the code of behavior allowed one to wear sorrow openly, instead of hiding it like a repugnant sore. In the West death was finality, a gate slammed forever shut. In the East it was a door left slightly ajar with the specter of the departed still visible through the narrow gap. The dead remained part of one's life, and their graveside places were frequently visited. One held picnics on them with food baskets unpacked in the shade of tombstones and quiet tears shed on the sausage, bread and *pogacha*. After the meal, the young played games or broke into songs. Widows never sang, certainly not during the first few years of mourning, but kept themselves apart, small black islands in the sea of colorful Sunday bests, swaying back and forth like poplars buffeted by the wind and giving voice to their grief in an eerie, monotonous wail. It was a sound that had belonged to Peter's childhood much like the rustle of reeds in the marshes along the gray, sluggish Danube or the village popes' banging on clapboards before mass, a custom left over from the time of the Turkish rule, when the ringing of church bells had been prohibited.

For widowers, it would have been unthinkable to bay like stray dogs. To express grief, they relied on their rifles. When unable to find rest or sleep, they left their solitary beds, stepped out into the night and aimed their rifles at the sky as though bent on evening up the score with the Man above the clouds. Their shots would pierce the dark silence, scare flocks of sleeping birds and convey the inconsolable burden of their sorrow to their neighbors. Peter suspected that his membership in the Geneva Rifle Club and the trophies he won at sharpshooting contests were signs of his reversion to the moods and practices of his faraway country.

It was twenty past five when his doorbell rang. He heard Albert, his valet of many years, shuffle through the hallway. Albert, especially since he was growing old, had the slow, plodding movements of an automaton, making one wonder how he managed to keep the house in such perfect order without ever seeming to work at it.

Not bothering to knock, Albert entered the drawing room with a telegram in his bearlike paws. During the past months, there had been an increase in telegrams, some delivered, to Albert's great annoyance, in the middle of the night.

"There." He handed the envelope to the prince. "I wonder who it is this time." What he meant was who had died. To his mind, someone's passing was the sole reason why a sensible person might revert to such an expensive means of communication.

Peter tore the envelope open, staring with a troubled frown at its message.

"I hope you don't have to go to another funeral," Albert muttered. "Won't be so bad, though, not at this time of the year. Although one can never tell. Remember the cold you brought home from old King Umberto's in Rome? And that, too, was in summer."

The word "funeral" grated on Peter's nerves. Dismissing Albert with an impatient grunt, he rose and went to his bedroom, where he dropped into the straight chair beside his simple soldier's bed and reread the message:

"Pigs safely sold stop buyer promises payment for tonight stop greetings Nenadovich."

The wire, the last one in the series of relayed messages, had first been telephoned by Colonel Mashin to a Smederevo cattle dealer, then forwarded via telegraph to a confederate in Zimony, from there to Nenadovich in Vienna and finally to Peter in Geneva. The cattle fair held at Smederevo on that day was to make the message appear harmless. The Serbian secret police, keeping close watch on all telegraphic communications between their country and the rest of Europe, were unlikely to connect a wire concerning a lifestock deal with the imminent *coup d'état*. They would have needed the gift of second sight to infer that the "pigs" of the wire referred to the King and Queen of Serbia.

There was no escape for him now, Peter conceded. He had to go through the process of becoming king. The speeches, the handshakes, the *zhiveo* shouts coming from what to his tired eyes were going to appear like a colorful hedge along the streets, a hedge of bodies and faces melting into a restless pattern, thousands of small flags fluttering in the wind like birds taking to the air. There would be an anointment, preceded and followed by receptions, all much too hard on his aching feet.

After years of dignified anonymity, he would suddenly find himself the center of every gathering, a living yardstick against which the status of every one of his subjects would be measured. It had been Zorka's passionate wish to see him anointed in the Belgrade Cathedral, yet, in her lifetime, while he still retained the vigor to accomplish it, he hadn't made the effort. But now he was embarking, a burned-out hull of a man, on the questionable adventure for the sake of some reckless strangers. What he found most disconcerting was that the men who had forced him into action didn't know him and had never cared to. The suspicion that they had chosen him not *despite*, but *because* of his age, hoping to turn the feebleness that went with it to their advantage, kept gnawing at him. He had reacted with steely defiance to this suspected scheme. He was going to be their king, there was no turning back now, but not a king patterned after their wishes. They would have to abide by his rules or kill him, because once placed on the throne, he would never vacate it voluntarily, at least not before forcing the reforms he considered vital for the future of the country down their throats.

Being old and disillusioned had one advantage: One was immune to flattery, bribe or threat. One had nothing to lose but one's life, and that wasn't worth the minutest compromise.

Before consenting to take on the burden of kingship, he had carefully examined all the men—and all the forms of government—that could serve Serbia in his own stead.

A republic would have been, under different circumstances, his preferred solution. After pondering all the pros and cons, he discarded the idea sadly. Democracy for the Serbs was like a loaded rifle in the hands of a small boy. They lacked the skill and discipline to handle it; they would have to outgrow their medieval penchant for tribalism and vendettas, accept the ballot instead of the bullet as the best means for settling a political dispute.

A traditional solution would have been his elder son, George, elected king with a regency ruling until his coming of age. Peter loved the boy with all his heart, more than his younger son and his daughter, because his love for George held touches of pity and anxiety. The blood of terrible Karageorge flowed in the boy's veins, as it did in his own, yet George was also

Nikita's grandchild, and to be burdened with two such ancestral lineages held not much hope for someone as neurotic and capricious as the boy.

Born twenty-nine years after Karageorge's assassination, Peter had no illusions about his grandfather, one of the most complex personages of Serbian history. After a modest beginning as swineherd and later corporal in the Austro-Hungarian army, Black George suddenly emerged as the heroic leader of the 1805 uprising against the Turks. He was a demigod and a monster; warlord, statesman, creator of modern Serbia, single-handed murderer of one hundred and twenty-five human beings, among them his own father and brother, cowardly defector of the cause of Serbia's freedom and finally the hapless victim of an assassination plot hatched by another swineherd turned statesman: Milosh Obrenovich.

Peter took no pride in the founder of his dynasty, only a painful and nervous foreboding about the harm that his savage ancestor's genes might do to future generations of Karageorgeviches. It had become almost a fixation with him to keep a close watch on himself and the members of his family for signs of the mental instability that had driven old George from feats of heroism to the most abysmal acts of infamy.

To Peter's great chagrin, young George was the most suspect of them all. As a small boy, he had often fallen into senseless rages, snarling and howling like a caged animal. As he grew older, the fits seemed to become less frequent. Now, at fourteen, reports on his conduct at the St. Petersburg École des Pages contained no indication of more trouble than could be expected from a spirited young boy suddenly subjected to the discipline of a rigorous military training. This, in a way, was encouraging.

The younger son, Alexander, a plain and unattractive child of twelve, had never given Peter any cause for either alarm or satisfaction. He felt that he must wait for both boys to grow into manhood before he could designate either as fit for the throne.

His brother, Alexis, his cousins Bozhidar and Arzen, the three male adults of his clan, seemed, except for petty eccentricities, as normal as exiles with death sentences *in contumaciam* hanging over their heads could be expected to be.

Of the three—all living in Paris—he felt most tolerant of Bozhidar. At least he had managed to find a place for himself, not as a Balkan prince, but as an individual, while Alexis, for instance, dedicated his entire life to the glorification of his title.

Alexis had married a rich American woman, hoping that her money would obtain for him precedence over Peter when the time came for the restoration of the Karageorgevich dynasty. Peter would have yielded the throne to him gladly if only this Karageorgevich had not been such a perfect ass. Though harmless and basically decent, he was a man of childlike vanity: insecure, fumbling and easily impressed.

As for his own brother, Arzen, he was a second Milan, but without the dead Obrenovich's brilliance and charm. His escapades had been the talk of Paris, not of its salons, but its bordellos and bohemian cafés. Divorced from his Russian wife, he lived with a fading Parisienne, whose oft-proclaimed ambition was to become a second Draga Mashin.

What finally caused Peter to decide in his own favor was his smoldering contempt for his ex-father-in-law, Nikita of Montenegro.

During his years in Cetinje, he had ample opportunity to observe the *modus operandi* of one of the most unscrupulous men the Balkans had ever produced. He used to marvel at the naïveté of the Montenegrins, a primitive, yet ferocious breed of Serbs, for tolerating Nikita on the throne. Before moving to Cetinje, Peter had considered education the magic lamp that threw its light not only on its possessor, but on all who came in contact with him. This was not true in Nikita's case. Although a scholar and poet with some passable verse dramas to his credit and probably better educated than most Western European princes, he did everything within his unlimited power to keep education, like a dangerous malaise, away from his people. If he hadn't been born a prince, he would probably have become one of the great adventurers of his century, a swindler on the grand scale, pursued, yet never caught by any police. As the descendant of the two-hundred-year-old Petrovich of Nyegosh dynasty, he considered himself the rightful claimant to the throne of Serbia. From his isolated mountain peak he kept a never-slackening watch on the political scene of Europe, boarding a train at a moment's notice whenever he felt that a call on a Western statesman or a royal personage would further his aims. While other Balkan princes tried hard to be taken for gentlemen, he chose to impersonate—in baggy linen trousers and embroidered vest—a lovable old goatherd whose earthbound equanimity could be shaken neither by the splendor of Czar Nicholas' court nor by the elegance of the French Riviera.

As all gifted scoundrels, he was blessed with irresistible charm. His daughters, distributed over the face of Europe, placed like watchtowers at strategic points where they could best further his aims, were no hindrance either. The ratio of two daughters to St. Petersburg and only one to Germany was to demonstrate Nikita's loyalty to, but not complete dependence on, Mother Russia. The Battenberg connection proved fruitful insofar as it secured him the friendship of such a hard-to-conquer old party as Queen Victoria. The Karageorgevich alliance through his daughter Zorka had been Nikita's sole miscalculation.

Peter had never seen larceny practiced with such shameless nonchalance as by his father-in-law. At regular intervals, Nikita invented a national disaster: Famine, forest fire, even earthquake befell Montenegro, and he turned to Mother Russia for emergency relief. To send investigators to Montenegro would have been too complicated, so in order to preserve the affection of its most loyal satellite, Russia sent to Cetinje freight-car-loads of grain, machinery, medicine and building material, which were promptly sold to Trieste or Zimony mechants and the purchase price deposited in Nikita's Swiss bank account. The crudest of his thieveries was pocketing money orders sent by expatriate Montenegrins to their relatives. The Cetinje post office had orders to pay them straight to the prince. As most recipients were illiterate, a receipt marked with a cross was sufficient to satisfy the sender that his gift had been delivered.

To Balkan Slavs, conditioned over several centuries to the lawless rule of Janizaries, pashas and even sultan-appointed princes of their own blood, Nikita's practices seemed as natural and uncontrollable as floods, snowstorms and epidemics. To Peter, they were criminal acts perpetrated by a scoundrel ready to move to even more lucrative heights. Nikita's burning ambition to unite all Southern Slavs under his rule terrified Peter, because he knew that, although sixty-two years old, the man possessed enough vigor, guile and connections to realize his dream. His reign would prove even more harmful than inept little Alexander's; nevertheless, Serbia's crown, if refused by Peter Karageorgevich, would sooner or later become old Nikita's booty.

Engrossed in his thoughts, he failed to hear the doorbell or the sounds of Albert's heavy steps trudging through the hallway or the medley of strange male voices.

Albert entered the bedroom, handing him two visiting cards. "These men want to see you. I told them you were resting, but they won't go away."

Peter slipped on his glasses to read the names. One, René Duplessis, sounded familiar. He remembered having come across it on the financial pages of Swiss newspapers. Yes, he decided, it was the name of a Belgian banking house. The other visitor, Dr. Pollack, he couldn't place.

"Did they tell you what they wanted?" he asked Albert.

"Not exactly. That is, they promised me ten francs if I talked you into receiving them. I told them to keep their money. I was hired to press your suits, polish your shoes, clean your house. Whom you do or don't receive is none of my business."

"Tell them I am busy," the prince said, then reconsidered. It would be unfair to deprive Albert of ten francs; besides, he wasn't really busy, and what's more, he was too restless to read or ask a friend over for a game of chess. "Wait," he called out. "I've changed my mind. I'll see them." Then, as an afterthought: "And don't be too proud. Take their ten francs."

As the names of Duplessis and Pollack had foretold, there was nothing in common between the two men, either in looks or age or manners. Small and somewhat effeminate, wearing a masterfully cut redingote and striped trousers, Duplessis reminded Peter of the blackbirds that descend every springtime upon Geneva's public parks, trying, without much success, to strike awe into the population of sparrows, squirrels and small children. It might have been Dr. Pollack's bulk that made René Duplessis seem more diminutive than he really was. Six feet tall, with a large, moonlike face that sat neckless on his heavy trunk, Pollack resembled a hog butcher more than an attorney. He was Jewish; Duplessis was not. Even before he opened his mouth, Peter guessed that Pollack was Viennese. There was something oddly revealing about Viennese Jews. Probably because of the relatively tolerant atmosphere of their city, they seemed more self-assured and secure than their brethren in other countries of the Continent, especially Russia and Poland.

The two men halted at the door and bowed stiffly from the waist. Neither spoke, but each kept his eyes fixed on Peter as if he were a statue in a museum.

"What can I do for you, gentlemen?" Peter asked when the silence threatened to stretch interminably.

"Your majesty, permit us to offer our heartiest congratulations," Duplessis said. He had the voice Peter expected: high-pitched and reedy.

Peter frowned. He disliked the man. His logical reply would have been to ask Duplessis what had prompted the title and the congratulations but decided against cuing him.

"Would you, please, come to the point. What do you want from me?" He offered them no seats and kept his arms to his side, to forestall a handshake.

"We wish to express our pleasure over the recent turn of events, your majesty," Duplessis said. "It makes one believe in divine justice."

Peter pulled out his watch and held it in the palm of his hand. "I'll give you one minute. Either you tell me what you want or I'll ring for my man to show you out." He could be gruff when called upon, and this was, he decided, the proper occasion for gruffness.

The tone had the hoped-for effect on both men. It made the short one shrink a size, while the large one pushed his partner out of the way and moved toward Peter. "It's about the Casino at Topcider. Monsieur Duplessis and my humble person are representing the group that conducted negotiations with Queen Draga in Belgrade. Considering last night's events, a sad waste of time, if I may say so."

"What events?" Peter asked puzzled.

The men stared at him, confused.

"And what casino? What negotiations?"

"Your majesty might not have been informed about them. I

mean, about the Topcider plans. The matter had been discussed with the late queen, but in view of last night's events. . . ."

"What events?" Peter shouted. Intuitively he knew what the man was talking about, but it made him uncomfortable and, at the same time, extremely angry.

The men, startled at his outburst, exchanged bewildered glances. This time it was Duplessis who picked up the thread, his manner losing much of its former smoothness.

"The—the"—he searched for the right word—"the dethronement of the royal couple." As though becoming dehydrated under the prince's stare, he began to wilt. "I mean, the *coup d'état.*"

Dr. Pollack came to his aid. "It seems there is some news of major importance that has not yet reached your highness." He halted, waiting for Peter's reaction. When it failed to come, he decided to drop his bomb. "We have received word from our Belgrade associates that King Alexander and Queen Draga have fallen victim to a *coup d'état.*"

"*Coup d'état?* When?" Peter asked, aware of a nervous tremor at the pit of his stomach. Was he mad or were they? Had he misread the date on the telegram? Could there have been a change in the conspirators' plans?

His tone, conveying to Dr. Pollack that something was wrong, caused him to remain silent. He was after all an attorney at law.

Duplessis, lacking his partner's sharp legal instincts, plunged headlong into the fire. "Last night, sire."

"You mean, Tuesday night?"

"Yes, sire. Tuesday, the tenth of June. In Belgrade the twenty-ninth of May, according to the Old Style calendar."

Unable any longer to bear the sight of the two men, Peter turned his back on them. At last, he understood fully what he had merely guessed at a moment earlier. "According to the Old Style or Julian calendar, yesterday was the twenty-eighth of May, not the twenty-ninth," he told him. "You gentlemen seem to be unaware of the fact that since 1900 the difference between the two calendars—the Julian used in Serbia and the Gregorian used here—is not twelve but thirteen days. Well, so much for calendars. As for the *coup d'état* in Belgrade, your information is equally incorrect. No such event has taken place in Belgrade. Either yesterday or today. Consequently, you may advise your associates to continue their negotiations with the present government there. It is more than corrupt enough to grant you a license for a casino in Topcider." With this, he stepped to the desk and pressed the bell button. When Albert entered, he told him, "The gentlemen are leaving."

They exited in complete silence, or perhaps, as Peter was to muse later, he had been too perturbed to hear their adieus. The picture was clear. A confederate had notified the two hyenas that on May 29, Belgrade time, the King and Queen of Serbia would be assassinated. Not wanting to lose a second and determined to conclude the deal negotiated with the couple presumed dead by them, they rushed to the new king. Their haste indicated that other groups had also become interested in the project. They had undertaken a bold gesture in trying to obtain the license before the competition became reoriented.

Peter felt as though their short visit had filled the room with the stench of rot and opened the window to air it.

The realization that he had been deceiving himself about the nature of the coup hit him like a knife. He had naïvely believed that his warning to Mashin would prevent things from getting out of hand. He had expressed his wish, confident it would be respected. But now Duplessis' and Pollack's visit made it clear that the slaughter of the Obrenovich couple was a foregone conclusion. He panicked. Was his road to power going to lead through puddles of blood? Did he have murderers for partisans? What would his Socialist friends think of him? Would they and the rest of the world believe in his innocence when he himself doubted it?

Even more disturbing than his friends' future reaction was his concern for the condemned couple. Had they received a warning and disregarded it, or were they completely unaware of the threat? Evidently they were; otherwise, they would have tried to avert it. Alexander was a fool and Draga a greedy slut, still they were too young to die. He had never met them and up to now considered them only the symbols of an objectionable system. Their imminent death, however, suddenly turned them from symbols into flesh and blood.

He wondered what steps he could take to prevent their assassination. A telegram to the conspirators? Certainly not. It would fall into the hands of Alexander's police. The Obreno-vich couple might be saved, but at the cost of dozens of good Serbs being imprisoned, tortured and no doubt garroted.

Precious minutes were ticking away on Czar Alexander III's ornate clock. As though trying to humor him, the clock, usually slow, proved to be fifteen minutes fast on this day. Nenado-vich's telegram mentioned "tonight," which could be any time between sunset and dawn. With sudden decisiveness, he rose, collected his hat and cane and left the house.

The sole person he could safely turn to and also expect help from was his good friend, the Russian Prince Oldenburg, who, although an apparent political exile, maintained surprisingly amicable relations with his country's foreign service. The prince, being a private citizen, could do what he, Peter, couldn't, and that was induce the Russian minister to Switzer-land to send a coded message to the legation in Belgrade warn-ing of the danger threatening the royal couple. Peter had no doubt that Czar Nicholas II's envoy to Serbia, the cultured and fastidious Minister Tcharikoff, would promptly take the neces-sary steps to prevent a crime that might in the long run throw a dubious light on the very person of the czar.

Prince Oldenburg was most accommodating, as always, assist-ing Peter in composing the message, then personally phoning the Russian Legation in Bern and reading the text to the min-ister, who, in turn, promised to dispatch it without further delay.

Peter Karageorgevich then went home to the Rue de Bellat house, if not completely relieved, at least at peace with himself.

6 P.M.

THE sentry, posted at the seldom-used rear entrance to the Konak, a heavy oak door, padlocked and rein-forced with wrought-iron bands, reacted with a perplexed stare when he was suddenly confronted by the queen, materializing

large as life in the bright afternoon sunshine. It took him quite
some time to collect his wits and execute a nervous salute. He
had, of course, seen her before, but always from a distance, and
her unexpected proximity caused him to feel suddenly weak in
the knees. His two-month army training having failed to prepare him for emergencies such as the present one, he gave vent
to his utter bewilderment with a stentorian bellow of "Long
live the queen!"

"No, no, hush!" Draga implored and, looking around, saw
that the young man was the only guard in sight. "When will
you be relieved? What time?"

He kept staring at her. His lips moved, but no sound
emerged. She gave his arm a motherly pat.

"All right. Never mind. Just stay here and keep still. Don't
tell anyone you saw me. Either now or later. You understand?"

Holding his breath, the boy, still stunned, nodded and muttered, "Yes, your majesty," choking on the words. Openmouthed, he watched her start out in the direction of the rear
gate.

She reached it without encountering a soul. Both sentry
boxes, one on either side of the gate, were deserted. Taking a
peek over a cluster of lilac bushes planted along the wall, she
spotted the soldiers squatting in the grass, engaged in a spirited
card game with members of the squad supposed to guard the
service entrance to the stables. Infuriated by their dereliction of
duty, she made a mental note to denounce them to Laza. Soldiers posted at the Konaks formed a select group. The entire
army must really have gone to the dogs, she fumed, if even
these men failed to fulfill their duty.

For her mission she had chosen a voluminous dust cloak and
a straw hat with a flopping brim that shaded her face, even
though none of the passersby expected to see the queen slipping through the small gate, then hurriedly crossing the street
and ringing—as unceremoniously as if she were a house-to-house
peddler—the doorbell of the Russian Legation.

She had to ring twice before the door was opened a cautious
gap by a towering footman, one of the bearded, bearlike
muzhiks employed by the legation who in reality were not
muzhiks at all, but carefully selected graduates of the Asian
Department's school for spies.

"I've come to see Minister Tcharikoff," Draga announced in her most commanding tone.

The man stared at her in disbelief. For a long moment, he kept the door only half open, his hand still on the knob.

"Whom may I announce, madame?" he asked, his polished accent in crass contrast with his homespun appearance.

"The Queen of Serbia."

The man made no move to let her enter, and she felt herself beginning to lose her composure. "What are you waiting for? I want to see the minister."

At long last, the man threw the door open, inviting her in with a gesture. When she started down the long stone-floored corridor leading to the offices of the staff, he quickly intercepted her, steering her toward the small waiting room in the forepart of the building.

"Will your majesty kindly wait here till I inform the honorable minister?" he said, bowing deeply, his tone suggesting a command rather than a request.

Left alone, Draga strained her ears to catch and sort out the sounds of the house. Having visited it innumerable times in the past, she was familiar with its floorplan and the allotment of its rooms to the various staff members. When she heard a door creak, she knew it was the one leading to the military attaché's office. The nervous tap-tap coming from above betrayed the presence of people in the upstairs conference room. Outside of these and the footman's steps mounting and later descending the carpeted stairway, silence reigned in the building. Considering that at this afternoon hour the staff still had to be at work, the lack of activity surprised her. The walls were thick and most floors covered with Oriental rugs; nevertheless, the quiet seemed unnatural, as she remembered the anthill bustle of the house during her previous visits. Now the only sound she could hear was that of her own heartbeat.

The footman returned at last.

"Will your majesty kindly follow me?" He opened the door for her, allowing her to precede him. In the corridor, she started in the direction of Minister Tcharikoff's office, but the footman lowered his long arm in her path as if it were a railroad barrier.

"This way, your majesty." He directed her toward the stairway. On the second floor he opened the door of the small salon that belonged to the suite reserved for distinguished house guests.

"Kindly take a seat, madame; the colonel will be with you shortly."

Draga veered to face the man. "Colonel who? I told you I wanted to see Minister Tcharikoff."

"The honorable minister is sick in bed."

"I don't care. Tell him to get out of bed."

The man bowed. "As your majesty wishes." He left, closing the door behind him. Draga heard the sound of his heavy steps recede through the upstairs hallway, then other, lighter footsteps approaching.

The person who entered was not Minister Tcharikoff. He was a square clump of a man, wide-shouldered, without neck or waist, all massive muscle, whose grayish-yellow eyes bored into Draga like two twist drills. He remained standing in front of the door, rocking back and forth on his heels like a tumbler toy.

"Well, well, the Queen of Serbia."

Draga had never before seen either him or his photograph, but she had not the slightest doubt about his identity. She now faced the much-feared Colonel Grabov, the man in charge of Russian espionage activities in the Balkans. Keeping an enormously complex organization under his watchful control, he had the reputation of being ruthless, inhuman and thoroughly professional. So were his agents. No sadists prone to being carried away by their sick passions, but cool experts who knew how to derive the most benefit from physical or mental torture. The colonel, it was rumored, never attended these investigations. Sensitive to unpleasant sounds, sights or odors, he preferred to study the suspect's utterances, recorded verbatim by a stenographer, in the seclusion of his office. As his long career had been marred by few such failures as the bungled assassination of ex-King Milan by Knezevich, he moved in an aura of respect and infallibility. Carefully guarding his incognito and having personal contact with no one but the top echelon in his organization, he had become a mythical personage, even to people, like Draga Mashin, who were fully aware of his existence. His past, even his present, seemed shrouded in mystery. He was supposed to be a widower of many years, with no children or relatives, no hobbies or outside interests, a nondrinker and a moderate eater, healthy, even-tempered, deeply religious and—by all appearances—asexual. His presence in Belgrade indicated that events of the utmost importance were in the making, and to Draga, it was cause for alarm.

"I demanded to see Minister Tcharikoff," she repeated, glowering at him.

"I am afraid that won't be possible. The minister sends his regrets. He entrusted me to ask you about the purpose of your puzzling visit."

Draga started for the door. "I have no intention of telling you."

Grabov barred her way. "May I present myself. I am Feodor Vasilievich Grabov."

"I know," she told him. "I also know that talking to you would be a waste of time. And I don't have too much time to waste."

"I am surprised to hear you say that. It indicates that you have at long last awakened to the realities of life. I wish you'd gained this insight much sooner. You'd have saved us a lot of trouble. And yourself as well."

She felt her eyes fill with angry tears. "I didn't come here to be lectured, Colonel. I can't believe that Minister Tcharikoff really refuses to see me. I've known him to be a man of conscience, of human feelings. I doubt that he's been told that I am here. Or of the conspiracy your department is plotting against us." She raised her voice. "You want us out and the Karageorgeviches in. Don't think we haven't been warned. We still have a few loyal men on our side. So don't expect the transition to be child's play. We can be as tough as you. If you want violence, we'll give it to you. But it won't be our blood alone that will be shed."

"Is that what you wanted to tell Tcharikoff?"

"No. This is what I am telling you. Him, I would simply remind that my husband happens to be the godson of Czar Nicholas II's grandfather and that the czar has in letters and speeches repeatedly referred to him as his beloved brother. I want the minister to warn Czar Nicholas of the dishonor the assassination of a man he's called his beloved brother would cast on his name. What the world press would make of it. Or future history books."

The colonel sat down and pensively rubbed his chin, which sprouted a day's growth of stubble. His eyes were red-rimmed, and his black serge suit was as rumpled as if he'd slept in it, as he probably had. He must have arrived in Belgrade shortly before, Draga thought, and had no doubt been taking a nap when her unexpected visit was announced.

"Well," he said, stifling a yawn, "the press, foreign or domestic, can be bought, and as far as history books are concerned, they abound in kings and emperors who had their beloved brothers murdered." Draga noted that the word "assassination" had elicited no protest from him.

"But let's skip the dramatics," he went on. "You cannot expect his imperial majesty's government to stand by calmly while you and your little husband commit one treachery after the other."

"What treachery? We've done more for your cause in Serbia than anyone else, dead or alive, including your favorite, Natalie Kechko."

"Come now—she tried very hard."

"She tried, but we succeeded. And there is the difference. To mention only one thing, I managed to eliminate King Milan, a feat your department and Madame Kechko were unable to accomplish."

The colonel leaned back in his chair, resting his head on its high back.

"No use denying you did render us important services." He paused for a moment, then closed his eyes. He looked as though he were about to fall asleep in the middle of the sentence. No doubt, he'd been called to Belgrade in a great hurry and had had a tiring journey. Even spies were human. Sitting up in crowded trains for nights in a row would prove as wearying for them as for any harmless traveler. "Yet," he went on, "you violated our agreement regarding the succession to your husband's throne. What on earth made you try that ridiculous pregnancy trick? We knew you were as sterile as a spayed sow. Did you expect us to believe that hoax?"

"I honestly thought I was pregnant."

"It would've been a miracle."

"I happen to believe in miracles. And in the power of prayer. God, how I prayed."

The colonel stared at her dully. "Yes, yes, you prayed. And had the famous Dr. Coulet of France confirm your pregnancy. Probably he, too, prayed. You even succeeded in fooling your husband. Too bad, you forgot to fool Rosa Volko."

"Rosa who?"

"Volko. A laundress employed by your household. A very observant young woman."

"Good God! You certainly believe in the end justifying the means."

The colonel dismissed her remark with a light shrug of his shoulders. "We select our people regardless of social standing, race or profession. Remember the Viennese engraver Scharff?"

"Scharff? But certainly. He was commissioned by my husband to carve a medallion portrait of me."

"He found your husband's blind trust in you very touching. The king kept warning him not to tire you with the sittings on account of your advanced pregnancy. And you didn't even go to the trouble of slipping a cushion under your corset."

"No. Because not only Dr. Coulet, but two other gynecologists considered me pregnant."

"You weren't, and that's that," the colonel snapped irritably. "I suspected you from the beginning and was very much disturbed when her majesty Czarina Alexandra expressed her willingness to be godmother to the nonexistent child. To be involved in a hoax would have reflected badly on her. That's why I insisted on sending two of our own physicians to Belgrade. Once I had Professor Stegiret's report I didn't even wait for Dr. Bubareff's—I submitted it to the czarina. She was deeply shocked. Both she and the czar had gone out of their way to make allowances for you. Incidentally, had you really gotten yourself with child, even that would have been a breach of promise on your part. You were supposed to make your husband declare our chosen candidate heir to his throne. We had even thought of the eldest son of Prince Peter Karageorgevich. That was the deal."

"Only in case I produced no heir."

Grabov struggled slowly to his feet and stretched his compact body, trying to shake off a drowsiness that threatened to befuddle his thinking. "And what about the idiotic plan to palm off your little brother on your unfortunate country? Good God, woman, did you expect us to approve or his imperial majesty's government to endure such a slap in the face?"

"His imperial majesty let us down miserably. You don't seem to remember that ours was a bilateral agreement. I was supposed to bring about the reconciliation between the Houses of Karageorgevich and Obrenovich and put the Radical Party in power. In return, Nicholas and Alexandra were to invite us to Livadiya, meet our train at the Simferopol station and take the four-hour drive to the castle in an open carriage with us. The czarina was to kiss me on both cheeks and call me 'sister' in front of the court."

"The czarina is a great lady, but even her kiss would have failed to turn you into a queen."

"Your people thought otherwise, or they wouldn't have promised me that kiss," she said irritably. "What is more, the entire marriage was their idea. Despite his love for me, the king wouldn't have married me without Colonel Taube's assurance that the stunt could be pulled off. As for me, I was perfectly satisfied with the role of royal concubine. I didn't, of course, expect it to last forever, so I made plans to save some money and retire to the south of France when the time came. I'd still prefer that to being queen and having my reputation ruined by your agents."

"You've ruined that yourself. You've robbed the treasury, persecuted innocent people, forced your husband to change the constitution more often than his shirt. He has antagonized the army by cashiering its best officers simply because they refused to kowtow to you. Now the entire officers' corps has turned against you both."

"Yes, he cashiered a few. They had used my picture for target practice in mess halls and had the troops sing their old marching songs with pornographic lyrics about me. No honorable man would tolerate such insults against his wife."

"Honorable man! What about the two francs the honorable man pocketed from the price of every repeating rifle ordered from the Skoda factory for the army? You think such deals remain secret? When speaking of bribery and graft in the highest places, people no longer hint at generalities but name you and the king. All that while your country is on the brink of bankruptcy with the minister of finances running from one international banking house to another begging for loans like a luckless gambler. Czar Nicholas entrusted you with the mission of bringing freedom and prosperity to your long-suffering people, and you failed him disgracefully."

Draga's green eyes flashed with anger.

"Freedom and prosperity! You don't even know the meaning of those words! You and your czar! Why do always the cruelest, most despotic regimes protest the oppression of peoples other than their own? And embark on holy crusades for their liberation? Why? The political prisoners held in *all* our jails wouldn't fill a single building in one of your many camps for deportees in Siberia. If your government is such a great champion of freedom, why the hell doesn't it start setting its own people free?"

Grabov pulled his watch from his vest pocket and threw a glance at it. "You'd better leave now, madame. I didn't come to Belgrade to engage in futile debates with you."

"I won't go unless you let me talk to Tcharikoff."

"Don't be ridiculous. Do you want me to have you thrown out bodily?"

"I dare you."

"My good woman, be sensible. You've been around too long to have illusions about men like Tcharikoff. What makes you believe that he'd go over our heads to plead with the czar in your behalf? Or even with Minister of Foreign Affairs Count Lamsdorf? He'll remain in his quarters nursing his influenza, and should anything unpleasant happen to you, he'd be the first to express his shocked disapproval. He'd publicly snub the new Serbian government by having an obscure counselor represent him at the inaugural ceremonies. And as for his imperial majesty's government, it would never admit having had a hand in the revolt against you. Should the events take a tragic turn, the czar would order all flags flown at half-mast clear across Russia and a twenty-seven-day court mourning for his beloved brother and wife. It would be duly recorded in the newspapers that he and the czarina had shed tears of deep sympathy and prayed for the souls of the departed in the privacy of the small chapel adjoining their bedroom in the Tsarskoye Selo Palace."

Draga listened, more fascinated than stunned. "So this is how it's going to be," she stated rather than asked. The tension of the past weeks was beginning to have a numbing effect on her, causing her panic to be replaced by a deadly calm. She even managed a smile for Grabov.

"You're trying hard to scare me, Colonel, although your mere arrival in Belgrade ought to be enough to frighten me out of my wits. I'm really amazed that you've managed to slip into the country unnoticed by Prefect Marshityanin's agents. However, I am sure that the more efficient Austrian secret service has become aware of your presence. Since Franz Josef's government would hate to see a Russian puppet occupy Serbia's throne, they'll do everything in their power to prevent a coup against us. Don't forget, their monitors are anchored a spitting distance from here on the opposite shore of the Sava."

The colonel heaved a sigh of bored impatience. "I wouldn't count on the monarchy if I were you. You've long exhausted your usefulness to them. Count Goluchowski would rather see Peter Kara, a confirmed Austrophobe, on the Serbian throne than you and your Sasha. With Peter he knows where he stands, but your foreign policy changes with every birthday greeting that some foreign royalty has remembered or forgotten to send you. For an invitation to tea at a king's palace you'd be willing to sign a ten-year friendship treaty with the devil himself and for a dinner party in your honor deliver Serbia lock, stock and barrel. No, Austrians may be easygoing, but fools they are not. So don't wait for the monitors to cross the Sava full speed, because they won't."

The heat in the room with all its windows and doors closed was beginning to feel oppressive. Earlier she had thrown her duster and hat on a chair and now went over to collect them. Nervously, she slipped her right arm in the sleeve of the coat and struggled awkwardly as the other one turned inside out. Grabov watched her dully, without making the slightest effort to help.

"Aren't you the paragon of gallantry?" she asked with an acrid smile, finally donning the garment.

"That I am not," he muttered. "I was never hired for my manners."

"Not like Colonel Taube." She laughed. "Wasn't he the perfect gentleman? Considerate, suave, gracious. I had the most enjoyable time three years ago when I discussed the planned assassination of my then future father-in-law with him." Her voice took on a sharp edge. "You know, Colonel, it could cause your government a measure of embarrassment if a memorandum, giving the details of that venture fell into the hands of your enemies. Or even some important newspaperman."

He gave her a long look. "I've been expecting that."

"Expecting what?"

"That you'd resort to blackmail when everything else failed. But it won't work. I know there is no such memorandum."

"There could be. In the safe of some trusted friend abroad. With instructions how and when to make it public."

"Supposing you did put things into writing—things that should've remained forgotten—aren't you aware that their disclosure would be more damaging for your reputation than for ours?"

"I've been called so many bad names that one more won't make much difference."

"That's where you are wrong. Of course, you're hated by the common people, who blame you for crimes and blunders committed long before you appeared on the scene. The intelligent minority, however, both here and abroad, sees you for what you really are: a very ordinary woman unable to cope with an extraordinary role thrust upon her by destiny. You are not a bad sort, Draga. Unfortunately, fate has played a nasty trick on you."

He had delivered his little speech in a dull mumble, punctuating it with stifled yawns; nevertheless, she sensed that his drowsiness was no longer real and that his gaze directed at her from under half-closed lids was searching and intense. She had been at the door, ready to go. Not long before, he'd threatened to have her thrown out, but he was deliberately detaining her now. Had he been putting on an act then, or was he now? Was he paving the way for a proposition? If so, it was going to be a difficult one to accept; otherwise, he wouldn't waste his energy and time on meaningless chatter.

"Nasty trick, is right. Yet fate had nothing to do with it. Not half as much as Colonel Taube."

Grabov began pacing the floor, his hands clasped behind his

back, his eyes on the ceiling, giving the impression of a man contemplating a very important decision, which, Draga felt, had been ready in his mind when he had entered the room. Watching him, she was amazed at the easy grace of his square-framed body. It was a body trained in athletics and in the endurance of physical hardship, able to climb snowy peaks, swim raging rivers, vault six-foot fences and scale the walls of otherwise-inaccessible buildings.

He suddenly halted to face her. "I'll tell you what. You may stay here. We'd say you wanted to run away from your husband and asked for political asylum from us."

She blinked nervously, wondering if she'd heard correctly. Unmindful of her puzzled expression, he continued in a tired monotone.

"For quite some time, you've disapproved of your husband's foreign policy and shady practices. When you summoned up enough courage to tell him that, he decided to get rid of you. By means of divorce or any other method available to him. You've had access to state secrets, so he could ill afford an open scandal. You were beginning to fear for your life. And with reason, too. In desperation you found no other escape, but to sneak from the Konak, dash across the park and knock on our door. Isn't that the way it happened?"

"No!" she said, her voice muffled with indignation. "Certainly not! What are you driving at?"

"Offering you a way out of the mess you've got yourself in."

"At what cost?"

"Free of charge."

"What interest do you have in protecting me?"

"None whatsoever. Except—"

"Except—"

"We want to avoid distressing Prince Peter. He is a man of great sensitivity. We know that it would upset him if he heard that you, a woman, were harmed or maltreated. He has let his partisans know that unless the transition were engineered in a dignified manner, he would refuse to accept the throne."

"How noble of him," she said sarcastically.

"Besides it would help disillusion all Obrenovich sympathizers to hear Alexander's misdeeds related by such a knowledgeable source as yourself."

To her amazement, Draga found she wasn't even shocked. "As for Prince Peter's sensitivity, he should stick to his clerking in Geneva and not try to jerk out the throne from under us. As for my informing on my husband—"

Grabov cut her short. "Aren't you accepting my offer?"

"No. I am not going to save my skin and leave my husband to whatever fate you have chosen for him."

"He'll be better off without you. You've been a millstone around his neck."

"I am his wife, and I am the Queen of Serbia. If he has to go, I want to go with him. With him and with some integrity and dignity preserved."

He emitted a cackling sound, half laughter, half snarl, and took a step toward her as though trying to bar her way. She was gripped by sudden panic. Men like Grabov didn't make offers; they issued orders.

The thought that the door might be locked, making her his prisoner, flashed through her mind. She grabbed the handle and was relieved to feel it move. With one nervous step she cleared the threshold and was storming down the stairs when halfway down, she crashed into a man on his way up. For a second, he held her in his arms, whether to save her from stumbling or to detain her, she couldn't tell. She extricated herself from his clutches and continued downward. The bearded footman who'd let her in sat in the doorkeeper's cubicle, reading a newspaper. He had obviously been unaware of her descending the carpeted stairway and stared now openmouthed as she flung herself at the exit door trying to jerk it open.

When the door resisted her pull, she shouted at him, "Let me out."

He slowly lumbered to his feet, then stopped, listening. The sound of agitated voices came from above, followed by steps descending the stairway. Draga heard it, too. The noises fused into a cacophony of pursuit like the bay of hounds at a fox hunt. Later she tried in vain to recall how she had managed to throw the door open and catapult herself into the street.

About the next few minutes, also, her memory remained a blank. She must have crossed the street, giving no thought to Laza Petrovich's warning about a gunman lying in ambush for her. At the gate to the Konak park she was suddenly confronted by the two sentries, who, in the meantime, had returned to their posts. They failed to recognize her and pointed their rifles at her.

"Let me pass, you idiots!" she cried angrily as one of the fixed bayonets came dangerously close to her breast. "Don't you know who I am?"

They scowled at her, their young, suntanned faces two scary' masks. When she took another step forward, the younger soldier uncocked his rifle.

"Get out of my way!" she shouted at him. "Don't you recognize me? I am your queen!"

"The queen!" the older man muttered. "She is the queen!"

The other soldier remained doubtful. Thinking back later, she wondered with bitter *Galgenhumor* if he ever realized how close he had come—a mere trigger's click away—to assuring himself a place in Serbian history as the queen's executioner. It was only after another long scrutinizing look that he decided to shoulder his rifle and—with a stiff salute—step out of her path.

7 P.M.

"OPEN the window, Apis," Colonel Mashin ordered. "It's getting too close in here."

"Jesus, it still feels like an oven out there!" Captain Dimitriyevich lifted the latch and let the hot air in through a narrow gap. The noise of the name-day party in the barracks yard invaded the room despite the closed shutters. The office, used on workdays by a quartermaster sergeant, was selected by the colonel for the convenience of its location: It was in the back of the building with an exit to a narrow alley descending to the Kalemegdan Gardens. Here, in the sheltered dimness, the ten men huddled over a map of the inner city with the two Konaks in its very center.

"No move must be made before midnight," Colonel Mishich said. "I've just learned that Alexander has ordered Paul Marinkovich to the Konak for seven forty-five in the evening."

"They already had a meeting around noon," Captain Ljuba Kostich of the Royal Guards told them.

"He is to report on the latest developments in Sofia," Naumovich explained. He seemed sober and collected, though his eyes were bloodshot and a slight tremor vibrated around his lips. "Alexander has been toying with the idea of a surprise attack on Turkey. Has put out feelers to Bulgaria about making it a joint effort."

"What does he hope to gain by attacking Turkey?" Lieutenant Bogdanovich asked.

"Time, what else? To have a war to divert the country's attention from his domestic problems."

"We're not ready for a war," Apis observed. "Christ, the man has no honor. Willing to risk a national catastrophe to save his lousy skin."

"Let's not digress, gentlemen," Mishich admonished them. "As I was saying, Marinkovich was ordered to report at seven forty-five. They'll probably have a long conference—"

"He will also be received by the queen," Naumovich cut in. "Oh, it just occurs to me. Three Cabinet members, too, have been sent word to be at the Konak tonight. Alexander wants to see them after having talked to Marinkovich. That may delay supper."

"What time do you think they'll eat?" Mashin asked.

"Not before ten thirty. There'll be twelve at the table, including the four Lunyevitzas—that is, the two girls and the captains. Sasha, I mean, the king, told me he might ask Marinkovich to join them for supper. I doubt that, because that would make thirteen at the table."

"Will you eat with them?" Mashin asked.

Naumovich threw an unhappy look at him. "I am afraid so. The equerry on duty always does."

"It sounds as though it might turn into a jolly little party to last till after midnight," Colonel Mashin said. "We'd better wait till the guests have departed, the king and the woman retired to their apartment and the staff gone to bed. We don't want any confusion; innocent people or our own men killed by some stupid mistake. Let's go over the plans once more, gentlemen." He gestured at Mishich.

"I'll have supper at the Kolaratz with my brother-in-law," the colonel said on cue, "and leave the restaurant at midnight and come up here. By then two battalions will have received marching orders and be assembled in the yard. I'll start downhill with them at twelve thirty sharp, bring them to the back of the Konak and deploy them between the Russian Legation and the palace grounds to bar all access from the west. Correct?"

"Correct." Mashin nodded, then turned to a tall, hawk-faced major. "We must be ready somewhat earlier than the Sixth Infantry, because it will take us about ten minutes longer to reach the Konak from the Palilula Barracks than it will Colonel Mishich and his battalions from here. Have you made sure there are no dissenters among your subalterns?"

"There isn't one in the entire Seventh Regiment, Colonel. I can vouch for that. The Eighth, of course, is another kettle of fish. Colonel Nikolich has repeatedly declared that he considers his pledge of allegiance binding unless released by the king himself. He is very much liked by his officers, so he might be a problem."

"We won't worry about him, now," Mashin decided gruffly. Whenever the possibility of some unexpected obstacle was mentioned, he reacted with an unsoldierly pique. "We'll go ahead without him and his Eighth. Faced with a *fait accompli* after the coup, they will have no choice but to swear obedience to Prince Peter. I mean, King Peter."

Colonel Mishich turned to the hawk-faced major. "Have you tried to feel out the ranks?"

"What for? What good would that do?" Mashin asked irritably, leaving the major no time to answer. "You don't ask cattle how they feel when taken to market. As far as the Seventh Infantry is concerned, we've agreed with Milivoy"—he indicated the major—"that he will introduce me as their new commander freshly appointed by King Alexander. Then we'll march into town and surround the Konak on the east, west and south sides."

"Won't the men ask questions?" Michael asked.

"No. Each time there were demonstrations in the city, they were mobilized and marched to the Konak. It'll be an old routine for them. The only difference is that this time they won't be ordered out to prevent a coup, but to participate in one. Yet they won't know it till it's all over. All we have to worry about is that they march as quietly as possible. We mustn't wake up the town."

"Have you ever seen cattle march on tiptoes?" Apis asked sarcastically.

Before coming to the quartermaster sergeant's office for the meeting, Michael and Apis had met at the veranda of the Serbian Crown. They had a few minutes to spare, so Captain Dimitriyevich gave Michael short character sketches of the men they were going to see.

Though he didn't say so, it was obvious that Apis bore no great love for Colonel Mashin. He sensed what had escaped most people, that Mashin felt a deep and irrepressible contempt for Serbia and everything Serbian.

The son of a Czech physician, the colonel could never forget that he was a Westerner among Easterners, the descendant of scientists and professional men among the sons of pig breeders and highwaymen. As an adolescent, he had spent his vacations with his maternal grandparents in Prague, and he felt more at home in the old city's crooked streets than in Belgrade's tree-lined avenues. Though his father had been court physician and friend to Prince Alexander Karageorgevich, he entered the service of Milan Obrenovich to become a member of his inner circle.

Prince Milan, later by the grace of Austria King Milan, failed to gain more than token loyalty from him. For Alexander, the son, Mashin had nothing but ill-concealed disdain. Convinced of his own superiority, he had taken a brilliant career for granted. Then suddenly, owing to the most unlikely coincidence of the young king's falling in love with Svetozar Mashin's widow, the colonel's high hopes went up in smoke. The *coup d'état* had one sole aim for him: to raise him to the heights he had always considered his proper place. He insisted on leadership in the conspiracy. To take orders from a Mishich or even a Dimitriyevich would have been unacceptable to him.

As a whole, the conspirators were rather a mixed bag. Apis

and Colonel Mishich were the only ones to come from the middle classes, which meant two generations away from illiteracy and the soil. Pockmarked little Lieutenant Bogdanovich's father was a known jatak, friend and fence to highwaymen, convicted and sentenced to death, yet never executed since the local gendarmes never went to his house to arrest him without first warning him to leave town.

As for Milivoy Angyelkovich, his family had apparently failed to win their local gendarmes' goodwill. After a three-year pursuit, the major's grandfather was captured and dragged before a judge. Young Angyelkovich experienced the dubious thrill of seeing his grandfather executed on the very spot where the old man had cut the throat of a Jewish merchant on his way home from the Valjevo county fair.

Although he was to pay with his life for the murder of a Jew, Grandfather's sentence was carried out in a most humane manner. The gendarmes took along two full bottles of slivovitz for the cart ride to the scene. The party arrived on the bleak meadow in the highest of spirits, with lively banter flashing back and forth between the men of the law and the convict, the latter having consumed one full bottle while the gendarmes shared the other one. The gravedigging was done as zestfully as if the hole in the ground were to receive a young tree and not an old body. The gendarmes' merriment disturbed young Milivoy, for he feared they might miss their mark and cause his beloved grandfather unnecessary suffering. He needn't have worried, because their aim was perfect. His heart pierced by three bullets, old Angyelkovich crumpled to the ground like a rag doll.

"Now let's recapitulate the individual orders," Colonel Mashin said to a heavyset, cross-eyed captain, the front of whose dark-blue tunic was decorated with a row of medals and also with a number of greasy spots, paprika-colored reminders of past meals. "You'll wait fifteen minutes after Colonel Mishich's departure, then descend to Premier Tzintzar-Markovich's house. Either at one thirty A.M. sharp or upon receiving a message from me, you enter the house and execute the general."

"Yes, sir," the captain answered in a voice loud enough to be heard across a drill yard.

Michael Vassilovich stared first at Mashin, then at the man. He was hearing, for the first time, that the premier's murder actually had been contemplated. He could understand neither the nonchalance with which Mashin pronounced the death sentence nor the captain's eagerness to play executioner to the commander he had served under and been decorated by during the 1885 Serbo-Bulgarian War.

Captain Svetozar Radakovich's fame as a war hero had been somewhat marred by his participation in atrocities that had made the 1885 conflict an especially bloody page in the history of the terrible Balkans. No man, woman or child, not even a sheep or dog, survived in the Bulgarian frontier village Radakovich had stormed with his squad; no house remained standing; no orchard was spared. Yet Radakovich had been a green sublieutenant fresh from the Military Academy then, trained for the pitiless and sadistic warfare practiced through five centuries of Serbia's struggle for survival. Eighteen peaceful years had passed since then without his ever having to shoot at a human target. He was a family man now, the father of seven children.

"Colonel," Michael asked Mashin, "when was it decided that the prime minister be executed? When and why?"

Michael felt the eyes of nine men fixed on his face. Not all were friendly. For a while no one spoke. Mashin finally broke the silence.

"As for the when, we had a brief meeting with Colonel Mishich at the Officers' Club this afternoon. With him and a few fellow officers. As for the why, we've come to the conclusion that it has to be done. Any more questions?"

Michael turned to Apis. "Did you know about this?"

"No. It's news to me, too. And I can't say I approve. General Tzintzar-Markovich has a fine service record as one of our best chiefs of staff. He should never have got mixed up in politics. A lousy politician, but a fine soldier."

Mashin's face paled, but he was careful to conceal his annoyance with Apis. The captain was much too popular among the young men of the conspiracy to be openly crossed. "The coup can succeed only if the Obrenovich clique is left without leadership," he said in the tone of a patient teacher.

"Even after Alexander's abdication?" Michael asked.

"Even after his death. The clique might grasp at any straw to stay in power. Might rally around the Lunyevitzas or Milan's bastard son by Artemisia Johannidi. No, they must go. The whole set. We can't risk a civil war. It would be an excuse for Austria to occupy us, as it did Bosnia. They all must go," he repeated, stressing every word.

"Not Tzintzar-Markovich." Apis insisted.

Mashin was turning red in the face. "What are you suddenly so squeamish about? You've never had any objection to doing away with Alexander."

"That's different," Apis argued. "History has proved that abdicated kings can cause as much trouble as ruling ones. Think of King Milan. Yet dead kings have never returned from their graves except in Shakespeare's tragedies."

"Sorry, Dimitriyevich," Mashin said with finality. "The decision has been approved by the majority of our men. You and Vassilovich are in the minority."

Michael listened in shocked silence, unable to comprehend what had disgusted him more, the prime minister's unwarranted death sentence or Apis' reply to Mashin's casual pronouncement of "doing away with Alexander" with a bon mot about dead kings and Shakespeare. The realization of having been misled from the very beginning dawned on him with sickening force. He felt the impotent fury of a shackled prisoner. Yes, his hands were bound. To take action against the plan now would prove suicidal. Mashin would deal with him as he had with Captain Gagovich. The sole alternative left was the betrayal of the coup to Alexander, to prevent one bloodshed by triggering another. In that case, not only the men facing him would die, but dozens more, regardless of whether or not they had conspired against Alexander. It would furnish the king with a ready excuse for doing away with his not so loyal opposition.

Captain Mika Yosipovich was assigned the summary execution of the minister of war and Lieutenant Milosh Popovich of the minister of home affairs. The two officers were on duty and unable to attend the meeting. Both served in the Seventh Infantry Regiment, the command of which was to be assumed by Colonel Mashin later that night, thus their absence constituted no problem.

"I talked to them in the afternoon, and both assured me that we could count on them," Mashin reported. "I'll speak to them once more at the Palilula Barracks."

"Did you know, Colonel," Radakovich inquired, "that Lieutenant Popovich is rumored to have been engaged to the home minister's daughter?"

Mashin's reaction was an annoyed look. As he had personally selected Lieutenant Popovich for the task, he resented having his judgment questioned. "The trouble with you gentlemen is that you have too much time on your hands. So you spend it gossiping like old women. Yes, I've heard the rumor, but Popovich assured me it wasn't true. He'd danced with her once or twice, that was all." He turned to a young infantry officer with deep set green eyes and a permanent expression of discontent on his foxlike, suntanned face. "I don't have to remind you of your assignment, Tankossich, do I?"

"No, sir," the lieutenant answered with a strange, animal grin that bared his upper gums to reveal a row of decaying incisors and large, pointed canines. "It'll be a pleasure to take care of them. Why, only last week that little bastard Nikodiye ordered me and a fellow officer to stand at attention for ten minutes at the Kolaratz because we hadn't risen fast enough when he entered the place. Half of the civilians thought it a great joke, but the other half got up and left, which made the fools stop laughing. Rest assured, sir, before I blow out his brains, I'll make him regret he was ever born."

"You won't lay a hand on the man, if that's what you mean. The executions will be carried out in a proper military manner. And that goes for all of you. The sentenced men will be informed of the judgment passed on them and promptly put to death. No insults, no recriminations and certainly no brutality. Am I understood, Lieutenant?"

Lieutenant Tankossich snapped to attention. "Yes, sir." He grinned at Mashin. If he was displeased with the colonel's instructions, he was cautious enough not to show it. The task assigned to him was evidently much too important to risk with a show of insubordination.

"The younger Lunyevitzas, too?" Michael asked tensely. He had known them as small boys and later, when he lived with Draga in the cottage behind the Officers' Club, had often taken them to soccer games and afterward to restaurants to fill their ever-empty bellies with some decent food. They had incredible appetites and atrocious table manners. He was nevertheless very fond of them, enjoying their wry wit and boldly flaunted irreverence for age, wealth and authority. Evidently, men like Mashin and Mishich had failed to develop a taste for the boys' sense of humor.

Michael rose. "I protest. In my name, as well as Prince Peter's." He raised his voice. "How many times must I repeat: He agreed to a coup, not a massacre."

His anger seemed to make no impression on Mashin or the others. The colonel began to fold up the city map.

"Even if I didn't approve, the Lunyevitzas' execution happens to be one of the conditions a number of our men have set in return for their participation in the coup. Well, that takes care of secondary matters." He turned to the group. "As you know, Captain Ljuba Kostich will bring in the Royal Guards once the Sixth and Seventh infantries have taken up their respective positions. He'll be backed by Captain Janovich's battery of four seventy-five mm field guns."

"Pardon me, sir," Captain Radakovich interrupted. "Let's suppose—I mean, just suppose, that the action at the Konak isn't carried out according to plan. That there is some delay, unexpected obstacle or a complete—" He almost uttered the word "failure," but the colonel's scowl caused him to substitute it with the more cautious "confusion." "We would have to be informed whether to wait or—" As Mashin's scowl darkened, he quickly added, "What I mean, sir, it would put you in jeopardy if we acted too hastily."

"You weren't at the Officers' Club this morning, were you?"

"No, sir. I was on duty."

"Nevertheless, you ought to have managed to come. Then you'd know that there will be liaison maintained between us at the Konak and your individual groups. I have men assigned to that task. Should you have any qualms about the operation entrusted to you, speak up and you'll be relieved. With no hard feelings."

The captain blushed, and beads of perspiration appeared on his forehead. The heat in the room was becoming murderous. Nervously he reached for the high collar of his tunic to loosen it, then thought better of it. During the planning sessions, the colonel had repeatedly pronounced that after the coup only officers of proper military bearing were to retain their command. The army was going to be—in appearance, as well as attitudes—as professional and disciplined as it had been in Milan's time.

"No qualms, sir. On the contrary. I am proud of your trust. I was merely asking."

Mashin dismissed the apology with an impatient wave of his hand. "And as for you, Mika," he turned to Colonel Naumovich, who had been sitting hunched and comatose at the far corner of the room, "I want to remind you that the success of the coup depends upon you. That means the lives of close to one hundred and fifty fellow officers and cadets of the Military Academy."

Naumovich looked up with a start. "One hundred and fifty?" he repeated in a surprised falsetto. "Last time it was thirty-five."

Mashin glared at him. "So it was. But that was days ago. Since then more have joined up. But what the hell difference does it make to you? Be at the goddamn door on time, or you won't see another day. At one A.M. And wait for us till two A.M. If we don't appear by then, you'll know the plan was canceled."

Naumovich rose laboriously. An uneasy smile spread across his large, ageless baby face. "Who said I wouldn't be there?" His eyes combed the room, halting on Captain Dimitriyevich. "Didn't I tell you this morning that I would be there?"

"You saw Apis this morning?" Mashin asked.

"Yes, sir."

"Where?"

"At my house."

"I warned you not to be seen together."

Naumovich, like a schoolboy reprimanded by his teacher, eagerly volunteered the explanation. "It wasn't planned, Alex. I went home to change and there he—" His voice trailed off as he realized the implications.

"What business did he—" Mashin began, then suddenly stopped. Several of the men found it necessary to inspect their fingernails or brush bits of lint off their tunics; others, unaware of Mika Naumovich and Apis Dragutin Dimitriyevich being the two intersecting lines of a triangle in which Anka Naumo-vich happened to be the hypotenuse, looked baffled. Six feet tall, with the strength of the bull he'd been nicknamed after, Apis was the embodiment of seduction, and flabby Naumovich the very picture of inescapable cuckoldry.

The sight of the fat man standing disgraced in the circle of his brother officers, members of a male-oriented society, who looked at him as if he were the evildoer and not the victim, disturbed Mashin. Naumovich was the key to their success, their lives were entrusted to him, yet he was openly despised by all because his wife was sleeping with his friend and he had shut his eyes instead of killing them both.

In order to change the subject and put an end to the perni-cious silence, Mashin asked, "Have you talked to Lieutenant Zivkovich?"

As if awakened from deep sleep, Naumovich looked at him, blinking. "Talked? What about?"

Mashin frowned. "About Captain Panayotovich. Who else?"

"But of course." Once again Naumovich was the schoolboy eager to please. "I will send him two bottles of vintage Pom-mard from the royal cellars. He'll tell Panayotovich that he is celebrating something—name day—anniversary—whatever. He'll persuade Panayotovich to drink with him. I've already given Zivkovich the sleeping pills I got from my doctor. And instructions on how many to use."

"What if the captain refuses the wine?"

"Not Panayotovich. Especially not after a hot day like this. The man has a thirst like a camel. I once watched him down two liters of wine in one sitting."

"Not like you," Bogdanovich said. "I understand you prefer champagne. And cognac. There's not a bottle left of King Mi-lan's old Napoleon *fine*. What will you do if King Peter refuses to let you have the keys to the royal cellars? That'll be tough on you, won't it?"

The laughter swelling in the room was much louder than the jibe warranted. Naumovich threw a sly, smoldering glance at Bogdanovich but remained silent.

"I'd stay away from the bottle if I were you," Mashin told him. "At least tonight. Tomorrow you may roll in the gutter as far as I am concerned."

Once again, there were guffaws. As before, Apis refrained

from laughing. Intermittently, he cast quick, nervous glances at Naumovich as though trying to catch some expression on his face, but it remained masklike and unemotional.

"Well, gentlemen," Mashin said in a tone solemn and sonorous enough for a bishop conferring his blessing upon a congregation, "that's about all. You know your duties. Ours is a just cause. God be with you tonight. Yet"—he grimaced as though the thought gave him a stomachache—"yet should we by some tragic turn of events fail in our task, we shall take the consequences like men and soldiers. Dying by our own hands rather than be captured. This sacred duty we shall carry out in order to save our fellow conspirators from persecution and death. So help us God."

He crossed himself, then embraced and kissed everyone present, the signal for each man to follow his example.

While all were milling about, Mika Naumovich stood in the center of the room, a fixed star amid swirling nebulae. He, too, went through the motions of brotherly bear hugs later, yet performed them with the mechanical exactitude of an automaton. Except that no automaton ever felt as soft and rubbery to the muscular arms encircling him as he did. His pale, clean-shaved skin turned red in spots as the stubble-covered faces brushed against his. Mashin alone noticed that no hugs and kisses were exchanged between him and Apis. He decided not to make a point of it.

"In case any one of you wishes to reach me," Mashin told them, "I'll be at George Genchich's house. I want to feel him out about his participation in the future Avakumovich Cabinet. Don't contact me, though, unless it's a matter of life or death. From now on, we'll have to be especially careful."

Colonel Mashin unlocked the door to the alley, and the men slipped out one by one.

Desperately wishing to be left alone, Michael cut loose from the group and hurriedly crossed the lawns and flower beds of the Kalemegdan Gardens, accelerating his steps as he approached crowded Prince Michael Street. As he passed the spot of Knezevich's unsuccessful attempt on Milan's life, the memory of that unfortunate episode brought him to a sudden halt.

Why the breathless hurry? he asked himself. Was he running from Mashin, his men or himself? Was it the heat, the pain at his temples or remorse over having become involved in the conspiracy that caused him to wander with the aimlessness of an amnesiac through the city?

But somehow, deep within himself, Michael knew what he wanted, or rather what he did not want. Even though his absence would fail to absolve him from guilt, he would have to get away before the denouement of the drama. Whether he would be labeled a coward or a traitor made little difference to him now.

He glanced at his watch. It showed a quarter to eight. If he hurried, he could still catch the eight o'clock steamer to Zimony, cross to Hungary and decide about his next move later.

His dilemma, though bewildering to him, was far from unique. A Serbian Jean Marie Roland, he recognized himself as one of those well-meaning idealists who refuse to believe that their gentle torch, lighted for the good of humanity, could explode into a conflagration, thereby causing the worst offenses of the *ancien régime* to seem like harmless bonfires. He wondered what the unfortunate Girondist had felt about *liberté, égalite, fraternité* when the news of his wife's death under Dr. Guillotine's ax sent him to a frost-beaded meadow near Rouen, where he ended it all by falling onto the thin, sharp blade of his unsheathed sword stick.

No sword stick for him, Michael told himself. He would take the first train from Zimony to Vienna, stop at a hotel, hang the Don't Disturb sign on his door and leave it there for days. By the time he emerged from seclusion there would be no newspaper headlines and the coup would no longer be fodder for self-styled political analysts in the cafés.

After a breathless downhill race, he reached the pier in eight minutes. The steamer, still moored to the wharf boat, quietly bobbed up and down in the water. It surprised him to see no passengers on board. On closer inspection, he noticed that the ticket seller's booth was empty, its windows pulled shut. A squad of gendarmes, under the command of a young lieutenant, was guarding the approaches to the gangplank. A group of civilians, some incensed, others merely baffled, were engaged in a dispute with the lieutenant.

Michael walked up to the officer. "What's the matter? When is the next crossing?"

The lieutenant shrugged. "No idea, sir. I'm afraid there

won't be any more crossings tonight. Perhaps tomorrow morning. But that depends—"

"On what?"

"Orders from the Konak. All travel to and from Zimony has been halted till further notice. I imagine the same order went out to frontier guards at all crossing points along the border."

"What about trains?"

"Same thing. Of course, the international trains are allowed through. But no passengers can get on or off them here in Belgrade."

"When exactly were these orders issued?" Michael asked.

"We received ours a little after seven. We got here in time to prevent the docking of the seven thirty from Zimony. You should've heard the passengers, sir, when they were told they couldn't disembark. They cursed my entire family line from my great-great-grandfather to my unborn children. Sometimes, it's no fun to be a Serbian gendarme."

Michael thanked the lieutenant for the information, assuring him that he sympathized with his predicament, then slowly, pensively, turned into the narrow street leading uphill to the city. He wondered what had prompted Laza to seal up the country. Had he received a warning about the coup and decided to swoop down on its participants before they could strike? If so, how complete a list of names did he have? Was Michael Vassilovich on the list?

The uphill walk, because of the exertions of his long day, began to tire him. Leaning against a wall, he rested momentarily, wondering what to do next. His leaving the country had become impossible or, at best, risky. He could hide out, but where and for how long and from whom? If the coup succeeded, Mashin's men would track him down; if it failed, Alexander's police would. In both cases, he would be hanged or shot as a traitor. The sole choice left for him was to bear the consequences of his fateful decision to join the conspiracy and let the current take him wherever it chose.

8 P.M.

THE evening brought no relief to the city sweltering in the unseasonal heat wave. Despite the weather, Belgrade enjoyed, with the Slava of the Sixth Infantry and the Song Festival on the parade grounds, an unusually busy day. Visitors from the country, as well as from across the Hungarian border, joined the crowd of locals on the main boulevards, causing traffic to move at a snail's pace. The people were well behaved, but tense, probably because of the oppressive humidity in the air. All afternoon dark clouds had clustered over the flat lands on the opposite shore of the Sava. Intermittent flashes of lightning flickered, followed by the low, ominous grumble of faraway thunder. A storm was brewing somewhere, yet no one could predict how soon it would break over the city, if ever.

Michael stopped at the Serbian Crown for a quick meal but found no empty table. The Crown had always been very popular with officers, especially the younger set. On this evening, the corps had taken it over, or so it seemed because of the boisterous mood of the men. Michael recognized a few conspirators among them. They must have started drinking early and were on the verge of getting drunk, which disturbed him.

He tried two more cafés and finally wound up at the Kolaratz, where the headwaiter knew him and squeezed in an extra table. Under an arbor of wine-covered latticework, he saw Colonel Mishich in deep conversation with a civilian half-hidden by the branches. When the man rose and crossed over to

232

another table, Michael recognized him as the attorney Ljuba
Zivkovich, a fighting Radical, who had been sentenced to
twenty years in prison after the Knezevich assassination attempt
upon ex-King Milan's life, but pardoned during the pro-
Russian trend that followed Alexander's marriage to Draga
Mashin. Now, should the *coup d'état* succeed, the plan was to
appoint him minister of home affairs in the Avakumovich Cabinet. A Serbian politician's life was no bed of roses, Michael
concluded with a wry grin.

At the Kolaratz, as at the Crown, uniforms outnumbered
mufties. Probably because of Colonel Mishich's presence, voices
were kept low. Also, there were more ranks above captain and
less heavy drinking than at the Crown. A gypsy band was playing on a dais at the end of the garden, with the great Mija,
Serbia's famous gypsy violinist, leading it.

As though sensing the tension in the air, he offered a selection of old, mournful folk songs relating of dead heroes, widows'
tears and ill-fated lovers. It was either the lugubrious music or
the subdued atmosphere, so different from the riotous mood at
the Serbian Crown, which made Michael feel uncontrollably
restless. The food stuck in his throat, and when he tried to lift
his glass, it slipped from his trembling fingers spilling its con-
tents on the tablecloth. He stared befuddled at the thick, homespun linen soaking up the red wine. The sight made him
nauseated. He asked the waiter to change the cloth, which cost
him an extra tip, for Belgrade waiters didn't consider a tablecloth soiled unless it contained more spots than a Dalmatian.

There were four more hours to go till twelve thirty, and he
wondered how to live through them without losing his mind.
He should have gone home and snatched a nap, yet knew that
the calm of the Vassilovich compound, untouched by preparations for the night's drama, would, instead of inducing sleep,
ruffle his nerves even more. Then there was the danger that he
might be cut off once he left the city center. The troops, com-
mandeered by the conspirators, might, like a flash flood, turn
the vicinity of the Konak into an unapproachable island.

He envied the young men at the Serbian Crown for being
able to get drunk. He wished he could follow their example,
but now that he had resolved to remain in league with the
rebels, he had to see things through, if for no other reason than

to save his self-respect. Drinking himself into a stupor would be the coward's way out.

He saw a party of civilians, all in their twenties, unknown to him, enter the garden and surge up to Colonel Mishich's table. Judging by their shabby, though neat, suits and crude white shirts open at the necks, they were students or teachers, an element most passionately devoted to the Radical Party. They were greeted cordially by the colonel and invited to join him.

Michael wondered whether Mishich's fraternization with an element usually ignored by the officers' corp would not awaken the suspicion of the ever-present secret service men, probably seated within earshot of the party. Colonel Mishich had to assume that he might be watched, but he seemed not to care. By the time the agents' report could reach the Konak it would have little influence on the night's events, whatever they might be.

Colonel Jankowski was not a happy man. He had sold the last three hundred morgen of the Jankowski estate in the Galician village of Brzesko, his peptic ulcer was acting up again and he loathed Belgrade. When, twenty-eight years before, he had graduated second in his class from Vienna's War College and when four years later he became permanently assigned to the Austro-Hungarian General Staff, he had every reason to take for granted a brilliant military career, culminating in the field marshal's baton. Then, halfway between major and lieutenant colonel, things went wrong: gambling, heavy debts, involvement with a general's wife, finally incurring Archduke Franz Ferdinand's displeasure during the 1896 maneuvers when a company of Reds under his command captured a battery of Blue field guns, thus frustrating a Blue division attack led by the archduke himself. The emperor personally congratulated him on his splendid performance right there on the mock battlefield, yet that did little to help. After the maneuvers, the old man returned to his Mount Olympus in Vienna's Burg, while the archduke remained a very intensely felt presence in the offices of the General Staff. After some unrewarding assignments, Jankowski was named military attaché to the Belgrade Legation. A few years before, the post would have held some importance, but he was sent to Belgrade at a time when the monarchy was losing interest in Serbia, a fickle and expensive ward.

The secret order sent to the legation from Vienna was to sit it out till some internal development caused the country to dance to a different—and, it was hoped, more consistent—tune. Hands off, watch and wait, the instructions read, and Jankowski had no choice but to abide by them. Anyway, he had no taste for the kind of politics practiced in Serbia. When granted a farewell interview with Chief of Staff General Beck, the lame excuse given him for the assignment in Belgrade was that he, as a Pole, would be able to establish rapport with his fellow Slavs. This, of course, he knew to be sheer nonsense.

A Pole, especially a Vienna-oriented Pole, urbane, baroque and slightly decadent, and a Southern Slav, backward and savage, half swineherd and half highwayman, were light-years apart. He regarded his stay in Belgrade not as a tour of duty, but an exile in punishment for past and future derelictions. He attended receptions and public occasions only when unavoidable and spent his days reading and listening to phonograph records. The book-lined walls of his four-room flat in a side street off Teraziya were the ramparts that guarded him against the onslaught of barbarians. The music of Mozart, Beethoven and Johann Strauss, emanating from the horn of his never-silent machine, acoustically isolated his world from the bedlam beyond.

Now he'd been summoned to an audience with the woman whom he considered the very incarnation of the tawdriness that caused his present post to be so detestable. In happier years, he had known ladies with mile-long lineages, among them the Princess Paula Metternich, acknowledged social leader of Vienna. He had mingled with real queens; consequently, he felt nothing but bored contempt for the counterfeit queen who faced him now. He considered not only her, but the entire Obrenovich dynasty a sad joke, except for the late King Milan, whom he revered not because of his royal title, but for his great talent in giving a most genial impersonation of a sovereign. To be king had been a lark for Milan; he played at it while it amused him and abandoned it the moment he found it boring, never having taken the role seriously. To poor little Alexander, on the other hand, kingship appeared to be part of his entire being. In Jankoski's eyes he pranced about, blown up with the dignity of his title like a toy balloon filled with hot air, never realizing that he had long sprung a leak and was becoming more and more deflated.

"I've called you, Colonel, to remind you that it is your government's duty to help us," Queen Draga said to him without allowing him to finish his apology for having excused himself from her *déjeuner*. He tried to tell her that he had suffered one of his frequent migraine attacks, but she was clearly not interested.

"Help you in what way, madame?" he asked, although he knew what she was driving at. "If you mean His Majesty King Alexander's attempts to secure a loan from a certain Viennese banking house. . . ."

She cut him short. "It's not the loan. And don't act as though you didn't know." She leaned close to his face and shouted, "We're going to be slaughtered by a gang of cutthroats unless your government takes steps to defend us."

Jankowski drew back and succeeded in looking baffled. "Slaughtered? What an expression, madame. And cutthroats? If you fear an assassination attempt—granted they aren't unusual in this part of the world—you have a very efficient and, at times, ruthless police to prevent it."

Draga rose abruptly. The colonel jumped to his feet as though there were springs built into the seat of his pants. Despite his personal feelings about her, he never forgot she was a woman and he an officer in Franz Josef's army.

"For God's sake, Colonel!" she exclaimed. "Don't act as if you didn't know. There is a conspiracy brewing in this town with dozens, perhaps even hundreds involved. Probably the entire Radical Party."

"Madame—" he tried to interrupt her.

She refused to be diverted. "I know what you are going to say. That conspiracies have always been indigenous to Serbia. But *always* isn't true. Only since Russia decided to take an interest in the Balkans. You know as well as I do that without its meddling there would be perfect harmony between King Alexander and his people."

"Madame, my government has reason to believe that for the moment Russia prefers to keep out of the internal affairs of the Balkans."

"And I have it from the most authentic source that she does not. Don't you know that Colonel Grabov is in town?"

There was a long pause. "Yes, I've heard. Frankly, I never believed he really existed. Mysticism is something the Russians revel in. Their government often invents fictitious organizations, even persons, to impress the people and gullible elements abroad. Yes, I've heard stories of Colonel Grabov and his Asian Department, but I never had the pleasure of meeting him or his mythical associates."

"It so happens that I've had the pleasure, if you can call it that. And he is very real. So is the conspiracy. He didn't bother to deny it, so—" Her voice broke in the middle of the sentence.

Jankowski gave her a pained look. "But, madame, don't you see the strategy? He is trying to intimidate you. I have no idea to what purpose, but that's how the Russians operate. Spreading rumors, dropping hints, obscuring issues. If they had as many spies loose as they want us to believe, there wouldn't be any people left in Russia."

His slightly nasal French with a touch of a Polish accent began to grate on her nerves. She raised her voice. "Now look here, Colonel! I demand that you take some action to protect us. You have four monitors anchored at Zimony. You also have two infantry regiments stationed there. In consideration of the long and loyal friendship the Obrenovich dynasty has displayed for the monarchy, it's that government's God-imposed duty to save us."

"But how, madame?"

"If there is no other way, have your military occupy Belgrade."

He stared at her, this time genuinely baffled. "Occupy Belgrade! Invade Serbia! Madame, you can't be serious!"

"I am perfectly serious."

"Do you realize, madame," he asked with a wry smile, "that you have just offered my government the kingdom of Serbia?"

"I do." She dropped wearily into a chair as though the talk had drained her of her strength.

"What about the king? Will he give his consent to such a preposterous suggestion?"

"He always takes my advice. Besides, I don't see anything preposterous about your troops occupying the city. Temporarily, that is. Till order and stability are restored."

Though he knew that Count Goluchowski would dismiss the offer with a tired wave of his hands, he decided to report it in a coded wire to the Ministry of Foreign Affairs. "I shall contact my superiors, madame, though I can't promise you any immediate results." He hoped the audience would soon be terminated.

"Oh, but you must make them understand that there is no time left for vacillations. They might wake up tomorrow and find us gone and Peter Karageorgevich seated on the throne. Do they want him? Don't they know he is the czar's man? Once he is established here, the monarchy has lost Serbia and all Southern Slavs to Russia. That would be a fatal blow to the monarchy. To find itself hemmed in between two such formidable powers as Germany and Russia. Don't you see the danger of that?"

"Heavens no, madame. Germany is a friendly state, and as for the Russians, they have enough domestic problems without taking on the Balkans' woes as well. Anyway, I don't think they are a threat to the monarchy."

He was lying. He did consider the Russians a threat, not only to Austria-Hungary, but to the rest of Europe. In his younger years he had been repeatedly dispatched as observer of their winter maneuvers. Watching their troops take part in mock assaults, he saw tidal wave after tidal wave of blank-faced men advance on a make-believe enemy like an enormous harrow leveling everything in its way. If sent into real battle, he thought, that human juggernaut would never retreat, because if its front lines were routed, the next wave of men would roll up from behind and trample the retreating front line into the ground. Russia, Jankowski felt, was a death threat to the world. Not a violent fiery death, but the slow, white death of the Arctic that overtakes the traveler on his sledge, thinning out his team of huskies one by one.

Draga's muffled, desperate voice stirred him from his musing. "For heaven's sake, Colonel, let's not digress. This isn't the moment to discuss politics. We are in mortal danger. Something's got to be done. Or—" She stopped and gave him a long, inquisitive look. "Are you listening, Colonel? I have a feeling I've been talking to a blank wall."

You are, poor woman, you are, he thought. Aloud he said,

"Of course, I am listening. I was merely thinking of some practical way to handle the matter. Mind you, I'm still convinced your fears are unfounded, yet supposing they aren't—"

She cut into his speech. "Sasha is only twenty-seven. Isn't he too young to die?" Her anxious gaze was beginning to make him feel ill at ease. He no longer saw the troublesome female upstart who used to irritate him with her hopeless demands for invitations to the imperial Burg and archducal palaces, but a condemned prisoner waiting for her executioners.

"Madame," Jankowski began. This time he was not the military attaché talking, but the man. "I'll do all I can to convey your apprehensions to my government. Even if I succeed in convincing them that your fears are well founded, it'll be some time before they can take action. So, for the moment there is only one solution I am in the position to offer: political asylum at our legation and finding a way to escort you to Zimony, where you may board one of our monitors."

Her shrill, hysterical laughter caught him unawares. He sat bolt upright and looked at her with hurt indignation. "What's so funny, madame?"

"Are all spies alike?" she asked, still choking with a strange, joyless merriment. Tears, of either mirth or anger, were streaming down her face, marking her cheeks with thin, discolored lines of rouge. "Grabov offered me the same thing. Except for the monitors." She chuckled. "But only because he doesn't have any. Not on the Danube. But soon he will. Just wait. Their gunboats will be cruising on your blue Danube. You'll be left with nothing but the waltz." She hummed a few bars of a Johann Strauss melody. "You know, Colonel, come to think of it, perhaps that's all you have ever wanted. A cup of coffee with whipped cream and a hundred violins playing the 'Blue Danube Waltz.' To hell with Belgrade, its guzlas and kolos and its worn-out old mare queen."

He wondered momentarily if she were drunk. He was at a loss about how to react to her incoherent ramblings. At last, she rose, signaling the end of the audience.

"I've made my offer, madame, and without the knowledge of my government," he told her stiffly. He regretted having taken pity on the foolish woman. "Should my government disapprove, it might mean the end of my career. Ever since the 1897

Austro-Russian agreement, both powers have observed an attitude of strict noninvolvement in Balkan affairs. Opening the door of our legation to you would be tantamount to breaking that agreement. That is, in case you decide to accept my offer."

"I do not, Colonel. I see you're hurt because you think I was making fun of you. I wasn't really. I laughed because Colonel Grabov made the same offer. But only after I'd threatened him with blackmail. Your offer, on the other hand, was dictated by the goodness of your heart. Yet it is not my own fate that worries me. I am concerned about the king. If my leaving the country would save him, I'd grab at your offer and go. It might have helped some time ago. Not anymore, though. If I went now, it would be desertion. And that would be worse than perishing with him."

He was awed despite himself. He had had many talks with her in the past and at times been aware of her cleverness, even wit, but his basic prejudices caused him to overlook her merits and notice only her faults. Now he wished he could turn the clock back so he could have time to put in a few good words in her behalf that would influence his old friend and *Landsman* Goluchowski in her favor. She was evidently loyal to her gauche little king and—given a fair chance and some expert advice—might have made an acceptable queen. Well, it was too late now.

"I shall take the liberty of reporting to you, madame, as soon as I have discussed the matter with my superiors. I shall impress the need of urgency upon them. I'm certain we'll have a reply from Vienna within a few days."

She nodded with a feeble smile. "Thank you so much, Colonel. I know you'll do your best."

She proffered her hand, and as he bent low to kiss it, she noticed a bald circle covered by combed-over wisps of hair. Tall, elegant Colonel Ladislav Jankowski was considered the handsomest man in the entire diplomatic corps in Belgrade. She didn't know why, but the bald spot distressed her. It was like detecting a crack in a fine, old piece of china one believed to be unmarked by the passing of time.

9 P.M.

A PATROL consisting of a corporal and two privates in the Royal Guards entered the garden. Their appearance caused no ripples among the diners. Searching parties, even arrests, were the order of the day in Belgrade's cafés and restaurants. A few forks might have been laid down, a few heads turned and a few sentences left unfinished; but the gypsies played on, and the hum of conversation hardly diminished in volume. The three uniforms halted in the entrance. The corporal motioned to the headwaiter. They spoke for a few seconds; then the corporal started up the aisle between the tables. Eyes followed him across the garden. Here and there officers rose to get a better look at the man who was to be singled out. Civilians remained glued to their seats, some slid lower, hunching their backs as though trying to become invisible.

The corporal halted a few steps from Michael and executed a stiff military salute.

"Corporal Ristich reporting, sir. Would the captain be so kind as to present himself at the office of her majesty the queen's court marshal?"

It took a puzzled Michael a few seconds to understand. "Did you say the office of the queen's court marshal?"

"Yes, sir."

"When?"

"Now, sir. I have a carriage waiting."

"All right. Just wait a minute till I pay my bill."

"Yes, sir." The corporal saluted, and was about to walk away when Michael called after him.

"How did you know where to look for me?"

The man turned back. "I didn't know, sir. I was told to go first to the captain's house and if I didn't find the captain home, to look in all the places along Teraziya and the boulevards till I found the captain."

Buildings, like women, have their individual time of day when they look their best. With the Old Konak, it was the twilight hours during June (the end of May, according to the Old Style calendar) when the sunset, reflected in its window-panes, turned each into an enormous, burning ruby. The approaching night managed to cover its cracks, discolorations and peeling paint with a crepuscular net. The gate and the guard-house were dimly lighted because expenses had to be cut. Since time immemorial, the civil list had always been exhausted by the end of May, which in turn unleashed venomous attacks by the Radical press on the court. In the past, these clamors died down in a week or two, but would they this year? Michael wondered.

The carriage deposited him under the marquee, the sole elegant feature of the building. The front door to the vestibule was already locked, but before he could ring, a footman, evidently alerted for his arrival, opened it for him.

"Her majesty is expecting the captain." The man addressed him in Hungarian-accented German. The queen preferred domestics formerly employed by aristocrats residing in Vienna or Budapest to native servants, as Serbs had proved practically untrainable for gracious and polished performances. "The queen is in her boudoir. Will the captain kindly follow me?"

The footman must have been a new acquisition, Michael guessed; otherwise, he would have known that the captain needed no guidance through the maze of the Old Konak. They passed the ground-floor offices and mounted the steps leading to the entrance hall and from there to the royal apartments. Three double-winged doors opened from the entrance hall, one onto the dining room, the second to the audience wing and the middle one to the couple's private suite. As always, the faint odor of cooking lingered in the entrance hall. In the nearly twenty years since he had first set foot on the timeworn parquet floor, the character of the odors emanating from the kitchen changed according to the political party in power. During the reign of Milan, the odors were definitely French, spiced with thyme, sage, a *soupçon* of garlic, at times overpowered by the fragrance of oven-baked *pâte feuilletée* for Milan had a sweet tooth. Under the regents, the pungency of onions sautéed in lard invaded every nook and cranny of the house. It was only years later at the time of Milan's return as king-father, that constant airings took place. Now, as far as Michael's experienced nose could judge, the smell of *Wiener schnitzel* prevailed for the present chef of the royal household was an Austrian formerly employed by a Duke Festetich.

The footman halted at the door to the boudoir, knocked, then waited for the queen's *"Entrez,"* after which he flung the door wide, calling out in the stentorian tone of an amusement park barker: "Captain Michael Vassilovich."

Michael suddenly felt his body grow cold and heavy like stone. It was a fleeting sensation, immediately gone, as though he had died and been resurrected within seconds. He could recall only one similar attack of nerves in his life, though under entirely different circumstances. It had happened during the Serbo-Bulgarian War when he had led his platoon into his first battle. For a moment he had thought that he had suffered a stroke and would never be able to move his limbs again. The next thing he remembered were bullets whizzing past him as he stormed the enemy stronghold meters ahead of his men.

He found Draga standing in the middle of the room, looking lost and strangely out of place like a guest at the wrong party. He entered, bowing stiffly, then halted. The three of them, footman, queen and visitor, stared at one another in strange silence like actors who had forgotten their lines. Then the queen collected herself and, with a wave of her hand, dismissed the footman.

"Thank you for coming, Mika," she said. Her use of the nickname caught him off his guard; it had slipped so easily from her lips.

"You left me no choice, madame. One can't possibly turn down an invitation delivered by an armed patrol." He waited for a reply. The silence disconcerted him. "What can I do for you?"

She gazed at him intently. "You haven't changed much, Mika. You look even younger than when I last saw you. Not like me. I am falling apart. But of course, I haven't spent the last three years in Switzerland."

He had been prepared by gossiping friends to find her aged, her prettiness vanished, and was surprised to see how wrong they had been. The excitement of their meeting and some boldly applied rouge added color to her cheeks and her eyes shone like emeralds changing to topazes when the light of the chandelier hit them. True, she had put on weight, acquired the hint of a double chin, but the years had failed to affect her voice, still warm and melodious, even the harsh Slav consonants abrading to an easy softness. Her voice had always held a strange power over him. Her calling "Is that you, Mika?" in answer to his key turning in the lock of their cottage, had sent a flash of desire to his loins. Never since those days had homecoming to any of his mistresses been such pleasure.

Now the magic worked once again, but only for a second, for he hastily reminded himself that the woman facing him now was not the Draga of six years before and never again would be. "What is it you wanted to see me about?"

"I understand you've been appointed equerry to the king. I must say, it took me by surprise."

"Me, too. And I haven't stopped being surprised."

"It was General Petrovich's idea. He knew you had once belonged to the Milan clique and hoped that you might be helpful in bringing about a reconciliation between the king and the army."

"I didn't know they were estranged."

Her eyes flashed like a cat's about to pounce on a bird. "Good God, where have you been?"

"In Switzerland, madame."

"Don't you 'madame' me!" The unexpected outburst was like a bridge to the past. Her angers had always exploded with the abruptness of gunshots, their sound and fury dying just as abruptly, leaving not the faintest echo behind. This time, however, her frown, more hurt than angry, failed to turn into the placating smile of the old days, and she was close to tears.

"What else can I call you without committing *lèse majesté*?" he asked.

She had seated herself on a fauteuil, upholstered in the same pink brocade as the wall covering. Even the Aubusson carpet on the floor, Michael noted, contained dainty pink flowers. During the two-king reign this room had been part of Alexander's bachelor quarters, furnished with odds and ends, bearskins and homespun fabrics, and used by father and son and their intimates as a haven from the bustle of the public Konak. The sole item left over from Milan's days was the late king's handsome portrait looking laughably out of place in the midst of all the pink fluff. Even Draga herself, Michael mused, seemed out of place in this strawberry-ice ambiance, the fairytale dream of a sixteen-year-old come true twenty years too late.

"Oh, Mika," she said in a tired whisper, "do you hate me, too?" From anyone else the cry would have sounded like a cunning plea for sympathy, but her tone was weighted down with such despair that it touched him deeply. This wasn't the giddy white rabbit munching on the lettuce leaf oblivious of the boa constrictor; this was a poor wretched soul staring straight into the rapacious jaws.

"I don't hate you, Draga, though God knows I have reason to."

"Why? Because I left you? But, Mika, whatever was between us—it had no future—if only you had said something. A hint. I would still be with you. You know that, don't you, Mika?"

God help them, Michael prayed, they were not going to go into that. "If you had been in that Johannesgasse apartment in Vienna watching King Milan die as I did—"

"He loathed me," she cut in.

"With reason, too. First the Knezevich assassination attempt, then your husband's order to shoot him if he tried to return to Serbia. And you had a hand in both."

"And if I did! It was one crisis after the other. My nerves were wearing thin. I wasn't really myself. Good God, I'd been sleeping with Sasha for three years, and what did it get me? A house on Crown Street, a few trinkets and the shady title of king's official mistress. People kowtowed to me, but deep down they had nothing but contempt. Don't think I didn't know it. I was thirty-four years old. What future could I expect if Sasha tired of me? Then he offered to make me his queen. Only a saint or a fool would have refused, and I am neither."

"Saint, no, fool, yes. You were given a great opportunity, and you made a mess of it."

"Oh, God, Mika, I tried! To be like those ancient heroines, Milica or even old Milosh's Ljubica. I wore national costumes to receptions and served *chorba* and *djuvech* at state dinners. I visited the grave of that scoundrel Kara George to show the Russians my aim was to be queen to all Serbs, even to the Karageorgeviches. To placate the Milan clique, I talked Sasha into making a pilgrimage with me to his father's grave. It was a mistake. On my first visit as a queen to the monarchy's soil I was greeted not by the emperor or even an archduke, no! It was the ban of Croatia who welcomed me! A magistrate. A nobody! He didn't even bother to bring his wife along, as though it would've been beneath the lady's station to curtsy to me!"

"Draga, there is more to being a good queen than having Emperor Franz Josef greet you at the border."

"Oh, but I didn't want it for myself. I wanted it for Serbia. So that people all over the world would learn that it is no longer a Turkish province, but a proud and independent country. The last slap to my face was the canceled invitation to Livadiya. Was it so terrible that I wanted to adopt a child and call it my own? Had I borne Sasha a son, would all the men I'd slept with over the years become nonexistent? Nicholas and Alexandra didn't snub me because of the pregnancy muddle. They dropped me because their government no longer needed my services."

The puzzle of Draga Mashin, this woman he had alternately loved and hated, her successes and blunders, suddenly became clear to Michael. What had caused her to fail in her role as Queen of Serbia was not excessive greed, recklessness or even megalomania, but her unshakable desire for bourgeois values. She wanted a husband, a family, security and, above all, respect —blessings within easy reach of any woman save the one who married a Balkan king ten years her junior. The peace of mind and fulfillment for which she now waged a losing battle could have been hers had she settled with Michael Vassilovich in one of the little whitewashed houses on the hill by the cathedral. She would have charmed the neighbors, and she would have belonged. As Queen of Serbia, her friendly overtures were wasted on royal neighbors, who looked the other way when she proffered them her hand. She had made a fool of herself in their eyes, as well as in her subjects'.

They were silent, he trying to sort out his feelings for her, she wondering what those feelings were.

"There is one more thing I want you to know, Mika." Her voice pleaded for credence. "Since I left you, I haven't slept with anyone but Sasha."

"Draga, what difference does that make?"

"You'll hear nasty stories about me. They are lies, Michael. I admit, it wasn't always easy for me. I am very devoted to him, grateful, but—"

"Draga, that's between him and you. Let's not digress. What did you call me for?"

She had buried her tired face in her hands, the fabulous diamond of her engagement ring sparkling with a defiant luster on her finger. "Save us, Mika! Talk to them!"

"Talk to whom?"

"Them. That's who they are. Them." She rose wearily. "Don't tell me it's a coincidence that you arrived home from Geneva the day the *coup d'état* had been planned for." He tried to interrupt, but she went on. "You were King Milan's man and still are. And so are they. They have sentenced us to death. Please, please. Mika, go and tell them that we are ready to surrender. Grant us *sauf-conduit*, and we will leave. They may bring in Peter Kara or Nikita of Montenegro. We won't lift a finger. What's more, we'll pass the word to the few friends we have left to offer their loyalty to your man. Give us a few days, and we'll be out of the Konak. And the country. I've been ready to leave for quite some time. I hoped I could go with my head held high. Now I no longer care."

He wondered if she meant what she said. He could not recall her ever having lied to him, silent about things, yes, but lies, never. His eyes searched her face. He found misery and resignation there. Inexplicably even to himself, he pulled out his handkerchief and, gripping her chin with one hand, wiped the rouge from her face. It was something he had often done in the past when she tried to improve upon nature. No matter how careful she was, he always detected the rouge and, without a word, simply removed it. She never protested, accepting his ministrations as good-naturedly as his other whims. The next day, she reddened her cheeks again, and the game repeated itself without casting the slightest shadow on their relationship.

His unexpected reversion to the old routine was like a bridge thrown over a marshland of six years, stronger than any word, kiss or lovemaking could have been. Taken completely unaware, resentment built up against him during their estrangement dispelled, Draga threw herself in his arms, savoring a sensation of immense relief. Then she remembered that she was no longer entitled to such comfort and self-consciously withdrew.

"Can you help us, Mika?" She asked the question anyway, knowing that it would destroy a mood that could never be recaptured.

The moment of their embrace had left him with a not entirely unpleasant pain. Since their last time together he had had affairs with a number of women and loved none, which fact, however, had not failed to keep him from enjoying what they had to offer: sex, fun, companionship. Holding Draga in his arms, her soft brown hair with its bittersweet fragrance brushing against his cheek, he felt a strange nostalgia for the passion he once had for this woman and for no one else. It was the recognition of loss, of having missed or spoiled something that could have given substance to his life. Gazing into her still beautiful green eyes with the fine crows' feet at their corners, he almost uttered the stereotyped line that men nearing middle age often say to attractive women past their first bloom: "I wish I had met you when you were eighteen." The trouble with him and Draga, Michael knew, was that they *had* met when she was eighteen.

"I am not sure that I can help you, but I'll try," he said finally.

"So you *are* one of them," she said, moving away.

"Isn't that why you ordered me here? Wouldn't it disappoint you if I weren't."

Subdued now, she shrugged. "It still hurts. You of all people."

"This is what I call Draga logic." He reached out to stroke her cheek. "Of course, logic was never your strong point."

"I was never a thinker," she admitted. "I'm afraid, my decisions were always the spur-of-the-moment kind. Unfortunately, Sasha is the same. Whenever an idea strikes him, he carries it out without weighing the consequences. Let's put the Radicals in power—the Liberals—the Conservatives. Kick out the Radicals—appease Russia—snub Russia—close a treaty with Austria —break a treaty. He is a juggler; only he juggles with constitutions. The New, the Old, the 1880, 1901. He calls it being flexible. I am afraid, the word is 'unbalanced.' And the same goes for me."

Michael pulled out his watch and glanced at it. "We're wasting time. You've told me you are ready to give up. What about the king?"

"He is, too."

"What makes you so sure?"

"He won't stay without me. He was ready to pack up and leave when it looked as though the country wouldn't let him marry me."

"That was three years ago."

"He's more attached to me than ever before."

"Don't you understand? I need more than a vague promise from you."

"What else can I give you? Besides, it isn't a vague promise. I mean it. So help me God."

"I must have a signed statement that within a short time he will proclaim his abdication."

She stared at him numbly, considering. "I don't know. His pride. He may not have the wisdom of the great Nemanyich kings, but he certainly has their pride."

"But you said he was ready to abdicate."

"I believe he is, but to put it in writing? To them?" She flared. "It would sound like crying for mercy."

"Aren't you?"

She threw a suspicious glance at him. "You're not trying to force us into something that we might regret later, are you?"

He was beginning to lose his patience. "Draga, I didn't tell you there was a coup in the making, *you* told *me*. And asked for my help. But now—"

She placed a placating hand on his arm. "You are right, Mika. Stay here. I'll talk to Sasha. You see, I hoped it would be enough to give them *my* promise. After all, I am the bone of contention in this whole wretched affair. I wanted to work on Sasha, slowly, cautiously. He hates to be pressured. Besides, he isn't afraid of them. He still thinks he can outwit or outscare them."

"Take my word for it. He can't."

She took a deep breath. "Oh, Mika." She started to say something, quickly reconsidered and left the room.

Since seven forty-five that evening, the king had been in conference with Paul Marinkovich, his envoy to Sofia. The idea of an invasion of Turkey's European holding with the aim of liberating Old Serbia and Macedonia had been haunting Alexander for some time. A popular and successful war seemed to him the sole remaining way of closing the breach between him and the country. Marinkovich had been entrusted with negotiating power for a secret treaty with Bulgaria so that Alexander could be safe from a stab in the back by an old enemy while attacking an even older one.

Three Cabinet ministers and the now gala-uniformed but still distraught Colonel Naumovich were in the small anteroom when the queen stormed in. Draga acknowledged their somewhat startled greetings with an impatient wave of her hand and was about to enter the king's study when Naumovich barred her way.

"His majesty doesn't wish to be disturbed, madame," he said, swaying slightly and puffing whiffs of brandy vapor into her face. "Not by anyone."

"Don't be ridiculous," she snapped. "I am not anyone."

"These gentlemen have been waiting for hours to be received." He indicated the ministers. "They haven't even had supper yet."

"I am sure their wives will keep their suppers warm. But as for you, you'd better have some strong coffee." She glared at him. "What's the matter with you, Colonel? You've always been a lush, but not a falling-down drunk. Now get out of my way."

Her sudden entrance caught the king in midsentence. The minister leaped to his feet and bowed from the waist.

"What's the matter, madame?" the king asked, not attempting to hide his displeasure at the interruption.

"I must speak to you."

"I am having a very important talk with Paul and—"

"Please, Sasha, it's urgent."

Alexander thought for a moment, then said with a wry smile, "Women's wishes are God's wishes." He turned to the envoy. "We shall continue later, Paul. Would you mind stepping out for a minute?" When the envoy bowed and started backing out of the room, the king stopped him with a gesture. "Please, wait in the conference room. Half the Cabinet is out there in the anteroom. I don't want you to be cross-examined by them about our meeting."

Marinkovich knew of Alexander's obsession for secrecy. He executed two more deep bows, one to the king and one to the queen, before backing out of the room. An ambitious young man, he had been warned that advancement in Alexander's service depended on the queen's approval.

Alexander waited for the door to close. "What's wrong, madame?" he asked in a coolly official tone, the sign of an imminent royal tiff.

She sensed that she must proceed with caution. "Have you talked to Laza?"

"What about?"

"The coup."

"What coup?"

"For God's sake, Sasha, don't act as if you didn't know." She took a deep breath and plunged. "You'd better face it. Time is running out on us."

He gave her a searching look from behind the thick lenses of his glasses. "Running out?" he repeated shrilly, removing his pince-nez and rubbing it against the sleeve of his uniform.

"You must abdicate, Sasha."

"Abdicate? What a preposterous idea! And coming from you of all people." He carefully replaced the glasses. "You must be out of your mind."

Draga placed her hands on his shoulders. "Sasha, please, be sensible. No use fooling ourselves. There's only a handful of men still loyal to us. And they're not exactly the cream of the crop. Even if we aren't murdered tonight or tomorrow night, there is no sense in clinging to something that has no future. And gives us no happiness. You keep telling me that you love me, that your most fervent wish is to make me happy. You won't ever if we stay here. We have so much to live for. This isn't it—this isn't."

He listened, his face frozen; then slithered out of her grasp and stepped back. *"Reviens à toi, Draga.* You aren't making sense. Murdered tonight! What absolute nonsense."

In a few breathless words she recounted the events of the afternoon, including the incidents with Savka and Milica, her meeting with Colonel Grabov and Jankowski and finally with Michael Vassilovich. His reaction to the latter's name was a slight twitch of his narrow lips. Once more, he removed his pince-nez, his naked face with its expression of petulance and vindictiveness reminding her again of the small boy who used to throw wild tantrums whenever he was denied a wish.

"So that's what it is," he said. "That bastard. Captain Vassilovich. I told Laza not to let him set foot in the Konak." Turning, he strutted to the door and threw it open.

"Naumovich," he screamed in the shrill, feline tone his court had learned to recognize as a warning signal.

The queen tried to intercept him. "What are you going to do?"

"Naumovich!" he shouted again. By then the whole ante-room was staring at him in frozen silence. "In here!" he pointed at the floor as though he were commanding a dog.

Naumovich had been dozing in a dainty Louis XV chair much too narrow to hold his bulk that spread beyond the breadth of the seat like overrisen bread dough. With difficulty, he lumbered to his feet and shuffled to the study.

"Close the damn door," the king barked at him.

Obediently, he pulled the door shut, then, eyes lowered, ambled up to his master. "Yes, sire," he muttered. "At your service, sire."

"I want Captain Vassilovich arrested."

The queen reached out nervously for his arm. "Please, Sasha."

Ignoring her, Alexander went on. "You'll find him in the queen's suite. Go and take him to the guardhouse, where he is to be kept till further orders. Should he offer resistance, you're hereby instructed to shoot him."

Naumovich stared at his king in utter bewilderment. "Shoot him? I don't have a gun on me, sire."

"Then get one, damn it. It shouldn't be such an insurmountable problem in this bloody caravanserai."

With a shrug, Naumovich turned to the door. Conscious of the king's vicious mood, however, he made a feeble attempt at backing out; then, realizing that in his present condition even a straight walk presented some hazards, he decided to dispense with court etiquette and make his exit unceremoniously but fast.

"Naumovich! Stop!" The queen's voice halted him as he was already outside.

"Go on! You heard me!" The king outshouted his wife.

Exasperated, Naumovich stood still. Past experiences had taught him that whenever there was a conflict between the royal couple, it always ended in the queen's victory. All one had to do was to pretend to be deaf and wait.

"The man wants to help us, Sasha," the queen told him. The expression of bored petulance gave way to watchful alertness on Naumovich's face.

"Some help," the king grumbled. "I ought to break every bone in Laza's body for bringing him to the Konak. Shut the bloody door!" This was directed to Naumovich. "I knew it from the very first," he continued to the queen, "that it was a damned stupid thing to do. Don't you see Vassilovich's strategy? He is a Karageorgevich man. His chums know they can't win in a fair fight, so they are fighting underhandedly. Savka, Grabov, Jankowski and now Vassilovich. They're all part of a conspiracy that aims lies instead of guns at us."

"Please, Sasha. I told you. He didn't come to me. I sent for him."

"If you hadn't sent for him tonight, he would've come to you tomorrow. What disturbs me in this whole bloody idiocy is Laza's role. Is he, too, part of a conspiracy?"

"Sasha, for God's sake, how can you say that? There isn't anyone more loyal than Laza."

"I've heard that before. Let me tell you, there is only one man in this anthill I have implicit faith in, and that is Mika Naumovich." Ignoring the low moan which escaped the colonel's mouth, he added, "The rest, *chérie*? They're nothing, but flunkeys. Loyal to the highest bidder. They—" He was interrupted by a chuckle from Naumovich. Still standing at the door, his back to the royal couple, his fat shoulders began to shake as though he were in the grip of an uncontrollable laughing fit.

"What's so funny, Colonel?" the king asked sharply.

Naumovich turned now to face him, unashamedly sobbing. Fat, pear-shaped tears rolled down his cheeks, dripping into the stiff collar of his gala uniform.

"*Sacré bleu*, Mika, what's the matter with you?" Alexander asked, startled.

"Your majesties have been too good to me!" Naumovich stuttered. "I don't deserve it. I wish you weren't so good to me."

"*Tiens, que c'est agaçant!*" the king muttered, annoyed. Any other time such an outpouring of gratitude would have flattered him; now it interfered with the business at hand. "I appreciate your loyalty, Colonel. I'm sure you'll have ample opportunity to prove it to us, but now will you please pull yourself together and arrest Captain Vassilovich."

"Wait!" The queen was not ready to give in. "What do you want him arrested for? What will you gain by it?"

"The names of his contacts. If there really is a conspiracy and he is part of it, then he certainly knows who else is involved."

"He won't betray them."

"We can make him. You know we can."

Naumovich was no longer sobbing. Dry-eyed and seemingly sobered, he was listening avidly.

"That's what I've been waiting for," the king confessed. "To get one of them. Now we'll have the rest. Leave it to Prefect Marshityanin."

"I won't have it." The queen raised her voice. "You'd be making a horrible mistake. Good God, Sasha, wake up. The days are over when problems could be solved by putting a man in irons. We don't have jails large enough to hold all the people who are against us. Give up. There is such a thing as honorable retreat."

Alexander, glaring at her with his lips pressed into a thin line of reproof, began pacing the floor. After a few turns, with an abruptness that caused Naumovich to recoil, he halted in front of him. "Bring the man here!"

"And if he refuses, sire?" Naumovich asked, a glint of speculation in his eyes. "Is your order to shoot him still valid?" The eagerness of his tone indicated to Draga that he no longer considered the shooting of the captain to be beyond his capability.

"No," the queen answered quickly. "It is not. Anyway, he won't refuse. Tell him *I* want him to have a talk with the king."

Naumovich took a deep breath as though about to say something; then reconsidering, he made a quick exit. Immediately the king pounced upon Draga. "So he'll come for you! I must say, madame, it didn't take you long to reestablish rapport with the captain."

Exasperated, she shook her head. "Won't you ever grow up, Sasha? Yes, the man was my lover. He was also your father's best friend. He does have a grudge against you, not because of me, but because of your father. Yet he wants to help you. You told me yourself that Vassilovich used to give you riding lessons when you were a boy, taught you to play tennis. I have a feeling that the memory of you as a small child outweighs any animosity he's had against you these past years. Don't try to make him betray his friends, whoever they are. He won't. He is a very stubborn man."

"No more stubborn than I," the king mumbled, then raised his voice. "Once and for all. I am not going to abdicate. But to please you, I shall tell him that I am considering it."

"But—"

"That's not cricket? Of course, it's not, but we're not playing a gentleman's game. I am getting fed up with all these stupid rumors. Everyone I've talked to dispenses different advice. 'Stamp out the nest of snakes!' 'Wait!' 'Don't wait!' As if everyone had one purpose; to drive me out of my mind. I haven't told you this, but just the other day Boza Marshityanin suggested I get rid of Mika Naumovich. He'd received some confidential information that Naumovich is in collusion with the Karageorgevich camp. This certainly proves the extent of the hysteria people have succumbed to around here. That Boza can come to me and accuse his and my best friend of treason!"

"I don't know, Sasha, Naumovich has acted rather strangely lately."

The king whirled about, pointing an accusing finger at his wife. "See? You too! Exactly what I was saying! All one has to do is drop a hint and it's taken for gospel truth. No, I won't be maneuvered into turning tail. No, *j'y suis, j'y reste*. But I'll see to it that we find the source of the rumors. And if we do, I won't show pity. That I promise you."

A knock on the door interrupted them. Draga closed her eyes and clasped her hands together till her nails cut painfully into the flesh of her palms. She heard the king call, *"Entrez,"* and Naumovich solemnly announced Captain Michael Vassilovich, an unnecessary formality considering the circumstances.

As always, constant confusion reigned in the palace staffs about who was and was not to be announced formally before being admitted to the king's or queen's presence. Frequently, sightseers were allowed to wander freely through the Konak, while the queen's masseuse would be ushered into her bedroom with the ceremony prescribed for foreign envoys presenting their credentials. It was a malaise that was to plague all young kingdoms lacking in tradition.

The two men entered, halted at the door, then bowed to both king and queen. Alexander eyed them morosely, his gaze shifting from one to the other.

"You have my permission to leave, Colonel," he told Naumovich.

The equerry reacted with a nervous twitch of his lips. Quite clearly, the king's dismissal displeased him. He stood behind Vassilovich, his right hand moving to the bulge in his right trouser pocket caused by a small gun he had managed to borrow from someone before escorting in the captain, and he flashed a conspiratory wink at the king.

"Wouldn't it be advisable if I stayed, sire?" he asked.

"That won't be necessary," the king said. Then, with an impatient wave of the royal hand. "Out!"

This time, there could be no doubt in Naumovich's mind that an order had been issued. Bowing with a sigh, he left. Draga wondered what had caused the usually so apathetic Mika's sudden interest in what Michael and the king were about to discuss.

Michael advanced a few steps and halted at the required three-meter distance from the king. "Captain Vassilovich respectfully reporting, your majesty."

The king's expression darkened a few shades. "I ought to have you arrested, Vassilovich. Court-martialled and hanged for

treason. I have a mind to do it, too, because I am not frightened
of you and your fellow traitors. I am not as dumb as you think.
I happen to know who they are and will swoop down on them
and burn out the entire hornets' nest. I have two thousand
officers in my army, loyal and honorable men, and I shan't
allow a small group of rotters to alienate them from me by
spreading filthy lies about my regime. They say that I withhold
their pay, don't grant them promotions and refuse them entrée
into the Konak. Yes, their pay is withheld if they're caught
embezzling regimental funds, they're granted no promotions if
they're unable to pass the required examinations, and they're
barred from my court if they have the manners of swineherds
and smell of sweat and horse manure."

Standing at rigid attention, Michael stared fixedly at the
royal face as it turned livid with self-willed indignation. The
queen, curled up on the sofa, looked on with the frustration of
a guest trapped into listening to a piano recital by the son of
the house.

"I don't spend my days at racetracks and my nights in gambling casinos like Papa. I work eighteen hours a day and stay
awake at nights worrying about the country's ills, yet nothing I
do is right and everything Papa did was splendid." Alexander
halted, waiting for some reaction from Michael. When the captain maintained a noncommittal silence, he went on. "I'm getting tired of this joyless struggle, this uphill fight. I am now
suggesting a truce. Extending an olive branch to the officers'
corps. If your friends will give me a short time in which to
settle things my way, I shall—"

The queen, both hands raised as though warding off a suddenly materialized ghost, rose to her feet. "Stop it, Sasha. Let's
not resort to schemes. They won't work. I want out, and I want
you out with me."

Alexander glared at her indignantly. "I don't know what
you're talking about, madame."

"Of course, you do. You're no longer in a position to propose
deals. Or ask for another reprieve."

"Madame, you're forgetting that you are the Queen of Serbia."

"Of course, I am the Queen of Serbia. Née Lunyevitza. That
is something *you* seem to be forgetting. I am not Marie Antoi-
nette, daughter of an empress, but the daughter of the poor and

wretched Lunyevitzas. Consequently, when it'll come to my being guillotined, you won't see me mount the scaffold in royal dignity— No, Sasha. I'll be dragged up there, pleading and screaming like another king's whore, Madame du Barry."

The king turned purple with rage. "Madame, what language!"

"Sasha, I am frightened. For you and for myself. Let's just pack and go."

Alexander looked at her icily. *"Dois-je comprend, madame, que vous voulez quitter le pays?"*

"You know very well what I mean."

"I am shocked, madame," Alexander screeched. "After what I've done for you. You've conspired with the enemies of my house. And that amounts to treason. For that I shall have you arrested and tried. I can do it because I am still king. You won't be the first queen to be tried and found guilty. Look into the history books. You'll find more than one example. Just look and—" Suddenly, choking as though a lump had lodged itself in his throat, he grew pale and stumbled. Michael leaped to his side, catching him before he could fall, then helped him to the sofa. For a long moment, Alexander sat inertly, his large head hanging from his thin neck like an oversize squash from its vine. The queen kneeled down before him, cradling him in her arms.

"Sasha, dearest, what's the matter? Are you feeling ill? Shall I fetch your drops?" Quite obviously, his threats of arrest and trial had failed to make an impression on her.

He whimpered like a small boy. "How could I ever say such horrible things to you, Draga, *chérie*? Will you ever forgive me?" Suddenly, he remembered that they weren't alone, and pushing her away gently, he rose.

"The queen is right, Vassilovich." His voice was now calm. "I must abdicate. But don't for a moment think that I am fleeing before a revolt. If it weren't for the queen, I'd stay and face it. But she is the most important human being in the world to me. If I can't make her happy, my life is not worth living." He paused to remove his tear-streaked pince-nez and with it ten years of his age. His pudgy face, unlined except for the two frown wrinkles on his forehead, became surprisingly young, his myopic eyes giving it the vulnerable quality of the mentally retarded. The glasses, Michael realized, were a mask behind which a small boy lost in the world of adults tried to hide. "You're familiar with my life, Vassilovich, so you'll believe that before meeting Queen Draga, I didn't know what happiness was. I was born under an unlucky star, on the day my father's army suffered a most humiliating defeat. I grew up like no other boy in the country, not because I was a prince, but because I had a battlefield for a home, where Mama and Papa fought till death did them part. I wasn't their child. I was their prey to be carried off after a successful raid. Then I found a peaceful haven in the love of a good woman. The tragedy of my life isn't that I've failed to be a great king, but that I've failed to be a good husband."

"Dearest, that's not true," Draga murmured. "You've done more for me than you should've."

Alexander breathed a kiss on her hair. "I am crushed, Vassilovich. I was given a chance for a happy life and I've botched it. I thought that by making her my queen, I was doing the right thing for her. Instead, I exposed her to the murderous hatred of the whole country." He turned to her. "Queen of Serbia, tell us now: Whom do you hate?"

Draga smiled nervously. His performance embarrassed her. "What's the matter with you, Sasha? I don't hate anyone. Why should I?"

Alexander turned to Michael. "I don't either. Yet I am hated. Even by those who've received nothing but kindness from me. Why? Because I am the son of a king and a king myself? Because I wasn't born in a fisherman's hut somewhere on the Danube? All right. Let's suppose that by exercising my royal prerogatives, I've antagonized a few. But what has she done? A gentle, lovely woman? Good God, I should never have made her queen. The world is full of beautiful places. 'Know'st thou the land where the lemon trees bloom and the golden orange glows in the thicket's dark gloom?' " He paused dramatically to brush away a tear.

Michael listened with a mixture of embarrassment and compassion, feeling like someone who, by accident, has glimpsed the physical disability of a man hitherto considered sound of limb. Self-pity always rubbed him the wrong way, especially when it was as misguided as Alexander's, yet the young man's blind and destructive devotion to his wife touched him despite his better judgment.

"Has it ever happened to you, Vassilovich?" the king asked. "Have you ever realized too late you missed a fork in a road from a path that could have led you to happiness?"

"It certainly has," Michael answered truthfully, failing to add it was the same fork, the same path and the same woman.

"You told me you were willing to inform your friends of the king's decision to abdicate," Draga reminded him. "Do you want a formal letter?"

"A line with his majesty's signature will do."

Deep in thought, the king began pacing the floor. Reaching an important decision was always a nerve-racking experience for him. To move about helped him hide his confusion. Michael was amused to find himself comparing the king's comical half limp to that of a kangaroo. He had once heard that the famous actor Coquelin appearing in Molière's *Misanthrope* at the Belgrade National Theater, had copied the king's walk for the part, causing royal indignation and more than a few snickers.

Alexander spoke at last. "It's a fact known in Belgrade and also mentioned in the foreign press that the queen is planning to take the cure in Franzensbad during the summer. So we shall issue a court bulletin announcing the queen's departure, let's say, by the end of the week."

"I'd suggest forty-eight hours, your majesty," Michael replied curtly.

The king gave him a long look. "All right, forty-eight hours. We shall add that being concerned about her majesty's health, we shall accompany her on the trip. While she is taking the cure, I'll remain abroad to negotiate with the Skoda factory for the new seventy-five mm field guns. Yes, it will seem like a plausible explanation for our leaving the country and allow your friends to stage their *coup d'état* in our absence. It will naturally prevent us from returning to Serbia." He halted in his perambulation to ask, "Does that appear sensible to you?"

"Perfectly, your majesty."

"At least, it won't look as though we were running for our lives, and it gives us a dignified way out." He turned to the queen. "I'd better write that note now. Where do you keep paper and pen?"

"On my desk. You'll find some of your own stationery in the drawer."

After the king had left for her bedroom, Draga turned to Michael.

"I've done my part, Mika. Now you'll have to do yours."

"I shall, Draga."

She gave him a sad smile. "I once loved you very much. If you had only loved me a little more—"

He felt a nervous, throbbing sensation at the pit of his stomach. It had been a long, trying day, and its frustrations were beginning to take their toll. "More than a little. I was a damn fool, Draga. Will it make you feel any better if I tell you that I am sorry for both of us."

She emitted a tired laugh. "Not for me! Had I stayed with you, I would never have become Queen of Serbia."

The door creaked open behind them as the king reentered. With a jaunty gesture, he handed Michael a page on which were scrawled a few lines: "I hereby solemnly swear to leave Serbia together with my beloved wife, Queen Draga, not later than May 31, 1903 (O.S. calendar) June 13, 1903 (N.S. calendar) and subsequently abdicate my throne." It bore the date and the royal signature.

"Are you satisfied?" he asked Michael. "We'll need to give ourselves three days. After all, we have to pack. There are a few things I'd hate to leave behind. The crown jewels, for instance." He wore the carefree grin of a schoolboy on the first day of school vacation.

His cheerful mood disturbed Michael. Did it mean that Alexander was merely playing one of his deceitful little tricks and that there were more surprises to follow? The smile, however, faded from the king's face, giving way to an unhappy grimace.

"It's done, Draga," he said. "There is no way back." He took her hand and lifted it to his lips. "Will you have regrets?"

She stroked his face. "Never. And I promise you that you won't have any either."

"You have my permission to leave, Vassilovich," Alexander said in a suddenly hostile tone, and turning his back on Michael, he pointedly ignored the captain's parting salute.

As Michael crossed the entrance hall on his way out, his glance fell on Milan's large stuffed bear, and he felt the sting of

an old sorrow. For some time after Milan's death, the image he
had been able to conjure up of him was one of a dying man,
pale, emaciated, broken in spirit. Now suddenly, in his mind's
eye, the ghost took on the appearance of its most vigorous years.
Once again, Milan seemed very much alive. Alive and immortal as only the deeply loved dead can be.

The bear in its monstrosity was an odd memorial to the ex-
king, yet in Michael's sight it *was* a memorial, more fitting than
any statue or plaque. He paused in front of it, venerating his
dead friend's spirit with a moment of silence.

As he stood quietly, a hand clamped on his shoulder, and he
turned to face a visibly perturbed Naumovich.

"What did they want from you?" he asked, keeping his voice
down. They were alone in the entrance hall, but the door to
the crowded anteroom was open and people moved in and out
of the various offices.

"What did who want from me?" Michael asked, though he
understood the colonel's question.

"The king and the queen. What did they want?" It was the
voice of a badly frightened and desperate man, but Michael also
realized that Naumovich was very drunk.

Ever since the seven o'clock meeting at the fortress, Michael
had had his doubts about the wisdom of Naumovich's enlist-
ment in the conspiracy. He was familiar with the man's shady
reputation, and Naumovich's behavior at the meeting had only
served to aggravate his apprehensions.

"They wanted to talk to me," he answered testily.

"Did you tell them about tonight. About me?" In Naumovich's shifting eyes Michael recognized madness. He knew he
had to proceed with great caution, as if he were defusing a
bomb.

"Don't be ridiculous, Colonel," he said, feigning nonchalance. "They found out I'd been to Geneva and tried to get
some information about Prince Peter. They suspected that I'd
brought a message from him. Of course, I denied it. They had
no proof, so at the end they believed me and let me go. That
was all."

Naumovich clung to his doubts. "They know."

"Of course not."

"Maybe he doesn't, but she does. She is not stupid, you know.

I sometimes have the feeling that she suspects me." Seized by a sudden attack of dizziness, he reached out for Michael, grabbing his arms with both hands and almost knocking him off his feet. "Oh God, this terrible day. How I wish it were over. How I wish I'd never lived to see it."

10 P.M.

IT HAD been a trying day for the men in the Konak guardhouse. For one thing, all leaves had been canceled, officers ordered to remain on duty, or if relieved earlier, to return to the palace grounds.

A mood of nervous irritability prevailed. There had been too many false alarms during the past weeks and their effect was showing on the general morale. Colonel Naumovich had sent down a few bottles of wine to the officers' room earlier in the evening with an accompanying note which stated that the gentlemen deserved some refreshment to make their overlong duty hours bearable.

The colonel had put Lieutenant Peter Zivkovich in charge of doling out the wine. Two vintage bottles of rare Pommard, already uncorked, were especially marked for the commander of the Palace Guards, Captain Panayotovich. Despite the captain's mild protest that he wanted to keep a clear head, the lieutenant poured out a large tumblerful for him.

"You must be parched, Captain, the way you have been on your feet all day in this terrible heat. You might as well take a short nap now. It's not as if you were alone in the guardhouse. If you ask me, the whole alert is one of General Laza's whims. To make himself important, to prove to the king that he is constantly on the lookout. Yovan Miljkovich has just reported in. He says there is absolute quiet in the city. Couldn't be more peaceful."

"Wasn't Yovan supposed to be off tonight?"

"Yes, he was. Poor fellow. He's very worried. His wife is days overdue. The doctors told him if she doesn't give birth tonight, they'll have to operate. He should've stayed home, but you know how he is. Sensitive about being the premier's son-in-law. Service above and beyond the call of duty."

The commander thirstily emptied his tumbler and made a wry face. "What sort of wine is this? It has an odd taste."

"It's a great wine," Zivkovich assured him eagerly, holding up the bottle. "A Pommard. French. The best. That's why it seems different. Not like our wines. That odd taste is really the mark of quality."

Panayotovich threw a doubtful glance at the bottle. It was probably the first Pommard of his life. A captain of the Serbian Palace Guards could ill afford French wines. Even the domestic product had become expensive since the phylloxera scourge of the 1880's had laid waste most of Serbia's vineyards.

Zivkovich refilled the tumbler. "You'll see. A few more sips and you'll love it."

"A few more sips and I'll keel over," the captain protested. "Jesus, Maria, Joseph, am I tired! It has certainly been a long day." He emptied his glass. "You are right. It sort of grows on you. Why don't you have some?" He poured out half a glass for the lieutenant.

Zivkovich shied from it as if the dusty tumbler were about to explode. "Better not. One of us has to stay sober."

"I am sober," the captain snapped. "You won't find a man in this whole goddamn army who's ever seen me drunk on duty. And certainly not after two glasses of some fancy wine." He examined the bottle. "Pommard!" He spat out the name with the fierce chauvinism of the Serb patriot.

"Certainly not, Captain." Zivkovich grinned placatingly. While busying himself with order blanks on the desk, he threw furtive glances at the older man. Slumped down on the leather sofa, the commander now reached for the wine he had poured for the lieutenant. Discreetly Zivkovich turned away. He heard the captain gulp down the wine, then drop the tumbler to the floor. There was a long silence, then the sound of muffled snores, which announced clearly that Captain Panayotovich had fallen asleep.

The small white house built in one of the side streets of Teraziya boasted a picket fence around its front yard in which a cluster of lilac and jasmine bushes grew like a veritable jungle. The house belonged to George Genchich, ex-home minister, since his loudly voiced objection to Alexander and Draga's marriage one of the "untouchables." Like Colonel Mashin, he, too, had been placed on the retired list and was shunned by all who still enjoyed or hoped to enjoy royal favors.

Michael had to knock twice on the front door before it was finally opened by Madame Genchich. He had been to the house in the past, usually in the company of King Milan or carrying messages for him, but it took the woman some time to recognize him.

Unless invited, people seldom made social calls at such late hours, and a persistent knocking on a door, especially on the door of a politician fallen from grace, portended no good.

When told by Michael that he wished to speak to Colonel Mashin, Gordana Genchich answered that she would look into the backyard, where her husband was cooling off after the hot day in the company of friends and see if the colonel was among them. Still suspicious of the late visitor, she asked him to wait outside on the small front porch. A few minutes later she returned to invite him into the parlor.

"Sorry for having been so inhospitable," she apologized. "You must understand how things are nowadays. You can't trust your own brother. I know you were King Milan's man, but so many people change sides, sell their loyalties for a mess of pottage." She threw an anxious glance at the door leading to the backyard, where the men sat around a rough-hewn table with bottles of schnapps before them. "I shouldn't have said that. My husband gets angry with me when I talk too much."

After a day spent in Belgrade, the deferential attitude of the women still embarrassed Michael. He had lived too long in the West to allow a friend's wife or mother to kiss his hand or to hover humbly behind his chair throughout a visit while he remained seated. Of course, there were women who, under the court's influence, had become boldly emancipated, attended social functions with their husbands, drank with the men and talked politics in public. But Gordana Genchich was not one of them.

Colonel Mashin strode in from the garden. "What is it now, Captain?" he asked in a harshly reprimanding tone.

The hostess' timid glance flickered from one man to the other; then she scurried from the room.

"You must know it's important; otherwise, I wouldn't have come here," Michael told him, annoyed. His nerves were wearing thin. "Here, read this." He proffered the king's note to Mashin, too irked to add the obligatory "sir."

Recognizing the letterhead, Mashin shrank from the note as if it had come from a plague-infested house. "What is it?" he asked.

"Read it, then you'll know."

Mashin pulled a case holding a pair of metal-framed glasses from his breast pocket. The caution with which he handled the spectacles bespoke a man in strained circumstances who could ill afford to have them replaced should they break. Having hooked them safely behind his ears, he reached for the note. For an interminably long time, he stared at the scrawled longhand in silence. "What is this supposed to mean?" he asked without looking up.

"Just what it says, sir. That King Alexander is willing to leave the country voluntarily."

"In three days." The colonel shifted his glance from the paper to Michael's face.

"Exactly."

"But he might be dead in three days." He spoke with clarity and finality, like a judge pronouncing sentence.

"Not if you call off the coup tonight," Michael retorted, realizing that he was now arguing a lost case, not only Alexander's, but his own. Still, his steadily growing dislike for Mashin forced him to continue. "I've talked to both Queen Draga and King Alexander. I didn't approach them; the queen sent for me. She's received repeated warnings about a possible coup and is terrified. She knows no details, only that their lives are in danger. Her influence over Alexander is still enormously strong, and though he first showed some resistance, she convinced him that he must get out." Michael paused for Mashin's reaction. Receiving only a blank stare, he went on. "We all know Prince Peter's attitude. I feel this note from Alexander is what he had hoped for: a chance for an orderly transition of power. I am sure you recognize the handwriting and can tell it is not forged."

Mashin nodded. "It's genuine, all right." He gave the paper a second look, then slowly, pensively tore it into small pieces. He grinned at Michael, the waxen hardness of his features melting into a small boy's waggish deviltry. "That takes care of his majesty's *billet-doux*. Any more messages up your sleeve, Captain? From the gallant Lunyevitza brothers? Or perhaps his excellency General Tzintzar-Markovich?"

The sight of the grinning face engendered a rage close to insanity in Michael. Gripping the guard of his sword, he shouted at Mashin in a voice choked with hatred.

"You bloody maniac, you want them all slaughtered because of her. You couldn't fuck her, so now she must die. You've been waiting nineteen years to have your revenge. That's what your whole coup is about. Not Prince Peter, patriotism, desire for a better government. That's all rot. You may fool Mishich and the rest, but not me. I know better."

The outbreak had taken Mashin by surprise. He tried to answer, but only a hoarse gurgle came from his throat, as he watched Michael struggle to whip out his sword, which refused to leave its sheath. For the past three years it had been hanging in a moldy cabinet in the Vassilovich house and become encrusted with rust. When girthing himself with it, the symbol of his officer's rank, in the morning, Michael did it mechanically, failing to realize that the need might arise for it as a weapon. Now the need had arisen, but the sword refused to serve him. Furiously, he emitted a stream of frustrated curses.

Mashin stirred from his numbness. His hand moved to the slightly bulging hip pocket of his black serge suit, fingers closing in on the small gun it held.

"Take back that muck or I'll kill you." He pointed the gun at Michael.

Michael had given up the hopeless struggle with the sword. Still blind with fury, he advanced on the colonel.

"The hell I will. And let me warn you, Mashin. If you go ahead with the coup despite the king's promise to step down, I'll—"

The colonel took a step back and cocked the gun. "*You* dare warn *me*? Who do you think you are? What right do you have to tell me how to handle this goddamn venture? I've lived with it for two years. Risked my life, risked my friends' lives. You

walked into it this morning. All right, you've brought a message from Prince Peter, who knows as little about Alexander's
machinations and trickery as you do. Don't either of you tell me
how to deal with him. And if Prince Peter doesn't approve of
my methods, I can always find a pretender who will."

"You're evading the issue, Colonel."

"I am not. I just don't think that your ridiculous accusation
merits the effort of a denial on my part. Yes, I hate the whore,
but only because I hold her responsible for my brother's death
and for the ruin of the country. Two very good reasons."

His suddenly avuncular, almost friendly tone had been in
odd contrast with the cocked gun. Michael sensed the effort
behind the forced calmness.

"We have laws. The severest sentence for a woman found
guilty of murdering her husband is twenty years, not death.
Found guilty by a court and not her brother-in-law."

"She probably told you some atrocious lies. And you believed
her, because you're a fool. And let me tell you something. It's
not I, but you who is still horny about her." He lowered the
gun. "Nevertheless, I won't shoot you, Vassilovich. It would
cause complications, possibly the postponement of the coup. It's
funny. That rust on your sword probably saved your life."

"Or yours."

"I don't think so. You might have wounded me, but I would
sure as hell have shot you. So let's just draw a veil over the
whole goddamn nonsense for the moment and concentrate on
the business at hand."

Somewhat calmer, Michael gave him a long look, trying to
find behind the pink-cheeked, thick-nosed Czech countenance
the secret man.

"God is my witness, I don't understand you. Why expose
yourself and your men to danger when there is a chance for a
bloodless coup? You don't trust Alexander. You may be right.
But what if you're wrong? Would a three-day postponement
make such a difference? Isn't a dignified and respectable take-
over worth waiting for? On my way here I've passed the Serbian
Crown. Do you know that about fourteen or fifteen of your
men, mostly subalterns, are staging a revelry that's scaring the
piss out of the civilians? They're so drunk already that by midnight they'll either pass out cold or go completely berserk.

Right now they're making enough noise to wake up both the living and dead in Belgrade."

The belligerence also seemed to have left Mashin. "No, Vassilovich," he said in an amicable tone. "The coup can't be called off. Not at this stage. Not without disastrous consequences. Orders have been dispatched to out-of-town posts to men who can no longer be contacted. They'll go ahead doing what was assigned to them, and if they're not backed up by us here in the city, they'll be in trouble. I don't have to tell you what it will mean for all of us if they fall into the hands of the secret police." He stuffed the shreds of the note into his coat pocket. "If little Sasha is really serious about the abdication, he can say so when we meet him face to face tonight. We're patriots, not savages. He is the King of Serbia, the son of Milan, our first independent sovereign in five hundred years. We don't want to befoul the royal throne with his spilled blood."

"I am relieved to hear that, Colonel," Michael told him.

This wasn't true; he was far from being relieved, for he doubted Mashin's sincerity. Something had to be done, though, and without delay. Draga must not die, he told himself. Whether he wanted to save her because he loved her or merely because he found the part of the accessory before the fact he had been tricked into playing distasteful seemed of no importance at the moment. His immediate concern was his escape from Mashin. He was afraid the colonel might forestall his leaving or assign a man to follow him.

George Genchich, the host, came in from the garden.

"It *is* you, Mika," he exclaimed jovially. "When Gordana told me that a Captain Vassilovich was looking for Mashin, I didn't believe it was you. I assumed you were still abroad."

"It is me all right," Michael said, annoyed. Damned politicians, he thought. Genchich with his violent anti-Alexander feelings had to be a member of the conspiracy, but he was still playing it safe. The fewer people knew about his involvement, the better for him should the coup fail.

"Come on, have a drink. You look as if you could use one." Putting his arms around the younger man's shoulders, he steered him toward the garden.

"Some other time. I was just leaving. Thank you anyway."

"Where are you going?" Mashin asked sharply.

"To meet my brother Voyislav at the Serbian Crown." On the spur of the moment, he could come up with no better excuse. Of course, Voyislav was home, no doubt fast asleep in bed.

"Go back to your guests, George, I'll see Vassilovich out." Mashin's tone, brisk and clear, parried all chances for an argument, leaving no doubt in Michael's mind that a man in command was talking to a subordinate. He wondered what portfolio Genchich was to be handed in the post *coup d'état* Cabinet.

"As long as you are going to the Serbian Crown," Mashin said to Michael after the ex-minister had obediently shuffled off, "I want you to have a talk with the men there. Warn them not to get out of line. Then join Dimitriyevich at the Officers' Club. The schedule is unchanged. We'll meet at one o'clock sharp in front of the South Gate to the Konak. And one more thing. I want no mention of the scribble from Alexander. To Apis or anyone else. Am I understood?"

"I am not deaf, Colonel," Michael replied testily.

As he turned toward the gate, Mashin's parting words caught up with him.

"That was an order, Captain, don't forget it."

"No, sir, I won't," Michael answered without looking back.

Fat, heavy raindrops cascaded off his shako, and looking up, he saw a flock of tattered clouds chased by a sudden squall, precursor of the long-overdue storm, waft across the sky. Where the clouds parted, stars twinkled with a brightness that caused them to seem almost reachable. He couldn't tell why, but the realization that the storm was merely brewing and wouldn't break for hours to come depressed him. Would a downpour disperse the conspirators before invading the Konak? he asked himself. Not likely. Ordinary demonstrators would probably run for cover before a threatening storm, but Colonel Mashin's men were more than demonstrators. They were hunters, eager enough to brave a Biblical deluge in the pursuit of their prey.

Walking down Mihajlova Boulevard, he had the sudden feeling of being followed. Despite the late hour, there were still people in the street, refugees from the unrelieved heat of their houses, stragglers from the Song Festival, peasants who had missed their trains or boats or simply couldn't tear themselves away from the wonders of the big city. From behind the open doors of the coffeehouses came the sound of cards being slammed down on tabletops by men who played with the imperturable taciturnity of deaf-mutes.

The lusty rhythm of a kolo, punctuated by the exuberant shouts of young male voices, could be heard from the direction of the Serbian Crown. As he was about to turn into a side street, a hack, drawn by a tired hag and with five lieutenants piled into it, passed him. To the accompaniment of an unhappy gypsy astride the nag and scraping away at his battered violin, the lieutenants bellowed a popular Suppé number. Michael thought he recognized pockmarked Lieutenant Bogdanovich among them. After waiting for them to pass, he hurriedly left the boulevard for an alley lined with chestnut trees. Even here, lights burned in several houses, as though people were staying awake waiting for some climactic event to end the day. Most likely, though, it was the heat that kept them up.

The sound of steps came from some distance away behind him. He halted under a streetlight and pretended to search in his wallet. His pursuer had stopped, too, melting into the shadows of a doorway. When Michael walked on, the man did, too. Michael wondered who had sent him, Alexander or Mashin, and what his orders were: merely to follow him or to do away with him.

He knew he had to shake off his pursuer and soon. A hack would have come in handy, yet the nearest stand was in front of the National Theater, and with the performance over, his chance of finding one seemed slim. Belgrade's cabbies were an independent breed. The fact that their services were most in demand on the night of a Song Festival failed to induce them to change their regular bedtime hours.

Michael passed the house belonging to a rich wine merchant with a store on the former Crown Street, now called Draga Street. He had known the family from the time when he had briefly courted one of the daughters, since married to another wine dealer and the mother of five future wine dealers. With sudden decision, he entered the yard through a small gate, passed the residence and headed for the stables that lay beyond a small flower garden.

No lights burned in the house or elsewhere on the grounds, with the exception of the small kerosene lamp hung from the ceiling in the stable. At the far end of the brick-paved center aisle, a farmhand lay snoring in a fodder box topped by a straw sack.

For a moment, Michael contemplated waking the man, but the loudness of his snores and the empty bottle at the foot of the fodder box changed his mind.

Six horses stood in the stalls along one side with young steers and milk cows bedded down in the straw across the aisle. Gently, so he wouldn't frighten the animals, Michael untied the gelding nearest the entrance and forced it to back out from its stall. His knowing touch and soft voice murmuring words of comfort into its ear worked like magic. He led the horse to the yard without waking the man or causing the rest of the animals to stir, except for a few low neighs from the gelding's teammate.

Outside, he stopped to listen. Behind the stable lay a vegetable garden which extended to the parallel side street. His ears picked up the snap of dry twigs breaking under a foot and the squeak of what must have been the rear gate. His pursuer had obviously failed to see him enter the stable, figuring that he had tried to elude him by crossing the merchant's property to the parallel street. He quickly swung himself onto the gelding's bare back, secretly pleased with his agility at the ripe age of thirty-seven, then steered the animal through the front gate, coaxing it into a fast gallop in the direction of Draga Street.

The neighborhood, only a few blocks from the main boulevards, seemed like another world, sleepy, serene and almost rural. As his thoughts vaulted the chasm of six years, he remembered that he had never passed the house he was now headed for without a twinge of pain and anger. It was the one, No. 16, where Draga had set up housekeeping when she became Alexander's official mistress. Since her marriage, the entire Lunyevitza tribe lived in it: her eldest sister, Maria Christina Petrovich with her son, George, the two younger sisters Voyka and Georgina and the brothers Nikola and Nikodiye.

As always, a lone soldier stood watch in front of the gate. He must have dozed standing like a horse, for he reacted to Michael's arrival with the torpor of a man roused from sleep by the ringing of an alarm clock. Confused, he stared at the dismounting captain, then whipped off his rifle with the fixed bayonet and pointed it at the intruder. As calmly, as if it were a tree branch obstructing his path, Michael pushed hand and rifle out of his way.

"At ease, man." He handed the horse's reins to the soldier. "Hold him for me. Is anyone still up in the house?"

The windows facing the street were dark. If there was light in the back, it didn't show.

The private's eyes shifted to the barebacked animal, then to Michael. For an officer in dress uniform he looked a bit rumpled, yet his tone left no doubt in the soldier's mind that he *was* an officer.

"I don't know, sir. The captains and the young ladies left some time ago, but Madame Petrovich is home."

Michael rang the bell, waited for a while, then rang again. At last, someone shuffled to the door and opened it to a narrow gap. Despite the poor light, Michael recognized the Croatian cook who had worked for him and Draga when they had lived in the cottage behind the Officers' Club.

"Jesus Maria, Captain Vassilovich!" the woman exclaimed. She was undecided whether to be pleased or apprehensive. After all, not only her mistress, but she too, had walked out on him.

Michael pushed the door open. "Let me in, Yovanka. I must see Madame Petrovich."

"She's gone to bed, Captain."

"Get her up. Quickly." When she hesitated, he raised his voice. "Go on!" Inside by then, he closed the door.

Before scurrying off, the woman switched on the light in the hallway. So this was the house, Michael thought, that a king had chosen for his nest of assignation. There were jars of home-made preserves on top of the wardrobes placed along the wall. Open double-winged doors led to salon and dining room, both furnished in a rather gaudy version of the Secession, a style he had always abhorred despite its great popularity among the rich of Vienna and Budapest. It was cold and *petit bourgeois,* the wrong background for a woman like Draga with the green eyes and soft, sensuous body of a sultan's concubine. It fitted Alexander, though, his pince-nez, long arms and legs with knobby knees and the grotesque thickness of his middle.

A door creaked, and lights were switched on amid a great

deal of excited female whispering. At long last, the eldest Lunyevitza sister, a middle-aged, plump and not entirely unpleasant caricature of Draga, came bounding out of her bedroom to
give him a a sharp look.

"I must say, this is an odd time for a visit, Captain." The first
session of the new Skupshtina was to enact a bill granting inviolability to the entire Lunyevitza tribe. She was already
adapting to conduct befitting her future royal status. "I asked
Yovanka if you'd been drinking. What on earth—"

He cut her short. "Let me have paper and pen. I have to
write a note to Draga."

Her eyebrows arched in reprimand; she crossed her arms
over the soft cushions of her breasts. "I don't think her majesty
would—"

He grabbed her by the shoulders. "Get some paper! A pencil
will do. And someone to take a note to Draga. Right now!
Don't you understand. It's important. Not for me, but for her!"

His tone broke down her resistance, and she crossed obediently to a console table in the salon, taking a pencil and a stack
of small cards with envelopes from its drawer. "Will these do?"

"Perfectly." He scribbled: "My mission unsuccessful, leave
immediately for Zimony. Mika," and slipped it into the envelope and sealed it. "Who can take this to her? It must be
someone with free access to the Konak whose appearance won't
attract notice. Someone who goes there all the time. What
about your brothers? The sentry said they'd gone out. Do you
expect them back shortly?"

"They are at the Konak. The girls, too. They were invited
for supper." She took the note and slipped it into the pocket of
her robe. "I had no idea you were in town. I thought you'd
settled abroad for good."

He grew impatient with her. "For God's sake, Maria, have
someone take this note to her right now! I would if it were
possible, but it is not."

"What is it all about?" she asked.

"Never mind that. It must reach her without delay. Delivered to her hands. It's a matter of life or death. Her life or
death!" For a moment, he wondered if he should tell the whole
story, then decided against it. Maria Christina was too much of
a goose to be trusted.

At last, she seemed to realize that the note was no social message. "My son, George. He's home, but he is sick. He's the only one I could send. Can't it wait till Nikodiye or Nikola come home?"

"Not one second! Get your son out of bed or go yourself."

"All right. I'll send him."

"And should he be asked at the Konak—by guards, staff, equerries—not a word about me. Understand?" She nodded. "Another thing. I left a horse with the sentry outside. Have your houseboy take it back to the Brankovich place. The wine dealer's. The boy is to say he found it loose in the street. But first, get George out of bed and off to the Konak."

At last the notion that Captain Vassilovich was neither drunk nor mad penetrated Maria Christina's easily confused mind. "All right, Mika, whatever you say." She started for her son's room. "Is Draga in some danger?" she asked, stopping at the door.

"Not if she gets that note," Michael told her. "I have to leave. Is there an exit through the back?"

"Yes, through the kitchen. Yovanka will show you."

The cook had remained in the hallway, eavesdropping. Now she drew her own conclusions. "They're in trouble, aren't they?" she asked Michael as she led him toward the back of the house. "I mean the king and Madame Mashin." It amused Michael to hear her refer to Draga by the old name evidently brought to the tip of her tongue by the ex-lover's unexpected reappearance. She had failed to notice the slip and went on chattering. "It's good of the captain to warn her. No other man would. I told her not to leave the captain for that young fellow. True, he was the king, but it's better to be village kmet and loved by the people than be the king and hated. Because he is hated like the plague, and so is she. And nobody makes a secret of it. I told my lady, Madame Petrovich, that I won't do the shopping anymore because of the filthy talk at the marketplace. People know I am working for the Lunyevitzas and keep harassing me. Call me names, slip rotten fruit and vegetables into my shopping bag. I once found a dead rat in it. I can pick the best cuts at the butcher's, but when I unwrap the meat at home, half of it is gristle. They also overcharge me. I have a hard time making my lady believe that it's not me cheating her. I would've quit long ago, but where can I go? Nobody wants to hire a person who's worked for the Lunyevitzas."

She let him out through the back door. "God be with you, Captain!" she called after him. "You are a good man!"

Headed for Milosh Boulevard, he groped his way through a maze of alleys. Not a living soul stirred in the neighborhood of one-story white houses with shingled roofs, set in neat green garden patches. They looked like the toys of a giant child left scattered on the carpet after their owner had gone to bed. It amazed him how little it all had changed since he'd last walked the crooked, unpaved streets untouched by the kind of urban development that inflicted some architectural monstrosities on the main boulevards. He wondered how the hatred engulfing the Konak could emanate from houses as clean, neat and guile- less as these. He, one man alone, was trying to stanch the flow of that murderous hatred, an act as desperate as that of the legend- ary Dutch boy who had saved his city by keeping his finger in the crack of the endangered dike.

He was willing to risk his life for a woman who moved in and out of his life like a stray cat, never losing her hold on him. He desperately wanted her saved, because he now realized that her death would burden him with an insupportable guilt, not so much for his participation in the coup, as for his failure to yield to her magnetic power in the past.

Her attraction had always been a riddle to him. No great beauty or brain, she nevertheless exuded an inexplicable magic to which men reacted with the most startling emotions. Did the wild young officers, drinking themselves into frenzy at the Ser- bian Crown, he wondered, hate her because she was an unfit queen or because she elicited feelings from them that embar- rassed them? Were they driven by the same lust as the Parisian Monsieur Jurieux, pounding on her door, screaming bloody murder because she had refused to give herself to him?

11 P.M.

THE band of the Royal Guards had taken its place in the corner of the entrance hall. As always, it was to entertain with a concert of popular music during supper. In the event the party stretched into the early morning hours, it would continue with either classical selections or dance numbers, according to the queen's mood. The program had been submitted to her for approval, yet this time she sent it back, leaving the choice to the conductor. There were rumors among the staff of her indisposition and the possibility that she might not appear at supper. The king had gone to her suite, keeping the guests and the kitchen staff waiting for what seemed an interminably long time.

Nicola Lunyevitza, looking as resplendent in his gala uniform as the *bon vivant* of a Millöcker operetta, was trying to relieve his hunger pangs by telling risqué jokes to middle-aged Ila Konstantinovich, the *mademoiselle d'honneur* on duty. Draga insisted on having only females of unblemished reputation in her entourage. Ila, a certified virgin, though blushing to the roots of her thinning hair, made no attempt to escape the young man.

His brother, Nikodiye, was in no mood for pleasantries. He was famished and grumbled loudly about his brother-in-law's lack of consideration.

"Sasha keeps complaining that he has no rapport with his Cabinet ministers," he told Naumovich. "He says they are stupid and comatose, unable to understand him. But how on

277

earth does he expect them to be bright and alert when they live by a different timetable. He rises when they go to bed and orders them to conferences when they are on their way home after a day's hard work. Just look at poor Marinkovich. Called home from Sofia in a hurry, he sat up all night on the train, has been at Sasha's beck and call since noon and will have another long talk with Sasha after supper."

Freshly shaved and wearing an immaculate dress uniform, Naumovich listened to the young man with a set grin that made him resemble a cheerful but unfathomable Buddha. He seemed sober, able to stand and walk without faltering, yet on the rare occasions when he opened his mouth, his speech was slurred and never quite to the point. His open-and-shut grin was too grotesque to escape Nikodiye's attention.

"What's the matter, Colonel? Anything wrong?"

Naumovich blinked. "Wrong? Why should anything be wrong? No—I was just wondering. Should I see what's keeping their majesties?"

Laza Petrovich now moved to them. He had been talking to the two Lunyevitza girls, both lovely, Voyka in pink and Georgina in pale blue. At eighteen, Georgina, nicknamed Golubche, little dove, was a real beauty with young Draga's sparkling eyes, rose-petal mouth and full-breasted slimness.

"The girls are inconsolable," Laza reported. "They were so much looking forward to meeting Lutchich Dalmatov. Now they hear he's sent his regrets. Won't come tonight. Caught the grippe on the train."

A Serb from Dalmatia and one of the leading actors in the Imperial Russian Court Theater, Dalmatov was scheduled to appear in Belgrade for a week beginning on June 11.

"If you ask me, it takes a bit of cheek from a Russian clown to turn down a supper invitation from the Queen of Serbia. If he is so sick, how will he play tomorrow night?"

Nicola, tired of shocking Ila, crossed over to them. "One of Chief Marshityanin's agents told me that Dalmatov had left for St. Petersburg."

"That's impossible!" Voyka said. "The city is full of placards announcing the engagement."

"The agent was quite positive. Said he'd seen him go through passport control this afternoon."

"That's odd," Georgina chimed in. "All performances are sold out. We have tickets for Saturday night. We want to go with Maria Christina and the Tzintzar-Markoviches."

"It seems you won't go," Nikodiye pointed out, "unless you want to sit through a performance of the local company—a punishment I wouldn't wish on my worst enemy." He pulled out his watch and glanced at it. "Speaking of punishment. It's fifteen past eleven. I am starved. Five more minutes and I'll die of hunger. If I do"—he turned to Laza—"don't give me a military funeral. Have the six prettiest girls of the Orpheum chorus line be my pallbearers. And the band play Offenbach's cancan while my coffin is lowered into the grave."

Everyone laughed except Naumovich, who glared at the young man with unconcealed distaste. "That was an unfunny joke, Captain," he muttered, walking away from the group.

Nikodiye looked after him, perplexed. "What's the matter with the fellow?"

"He's probably had one too many," Laza suggested.

"Or is sober for a change," Nicola suggested. "Yes, that's the trouble with him. A most unusual condition for Mika Naumovich."

The door to the royal apartments was thrown open by two footmen. Preceded by Court Marshal Nikoljevich, the king and queen entered the hall, Alexander wearing a general's undress uniform and Draga a gown made of lace-appliqued white voile, a masterpiece of the Viennese House of Drecoll.

"Oh, Draga, angel, you are beautiful!" Georgina exclaimed, forgetting to address her sister as prescribed by the rules of court etiquette. About to dash up to her, she caught sight of Voyka and Mademoiselle Konstantinovich executing deep curtsies and quickly followed suit.

Indeed, Draga looked unusually attractive and not only to Georgina's loving eyes. She was very pale, her cheeks unrouged and her dark hair gathered in a loose chignon on the top of her head. The lack of makeup, the disarray of her coiffure and the veiled sadness in her eyes caused her to seem younger than her age and strangely vulnerable. Even Envoy Marinkovich, who, like most people, had been at a loss to explain her power over the young king, felt strangely drawn to her, not only as a subject, but also as a man.

He was invited to join the party only after Dalmatov's note had reached the Konak. With his substitution for the actor they were to be twelve at the table.

"In case your majesties are interested"—Nikodiye unceremoniously outshouted the first strains of *Les Contes d'Hoffmann* overture intoned by the band—"I am starved."

Alexander frowned his disapproval. Though resigned to naming Nikodiye heir to the throne, he had never really liked the young man. In a way, he was attracted to him, telling himself that it was because of Nikodiye's resemblance to Draga. At times, in a drunken state, he had even felt a fleeting desire to have Nikodiye's masculine leanness replace Draga's eiderdown warmth in his bed, but exorcised the dangerous thoughts from his mind as he had so many similar ones in the past.

Draga represented safety and stability. As long as he held on to her, there could be no doubt about his manhood.

With the queen on his arm, Alexander led the way into the dining room. As they passed Nikodiye, Draga reached out and gently stroked the cheek of this brother, who could do no wrong.

"*Mon Prince*," she whispered with a melancholy smile. "I am sorry. We had something important to discuss with Sasha. You will be pleased when I tell you. It is something that concerns all of us." She changed to a lighter tone. "I've ordered your favorite dishes for supper. Young roast goose, a *primeur* from Hungary and *soufflé au chocolat*."

"The goose will be dry as an eagle and the soufflé flat as a pancake," Nikodiye said. "I wouldn't like to be your chef, that's for certain."

Alexander threw him a grim glance. "You might wish one day to have been only our chef."

Lieutenant George Petrovich had been fast asleep when his mother came into the room to shake him awake and tell him to dress and take a message to his Aunt Draga in the Konak. Ill with grippe and still running a fever, nevertheless, he obediently sat up and slipped to the edge of the bed, his feet probing for his pantoufles. As he tried to stand up, he was bathed in perspiration and seized by a dizzy spell.

"Hurry, George, it's a matter of life or death."

His mother, he knew, was fond of the dramatic and enjoyed crises. For the past week she had kept him covered with down-filled comforters, changing the cold compresses across his chest every two hours. She'd worried that his illness might turn into pneumonia or galloping consumption, but now, although he was too weak to stand, she was sending him out into the night.

"I am still feverish, Mama. Feel my forehead."

"You're not," she said after lightly touching his cheek. She made him take off his nightshirt, rubbed down his moist body with a bath towel, then helped him into his uniform.

"What is this all about?" he asked, peeved.

"Never mind that." She handed him the sealed envelope. "Just take this letter and hand it personally to Draga. Then come home."

"Is the carriage ready?"

"No. I don't want you to wake up the neighbors. It's just a few blocks. The walk won't kill you."

"But I am so weak."

"That's understandable. Anyone would be after ten days in bed. Dr. Gashich said this morning that the infection has completely cleared up except in the bronchial tubes, whatever they are."

As always, his mother won. A woman of iron will, she was the true head of the Lunyevitza tribe. Her sister's confidante and adviser, she was also responsible for many a royal decision, among them the prime ministerial appointment of General Tzintzar-Markovich, her ex-lover.

George Petrovich left the house through the back door. He took a deep breath of the balmy night air, hoping it would dispel his dizziness. Feeling a strange softness in his joints that caused his knees to buckle at each step, he was completely exhausted by the time he reached the Konak gates.

The guards were green recruits who didn't recognize him and refused to let him enter. After a long dispute, they agreed to call Lieutenant Zivkovich to the gate.

He and the lieutenant had been classmates and close friends at the Military Academy, both graduating at eighteen, he with barely passing marks, Zivkovich as number three. Nevertheless, it was he who was admitted to the War College, while Zivkovich was assigned to field duty and later transferred to the

Palace Guards. His preferential treatment by the throne antagonized his former classmates who ostentatiously avoided all contact with him. Zivkovich alone remained unchanged. Although they did not see each other as frequently as before, no dissonant note intruded upon their relationship.

Since Draga had become queen, George had free entry into the Konak any time of the day or the night. Now he expected Zivkovich to order the gate opened as usual. To his surprise, the lieutenant merely stared at him, visibly displeased.

"What do you want?" he asked.

"To see my aunt. What else?" He pointed at the guards. "These fellows don't seem to know who I am. They must be straight from the pasture."

"We've been ordered to apply special security measures tonight. No one is to be admitted without General Laza's permission."

It was George's turn to look displeased. "Damn it, Peter, you don't need anyone's permission to let *me* in."

"I'm afraid I do."

"So get it."

"The general can't be disturbed now. He's having supper with their majesties."

George felt his head spin. The scene had taken on an aspect of unreality. It seemed as though they were standing on the ocean floor and he were looking at Zivkovich and the guardsmen through a wall of undulating water.

"Don't be ridiculous, Peter. When Laza said to keep people out he didn't mean me." He raised his voice. "Let me in. That's an order!" As first lieutenant, he outranked Zivkovich. To give the order added emphasis, he grabbed the gate and shook it. This gesture, however, failing to make the hoped for impression on Zivkovich, merely caused his arms to hurt.

"Go home, George." His friend's tone held a pleading note.

"Get Captain Panayotovich. He'll let me in."

Zivkovich looked ill at ease. "He's busy right now."

A swift gust of wind swept down the boulevard. Despite his mother's rubdown, George felt clammy all over. A few seconds earlier he had been hot; now he shivered with cold. "I've brought a letter for my aunt. It's urgent. I was sick in bed for a week. My mother made me get up. Don't let me stand here in this wind. I'll catch my death."

"You do look sick," Zivkovich agreed. "Why don't you leave the letter with me? I'll give it to the queen. You go home. And stay there, will you?" Once again, there was an anxious undertone to Zivkovich's voice.

Later, when George replayed the scene in his memory, he grew angry with himself for having given the letter to the lieutenant. There couldn't have been an order issued to lock him, the queen's nephew, out of the Konak, it must have been Zivkovich's invention. For some reason his friend was determined to keep him away from the Konak. He had grown tense, almost panicky when insisting that he, George, go home. What could be the reason? A female visitor in the guardhouse or some other kind of irregularity? If he hadn't felt so wretched, he would have taken the trouble to find out. Instead, he considered the mission completed and started for home.

On the way back, he was halted by a fainting spell. He had to lean, like a drunk, against a wall till it passed. Although he saw a light in his mother's window, he tiptoed straight to the room he shared with his two uncles and crawled into bed. When Maria looked in on him a few minutes later, he feigned sleep and answered her question about the delivery of the letter with inarticulate mumbles.

When Michael entered the veranda of the Serbian Crown, he could tell by the heightened volume of the noise that a great deal of wine and schnapps had flown down thirsty throats during his absence. Most civilians had left the place, but the military seemed to have multiplied by amoeban division. Of the men present at the seven o'clock meeting at the quartermaster sergeant's office he saw only Lieutenants Bogdanovich and Tankossich, each the center of a loud and unruly group. For a moment it looked as though a fight might break out between the two tables over the piece of music the gypsy band was to play. Bogdanovich demanded a waltz and when the gypsies, their eyes bleary with boredom and fatigue, complied, Tankossich's party ordered them to stop that Austrian cat's miaow and intone a folk song written by the blind guzlar Filip Visnjich. The moment the dispute erupted, the fiddlers, their bows lowered, froze into a tableau of nonalignment. Let the sons of bitches kill one another, was written on their dark faces.

Gypsies bore an unconcealed contempt for obstreperous

young officers, what's more, for the entire Serbian officers' corps so free with saber whippings and so tightfisted with the dinar. Through the Romany grapevine they had heard of Hungarian hussars, Russian granddukes and American heiresses who, after an especially gratifying spree, would paste thousand franc notes on the foreheads of their favorite bandleaders or throw a handful of louis d'ors into the fountain on the Place de la Concorde and have the gypsies dive for it. Luck for a Belgrade gypsy was a swine dealer with a wad of Austro-Hungarian florins or an entrepreneur granted a government contract for building schools or supplying provisions for the army.

Before the debate over the band's selection could result in mass murder, someone suggested that the gypsies play "Queen Draga's Kolo."

After the royal marriage, when streets and public institutions were named after her, a few sycophant poets and musicians dedicated their works to her. Few were appreciated by the public. "Queen Draga's Kolo," a catchy tune, was the exception. It became popular not only in the capital, but throughout the country, played by guzlars, sung by marching soldiers and danced to by farm boys at rural festivals.

The captain who demanded the kolo was tall and gaunt, with the disturbingly fixed stare of a falcon. His face was very pale, except for two fever patches burning on his cheekbones. Lieutenant Bogdanovich introduced him to Michael as Mika Yosipovich. The name sounded familiar to Michael. After some rumination he remembered that this was the officer assigned the execution of the Minister of Defense.

In contrast with his comrades, Yosipovich was cold sober. Someone poured him a glass of *klekovacha,* the murderously strong juniper brandy. With trembling hands, he lifted the glass to his lips, took a small sip, then hastily replaced it on the table, grabbing one hand with the other to conceal its shaking.

Ever since he entered the veranda, Michael was debating with himself whether or not to tell the conspirators that the coup might as well be called off since the king's abdication had become a foregone conclusion. After his fruitless encounter with Colonel Mashin at the Genchich house, he had set out to comb the rendezvous places with the intention of giving the message to each group as if coming from Mashin, then leave town or hide out till things quieted down. There would be some confusion, he figured, probably sporadic violence, but the clockwork of conspiracy would suffer irreparable damage and the wanton slaughter would be prevented. Now, listening to the men's reckless talk, he realized that the revolt against Alexander Obrenovich was no longer the undertaking of one hundred and fifty officers, but a movement joined by the majority of the corps. There didn't seem to be a single man among the carousers at the Serbian Crown without, at least, a partial knowledge of the imminent coup. The oath of secrecy, sworn by the original participators, appeared no longer binding. There was a great deal of loose talk, braggadocio and profanity. If any of the civilians lingering at adjoining tables were secret police, they had to have cotton in their ears to miss what the shouting was about. Or were the police, too, involved in the conspiracy?

He walked over to the Kolaratz. The picture there was the same, though with less fire and fury. Colonel Mishich hadn't moved from his seat; only his companions had changed. Now he was surrounded by subaltern officers, all, if not completely sober, at least able to hold their liquor. Near the bandstand several tables had been pushed together for a party of about twenty young men, some in uniform. They, too, were drinking, but not quite as unrestrainedly as the men at the Serbian Crown. It might have been due to bandleader Mija's artistry or Mishich's presence that the men behaved. They listened misty-eyed to the violins and kept raising their glasses to the happiness of Mother Serbia. A cadet from the Military Academy was discreetly sick in a thicket of blooming jasmine bushes, and a few others, evidently not used to heavy drinking, had passed out or snored with their heads resting on the table. The picture was that of an average Saturday night, except that it wasn't Saturday.

As Michael stood in the entrance, surveying the scene, Artillery Lieutenant Milutin Lazarevich, a man he had known from past maneuvers, crossed to him. He wore a great coat buttoned up to his neck, and his oily skin glistened with perspiration.

"Where have you been, Mika?" Lazarevich asked. "Colonel Mashin was here a few minutes ago looking for you."

"At the Serbian Crown. Just coming from there."

"He'd been there, too, but didn't see you."

"What did he want me for?"

"I don't know. He seemed nervous about not finding you."

"Tell him to relax. I've been found. Now I'll go over to the Officers' Club and join Apis. Mashin may contact me there in case he gets worried again."

He no longer had any doubt that the man who'd shadowed him on his way to Maria Petrovich's house and whom he managed to escape had been dispatched by Mashin.

"If you go to the club, tell the men that the rendezvous is still set for one o'clock," Lazarevich told him, wiping his face with a handkerchief.

"What are you wearing that coat for in this heat?" Michael asked.

The lieutenant turned to face the high wall of the garden. With his back to the crowd, he unbuttoned the coat, allowing Michael a look at the thick cartridge belt around his middle.

"Just in case," he said, pointing at the dynamite patrons stuck into its loops. Milutin Lazarevich had enough explosive on him to blow up both the New and the Old Konak, as well as the entire inner city.

Midnight

AT THE sound of the cathedral bells striking midnight, Colonel Mishich rose from his seat. His companions were quick to leap to their feet, stirring the sleeping waiters into action. The colonel waited for all glasses to be filled, then raised his.

"God be with you, my friends," he told them, his gaze shifting from face to face. "May the dawn bring you the promise of a happy and honorable life." He had begun in a low tone that only the men close by could hear, then raised his voice to a loud "Long live our beloved motherland, Serbia!" Wishing his country well was every citizen's right. Not even eavesdropping secret agents could suspect treasonous intent behind the toast.

The response was thunderous *Zhiveo* shouts resounding from all corners of the garden. There was a round of glass clicking at the colonel's table, hugs and kisses with tears of *amor patriae* falling on perspiration-soaked tunics. The moment had a touch of the *morituri te salutamus* mood of gladiators about to enter the arena.

After leaving the garden, the colonel found a hack with the cabby fast asleep on the box at the stand in front of the restaurant. His unexpected luck cheered him. He had had a long day and was beginning to feel his age. It seemed like a good omen that he was saved the exertion of a fifteen-minute uphill walk.

The first two battalions of the Sixth Infantry Regiment were being assembled as he reached the fortress. Both commanding majors belonged to the group of thirty-five officers who had originally organized the conspiracy under Colonel Mashin's leadership. Most of their subalterns were aware of the purpose behind the midnight descent into town. The rest of the troops, however, were, as usual, issued marching orders without an explanation. There was some unavoidable ill humor, men awakened from deep sleep stumbling about in blind confusion, toes stepped on, faces slapped by impatient officers, drunk or merely cracking under the strain. The tension of the conspirators began to affect the men, spreading like a contagious disease.

Emerging from his quarters, where he had gone to relieve himself, kiss his wife and children good-bye and murmur a short prayer in front of the family icon, Colonel Mishich felt the general restlessness hit him in the face like steam from an overheated engine. He ordered all platoon commanders to step forward.

"Tell your men that the king has finally decided to expel Queen Draga from the country and has summoned us to stand by to protect him in case her partisans try to stir up trouble," he instructed them. The lie was no spur-of-the-moment invention; he had thought of it long before. Unlike Colonel Mashin, he considered the troops' refusal to participate in a coup against the sovereign a possibility to be reckoned with and to prepare for. While the king was still respected by some, Draga was hated by all. Mishich hoped that the prospect of having her, an ugly botch on Serbia's escutcheon, removed from the national scene might reconcile the men with the inconvenience of having to leave their bunks in the middle of the night.

The reaction of the troops was exactly what Colonel Mishich expected. A wave of *Zhiveo Kralj Alexander* rolled over the barracks yard as each lieutenant communicated the message to his men, turning their sullen moods into the cheerful expectation of schoolboys going to a football game. The unruly milling about ended; the squads fell in behind their corporals, the platoons behind their officers; and within five minutes both battalions were in proper marching formation.

As the first column reached the gate, the men broke into a lusty army song the lyrics of which contained a string of obscenities relating to Queen Draga's person and ancestry. They were immediately hushed and ordered to proceed in complete silence. Shod with opanki instead of the heavy boots of Western infantry, many even barefoot, the two thousand men moved through the deserted streets like a horde of monkeys, their intermittent chatter quickly repressed by watchful noncoms.

For the first time in three years, Colonel Mashin was changing into his gala uniform. A few days earlier he had taken the precaution of sending it to his tailor to have the seams let out. He was glad he had thought of it, because despite the alteration, the tunic fitted snugly around his middle. Forced idleness had caused not only his spirit to slacken, but his muscles as well.

Of his family, only his wife knew of the planned coup. With a heavy heart, she laid out his clothing, selecting the least frayed shirts, the most artfully mended shorts, and socks that she had intended as name-day gifts for him. Mashin, who had persistently refused to admit the possibility of failure to his fellow conspirators, was more truthful with her, and she was fully aware of the dangers facing him: death during the encounter, by his own hand should things take the wrong turn, by execution if taken alive.

As she looked at the man whom she had loved, served and respected throughout her adult life, the realization that within an hour he might be a corpse brought to mind all the indignities a body, especially an enemy's body, could be subjected to if allowed to fall into hostile hands. Thanks to her foresight, the king's men were not going to report that Colonel Mashin's wife was a woman who let her husband lead a revolt in soiled or torn underwear or socks that needed darning. It was shameful enough that a staff officer in the Serbian army, even though on the inactive list, was unable to afford a wardrobe befitting his status, that his gala uniform was in presentable condition only because he had been forbidden to wear it for three years.

Used to seeing him in shabby mufti, her heartbeat accelerated as she saw him emerge from the bedroom, resplendent in a light-blue tunic with heavy gold epaulets, red pantaloons and a row of glittering medals, among them the two-headed White Eagle and the Order of Milosh the Great, bestowed on him by the late King Milan. When he took her in his arms and kissed her, a sensation as sharp as the grip of a rough hand and at the same time strangely pleasant spread through her body. She knew it to be desire, a feeling she hadn't experienced since the birth of her youngest child and, even before that, only sporadically. She was glad it didn't show on her face, for she would have been ashamed if it had. She watched her husband leave the house perhaps never to return alive, as the storm slowly dulled in her old woman's body.

On his way to the Palilula Barracks, Mashin paid a brief call on an old friend, Colonel Ivan Pavlevich, also on the retired list since his stand against the royal marriage in the summer of 1900. The sight of Mashin in a gala uniform, with the once snow-white but now yellowed-with-age aigrette fluttering on his shako, conveyed to the older man that something portentous was in the making. When he was told about the coup which was to eliminate the Obrenovich dynasty in favor of the Karageorgevich, his reaction was a heated outburst.

"You're out of your mind! It's been barely twenty-five years since we ceased to be a Turkish province and became a fully independent European country. In the eyes of the world we must never revert to the old savagery. Alexander is a mean little bastard, but he is still our hereditary sovereign, and there have to be more civilized ways of easing him off the throne than a bullet in his guts. Don't do it, Mashin. Call off the coup. I implore you for the sake of God and common sense."

Mashin gave him a long, contemplative look. "And what if I tell you I won't? What will you do to prevent it?"

The colonel shrugged. "What can I do? Nothing. Lock myself in the house and pray. For both Alexander and you. Because if one of you has to die, rather him than you. I've always disliked him, long before the marriage, even when he was a small boy. He was a nasty little brat. Nevertheless, I still wish you'd reconsider the whole matter."

Slowly Mashin reached into his coat pocket. As though mesmerized, the colonel followed the movement of his hand. To his relief, it emerged holding a sheet of paper, not a gun.

"It's too late now. I couldn't call it off even if I wanted to, which, incidentally, isn't the case. However, as you've just said, I might be killed tonight. So here is my last will. I have very little wordly goods to leave to my wife and children, so look after them when I'm gone. My wife will be completely lost. I've never let her handle money or make decisions, even in the most trifling matters. Now I know it was a mistake, but it's too late to do anything about it." He paused, a wistful smile, so alien to his character, softening his features. "Too late for many things."

His friend embraced him, kissing him on both cheeks. "I'll do all I can for them. But see to it that you don't get killed. Even Peter Karageorgevich, a good man, isn't worth such a sublime sacrifice."

Michael reached the Officers' Club fifteen minutes after midnight. He was still a block away when a sudden gust of wind, harbinger of the brewing storm, wafted the strains of "Queen Draga's Kolo," played by a gypsy band and sung by a babble of male voices, through the sleeping streets.

He found the large dining room of the club deserted. Guests, band and orderlies had moved outdoors, where the air seemed less stifling, especially now with a fresh breeze stirring in the foliage of the tall chestnut trees. He entered the garden and was immediately halted in his tracks by the sight of thirty-odd officers, coatless, shirts open at the necks, their wine-reddened faces bathed in perspiration, stomping and kicking to the frenzied

music of seven gypsies. Men dancing was an everyday spectacle
in Serbia, for they danced when drunk or sober, happy or sad,
before or after a battle, but he'd never before seen the kolo
performed with such ferocious animal spirit as now. Their passion seemed to have mesmerized the band into drawing the
wildest and most disturbing sounds from their instruments.
The leader, his dark face illuminated by a white-toothed grin,
resembled a Hieronymus Bosch devil playing for the souls of
the damned.

Captain Dragutin Dimitriyevich, apparently as drunk as the
rest, appeared to be the nucleus of the demon-ridden group.
Apis' tall, muscular body, towering over heads, kept leaping
into the air with the resilience of a giant kangaroo, higher and
higher, untiring and with a youthful vehemence as though the
day had just begun. There was something endearing and at the
same time grotesque about the big man's revelry. Watching
him, Michael felt a touch of envy. Was it Apis' twenty-seven
years that gave him the energy of a demigod and his, Michael's,
thirty-seven that weighed, at this late hour, like a sack of stones
on his back? This wild celebration before the act seemed waste-
ful and ludicrous to him. After such exhausting physical exercise no one but a Serb would have the strength left to go
through with a *coup d'état.* An Austrian or a Russian would
no doubt postpone it or give it up entirely. What seemed so
disturbing about Dimitriyevich and his companions was that
their calisthenics were a mere warm-up for later action to be
performed with even greater vigor and fury.

Tables and chairs had been pushed helter-skelter into a corner. As if the shouts emanating from the strong, young throats
weren't forceful enough to express the dancers' emotions, there
were revolver shots fired at the stars blinking through the rents
in the wind-chased clouds. The air was heavy with the odor of
perspiring male bodies. The swirling dust stirred up by their
feet enclosed them like a mosquito net.

Suddenly, Apis froze, shouting at the gypsies, "Enough!"
The first violinist, his back curved like a frightened cat's, immediately lowered his bow. When the second violin continued
playing, he brought the man into line with a kick in the shin
that was answered with a string of choice obscenities. Apis
pulled a fifty-dinar bill from his pocket and threw it to the
leader. "Out! All of you! Out!"

By then the officers were scrambling for their coats, flung onto the jumbled mass of upturned chairs. Apis slipped on his tunic, leaving it unbuttoned while he wiped the sweat and smudges from his face with a handkerchief and brushed the dust off his trousers.

The gypsies scurried for the small gate leading to the street and disappeared. With a wave of his hand, Apis summoned the officers to follow him into the dining room. Erect and steady-footed, he walked without the slightest trace of drunkenness. Inside, he turned to the men as they staggered in one by one, puffing and mumbling, and formed a circle around him. Apis called to the orderlies to close the doors and leave, then addressed his comrades in a low, calm voice.

"The time has come, gentlemen. In five minutes we shall be on our way. But before we leave, let me ask you a question. Are all of you convinced of the justice of our act? If you are not, speak up now. No harm will befall the ones who do. They'll hand over their arms and remain here under guard till our mission is completed. There will be no repercussions or punishment either now or later. However, should any of you refuse to execute an order or show the slightest hesitation in the course of the action, he will be shot on the spot. I also strongly advise those who need sobering up to have their heads doused with a bucket of cold water. We're not going to a royal reception at the Konak; we're going there to make history. You'll need all your wits about you if you want to come out alive."

There was a moment of confused silence. Michael scanned the faces. He saw pensiveness on some, drunken vacuity or savage determination on others. A few stood like stacked sheaves of wheat leaning against one another for support. Nevertheless, no one announced his intention to stay behind or have his head doused.

A loud *Zhiveo Kralj Peter* shout from a tall lieutenant broke the silence. It was the signal for a medley of voices hailing Serbia, Prince Peter, Colonel Mashin and, above all, Apis, the hero of every Serb under twenty-five years of age. The orgy of camaraderie Michael had witnessed at the Kolaratz repeated itself under the smoke-grimed crossbeams of the big room. Men fell into each other's arms; kisses were planted on cheeks burning with patriotic fervor.

"For God's sake, gentlemen," Apis outshouted the babble, "get hold of yourselves. Let's not waste any more time." He looked around. "Have you checked your firearms?" He waited for the murmured affirmation, then continued: "As you know, we expect the gates to the Konak grounds to be opened for us by Lieutenant Zivkovich. Once inside, there might be some resistance from the Palace Guards. Also, there is the danger of betrayal or a trap. Nevertheless, don't shoot except in self-defense because you might hurt men who have already joined us or are inclined to. Yovan and Peter"—he pointed at two second lieutenants—"you remain at the gate and keep it open so we can retreat if we have to. Remember, no one is to be caught alive. If a man is captured, he knows it is his duty to shoot himself. It's not such a big thing; sooner or later we all have to die." Pulling out his watch, he glanced at it. "Let's break into groups of threes and fours. On the way to the Konak, we'll use the alleys and avoid the main streets. The rendezvous is at one sharp at the South Gate. If things go as planned, we should be out again by one thirty."

While the men were filing out, Apis crossed to Michael. "What was the trouble between you and Colonel Mashin?"

Michael tried to appear unconcerned, "What trouble?"

"He dropped in here on his way home. Asked if I'd seen you. I told him not since the meeting at the fortress. He said he'd sent someone to look for you, but you seemed to have vanished."

"Vanished! Jesus Christ! I saw him as late as ten thirty at the Genchiches', went from there to the Serbian Crown and to Kolaratz's. Now I am here. Is that vanished?"

The younger man screwed up his eyes. "You saw him at the Genchiches'? What for?"

Michael thought for a moment. "Apis, this is something I am not supposed to tell you. But I will. I delivered a message to him from Alexander. In his own hand. It said he'd resign within three days. Mashin tore up the letter and ordered me to keep my mouth shut about it."

Captain Dimitriyevich's eyes shifted from Michael to the watch he was holding in the palm of his hand. He started for the exit, signaling to Michael to follow him. They were already in the alley when he turned back. "Why didn't you?"

"Didn't I what?"

"Keep your mouth shut?"

"Because I felt you had as much right to know as Mashin."

"He gave you an order."

They began walking. A small group, including the lieutenants who were to keep the Konak yard gates open during the assault, followed at a short distance.

"I don't have to take orders from anyone, only from Prince Peter," Michael said. "I was sent here as his personal envoy; consequently, I shall conduct myself the way I know he would want me to. He, not Mashin."

For a while, they continued in silence. "Mashin told me to keep an eye on you," Apis informed him.

"Well, do," Michael snapped.

"Don't worry, I shall," the big man answered in a tone that was gruff but not hostile.

At the Palilula camp, Major Milivoy Angyelkovich was nervously pacing the shrubbery-lined path alongside the Seventh Infantry barracks. The first battalion was waiting in marching order on the dark drill grounds behind the buildings. Every time the major reached the end of the path and executed an about-face, he threw a glance at his watch in the light of the gas lamp burning at the corner. Colonel Mashin was ten minutes late. Angyelkovich felt a nervous throbbing in the pit of his stomach. Although all officers of the Seventh Infantry Regiment above the rank of captain, as well as many subalterns, had pledged their support to the coup, none was as inextricably involved as he. By tacit agreement, all battalion commanders and staff officers had gone home, leaving him in charge. If the coup failed, they could wriggle out of trouble by claiming ignorance of the plan, but not he, known as one of the chief Karageorgevich organizers within the corps. His grandfather's execution flashed through his mind. He wondered if he could accept death with the same admirable bonhomie as the old man. He thought of his children. Would their future be wrecked by poverty and disgrace should Alexander remain on the throne? Smoldering anger was building up inside him against Colonel Mashin, who had lured him into such a perilous adventure.

He felt that the colonel's tardiness could have only one explanation: The conspiracy had been discovered, all participants arrested and a squad of gendarmes dispatched to capture him, Angyelkovich, the last of Mashin's confederates. The coup had been sheer madness: the tragedy of fools sacrificed for one man's grudge against Alexander Obrenovich.

At that moment Colonel Mashin, tall and majestic in a bemedaled blue-and-gold uniform and aigrette-trimmed shako, strode through the main gate of the camp.

"You are late, Colonel!" Angyelkovich reproached him.

"It was a bloody damn long walk, Major," Mashin said, mopping his brow. "Couldn't find a hack. These bastard cabbies turn in with the hens. I made it as fast as I could. In this heat, too. I'm soaked to the skin. I'm sure to catch my death if I don't get out of these damp clothes soon."

"You'd better address the battalion first," the major said with a touch of irreverence. "The men are getting restless."

He escorted the colonel to the drill grounds, where the troops were indeed on the verge of a minor revolt. They had broken ranks, squatted in groups or lay stretched out on the grass, snoring. Five men were playing twenty-one under the open window of a still-lighted barracks. Their officers, probably haunted by the same doubts that had troubled Angyelkovich, clustered on a bench. Sighting the colonel, they snapped out of their stupor and quickly rejoined their stations. The soldiers, on the other hand, looked at him with the mild curiosity of uninvolved bystanders.

"Battalion! Attention!" Angyelkovich roared. Tucking away a stiff salute, he wheeled about to face Mashin. "Sir! The battalion stands ready! All present and accounted for!"

Mashin returned the salute. "Thank you, Major."

The troops clambered to their feet and fell in behind their officers. Thin-lipped and impatient, Mashin glared at them.

"A goddamn pack of sloths," he muttered under his breath. "Ought to be decimated. That would teach them discipline."

At last the drill grounds quieted down sufficiently for Major Angyelkovich's "Attention" to triumph over the shuffle of feet and low-toned grumbling.

"I've ordered you men assembled because I want to make an important announcement. The gentleman on my right is Colonel Alexander Mashin, the new commandant of the Danubian Division, appointed by His Majesty King Alexander I. His majesty has empowered Colonel Mashin to overrule all orders issued by Minister of Defense Milovan Pavlovich, who has been relieved of his duties as of midnight."

A rebellious murmur spread through the ranks. The battalion clearly resented having been pulled out of bed to hear an announcement that could easily have waited until morning. Mashin sensed the brewing mutiny and moved forward till he was almost touching the first line.

"Attention!" he shouted in a voice that carried to the far end of the grounds. "One more sound out of you and every tenth man will be taken to the guardhouse in irons." The threat produced results. As if a soundproof cover had been lowered on the yard, all talk and shuffling ceased. "Now hear this! You will march to the city and deploy on the northern, eastern and southern sides of the Old Konak. You will march noiselessly and in perfect formation. Under no circumstances will you use your firearms unless ordered to by your officers. Your mission is to offer protection to His Majesty King Alexander against a horde of civilian demonstrators who have threatened to invade the palace."

A loud *Zhiveo Colonel Mashin* swept through the ranks. At last, the men heard an address that not only made sense, but gave them cause to cheer. Nothing could bring more pleasure to these simple sons of the soil than to distribute a few hearty blows to a bunch of city slickers. The same men of the Seventh Infantry had taken part in and thoroughly enjoyed the routing of the March 6 protesters in front of the Konak gates. The prospect of a new free-for-all now caused their adrenaline to flow.

While the battalion was regrouping for the march, Colonel Mashin ordered the remainder of the regiment readied for combat duty but kept at the camp till further notice. Then he assumed command of the marchers and started with them toward the center of the still-sleeping city.

Police Commissioner Veljkovich, on night duty at the precinct station on Prince Michael Street, heard a noise that sounded like raindrops falling on the chestnut trees. Looking

out the front door to see if it was really raining, he caught sight
of a long column of soldiers emerging, in what seemed to him a
rather stealthy way, from behind the shadows of the Kalemegdan Gardens. The discovery stunned him. He knew of no reason why troops should be marching into town in the middle of
the night. No maneuvers were in progress, no demonstrations
reported. Pulling the door shut and locking it, he went to the
telephone and, in a voice raucous with excitement, ordered
Central to connect him with Prefect Marshityanin's house.

Aroused from deep sleep, even deeper than usual owing to
the pint of slivovitz he had downed to soothe a bad toothache,
the prefect first took the call for a practical joke. When he
finally realized that the man phoning was one of his commis-
sioners and that army units were moving toward the royal palace, he lost his head completely.

"What the hell you think I can do from here?" he shouted.
"If they're really headed for the Konak, they'll be there long
before me. Call up the Central Police Station and tell them to
send all the men they can scare up to the Old Konak. Bar all
accesses to it. Use force if necessary. Oh, yes, and notify the
Palace Guards. General Laza canceled all leaves and placed the
men on the alert, nevertheless, give them a ring. I'll come down
myself, now that you've awakened me. I only wish for your sake
that it doesn't turn out to be a false alarm."

Veljkovich heard the sharp click of the receiver and shook his
head in quiet exasperation. He went to the street door, opened
it to a narrow gap and peeked out just as the last stragglers of
the column turned the corner into Teraziya and disappeared
behind the row of one-story shop buildings. Though vexed
by Prefect Marshityanin's attitude, he cranked the phone
and had the operator connect him with the Central Police
Station.

The officer on duty there would ordinarily have been General Laza Petrovich's young brother-in-law, a well-known member of the Belgrade *jeunesse dorée*. Like most officials whose
careers were sustained by nepotism, he felt much too secure in
his position to take it seriously. Despite an earlier warning from
General Laza about possible unrest, when nothing unusual occurred by midnight, he decided to leave his post for a pleasant
hour with his current mistress, a French *diseuse* appearing at

the Orpheum, appointing a young clerk to hold the fort for him in his absence.

Commissioner Veljkovich's call completely unnerved the clerk. He had been on the force only a few months and had no experience in issuing orders to a staff of men twice his age. Half were on their regular rounds; the other half, including the reinforcement called in for the night, were playing cards or dozing in the guardroom. How was he to bar all accesses to the Konak with eighteen policemen? Was he supposed to shoot it out with the army? Like most Belgraders, he had heard the rumors of a brewing military revolt, and if this was it and if it had come to a bloody clash between the king's supporters and the rebels, was he going to be caught in the middle?

His first problem was how to break up a fiercely involved card game and arouse the sleepers. Without solving that, to shoot or not to shoot became a hypothetical question. He thought of calling the Konak for advice, but in that case he would be revealing his superior's dereliction of duty and lose his goodwill. He used to daydream about opportunities such as the present one when he would have a chance to impress the world with his quick thinking and heroism, but now that the opportunity had arrived it sent him into a sick torpor.

He could never remember if it was five or thirty minutes later that he heard the sound of marchers approaching from the direction of Teraziya. Rising, he crossed to the phone on the wall, but by the time he reached for the crank, the vanguard had passed the station. He dropped his hand and listened motionless as the column—he judged it to be several hundred men —trudged by in odd silence and, to his relief, unnoticed by the cardplayers in the next room. He waited for the return of quiet on the boulevard, then tiptoed back to his desk and dropped wearily into the armchair behind it.

After phoning the Central Station, Commissioner Veljkovich rang up the officers' room in the Palace Guard barracks on the Konak grounds and asked to speak to Captain Panayotovich. The voice at the other end belonged to Lieutenant Zivkovich, who told him that the commander was out inspecting the sentries and that he, Zivkovich, would go and promptly deliver the commissioner's message to him.

"I doubt that there is any cause for alarm," Lieutenant Zivkovich added before cranking off. "Maneuvers have been planned for the Sixth Infantry and the troop movement might be in preparation for that."

The answer, however, failed to allay the commissioner's forebodings. He waited a few minutes, then had Central ring the Palace Guards barracks again. This time, he received no answer. Alarmed, he tried Prefect Marshityanin's number. The result was the same, which meant that either the prefect had left his house or his phone was disconnected. Since Veljkovich couldn't leave his post, he sent out a police patrol with orders to proceed beyond their regular beat and report back any unusual activity in the vicinity of the royal palace.

It was twelve thirty when the queen rose from the table. Since this had been no state dinner, but an intimate family affair in the dining room of the Old Konak, she had allowed herself to linger a little longer than usual over the vintage Tokay served with petits fours. It was a habit dating back to the days before Alexander, when she was free to spend many a night with friends in some café where only the break of the new dawn reminded them that it was time to go home. Of course, these after-supper talks were never the same in Alexander's royal presence. He seemed unable to relax completely or appreciate a joke, no matter how tactful, directed at his person. Nevertheless, Draga enjoyed these sessions, and so did the king, though for different reasons. With the serving staff dismissed, he no longer felt self-conscious about how much he ate or drank.

During the supper, General Laza had repeatedly excused himself to leave the room. The last time he reappeared the royal couple were already bidding good-night to their guests. Yielding to Draga's request, Alexander agreed to allow Marinkovich to go home and come back for continued conferences in the morning. Embracing her sisters and brothers, the queen made the sign of the cross over each. In hushed tones, the envoy asked Mika Naumovich whether she did that every time she parted with them or only on special occasions. The equerry answered with an oddly tortured look and a shrug of his wide, bearlike shoulders. Marinkovich wondered what ailed the man. There were deep rings under his eyes, and although the heat was still oppressive in the room, with all the windows closed and the drapes drawn, he seemed to be shivering with cold.

Laza Petrovich, too, noticed Naumovich's unusual conduct, his uncharacteristic silences, his absentminded toying with his food and, above all, his unrestrained drinking which, he had to realize, would anger the queen. Sensing Laza's eyes on him, he hunched up his shoulders and, like a small boy caught in some mischief, blinked with embarrassment. Then, not waiting for the royal dismissal, he slouched from the room. Laza thought of following him out but was detained by Draga, who chose that moment to address him.

"What's the situation? Have you noticed anything?" she asked in a low voice.

He shook his head. "No, madame. Not a thing. I went repeatedly to the gates to talk to Lieutenant Zivkovich. He's seen no disturbing signs either. Earlier this evening, out of sheer precaution, I ordered the Palace Guards to be on the alert. So they're especially watchful, with all sentries doubled and extra patrols making the rounds. I think we have nothing to fear. At least, not tonight. Nevertheless, I'll stay in the adjutants' room for the night. I left word with Lieutenant Zivkovich to call me in case he notices the slightest disturbance."

He knew that he had failed to allay her apprehensions. When she extended her hand to be kissed, she managed a faint smile and gave his fingers a gentle squeeze. "I don't know what we'd do without you, Laza. I wanted to ask you to stay the night, then decided it would be an imposition. Now you're staying without being asked. I've been under such strain these past weeks. Forgive me if I've been rude to you at times. I didn't mean to be. It's just—" She stopped as she saw the king approaching. She could tell by his walk that he was drunk. She decided not to upbraid him for it this time, as she herself had drunk more than she should. She wondered if she should tell Laza about the note Sasha had sent to the rebels by Michael Vassilovich, then decided against it. There were too many people around.

Two footmen carrying lighted tall candles entered from the serving pantry where they had been awaiting the chamberlain's signal. They were to accompany the royal couple to their private suite, a ritual left over from the days without gas or elec-

tricity. A third footman escorted the guests to the exit where
Captain Miljkovich, on duty in the adjutants' room, was to bid
them good-night.

"Any news about Miljkovich junior?" Nikodiye asked the
captain.

Miljkovich shook his head. He looked tired, and his eyes
were red-rimmed from lack of sleep. "Nothing, though the doctors think it won't be long now. They're standing by."

Belgrade was still a small town. Births, deaths, engagements,
marriages never needed to be announced in the newspapers as
word of mouth was a perfect means of communication.

"You really should've asked to be relieved of duty," Voyka
told him. "A husband ought to be with his wife at a time
like this." The graduate of an exclusive girls' boarding school
in Vienna, Voyka was on the verge of becoming a suffra-
gette.

The captain blushed to the roots of his silky blond hair. He
had been constantly teased by his fellow officers for his infatuation with his wife. They considered it a weakness unbecoming a
real Serb. This and his blondness set him apart from them. He
was like an albino piglet in a litter of thick-skinned, wire-haired
wild boars. Feeling the Lunyevitza brothers' amused gazes on
his face, he blushed an even deeper red. He disliked them and
considered the prospect of having Nikodiye named heir to the
throne disastrous for the country; nevertheless, he had turned a
deaf ear to his friend Apis Dimitriyevich's cautious overtures to
join the group of officers dissatisfied with King Alexander's regime.

He let the guests out through the heavy oak door that shut
off the royal apartments from the vestibule. While locking it,
he heard the guards on duty open the main entrance door to
the palace and relock it after the departing guests. There was
the screech of carriage wheels and the babble of small talk followed by the clip-clop of the horses' hooves on the paved driveway and the clank of the heavy south gate opened and closed by
the sentries. After that, silence descended on the darkened
Konak grounds.

Draga found her personal maid, the Viennese Frau Weber,
stretched out fast asleep on the royal bed. It annoyed her that

the woman hadn't bothered to fold back the pink brocade comforter or remove her shoes. Feeling too tired to make a case of it, she let the woman undress her, then dismissed her with a curt good-night.

She slipped into the wide bed. Alexander entered from the bathroom, wearing, as usual, one of the long nightshirts his valet had laid out for him. For the sake of royal decorum he always put it on in the valet's presence but threw it off before getting into bed with her.

As a precautionary measure, the windows facing the garden had remained closed and their drapes drawn. The air was unbearably hot and heavy in the room. Draga kicked off the comforter and covered herself with the silk topsheet. Alexander removed his pince-nez and carefully deposited it on the bedside table. Then he slid under the sheet. Sensing his intent, his wife held out her hands to keep him away from her perspiration-soaked body.

"Sasha, *chéri*, not tonight!" she whispered. "I am tired. Besides, it's so beastly hot in here."

His arms entwined her despite her protests. "You just lie there and let me—" His breath was hot on her face, while his oddly cold and clammy hands unbuttoned her nightgown to free her breasts. His lips moved from nipple to nipple, and his fingers began to explore the soft hills and valleys of her body. She was forced to muster her self-control to keep from kicking his hands away and to lie, resigned and silent, in their trap. It always took him infuriatingly long to reach a climax or—as so frequently happened—to fall asleep without reaching it. He was a child and she his toy; it was his touching and hugging and fondling her, not her responses, that seemed to bring him pleasure and a belief in his own virility.

He must have had more to drink than she realized because suddenly his probing hands relaxed and came to rest on her belly. His head dropped back on the pillow, his mouth fell open and the frown lines on his forehead lost their sharpness.

This is how he will look when dead, she thought, and the word "dead" caused her to shiver despite the heat. Slyly, gently, she extricated herself from his embrace and slid to the far side of the bed. Exhausted, yet still not sleepy, she knew that she would lie listening to her own heartbeat if she turned off the light. A French book she had started reading the night before, a thin volume with the title *Le Trahison* printed in black letters across its binding, lay on her night table. Hoping it would make her drowsy, she decided to read for a while. As she reached for it, Alexander stirred. His eyes, cloudy with sleep and myopia, opened and he squirmed closer to her. Afraid of waking him fully, she dropped the book and turned off the light, preferring to lie sleepless in the dark than submit to his clumsy sex games. She stretched out, her head propped up by a small pillow, her ears tuned to the noises of the night. The closed windows and heavy drapes blocked out almost all sound except a strange rumbling that resembled the roll of faraway thunder, though much too even and continuous for that. When she could no longer hear it, she decided that it had been thunder after all and dozed off, only to feel as though she were floating through the air. Faces bobbed up around her like buoys on a sea. Savka, Milica, Colonel Grabov and Michael. His image, lean and sharp-featured, showing the wear and tear of his thirty-seven years, became superimposed on the ghost of the young cadet she had never quite forgotten. He walked in a meadow with a girl who resembled her but was younger and prettier. She felt a strange pity for the girl, which brought tears to her eyes. It was with these tears that she slipped from half-consciousness into a sleep as soothing and pleasant as a lukewarm bath.

1 A.M.

By THE light of a match, Colonel Mishich took a look at his heavy gold watch, a gift from the late King Milan. It showed ten minutes after one. The vanguard of his two battalions was passing the Russian Legation to take up a position along the western wall of the Konak grounds. Despite the order to move in silence, the two thousand men deployed with a great deal of tussle and scuffle. Straining his ears, the colonel tried to sort out other more distant noises from the hubbub around him, noises that would indicate that the men of the Seventh Infantry had also reached their destination at the South Gate. Either they had not or the racket of his own troops was screening out all other sounds. Delegating command to the ranking captain, he hurriedly started out along the east wall of the compound. He had to find out what was happening on the other side.

Michael and Apis had reached the South Gate and were now waiting in the shadows of the trees for the rest of the men assigned to action at the Konak. Time seemed to drag as group after group emerged from the dark that engulfed the neighborhood. Mumbling the names of the still missing, Apis counted heads, growing more and more impatient as precious minutes ticked away.

"What are we waiting for?" Lieutenant Milutin Lazarevich asked nervously. To reach the rendezvous, he had had to climb fences, clear ditches and cross vegetable gardens to avoid the still-lighted streets between the Kolaratz restaurant and the palace. And all this with enough explosives in his cartridge belt to blow up a city block.

"I've had this goddamn coat buttoned up since ten o'clock tonight," he grumbled. "I am so hot I wonder why these cartridges haven't exploded. They must be duds."

By one twenty, all men assigned to the Konak were present and accounted for. Except for peasant carts bringing vegetables and fodder to the central market, no traffic moved on the boulevard. Occasionally, a late pedestrian passed, invariably quickening his steps when catching sight of the officers. The civilians of Belgrade had learned to keep their distance from young army men prowling in packs through the night. Nevertheless, every passerby caused hearts to beat faster and breaths to become bated. The boulevard lights made the officers feel like figures in a shooting gallery. One by one, they withdrew into the narrow side street that ran behind the palace guardhouse.

The wait and the tension were beginning to show. With mind and vision befogged by wine, the men staggered about restlessly, some getting sick with loud retching and cursing.

"What swine," Apis muttered angrily. He and Michael had

remained at the gate. "Why the hell do they drink if they can't hold their liquor?" He wiped his perspiring forehead with the sleeve of his tunic. For the first time that night, Michael noticed that Apis was losing his usual composure. "If Mashin doesn't appear in five minutes, I'll go and take care of the whole goddamn business alone."

"Or give it up."

Apis' face froze. In the pale light of the streetlamp it looked like a bronze mask. "No," he said hoarsely. "Never."

Michael decided to take a chance. "I've told you that Alexander promised to leave within three days. What difference can three days make after three years? It's certainly not worth risking your own or your men's lives for. There are people inside the Konak who might very well shoot at you."

"Or shoot us in the back. For instance, you. Is that what you mean?"

"Don't be an ass. Besides, what would I shoot you with? I am not armed." He lifted the flaps of his tunic, exposing the flat pockets of his pants.

"What the hell did you come along for if you aren't armed?"

"To see things through for Peter Karageorgevich. If he were here tonight, he wouldn't be armed either."

"You goddamn humanitarians! You let us do the dirty work, so you won't soil your hands. Beg your pardon, your glacé leather gloves. Good old Peter. He'll have three choices: refuse the throne; accept it and reward us; accept it and have us court-martialed."

"He'll never do that."

"No. Because we, the leaders have a pact. We pledged to shoot ourselves should Peter refuse to accept the crown from us. Then it can be offered to him by unsoiled hands."

"Let's hope it won't come to that."

The Old Konak lay dark and mysterious at the far end of the curving carriageway. Light seeped through the closed blinds of a room on the ground floor. As always, someone was awake in the adjutants' office.

"Do you know who the officer on duty is tonight?" Michael asked.

"I am afraid it's Yovan Miljkovich. Unless he has requested to be relieved because of the birth of his child. I hope he has. If only he'll have sense enough not to do anything rash. I tried to talk to him, but it was no use. He is a good man. I don't want him hurt."

Michael looked at the dark bulk of the palace and wondered if the feminine quarry of all these young men thirsting for wine and blood was still behind its thick walls or had taken his advice and sneaked out before her escape route was cut off by three infantry battalions. Captain Ljuba Kostich of the Royal Guards had sent word to the Officers' Club around midnight that the music was still playing in the Konak dining room. Michael hoped that it had served as a camouflage and that the supper guests had been wined and dined in the hosts' absence. Still, he was bothered by strange premonitions. Perhaps Alexander had refused to believe the message and stayed on, or the message had been intercepted by someone siding with the conspirators. In that case he himself was in deep trouble. The smart thing would be to disappear before the arrival of Mashin and the Seventh Infantry. He could pretend to be sick or have to take a leak and melt into the shadows of the next alley. Even if Apis or the others noticed him gone, they wouldn't pursue him for fear of attracting attention.

Quick steps approached along the west wall. Apis tensed, then sighed with relief when he recognized Colonel Mishich's dark figure turning the corner. He was bringing the cheery news that the Sixth Infantry occupied the street between the Russian Legation and the Konak park. Mashin and the Seventh were still nowhere in sight.

It was one thirty, and the men were growing increasingly restless. Some had brought bottles of schnapps along and continued drinking. Instead of staying in the dark side street, they drifted up to the boulevard to see what was delaying the action. Their growing anxiety manifested itself in frictions, and smoldering feuds erupted in name-calling quarrels. Only the intervention of the older and more temperate men kept passions under control.

"Let's not wait for Mashin and the Seventh," Lazarevich urged Apis. "We are late already. I'm sure Zivkovich thinks the coup has been called off. I have enough dynamite on me to blow up the gate and the Konak entrance, too. Let's take a chance and make a dash for it. A few more minutes and we'll find half the men gone home and the other half at each other's throats."

A cadet of the Military Academy, one of the five accepted by the conspirators, called out "Hey! Listen! They are coming!"

"Not so loud, you fool," Apis growled.

The cadet grinned sheepishly. "Sorry, sir."

By then everyone heard the rumble of marching feet. "Let's hope it's really the Seventh," Apis said.

Michael glanced about. With everyone listening raptly to the sound, it was his chance to slip away. Once the Seventh deployed along Milan Boulevard, there was no escape for him. He made a tentative move toward the side street but bumped into the men now streaming toward the gate and realized he had waited too long.

Had he really wanted to leave? he asked himself. Or had he, from the very beginning, been determined to stay and wait out the end of the drama? And if so, where did he belong? Was his rightful place here, in front of the gate or behind it, ready to defend it against the mob of drunks and zealots?

He threw a quick look at Dimitriyevich, poised at the gate to be the first to enter. The expression on his face caused in Michael an awareness of his own painful shortcomings. Apis seemed on edge, like everyone else, but steeled to storm the Konak whatever the obstacles. The perfect revolutionary, Michael thought, propelled by a passionate belief in the justice of his cause. Passion, blind, unthinking passion, was the secret ingredient that he, Michael, lacked. Lacked it as a revolutionary, as well as a lover. Never quite certain of his own desires, always questioning, examining, doubting. Expecting time to solve problems that, like festering wounds, became more pernicious as time passed.

He had been playing a crooked game with his own conscience. All his plans for escape had been mere self-deceit. Had the eight o'clock steamer for Zimony left on schedule, he would still be in Belgrade, having found some excuse for staying. What kept him now was his anxiety to learn whether or not Draga had obeyed his warning and left or was still trapped in the Konak. In the latter case, helping her escape was impossible. All he could do for her was exercise a restraining influence on Mashin and his men when the confrontation between the royal couple and the conspirators occurred. A slim chance, yet worth a gamble.

The first squad of the Seventh Infantry, led by Colonel Mashin, emerged from behind the trees of Slavija Square and turned into the boulevard. After months—even years—of planning, the moment for action had arrived. The men were no longer able to control their excitement. In a confused mass they pressed against the still-locked gates, hands grabbing at the iron grillwork, shaking it violently.

"Zivkovich! Where the hell are you, Zivkovich?" Shouts and curses erupted from their group as though the danger of detection no longer existed. "Let us in, Zivkovich! Do you want us to blast our way in?"

Colonel Mashin rushed up to them. "Keep quiet! If you bring the police down on us, we'll never get inside the bloody gate."

There was another ten-minute wait for the Seventh Infantry to take up positions along the walls.

"What kept you?" Apis asked Colonel Mashin. "We thought you'd never come."

Mashin ignored the question. "Give the signal to Zivkovich," he ordered. The long walk had clearly exhausted him. He took off his shako to wipe the perspiration from it.

Two short and one long whistle sound was the signal to let Lieutenant Zivkovich know that the troops had surrounded the Konak compound and that the officers were assembled at the gate. While waiting for it in front of the Palace Guards' barracks, the lieutenant had heard the stomping and shouting and became increasingly infuriated at the carelessness of the men. When the prearranged signal finally came, he started for the gate, yet not without a touch of doubt about the wisdom of his own involvement in this conspiracy with a group of such undisciplined fools. He trusted Colonel Mashin's intelligence but now wondered if the colonel was in control of his men. If the conspiracy failed, it would mean the end of his, Zivkovich's, military career and no doubt his life. Alexander had always been kind to him, and so had Queen Draga. Why was he risking so much for a cause that promised such meager rewards? Rushing across the driveway, he stumbled, dropping the heavy key he had sneaked from the drugged Captain Panayotovich's pocket. With a mumbled curse, he retrieved it, still wondering if he should not alert General Petrovich instead of opening the gate.

"God damn it, Zivkovich, what's keeping you?" a drunken voice called from the street.

He realized that he had no choice but to unlock the gate as he made a perfect target in the wide driveway. The men would no doubt shoot him if they saw him turn back. With a leap, he reached the gate and inserted the key into the lock. Rattling and squeaking, the gate swung open, and he was knocked off his feet by the men streaming inward in a groaning, cursing mass. Disregarding all caution, they stormed, with guns held at the ready, toward the faintly lighted Konak as though it were a fortress to be taken in one mad onslaught. Trying in vain to keep up with them, the two colonels fell back, stage-whispering angry but ineffective orders for them to stop. Apis alone succeeded in getting ahead of the runners. Arms outstretched, his big bulk a dark stop sign silhouetted against the clair-obscure of the yard, he halted. His hissed obscenities at long last managed to penetrate the fog of alcohol and hysteria that had turned the men into stampeding cattle. Panting and wheezing, they halted in their tracks.

"What the hell you think you're doing? Be quiet and act like soldiers, or go home and forget the whole thing." He heard a door opening behind him and added, "That is, if it's not too late already."

Evidently alerted by the noise, the sergeant on duty in the Palace Guards' barracks stepped out to see what was happening. He stood on the threshold, staring in disbelief at the thirty-odd officers clustered in the carriageway and Lieutenant Zivkovich scrambling to his feet after what must have been a fall.

The sergeant turned back and bellowed a loud "At arms!" into the guardroom. His revolver drawn, he advanced toward the intruders. His men, like a swarm of enraged bees, poured from the building. At his signal, they aimed their rifles at the officers.

A revolver shot rang out from the group in the carriageway. The sergeant, emitting a high-pitched scream, collapsed at the feet of his onrushing men. For a moment, no one stirred. Confused, the guardsmen froze. It was only now that they realized the attackers were being led by two colonels in gala uniforms. The shot that had felled the sergeant had come from behind them. The night was too dark and everything had happened too fast for the guardsmen to be sure about who had fired the shot.

The first to regain his composure was Lieutenant Zivkovich. Drawing his sword and braving a possible crossfire, he moved to confront the guardsmen with a stentorian "Attention! Shoulder arms!"

Still baffled, the men obeyed. Simultaneously, a skirmish erupted among the officers. An enraged Apis grabbed hold of the lieutenant who had fired the shot and delivered two resounding slaps to his face, sending the man in a half faint to the ground. There was some grumbling from the lieutenant's friends, but Colonel Mashin silenced them with the threat to have them shot as mutineers. Apis crossed to the sergeant and bent over him.

"Have him taken inside. He is dead," he told Zivkovich. "And order your men to return to the guardhouse and stay indoors till further notice. You'd better remain with them to make sure they do."

Colonel Mashin, his voice hoarse with tension, was trying to restore order among his unruly cohorts.

"Remember your instructions, gentlemen. Keep to the plan, or all will be lost. First group: Round up and lock up the palace staff—footmen, cooks, maids. Mind you, no rough handling unless absolutely necessary. Second group: Disarm guards, orderlies or officers on duty in the vestibule. Third group: Arrest General Laza Petrovich. I want him taken alive. Fourth group: Watch exits and windows. Anyone trying to escape is to be arrested or—if unavoidable—shot. Fifth group: Follow Colonel Mishich, Captain Dimitriyevich and me to the royal suite. Let me remind you that time is of the essence. The operation must be concluded within thirty minutes. I shall hold the group leaders responsible for any slipups. To botch this task might bring about the bloodiest revolution the world has ever seen. So pull yourselves together and act like soldiers because the future of Serbia depends on you. And now, gentlemen, let's proceed. God bless you and keep you all." Crossing

himself, he started for the main entrance to the Old Konak but
halted after a few steps. With his raised hand, he signaled to the
men for quiet.

Seeping through the steady noise of the troops surrounding
the Konak compound, came the distant tremor of marchers. As
it became louder, the men tensed. Lieutenant Bogdanovich
ventured the guess that it might be the Eighth Infantry coming
to the king's rescue. The threat of panic hung heavy in the
air.

"Don't be an idiot, Bogdan," Mashin growled. "It's Captain
Ljuba Kostich bringing his battalion of the Royal Guards."

An officer entered the yard through the gate held open by the
two lieutenants assigned to guard it.

Sounding unquestionably relieved, Mashin said, "It *is* Kostich." No doubt, he had shared Bogdanovich's fears, even
though he was careful not to admit them.

"Why so late?" he asked Kostich as the captain reached him.

"Some minor surprises, but everything is under control
now." Kostich talked with the slightly nasal accent of an Austrian aristocrat, an affectation from the son of Bosnian peasants.
Not even the dark of the night could hide the elegance of his
appearance, the highly polished boots, the perfectly fitting
tunic, the razor-sharp creases of the trousers. He appeared to be
dressed for a parade, not a coup.

Mashin turned to the officers. "All right, gentlemen, let's
start."

This time the group moved in comparative silence, Michael
keeping to Apis' side. No doubt the big man was a zealot, yet
the most decent and selfless of the leaders. Not driven by personal grudge like Mashin or frustrated ambition like Mishich,
he would never stage a massacre for a massacre's sake or take the
life of a defeated enemy. Clinging to the last ray of hope for
Draga's safety, Michael chose to place his trust in Apis' sense of
humanity to keep the abdication bloodless, provided Alexander
didn't commit some blunder that would provide Mashin and
his friends with an excuse for violence. His heart throbbing in
his throat, Michael followed Apis up the steps to the main
Konak entrance sheltered by the elegant marquee.

Mashin pulled out his watch. "We're thirty minutes late," he
muttered.

"What if Naumovich thinks we aren't coming?" Lazarevich asked.

The colonel answered somewhat gruffly. "He has orders to wait till two o'clock. If we weren't here by two, he was to go back to sleep." As always, Mashin resented having the efficiency of his planning questioned. He looked at the windows to the right of the marquee. "He said he would watch for us from behind that window."

Seconds, then minutes passed while no one stirred inside the building. "What the devil—" Mashin mumbled, stepping to the door and knocking cautiously. Once, twice, three times. At last there was the sound of steps approaching on the stone floor.

A male voice asked, "Who is it?"

"That's not Naumovich," Mishich whispered.

"Must be a guardsman," Captain Kostich said. "There were rumors that General Petrovich ordered an extra security guard to remain in the vestibule during the night."

"Why didn't you let us know?" Mashin asked shrilly. "What are we to do now?"

"Leave it to me, Colonel," Kostich said with a patronizing smile as he stepped to the door and raised his voice. "It's me, Captain Kostich. Let me in, soldier. I have to see General Petrovich."

The door was promptly opened, and Kostich stepped across the threshold. "Disarm him," he ordered the officers pushing in behind him.

Before the guardsman could collect his wits, he was gripped from both sides and relieved of rifle and revolver. Captain Kostich, as relaxed as if he were making a social call, strolled to a small room which opened off the vestibule. Three guardsmen were seated around a table. They had been playing cards with the fourth who had answered the door. Jumping to their feet, they scrambled for their rifles stacked in the corner as Captain Kostich walked up to them, shaking his head in mock consternation.

"Playing cards on guard duty," he said. "I wonder what next. You ought to be put in irons for that. This once I am willing to overlook it though. Hand over your arms and get the hell out of here." When the men hesitated, he raised his voice. "Fast. Get to the guardhouse and report to Lieutenant Zivkovich."

They knew him well, he was their commander, and they had no reason to doubt his authority. Nevertheless, as they leaned their rifles against the wall and dropped their revolvers and cartridge belts on the table next to the unfinished card game, they threw suspicious glances at the officers lined up in a double cordon across the vestibule. Captain Kostich, noticing the change in their expressions, decided to put their distrust at rest.

"The king received word of a threat against his life and summoned the colonels and the gentlemen to the Konak. Luckily, we got here in time to protect him."

The guardsmen either believed or pretended to believe the explanation and quickly made their exit between the double file of officers. Captain Kostich followed them outside, keeping his eyes, but also his revolver, trained on them until they disappeared into the guardhouse. When he returned to the vestibule, a smug little smile played around his stiffly waxed mustache, the magician's smile after performing a difficult trick.

Looking around as though he expected applause, he informed them, "That takes care of the guards."

"What in the devil is keeping that bastard Naumovich?" Mashin asked as he led the group up the stairs to the heavy oak door which closed off the upper floor containing the royal apartments. Captain Kostich alone remained behind. It had been agreed that he would return to his battalion and stay with it until the business of Alexander's removal from the throne was successfully concluded.

"How long do you want to wait?" Apis asked Mashin. "I think it was a mistake to count on Naumovich. I told you in the very beginning not to trust the bastard."

"So you did—so you did—" Mashin murmured nervously. "I knew it was a one in a hundred chance. It didn't work, so we'll just have to go on with the alternative plan." He motioned to Lieutenant Lazarevich. "It's your turn, Milutin."

"Alternative plan," a captain named Ristich murmured under his breath. Dynamiting any of the entrance doors had been considered as a last, desperate measure in case everything else failed. Suddenly, because Colonel Mashin hated to admit a mistake, it became the alternative plan.

Some of the subalterns around Ristich exchanged disturbed

glances. Except for shooting the sergeant dead, nothing irreparable had occurred as yet, was the thought that flashed through their minds. After a hasty retreat across the palace yard a man could go home and pretend to have been fast asleep throughout the night.

Mashin sensed their doubts. "Get on with it, Milutin. We've wasted enough time already."

"Now you know why you had to sweat all night, Milutin," Lieutenant Bogdanovich said, grinning.

Lieutenant Lazarevich answered with a profanity, then pulled a cartridge from his belt. "Move back, all of you. Unless you want to get blown to hell."

"To heaven," Apis corrected him. "If you're killed tonight, you go straight to heaven. And your statue is erected in the Kalemegdan Gardens."

A stubby little cadet added acidly, "For the pigeons to shit on." He had quite openly lost his enthusiasm for the business at hand and was making no secret of it. The men around him appeared to be seconds away from bolting as they reacted with nervous laughter. The cadet belonged to the group assigned, under the command of Captain Ristich, to arrest General Laza. Ristich had joined the conspiracy to clear his name from an ugly stigma. Because of an act of cowardice allegedly committed in the course of a duel, he had been forced to resign from the Russian regiment in which he had served with the czar's special permission. Despite his tainted reputation, he was arrogant and argumentative, and he and Mashin had clashed several times during the planning sessions. But for some odd reason, he had great influence over his subalterns.

Ever since the rendezvous at the gate, Captain Ristich had kept up a running commentary on how and why the coup was to fail. Now, from the corner of his eye, Mashin noticed him edging toward the exit just as Lieutenant Lazarevich was ready to light the fuse.

The colonel bellowed at him, "Captain Ristich! You filthy coward! Are you trying to sneak away?"

Lazarevich screamed simultaneously. "Get back, Colonel! Don't you see I've lighted the goddamn fuse?"

By then everyone else had ducked behind a corner or flattened himself against a wall. Lazarevich placed the cartridge in front of the oak door, then darted behind the large tile stove in the vestibule. Mashin had barely reached the safety of the same niche when the cartridge went off with an ear-shattering blast.

For a moment it seemed as though the entire building were about to cave in. The air pressure blew out the windows facing the courtyard, shredded the drapes, ripped pictures off the walls and cracked the full-length mirrors on both sides of the oak door. The door itself was no longer there; what hadn't been burned lay scattered on the vestibule floor. Like a writhing snake, a long flame crept up its shattered frame. The air was filled with smoke, dust, pulverized brick and the suffocating odor of sulfur dioxide. After a few minutes, when the air had cleared somewhat and the boom's thundering echo died down, Colonel Mashin, shaken but unhurt, stepped from the niche to survey the scene. The men were stunned but unscathed. The shock of the explosion, combined with the effect of the alcohol they had consumed, had left them dazed, and they staggered about, eyes glazed and mouths babbling.

"Let's get on with it," Mashin said. At that very moment, the electric lights went out.

2 A.M.

THE flame, eating its way up the doorframe, was the sole source of illumination.

"What's that, for God's sake?" Mashin asked of no one in particular, then turned to Michael, who was busy stamping out a burning splinter of wood on the floor. "Captain Vassilovich, what the hell is this?"

"How should I know, Colonel? Either the explosion blew out the main fuse box or someone switched off the power."

"That does it!" Captain Ristich shouted. "Let's get out of here!"

With his group swarming after him, he started for the exit just as Apis Dimitriyevich materialized from the shadows and, brandishing his cocked revolver, confronted him.

"Get back, you sons of bitches! It's too late to clear out. We're in this together to the very end whether you goddamn bastards like it or not."

There was a moment's stunned quiet, then the disruption of gunfire coming from beyond the Konak courtyard. Petrified, the men listened.

"That sounds like the gendarmerie station on Milan Boulevard," Bogdanovich said.

Colonel Mishich agreed. "That's right. No need to worry, though. They're only about fifteen men strong. And completely surrounded by my two battalions." He paused as the noise of the battle continued with volley after volley shattering the silence. "I don't know what made them shoot. They have no chance. They'll be disarmed."

"Or slaughtered," Ristich grumbled. "All good Serbs. A waste that could've been prevented by better planning. I am sure they don't know what the hell is going on. I've said it time and time again, the gendarmerie must be won over or we have no chance."

"Shut your mouth, Ristich, or I'll shut it for you," Mashin shouted at him, his usually deep voice suddenly sounding like that of an old woman snapping at her grandchildren.

Michael was unable to recall later how much time elapsed between the explosion and the conspirators' streaming into the entrance hall to the royal apartments. Everything seemed to have happened simultaneously, the explosion, the sound of gunfire from the gendarmerie station, the incident with Ristich and the loss of electricity. Except for Mashin and probably Lazarevich, he alone was cold sober and able to watch the proceedings with a bystander's objectivity. He wondered what Prince Peter's reaction would be to the besotted horde that now wrecked and befouled the house that had so honorably sheltered a succession of Serb rulers, among them his own father, Prince Alexander Karageorgevich. And above all, what the queen, if still within its walls, was feeling at the moment. His hope was that the electricity would not come on again. While the conspirators, unfamiliar with their surroundings, groped their way around, the king and queen might flee under cover of darkness. He had heard stories of underground passages, of tunnels leading from the Old Konak to the Sava embankment. Now he fervently hoped the stories were true.

Once the explosion had informed the king and the queen of the enemy's presence within the Konak, Michael thought it best to remain with the men and see what developed. He followed them through the gaping hole between the vestibule and the entrance hall and was shocked by the devastation he found. Here and there, the dark damask wall-covering was afire; spots flamed up and went out like oversize glowworms. The enormous stuffed bear, Milan's trophy from Valjevo, remained strangely unscathed. It's dark bulk, illuminated by the burning doorpost, loomed up threateningly, as though about to attack the intruders.

The first man who entered the hall collided with a figure, man-shaped yet not quite human, which resembled the Turkish markers erected on the graves of fallen Mussulman soldiers along country roads. Clad in a long nightshirt, his eyes glassy, saliva trickling from the corner of his mouth, Mika Naumovich stared drunkenly at the onrushing officers. Apis Dimitriyevich grabbed him by the collar of his shirt.

"Where have you been, you bastard?" he screamed.

Naumovich lifted his empty gaze to the captain's face. As his eyes focused and there was a slow flicker of recognition, his drooling lips twitched in a triumphant smile.

"I fooled you, didn't I?" he asked in a high-pitched whine. "You thought I'd open the damned door for you? Just so that you'd have your *coup d'état* and be a hero and fuck every poor bastard's wife, as you've been fucking mine. But now you'll pay, all of you. You'll be caught and hanged."

Without uttering a word, Apis lifted his gun and shot the man point-blank in the head. Naumovich's grin widened as though he found Apis' reaction a splendid joke. He was still standing, half of his mouth twitching in silent amusement, while the right side of his face, from chin to forehead, slowly lifted from his bones like a mask. He fell forward with a lunge that caught Apis unawares. Cursing, he kicked the inert body away, then began disgustedly to wipe the blood and bits of torn flesh and bone from his tunic. By swallowing hard, he forced back the vomit that surged in his throat. His attention became diverted by a man suddenly emerging from the darkness of the equerries' office; he recognized Captain Yovan Miljkovich, the prime minister's son-in-law. Revolver in hand, the captain halted on the threshold, his blond hair turning gold in the light of the fire.

"Yovan!" Apis shouted at him. "Put that gun down. Don't shoot! For God's sake, be sensible." He raised his voice to a desperate howl.

Miljkovich seemed to hesitate, then lowered the gun, his blue eyes slowly combing the faces illuminated by the flames.

"What is this?" he asked shrilly. "Have you all gone mad? Haven't you sworn loyalty to your sovereign, King Alexander? Where is your decency and honor? Are you officers or highwaymen?"

Stepping to the archway leading to the Serbian room, he planted himself on its threshold and raised his gun. "No one's going to cross through here alive! Move back or I'll shoot."

"Don't be a fool, Yovan," Apis called out.

At the same moment, a shot was fired by someone in the group clustered a few steps away from Miljkovich. The captain wavered, then cocked his gun, aiming it at the nearest man. Another shot came from the group, then, in quick succession, a third and fourth. Sometime between the discharges, Miljkovich, too, fired. His bullet missed its mark and hit the cracked remnants of the crystal chandelier dangling at half-mast from the ceiling. Then, with a painful moan, he crumbled to the floor.

"Why the hell did you shoot him?" Apis screamed at the men.

Mashin confronted him petulantly. "Look who is talking. Why did you shoot Naumovich? So he overslept. All right, that was unpardonable, but to kill him like a dog. I am in command here, God damn it! I issue the orders. What did you expect these men to do? Wait for Miljkovich to pick them off one by one? He was your friend. That's too bad. We aren't playing games here. If you can't take orders get your ass out of here!"

Apis responded with a dark scowl but remained silent. Mashin had evidently missed Naumovich's little speech, and Apis was not going to enlighten him. He asked Michael to help him remove Miljkovich's body to the adjutants' office, where they laid him on the couch. Apis gently stroked Miljkovich's eyelids closed and smoothed his tousled hair.

Frantic shouts emanated from the Serbian room. "Light! Light! Get some lamps or candles! It's pitch-dark in here."

"Someone go and get the servants," Mashin shouted. "Tell them we need candles." When no one moved, he bellowed, "Get them! We don't have the whole night!"

To Michael he appeared like a man on the brink of losing his mind. The usually neatly waxed mustache hung limply, and pearls of spittle glistened on the short tousled beard. Sometime during the ingress he had lost the aigrette from his shako, his left epaulet had become singed and his tunic had been covered with brick dust. The row of medals across his chest reminded Michael of the decorations left on a desiccated Christmas tree. Things weren't progressing according to Mashin's schedule, and the fear of failure was beginning to numb the man.

A block away, the battle at the Milan Boulevard gendarmerie station still raged. With each volley fired the colonel grimaced nervously.

The men who had invaded the Serbian room were ripping off drapes and throwing open windows to dispel the darkness. There was a great deal of shouting and cursing and the crash of glass as bric-a-brac was knocked off tables. Windowpanes shattered, and an occasional shot was fired.

"Where the hell is Ristich?" Mashin shouted. "Ristich! Captain Ristich!"

His pockets bulging with knickknacks he had collected in the dark, Ristich emerged from the Serbian room. "What now, Colonel?"

Mashin's eyes focused on his pockets, narrowing to angry slits. "We didn't come here to loot, Ristich. Put those things back or I'll have you court-martialed. Almighty God, how low can you stoop!"

"These things were on the floor. I picked them up so they wouldn't get crushed underfoot," Ristich retorted righteously. "All right. I'll put them back." With this, he emptied his pockets of a collection of gold coins and miniatures painted on ivory and flung them over his shoulder. "What else do you want?"

"Have you looked for General Petrovich?"

"No."

"Why not! You had orders to."

"Because he's gone. You don't think he'd be fool enough to wait for us to catch him?"

"He might still be around. Go and look."

A commotion erupted at the door to the Arabian room. Someone had procured an ax and was attacking the door with fierce blows when suddenly it was thrown open from the inside. Laza Petrovich, immaculate in his white-and-gold gala uniform, stood on the threshold; his eyes, contemptuous and unafraid, coolly reviewed the scene. His unexpected appearance stunned the men, and they stared at him in disbelief. The lieutenant who had wielded the ax so valiantly dropped it on the foot of the man standing next to him.

"Why break down this door?" Laza asked. "It wasn't locked."

Someone snickered, and the ax-wielding lieutenant glared at Laza. Drawing his revolver from its holster, he raised it slowly and took aim. A split second before he fired, Michael, noticing his intent, bumped his arm. His action, though saving Laza from a shot between the eyes, failed to prevent a bullet from ripping through his left arm a few centimeters above the elbow, causing considerable bleeding.

Mashin stepped to the lieutenant and grabbed him by the shoulder. "Have you gone mad? I've told you I wanted him alive." He looked around. "Ristich! God damn it, Ristich. You were assigned the arrest of the general. He *was* in the house. Is that the way you execute orders?"

Laza Petrovich examined the wound on his arm. "Do any of you gentlemen carry a knife?" he asked, giving the word "gentlemen" a sarcastic emphasis. "I want to rip off this sleeve."

Lieutenant Bogdanovich handed him one, then helped him cut the sleeve open. As Laza bandaged his arm, he threw a scornful look at Lieutenant Bogdanovich. "So you're one of them. That's just fine. Now I know why I always hated your guts." He turned to Michael. "And you. Don't think you fooled me. I made one mistake, though. I should have had you arrested. As a matter of fact, I did send an order out for your arrest. Right after it was reported to me that you'd left Vienna for Belgrade. Then I rescinded the order, trying to play it smart. Frankly, I didn't believe things were at this advanced stage. Twist it around once more." This to Lieutenant Bogdanovich. "I don't want to bleed all over the place like a stuck pig. There's enough muck around here already." He glanced about, catching sight of Naumovich's shirt-clad body. "Mika! What did you have to butcher him for? He was no saint, only a harmless—"

"He was one of them," Michael told him quietly. "Then he went back on his word."

"Is that so?" Laza gave Michael a long probing look. The younger man's use of the pronoun "them," instead of "us," had failed to escape him. Michael wondered if Lieutenant Bogdanovich, still busy with the bandage, had noticed the blunder.

Mashin crossed to Laza. "We'll need light. Have the electricity turned on."

"I'm afraid you'll need the house electrician for that."

"Get him."

"Now? First of all, he doesn't live at the Konak; second, he won't come here in the middle of this lunacy. You should've brought your own electrician."

"Then get us lamps and candles. You must know where they're kept."

"Why? I'm the king's first aide-de-camp, not his housekeeper."

"Don't provoke me, General," Mashin warned him. "You are a shrewd fellow. You ought to know that you have no choice but to cooperate."

"You're mistaken, Colonel. I am not a shrewd fellow. If I were, I would've known that the revolt against the king would be organized by the very men whose duty it was to protect him, that Colonel Mishich and officers of the Royal Guards would turn conspirators. I was convinced that the king was perfectly safe as long as he stayed within the gates of the Konak compound. It never occurred to me that the very keepers of those gates would open them to a mob of renegades. No, I am hardly a shrewd fellow."

"Call the servants, General. We need light."

"Ring for them yourself. There is the bell." Laza grinned. "Sorry, I forgot you had the fuses blown out."

The officers assigned to guarding the exits herded in five terrified servants—the Austrian majordomo, two footmen, a laundress and Frau Weber, the queen's personal maid. All wore hastily donned jackets and wraps over their nightclothes. The younger footman was bleeding from a gash on his forehead, and the women were sobbing hysterically.

"We caught them just as they were trying to sneak out through the cellar," a cadet reported.

When she recognized Laza in the ring of strangers, Frau Weber wailed, "General, sir, they were threatening to shoot us."

"For God's sake, Mashin," Laza said, "don't hurt these people. They only work here."

"Get us lamps and candles. We need some light in this goddamn dump," Mashin ordered. When the five remained frozen in terror, he lowered his voice. "No one's going to harm you, just get the bloody candles."

Clicking his slippered heels together, the majordomo pulled himself to attention. In his youth he had served as a master sergeant in Franz Josef's army. "At your service, sir," he sputtered in his crispest Austro-Hungarian military manner, then disappeared to return immediately with six candles, which he handed to Mashin, again clicking his heels.

"That's not enough," Mashin told him.

The majordomo was all humble apologies. "Unfortunately, sir, that's all we have in reserve. We've placed an order for a new supply, but you know how things are around here, sir. I sent a man to the candlemaker only yesterday to tell him to—"

Mashin nervously cut him short. "All right, all right. Get them out of here," he said to the lieutenants who had brought them in. "Keep them under guard, but no brutality."

A flustered Colonel Mishich arrived from the Serbian room. "We need someone to lead the way. You can get hopelessly lost in this goddamn maze."

Mashin handed him the candles. A cadet interrupted to say he knew a Dr. Gashich, who lived across the street. Perhaps one could borrow some candles from him. Mashin thought it was a good idea and suggested the young man try.

Mashin turned to General Laza. "You know your way around here. Help Colonel Mishich find Alexander and his whore. In return I'll assure *sauf-conduit* for you. But no tricks, General, because this place is as good as any for a man to get shot."

Laza shrugged and, with a mocking flourish, motioned to Mishich to precede him. "After you, Colonel."

Michael followed them into the Serbian room. The devastation it had undergone in the few short minutes since the first men had entered it was beyond belief. Drapes slashed, furniture overturned, the Lunyevitza grandfather's likeness ripped from the wall, the portrait of beautiful Countess Julia Hunyady, Prince Michael's wife, peppered with bullets, doorframes splintered, spots smoldering on the Oriental rug, divan seats ripped open, their springs left obscenely exposed through loosened tufts of horsehair. The sound of voices, jingling spurs, trampling feet and crushed glass came from the adjoining salon. It was obvious that the same wrecking crew that had played havoc here was now at work in there. An arpeggio passage ending in a discordant boom vibrated through the air as someone attacked the keys of the upright piano.

"Order the gentlemen back, Colonel," Laza said to Mishich. "They won't find the king in there. We'll have to go the other way." He threw an inquisitive glance at Michael to see whether he would correct him. When Michael remained silent, he ushered Mishich and his men through the Arabian room and the entrance hall to the lower wing with its offices, storage rooms and staff quarters.

The group explored every nook, looked behind screens and drapes, opened wardrobes and crawled under beds. This time, probably because of Laza's reminder that the Konak and its furnishings belonged not to the king, but the nation, the search was conducted without devastation.

Despite the troops which encircled the palace compound— the two Konaks, guardhouses, barracks for guardsmen, stables, coachhouse, tennis court, croquet lawn, flower garden and park —most of the servants had succeeded in vanishing. The few who remained huddled in mute terror in the dark appeared anxious to cooperate, but all denied having seen the royal couple since the breakup of the supper party. The searchers found only one door locked, that of Mademoiselle d'Honneur Milica Petronovich, not because the room's occupant refused to open it, but because the soldier assigned to guard it took the key with him when he fled after the explosion. Colonel Mishich ordered one of his men to shoot off the lock.

When Milica recognized Colonel Mishich in the light of the dimly flickering candles, she jumped to her feet and greeted him, flushed with triumph. "Thank God, you've really done it!" she cried. "Long live King Peter Karageorgevich!"

Embarrassed, the colonel held up his hand to ward off the heat of her patriotic fervor. "Wait a minute— I mean, yes, long live King Peter— But first, we have to find King Alexander."

Baffled, Milica stared at him. "You mean you haven't"—she searched for the word—"you haven't—done it yet?"

"We don't know where he is," a lieutenant blurted. "We've been looking all over for him."

"This wretched darkness," Mishich said sheepishly as though apologizing for their failure in consummating the task at hand. "We hadn't counted on it."

"But why look here? What would the king be doing here?" Milica asked. "Have you searched the royal apartments?"

"Aren't we in the royal apartments?"

"Of course not. They're in the other wing. You can't even get there from here. Unless you go back to the vestibule or cross the yard."

Mishich turned angrily on Laza. "Did you hear that?"

It was only now that Milica caught sight of the general standing in the doorway. "What do you know! Lepi Laza! There's been quite a change since last we met."

Laza looked at her with unconcealed disgust. "So it seems for the moment. But I wouldn't count on its permanency if I were you. Wasn't Queen Draga paying you enough, Milica? What more could she give you? The shirt off her back, the diamond ring off her finger?"

Milica ignored him. "You'll find the king in her bedroom. Unless he's gotten away," she told Mishich.

The colonel looked at his watch. "Two thirty already," he said reproachfully as though the general were responsible for the wasted time. "Take us straight to the bedroom. And no more tricks."

"I'll lead you," Milica volunteered.

"No, thanks," Mishich said with finality. "You stay out of this."

"It would hurt the colonel's tender sensibilities to shoot people in a lady's presence, Milica," Laza quipped as he started for the vestibule.

Colonel Mashin had gone to the gendarmerie station to discover the outcome of the battle there and learned that six of the post's fifteen men had been killed and the rest disarmed by soldiers of the Sixth Infantry. The surviving gendarmes blamed the battalion commandants for the slaughter of their comrades. Had they known that the crowd prowling in the dark were soldiers, not demonstrators, they would have held their fire. Late in the evening they had received instructions from General Laza Petrovich that in case of any disturbance they were to shoot first and ask questions later. During the past weeks, a flow of contradictory orders from the Ministry of Home Affairs, the palace and their own commandant had caused them to become either trigger-happy or apathetic, according to each man's disposition. The gendarmes on duty that night had unfortunately chosen to be hotheaded and rash.

The cadet sent to Dr. Gashich's house returned with a box of candles, which he handed over to Colonel Mishich's search party. Once again, the officers stormed through the Serbian room and the adjoining salon and then entered Draga's boudoir. As though the slight fragrance that permeated these rooms were an added intoxicant, they lost all restraint and once again slashed at shadows, attacking chandeliers and stabbing at screens—two dozen demented Hamlets, searching for Polonius behind every drapery.

Discovering that the door from the boudoir into the bedroom was locked, they screamed for Lieutenant Lazarevich and his dynamite cartridges, then watched impatiently while he set off the charge. Not waiting for the dust and flying debris to settle, they pushed—in one surging mass—through the gaping hole into the bedroom.

All the candles except two were extinguished in the resulting melee. They were forced to halt and regain their bearings. As the candles were relighted, the wide connubial bed, its curtains of heavy silk bedecked with miniatures and framed pictures of saints, rose up before their bedazzled eyes like an exotic barge. With a wild animal scream, they attacked the empty bed like hyenas falling upon a carcass. Swords slashed at pillows, comforters, mattress and canopy. One blade's sweep cleared the bedside table of its bric-a-brac: a small rococo clock encrusted with diamonds, jars of face cream, bottles of perfume, more pictures of saints, more framed photos, the French novel *Le Trahison,* with its marker inserted at page 87.

Michael watched them in stunned silence. In their crazed onslaught he recognized his own rage that had wreaked vengeance on Draga's bed in their cottage six years before.

The realization that his anger against her had evidenced itself with the same savagery as theirs now caused him to cringe with shame and remorse. He had no right to despise them, for he was no better than they. They all were brothers under their skins, all sons of the same wild, hardhearted race. No matter where they were taken, how long they remained in a more civilized environment, culture was but a thin veneer capable of cracking at the slightest touch to reveal the roughness underneath.

The air, heavy with smoke, male perspiration, sulfur dioxide and the strong fragrance of spilled perfume, began to choke the men. Someone drew the draperies and opened the windows. The shredded curtains of the canopy fluttered like streamers in the breeze. The lace skirt of the queen's dressing table catching fire from a carelessly held candle was ripped off and trampled underfoot.

Finally the fresh air and sheer exhaustion brought the men to a standstill, and they glanced about wide-eyed, realization dawning on them that they had vented their fury on an empty bed.

"They're gone! Don't you see they're gone!" Mishich shouted as the bedlam subsided.

"They can't be far. This bed was slept in," a lieutenant pointed out. He turned to Laza. "They were right here, in this very bed while you made us chase our own tails through half the Konak." He reached up to grab the taller man by the neck. "Where are they?"

The general shook him off as if he were a yapping dog. "How should I know? I haven't seen them since supper."

Assigned to duty at the Old Konak, though never permitted into the royal apartments, Bogdanovich had a vague idea of the floor plan and now pointed to the bathroom door in the corner.

The men fell upon it, ready to smash it in, but to their surprise, a light push on the handle opened it. It turned out to be a good-sized room, neat, yet not luxurious. The royal couple were not hiding in it. Nor were they in the adjoining cubicle which held the toilet or the linen storage that opened off the bathroom. The only exit led through a corridor to the entrance hall, where men had been posted.

"By God, they're gone!" Colonel Mishich confirmed dejectedly.

"What now?" someone asked.

"We'll have to continue looking. They have to be somewhere in the house." In spite of an attempt to appear confident, apprehension was written all over his sharp-featured face. As long as the king was at large, he could get in touch with Colonel Nikolich, the loyal commandant of the Eighth Infantry Regiment at the Banjicki Barracks and order him to the rescue. In that case it was conceivable that the troops of the Sixth and Seventh infantries, learning the true reason for their presence at the Konak, might turn on their own officers and side with Colonel Nikolich. Nikolich could then get in touch with Alexander's allies at the Morava Division in Nish.

Mishich was painfully aware that *coups d'état* were delicate undertakings, based on the element of surprise. Participants were permitted only one try; if they botched that, they were doomed. Every member of the searching party knew that, and the realization of a possible defeat began to act like a depressant. Huddled like sheep in a thunderstorm in one bewildered flock, they glanced about, no longer searching for the enemy but for a way out.

"They must be here," Colonel Mishich repeated stubbornly. "They couldn't have escaped. The entire compound has been surrounded since one thirty. If they're not in the Old Konak, they might be in the New. Or the stables. The carriage house. The gazebo! No one's looked there yet. Let's go. Don't worry, we'll find them." Stepping jauntily, he led the way to the entrance hall, the men following him listlessly.

Michael was the last to leave the ravished bedroom. Dreading a drama, as he had, he hoped for a peaceful end to the night. Draga and her king had probably slipped out of the palace before it was surrounded by troops, and were now on their way to safety. His guess was that the bed had been turned down and pieces of clothing left scattered about to mislead the intruders, and he doubted that the couple were anywhere in the compound. Crossing the wide, empty space between the two palaces, they would have been sighted even in the dark of the night, a risk they would not have taken.

The noise of the search party receded through the entrance hall. There was quiet for a moment, followed by loud shouting in the front of the house.

"Apis has been shot! Apis has been shot!" Voices called for Colonel Mashin, for a doctor, for bandages.

Michael hurried—as fast as he could in the dark—in the direction of the uproar. "Is he dead?" he asked the first man he bumped into.

"No," the man said. "Wounded in the chest. Bleeding badly, but still alive. We found him standing on his feet, leaning against the wall. We'd been sent to search the attic; that's how we found him. Lieutenant Bogdanovich has gone to call Dr. Gashich."

Michael found Apis in the adjutants' room. They had had to move Captain Miljkovich's body from the couch and dump it on the floor in order to make room for Apis who lay wheezing and shivering, but fully conscious.

"What happened?" Michael asked him.

"This bloody blackout. I saw a shadow climbing the steps to the attic, called after him to stop, and when he didn't I fired. That's all I remember. I might have been shot by him or someone else. I don't know, because I passed out."

Colonel Mashin rushed into the room. He had been in the vestibule, engaged in keeping the communication lines open between the activists at the Konak and their confederates at the various camps and military posts by sending out messengers and receiving reports. Several police stations, as well as the Telephone Central, had been taken over by the conspirators.

At the sight of the wounded Apis, Mashin flew into a rage. "Damned idiots!" he shouted at the men drifting in and out of the office. "You were supposed to search the place and all the time there he was, bleeding to death. Why are you standing here like a herd of ruminating bullocks! Get a doctor!"

No one stirred, they sensed the panic behind his anger, and it made no impression on them.

"What about the king and queen?" Apis asked. "Have you found them?"

"Not yet," Mashin confessed in a suddenly subdued voice.

Apis responded with a string of curses and a complete disregard for the colonel's rank. "How is that possible? Letting them get away! Botching the whole damn thing!"

A lieutenant returned with the news that he'd found the Gashich house deserted and the doctor and his family gone. Cautiously Michael unbuttoned Apis' tunic to look at the chest wound. There were two small holes with no lacerations. One bullet had entered above the right nipple, the other under the collarbone. It was hard to estimate the damage. While another officer was dispatched to find a physician, Colonel Mishich's group, with Laza in tow, set out for the New Konak. Michael remained with Apis.

"They've left," Draga whispered.

"Yes, I think they have," Alexander agreed, pressing his lips to her cold cheek. Despite the sickening heat, she shivered.

They stood in the pitch dark, not really believing the enemy had withdrawn. After the first explosion they had leaped from bed and taken refuge in the small alcove.

The alcove was off the bedroom with access through a narrow iron door covered on the bedroom side with the same white- and pink-patterned silk as the walls, making it practically undetectable even in broad daylight. The door had no handle or knob and was opened and closed only with the help of the key.

It was the kind of useless nook found in old houses that had undergone successive remodelings by the generations occupying them. Draga had used the alcove as a sewing room where her maid ironed her clothes and did small alterations. It contained a full-length mirror, a sewing machine, ironing board and clothes rack. And one narrow window.

Both sovereigns had been asleep, he more deeply than she, when the shot that killed the sergeant was fired. She woke and shook Alexander awake. The bedroom lay in the wing which faced the park and beyond it the street with the Russian Legation, so their guess was that the sound had come from the front. Draga lay in bed, listening tensely till the blast of the explosion catapulted her to her feet.

"They are blowing up the palace and us with it."

"It might be an accident. An explosion in the electric installations."

"No. It's *them*."

It was Draga's idea that they hide in the alcove. She recalled that when Frau Weber had entered her service, she had had difficulty in finding the door. Later she jokingly used the command "Open Sesame" each time she entered the narrow cubicle.

Alexander had fumbled impatiently for his pince-nez, but his wife had grabbed him by the arms and pulled him into the alcove, where she took out the key, inserted it in the lock and turned it. At that moment the lights had gone out, and they stood rooted to the floor. After a moment, Draga had tiptoed to the window and cautiously parted the lace curtain. Except for dim light specks flickering in the distance, the night was inpenetrably dark. The Russian Legation loomed bulkily in front of her.

The iron door to the alcove, fitting tightly into its frame, was a blessing, for it screened all sounds except those of the gunshots in the entrance hall and the Serbian room.

"They are killing everyone," Draga whispered. "I've counted at least twenty shots. Those poor, poor people."

"No, I think it's the Palace Guard firing," Alexander told her. "I have great confidence in the Guard. Didn't they prove their loyalty during the demonstrations last March? Yes, I have implicit confidence in my guardsmen. And their officers."

As he put his arms around her soothingly, she realized that he was naked.

"For God's sake, Sasha, put something on," she said. Despite Alexander's reassurances, Draga expected the alcove to be stormed at any moment. The indignity of the king having to face his assailants in the nude disturbed her more than the imminent threat of danger. Clad only in a batiste nightgown, nevertheless her body would not be exposed to the intruders' leering curiosity.

Obediently, he felt his way to the door and was about to turn the key when she stopped him. "For God's sake, don't go out! They might be in the bedroom."

"You said I should put something on."

Remembering that Frau Weber had hung some freshly

pressed items of clothing on the coatrack in the corner, she groped her way to it and handed him a garment. It felt like silk.

"Take this. I think it's a shirt."

Alexander slipped it on. Then he exploded. "This isn't a shirt! It's your blouse."

"Never mind. It's made like a man's shirt. At least, it'll cover your private parts. If they see you naked, it might occur to them to shoot off your balls."

"Draga!" He sounded thoroughly shocked.

"What do you expect from a whore?" she asked bitterly.

"You're the Queen of Serbia."

"No, Sasha, I am not. When I was young, I thought if I tried really hard I could become anything. A famous actress, a doctor, even a queen."

"But you *are* a queen."

"No. Only the king's whore. Didn't you know?"

Several rooms away, additional shots rang out, their sharpness dulled by the thickness of the Konak walls.

"That was in the salon," Draga told him.

"No, it was farther away. Maybe in the dining room. They're being driven out. It won't be long now. You'll see."

"Whoever they are, I'll make them sorry they were born," Alexander sputtered. "And don't suggest I show compassion, because I won't. I'll have every one of them hanged publicly. We'll cut this festering boil open. Once and for all. It should've been done long ago."

"You've promised to abdicate."

"Abdicate? Never! I had no intention of abdicating!"

"You said you had. You promised me that tonight."

"Only to put your mind at ease. I made a big mistake, though. I should've had your Captain Vassilovich arrested and handed over to Boza Marshityanin. If Boza had gone to work on him, we'd have all his confederates by now. Boza never fails."

"He is not *my* Captain Vassilovich."

As she pulled away from him, he could tell by the sound of her voice that he had hurt her. "He was your lover, wasn't he?"

"He was. You always knew that. But let me tell you something, Sasha. And you'd better believe me because I may be dead by tomorrow morning and I fear God too much to tell a lie when I know I might face him soon."

"You won't be dead. I—"

Reaching out in the dark, she placed her hand on his lips to stifle his protests. "Listen to me. I've never denied that I had men before you. But once I moved to the Crown Street house—"

"Draga Street," he corrected her.

"It'll be Crown Street again. Ever since I moved into that house, there has been no one but you. I swear on my immortal soul, may I burn in hell for eternity if I am lying to you. I lived in sin with you for two and a half years, and if that made me a whore, I accept it, but I was *your* whore. I—"

She halted. There was a new upsurge of sound, louder in volume, animal shouts mixed with the rumble of furniture being knocked over. "They are closer," Draga whispered. "They are in the salon. They're banging the keys of the piano!"

Alexander chuckled. "They might not have a piano at home and want to practice."

"You're not frightened!" she told him, surprised.

"No. I am not. I am not supposed to be. I am the king." She heard him chuckle again and realized that he was telling the truth. He wasn't afraid, completely unmoved by the panic that benumbed her. Suddenly it struck her that except for that memorable night in Wiesbaden when he had crawled into her bed, she had never seen him betray any fear. Perhaps this was the key not only to his character, but to the puzzling uneven-ness of his reign. Since his thirteenth year he had been recog-nized as the king, even by his father, the only authority he had ever known. When Milan had kneeled before him and kissed his hand, the gesture had instilled the principle of his own infallibility in his adolescent mind. He was the king, and kings neither erred nor worried about the consequences of their deeds. The grace of God made him king. He was God's respon-sibility; consequently, God would guard him from any evil. The odd aspect of it was that Alexander didn't really believe in God, certainly not the way Draga did. Or did Alexander merely substitute fate for God, which, in the end, amounted to the same thing.

Draga spent most of the long period of relative quiet during which the intruders searched the service floor of the house, kneeling in prayer on the warped hardwood floor. At times, she rose and moved to the window, to peek out.

"Where is everyone? The Royal Guards? Where is Laza? Nicola? Nikodiye?" she asked Alexander. "Sasha, I know they are all dead. Otherwise, they would be here. I wish I had let Nicola go back to his Nanette. And Nikodiye. He didn't want to be heir to the throne. Only this morning he begged me to let him leave. He is clever, Nikodiye."

"If he is so clever, why did he behave like a jackass? He went out of his way to antagonize the officers' corps. As far as I am concerned, your brothers may settle in Paris or Brussels or wherever—I am not going to push that bill about the succession down the Skupshtina's throat."

"We won't get out of here alive," Draga moaned.

"We will," Alexander answered with absolute certainty.

"Oh, Sasha, I wish I had your courage!" For the first time in their long relationship, she felt him to be the adult and she the child.

They were standing, arms entwined, when they heard the approaching stampede of the search party.

"They are back!" she whispered.

"Wait! It might be the Palace Guard coming to our rescue."

The savage cacophony reverberating through the entire suite quickly indicated that it wasn't the guard, but renewed danger close to their hiding place, for the invaders had reached the boudoir. The clatter of smashed china mingled with the shouts of men gone berserk.

"That was the Sèvres vase given your father by President Carnot," Draga told him. "What a pity. It can never be replaced."

Alexander listened with deep concentration. "They must be drunk. Whoever they are. I'd say a small group. Not more than twenty. They got drunk together and decided to storm the Konak. It cannot be a planned revolt, just a spontaneous flare-up. They're drunk. They don't know what they're doing."

"Don't delude yourself, Sasha; they know. It's what we've feared. It seems as—" Her words were cut short by the blast of the explosion that smashed in the bedroom door. Emitting a frightened cry, she pressed her hands to her mouth to stifle the sobs that shook her body.

The reverberation of the explosion took a long time to die

down. Through the hairsbreadth crack between the iron door and its frame, every word spoken in the bedroom came to them distinctly. Alexander no longer could have any doubts about the nature of the mutiny. The intruders, venting their fury on the empty bed, shouted obscene curses against him and his wife. He recognized individual voices, the voices of men whose loyalty he had never questioned.

"That's Colonel Mishich," he told Draga.

"Good God, and they have Laza with them. They want him to tell where we are, but he won't. He won't. God bless dear Laza."

"Mishich," Alexander mused. "Mishich means the army. Oh, the bastards!"

"They don't know about this place. But someone will tell them."

"No one has up to now, so there is a chance."

"Sooner or later they will find out."

"By then there might be a change."

"If we're lucky."

"We've been up to now. If Laza had a chance to contact the Royal Guard, they'll drive out Mishich and his fine comrades."

They heard the men dart into the bathroom, then Colonel Mishich's flustered order to continue the search in the New Konak.

"We're saved," the king whispered.

There was the sound of retreating steps, then a period of silence, broken now and then by someone returning to the bedroom, pulling out drawers and rummaging in the rubble.

"What's that?" she asked.

"They're looting," Alexander told her angrily. "Tomorrow, there will be a purge. The first to go will be Laza."

"But Sasha, he refused to tell them where we were."

"It's his fault things have got to this stage. He was in charge of palace security. Some security! The king and queen crouching in a dark alcove like children afraid of being spanked. And a mob of drunken officers breaking into the palace as if it were an abandoned shack in the mountains! Don't ask me to spare him!"

The looters having moved from the bedroom, there was now a lull, which worried her more than the turmoil.

"Sasha, you're wrong. Laza is a good man," she told him, not wanting to protest more vigorously for fear of setting Alexander's jealousy ablaze.

"The next to be dealt with is Tzintzar-Markovich. I have a feeling he is behind tonight's events. That's why he tendered his resignation this noon. I should never have forgiven him his treasonous act at the time of our marriage. He was Papa's man. He still is. Papa! Wasn't he incredible? You know, at times I almost miss him."

Prime Minister General Tzintzar-Markovich had not gone to bed that night. No one in his household had. His wife had left to be with their eldest daughter, who was in labor. She had promised to phone, and when she hadn't, he had tried to call the Miljkovich house but was told by Central that the lines in that section of town were out of order. He was wondering what to do when his wife returned home with the news that an explosion followed by gunfire had been heard from the vicinity of the palace. The Miljkoviches lived in a quiet street a mere stone's throw from the Konak compound; that explained why she had heard the blast, while he, in the south end of town, had not. On her way home she discovered the main streets closed off by troops and had had to cut through alleys and backyards.

"I wonder what the bastard is up to now?" the Premier muttered. His wife didn't have to ask whom he meant by "bastard." Lately it had been his favorite pejorative for the king.

Madame Tzintzar-Markovich had left her daughter in the care of a doctor and a midwife. Although the birth was not imminent, the young woman kept asking for her husband, who was on night duty at the Old Konak.

"I tried to phone Yovan at the palace," Madame Tzintzar-Markovich reported, "but the Central operator told me the line was out of order."

"Something strange is happening," the general said. "I had better—" He halted as someone banged on their front door. "Here they are. The little scum hasn't wasted much time."

"Do you think they have come to arrest you?" his wife asked fearfully. When he nodded, she said. "The cellar," pausing to control the sobs that choked her. "You might get out through the cellar. If you can make it to the icehouse, you'll be safe. They won't find the tunnel."

The tunnel had been dug in the summer of 1900, when officers opposing the royal marriage had reason to fear for their lives. It led from the icehouse, a cemented hole under a double-thatched roof built flush with the ground, to the far end of the orchard. At the time of its excavation, it had proved an unnecessary precaution, yet Madame Tzintzar-Markovich kept it—with the help of her sons—in good repair for "just in case," as she had put it.

"No," the general said. "I won't crawl away like a scared mole. Let the king arrest me. It'll harm him more than me."

He went to the window, parted the draperies and looked out. "Yes," he said, "he's sent quite an honor guard for me. Go, tell Gordana to answer the door."

Captain Svetozar Radakovich was contemplating breaking the door down when it was opened by a smiling servant girl.

"Come in, sir. The general said he'll be glad to see you. He is in the front parlor. The first door to the right." Her polite curtsy disconcerted the captain as the purpose of his visit was not a social call. Motioning to his men to remain outside, he entered the house, walked to the door indicated by the girl and knocked.

"Well, well, if it isn't Captain Radakovich!" The general rose and extended his hand jovially. "It's been a long time since we last met." He threw a glance at the captain's insignia, then reached out and touched a medal on his visitor's chest. "So you're still with the Sixth Infantry. Didn't I pin that on you in 1885? Almost eighteen years ago. Would you believe that?"

Radakovich stared at the man, secretly wishing he would stop being so damn comradely. "General"—he managed to force an official tone from his parched throat—"I've been sent to you with a special communication." He halted to take a deep breath. "I've been ordered to arrest you and keep you under guard until further notice." This was the lie Colonel Mashin had instructed him to use. After the arrest, his orders were to lead the general from the house, stand him against the nearest convenient wall and shoot him dead.

"I am not in the least surprised, Radakovich," the premier replied cheerfully. "It serves me right. I let the king force me into heading his cabinet at a time when no honorable politician was willing. I've been expecting this from the king ever since I tendered my resignation this noon."

Completely flustered at news that the general had broken with the king, Radakovich repeated, "My orders are to arrest you, sir." He wondered what he should do. Execute the order anyway, or contact Mashin for new instructions. He felt his stomach churn alarmingly and swallowed nervously to avoid vomiting on the general's Persian rug.

"Don't take it too hard, Radakovich," the general went on in a brotherly tone. "I know how you feel, but you're an army man, and the army isn't supposed to question orders, just execute them. Yet there is no hurry about it, is there? No reason why we shouldn't have a glass of schnapps together for old times' sake. Do you smoke?" He picked up a small silver box from the table and proffered it to the captain. "Look at the engraving, Radakovich. 'In sincere acknowledgment of loyal services, Alexander.' Do you appreciate the irony?" He lighted the captain's cigarette, then poured two glasses from the slivovitz bottle on the table. "To your health!"

"Thank you, sir." The captain found himself unable to control his shaking hands as he lifted the schnapps to his lips.

Madame Tzintzar-Markovich, eavesdropping with her ears pressed to the door, tried to hear what the two men were saying. Though she wasn't able to catch every word, the friendly tone of the conversation served to allay some of her fears. She concluded that her husband had been wrong when he thought the king had ordered his arrest. Perhaps Alexander had merely sent a message now that the Konak telephones were out of order.

She had started from the house to return to her daughter's bedside when she was rudely stopped by Radakovich's men. Alarmed, she burst into the parlor.

"Mito," she said to her husband. "I was going to go back to Elena, but there are soldiers around the house, and they won't let me through."

"No one is to leave the house, madame," Radakovich told her.

"I must go, Captain. My daughter is in labor. There was an explosion at the Konak and a lot of shooting. Enough to frighten her badly. Do you know what's happening at the palace?"

After a long pause, he told her, "No, I don't, madame, I really don't."

"Please, tell your men to let me through. Do you have children?" The captain nodded. "Then you must understand. If you want to, send a soldier with me to see that I go straight to my daughter's."

"For God's sake, Radakovich," the general broke in testily. "She isn't going to demonstrate against the king. She wants to go to her daughter."

Radakovich heaved an unhappy sigh. "All right, General." Stepping to the window, he called out to his sergeant: "Madame Tzintzar-Markovich has my permission to go to Captain Miljkovich's house. Go with her and see that she gets there safely. And stay there so that neither she nor Captain Miljkovich's wife is harmed."

"Why should they be harmed?" the general asked, frowning. "What can the king have against two harmless women?"

"I hate to leave you, Mito," his wife said. "What is to happen to you?"

"Nothing much, my dear." The general patted her cheek. "I guess young Sasha is merely trying to show me who is master. Go on, Elena needs you. There is nothing much you can do here."

She embraced him, then shook hands with Radakovich. She was leaving as the general called after her, "Before I forget! If I am taken to the fortress, order the food sent in for me from Kolaratz's. Pashich told me they're more reliable than the Serbian Crown. He always got his dinner piping hot from them."

As soon as she was gone, he refilled the captain's glass.

"I'm afraid we ought to be going," Radakovich muttered feebly.

"No, no— When I leave here, I'll be your prisoner, but as long as you're here, you're my guest. And only a rude guest would refuse a third drink with his host. Tradition, remember?"

"Wasn't this a terrible day?" the captain asked, toying with his glass. "This heat makes you dizzy even without schnapps."

"How about a cup of coffee? Yes, that's what we both need.

At least I do. God only knows how long Chief Marshityanin's men will keep me awake with their idiotic questions."

He rose and started for the kitchen door at the far end of the room. The captain gazed wide-eyed at the tall, ramrod-straight figure. In his mind's eye it easily coalesced with the equally stiff-backed man-shaped boards used for target practice on his regimental drill grounds. As though hypnotized, he drew his gun and, still sitting, fired a shot at the wide tunic-clad back. The general halted but did not fall. Radakovich slowly rose from his seat and emptied the remaining chambers of the revolver into the motionless, still-erect figure. The general executed a grotesque *entrechat*, then slumped to the floor.

It had been a long time since the captain had killed a human being, and for a moment, the irrevocable finality of the act petrified him. Gasping at the corpse that only a few seconds before had been one of the most powerful personages in Serbia and realizing that a snap of his finger had achieved this transformation, he was filled with a strange elation. He had never before been aware of the identity of a victim, not even the woman he had raped after cutting her throat. Her death rattle had no more moved him than the agony of the Bulgar horse that had broken its leg when he rode it back to the Serbian front lines after an attack on an enemy village. He had put the horse out of its misery with a well-aimed shot but wasted no bullet on the woman. In his youth, he had killed with the detachment of a harvester swinging his scythe. This was the first time he had killed someone whom he knew, even respected. That he could do it, despite strong scruples, filled him with satisfaction. He and his gun were a force with close to godlike powers.

He was stirred from his ruminations by two young women, the general's unmarried daughters, bursting into the room. One threw herself across her father's body, emitting a demented wail, while the other huddled against the wall. A gurgling sound like water rushing down a drain, came from her mouth, and when the wail began to grate on his nerves, Radakovich raised his gun and pulled the trigger. There was a sharp click. Befuddled, he stared at the gun, finally realizing it was unloaded. With a disgusted snort he turned and walked from the room, the girls' screams ringing in his ears long after the front door had slammed shut behind him.

Maria Christina had been stirred from a deep sleep by her siblings' voices. She turned the light on. Voyka stuck her head in the door.

"Are you still awake?"

"How can anyone sleep with this racket? Can't you ever come home quietly? It's one thirty. Where have you been?"

"At the Konak. Draga just wouldn't get up from the table. I thought we were going to sit there all night. And you can't rise before the queen gives the signal. Court etiquette, you know."

Maria Christina dropped back on the pillow. "Oh, shit. Get to bed, both of you and let me sleep, for God's sake. I have to get up early in the morning. Can't stay in bed till noon like you two princesses."

Since her separation from her husband, Maria Christina had shared her bedroom with her sisters. The two Lunyevitza brothers and her son, George, slept in the other bedroom.

The girls undressed with the usual chatter and giggling. Impatiently, Maria Christina turned off the light.

"Will you stop that idiotic squawk and be quiet?" she scolded them. A few minutes later their even breathing told her that they had fallen asleep while she lay wide awake, ruminating on the thoughtlessness of the young.

She was still awake when she heard the shot. No. 16 Crown Street, now called Draga Street, was close enough to the Konak for her to know that the gunfire came from the compound. She listened, holding her breath, but there were no more shots. After a while, she relaxed, dozing off, when the explosion shattered the silence of the neighborhood. She sat up unhappily, concluding that not much sleep seemed to be in store for her that night.

The blast, followed by the sound of the battle at the gendarmerie station, woke everyone in the house.

"Good God, this is it!" Nikodiye said, already pulling on his pants.

"What now?" Nicola asked, as always, allowing Nikodiye to take the lead.

"We'll go to the Konak. What else? Find out what's happening. Whoever the attackers are have met with resistance. Probably from the Palace Guards. No, the shooting isn't at the Konak. It must be the gendarmerie station at the corner of the boulevard." While slipping on his tunic, he listened tensely. "That's odd. The explosion was at the Konak, but not the shooting. It's definitely on the boulevard. I wonder why?" He then answered himself. "The explosion was a time bomb! That's what it was. Jesus Christ, I hope it wasn't planted in Draga's bedroom. Oh, the bastards! The goddamn bastards trying to kill a woman!"

Their nephew, George, staggered sleepily from his bed. "I am going with you."

"No, you're not. I won't have your mother nagging us that we let you catch your death in that wind. Go back to bed and pull that eiderdown over your ears like a good boy."

"A little while ago my mother sent me to the Konak. That's how worried she is about me." Nevertheless, he obeyed his uncles. He was feeling groggy, and besides, he had no desire to be in the presence of gunfire.

Nicola, also dressed, was now rummaging in his bureau drawer. "Have you seen my medals?" he asked Nikodiye. "I had them on tonight."

"Never mind them. We might be late already. Come to think of it, Draga must have anticipated some kind of trouble. She was on edge all during supper."

The women of the house were in the salon, huddled at the window. Old Yovanka, the cook, was wailing hysterically, but the girls and Maria Christina seemed calm.

"The whole neighborhood is up," Voyka told them, leaning over the ledge. "Everyone's wondering about the explosion. There is a crowd coming this way." She strained her eyes. "Soldiers. Yes, I can see their bayonets glistening in the light of the streetlamp."

"We're leaving," Nicola called to them from the threshold. "Close the windows and lock the doors. And don't let anyone in. No matter what. We'll be back as soon as we can."

The brothers hurried from the house, Nicola lagging behind as he fumbled with the medals he had finally found in the bathroom. Halfway down Draga Street they collided with the soldiers, a detachment of the Seventh Infantry led by Lieutenant Tankossich. In the dark, the lieutenant recognized the brothers only when they asked him if he knew what was happening at the Konak.

Tankossich spit the words at them. "Alexander and his whore are dead, that's what's happening."

Nikodiye stared into the ugly face illuminated by a shaft of light coming through an open window. For the fraction of a second, he was back on the unpaved Shabats street in front of the elementary school and the face belonged to one of his schoolmate tormentors. His fist twitched with the desire to smash it, but his arms were pinned down by two of the soldiers. The sensation of *déjà vu* gave way to a stabbing pain. Draga was dead, probably torn to pieces by the bomb blast. He was stirred from his immobility by Nicola reaching for his gun.

"No, no, don't," he shouted, hoping to avoid the disgrace of being shot down in the street like stray dogs.

By then Nicola, too, was being held by restraining hands.

Tankossich signaled to the soldiers to form a tight ring around them. Nikodiye peered searchingly into the men's countenances, trying to detect any sign of emotion on them, but all he saw was a dumb indifference. It told him what he had always suspected, that these peasants, jerked from their simple existence in some godforsaken backwoods, didn't even know who the Lunyevitza brothers were. The city that lay beyond their barracks' walls with its problems and politics remained as alien to them as it had been before their two-year military service. They were taught to obey their officers, and that they did because it was the only way for them to be done with the army and return physically to a world that in spirit they had never left.

"Who told you that their majesties were dead?" Nicola asked, suspecting that the lieutenant was lying.

"*I* am telling you," Tankossich screeched; then remembering Mashin's warning to conduct his mission with dignity, he lowered his voice. "Will you gentlemen hand over your weapons?"

"What if we refuse?" Nicola asked.

"In that case, I'll be compelled to shoot you."

"On whose authority?"

The question confounded the lieutenant. The words, Colonel Mashin's were on the tip of his tongue when he realized the

343

name wouldn't carry enough weight, at least not without a lengthy explanation. "On the authority of His Majesty King Peter's government," he told them grandly. "I have orders to arrest you and take you to the regimental headquarters of the Seventh Infantry. Will you please comply?"

Nikodiye unfastened his belt with the holster and handed it, together with his sword, to the lieutenant. The information that they were going to be taken to the Palilula Barracks revealed the fact that the rebellion had the participation of the army or, at least, part of the army.

"I am waiting, Captain," Tankossich said to Nicola, who had failed to follow his brother's example and kept glaring at the lieutenant in mute defiance.

"Do as you're told, Nicola," his brother ordered. "Think what it would do to your sisters to find you dead in front of their doorstep."

With a groan, Nicola complied, and they started for the Palilula camp, Tankossich leading the way and the soldiers surrounding the two captives like a portable wall. They were still within earshot of the Konak when the second explosion occurred.

"They're blowing up the whole palace," Nikodiye groaned. The first fresh pain had dulled to a quiet unhappiness that seemed to have been a part of him all his life. He conjured up Draga's pouter-pigeon image full of angry, indignant love, the way she had appeared to him in the morning. What did they have to kill her for? She had never hurt anyone.

"You should've stayed in Paris," his brother said.

"And you in Brussels."

Nicola chuckled angrily. "Wasn't I psychic when I resigned my commission?"

"Save your breath, Captain," Tankossich said nastily. "Lies won't help you."

"I wasn't talking to you," Nicola snapped.

They continued in silence until they reached the camp. Tankossich left the brothers under guard in the yard to report to the regimental commandant, Colonel Solerovich, who had just returned to the barracks from his home, where he had spent the better part of the night. He belonged to the group of officers classified as "favorably inclined" by the conspirators, which meant that while he wasn't to take an active part in the coup, he had promised not to oppose it. After the second explosion at the Konak and a message from Colonel Mashin that things were developing according to schedule, Solerovich became confident that the rebels would succeed and decided to espouse their cause openly. Nevertheless, when Tankossich reported the brothers' arrest, he felt more disturbed than pleased. He was familiar with the order to have the Lunyevitzas summarily executed; still, the act seemed a bit premature to him. For one thing, he had received no positive evidence that all resistance to the coup had been put down. Mashin's message, delivered after one o'clock, was vague and left room for speculation.

"Have you ordered the firing squad assembled, sir?" Tankossich asked.

The colonel's fingers drummed a nervous tattoo on his desk top. "Now wait a second, Lieutenant. Let's not rush things."

"What are you waiting for, sir? Even if the king and queen were still alive—"

"So they *are* alive!" the colonel pounced.

For a fleeting moment, Tankossich pondered the possibility of shooting the man. He could always argue he did it because the colonel had betrayed the conspiracy. Then realizing that it would be too daring an act to perform on his own, he resorted to a lie instead.

"But, sir, they *are* dead. They were blown to bits by the dynamite Lieutenant Lazarevich exploded in their bedroom. I can name ten people who saw them die." When the colonel still hesitated, he pressed on. "We must dispose of the brothers, sir. If we don't, the Obrenovich partisans might rally around them. We cannot take such risks, sir."

The colonel shrugged. "All right, have them brought in."

The death sentence written in Colonel Mashin's longhand had lain in the desk drawer all night. After the brothers were escorted in, he unlocked the drawer and pulled out the paper with the three short paragraphs written on it. In a voice raucous with doubt, he read the order to the two handsome young men who faced him at stiff attention.

After the first few words, as the meaning of the ceremony became clear to him, Nicola threw a look of panic at his younger brother. Nikodiye, trying to communicate love and encouragement, kept his eyes fixed on Nicola's face throughout the reading. A patient smile lingered around his lips as though he were hearing a joke whose tag line he already knew. When the colonel finished with the recital of his and his brother's crimes against the nation and of the punishment to be meted out, he had only one question to ask: "How soon, sir?"

The colonel swallowed hard. "Now." He waited for the brothers' reaction, but none was forthcoming. "Do you have anything to say in your defense?"

Calmly Nikodiye shook his head. "No, sir. What good would it do at this stage?"

Nicola echoed him. "No, sir."

"Any wishes?"

"Perhaps a cigarette."

Nicola nodded assent.

"And one more thing, sir," Nikodiye said quickly. "That we be executed side by side and buried together."

"Both requests granted."

"Three," Nikodiye corrected him, counting on his fingers. "Cigarette, execution, burial."

"That's right, three." Ashen-faced, the colonel ordered Lieutenant Tankossich to take them to the courtyard behind the guardhouse. It was a grass-covered area enclosed on three sides by high walls, where, since the existence of the Palilula camp, dozens of soldier prisoners, convicted of various crimes, had met their deaths.

"Do you remember a week ago last Sunday night at the Kolaratz?" Tankossich asked Nikodiye as they walked through the alley alongside the guardhouse.

Nikodiye threw a surprised glance at the leering wolf face, then quickly turned his eyes away. It was hardly a sight he wished to take with him to the hereafter. "Should I?" he asked, not really caring.

"You ordered the national anthem played and every officer to rise in your honor. I was one of them. Do you remember it?"

Incredulous, Nikodiye asked, "Is this why we are going to be shot?"

"It is!" Tankossich told him acidly.

"The punishment hardly fits the crime," Nikodiye pointed out.

"Among other things. You heard the verdict."

Nikodiye felt no need to reply, and they continued in silence. Suddenly, Nicola halted.

"Oh, hell," he exclaimed. Immediately, the lieutenant's revolver was jabbed against his ribs, and simultaneously, six rifles were whipped off shoulders and held at the ready.

"What's the matter?" Nikodiye asked.

"I wrote a letter to Nanette this evening and forgot to mail it. It's on the table in the bedroom, all sealed and stamped."

"If you're lucky, some good soul will find it and mail it for you."

"If I am lucky," Nicola repeated.

They reached the yard. No stakes had been prepared. This left Tankossich no choice but to stand the brothers unceremoniously against the wall. He remembered that the colonel had granted them a last smoke and, taking a battered tin box from his pocket, held it out to them. "Cigarette, gentlemen?" he asked elegantly.

"If you don't mind, we prefer our own brand, don't we, Nikodiye?" Nicola asked.

Tankossich shrugged. "I don't blame you. I would, too, if I could afford your brand."

Nikodiye produced his silver case filled with Khedives and offered one to Nicola. The brothers smoked in silence, their arms about each other's shoulders, inhaling deeply, relishing every draft. Nicola finished first, and when he threw away the butt, Nikodiye dropped his.

Tankossich ordered the soldiers to move into line, then rescinded the order, remembering that the prisoners were supposed to be blindfolded. He asked the brothers if they had handkerchiefs.

"Forget it," Nikodiye told him with the impatience of a man about to miss his train. "Get on with the damned business, will you?"

While the soldiers formed the line, the brothers embraced and kissed each other. There was no fear on their faces, and as they linked arms, they turned to confront the firing squad.

Lieutenant Tankossich planted himself at a safe distance from the soldiers and raised his sword. At the final command of "Fire!" the blade flashed through the air and six shots rang out. Six bullets hit the brothers, tearing into their chests and faces.

They fell sideways like knocked over bowling pins. The lieutenant waited a moment, then stepped to them and delivered the *coups de grâce* to the napes of their necks.

He had expected to derive a triumphant satisfaction from their deaths, yet all he felt was the emptiness of anticlimax. He had hoped for a plea for mercy or, at least, an indignant outburst and felt cheated that it never came. They had been the wrongdoers and he the avenger; nevertheless, the sight of their lifeless bodies with the horribly disfigured faces suddenly filled him with a strange remorse.

He ordered the squad to break rank. Alone and unobserved, he stepped to the bodies and leaned over them. Turning them over on their backs, he emptied their pockets of cigarette cases, money, matches, then removed the rings from their fingers. He stuffed the valuables into his own pocket, then started away when, with sudden decision, he returned to pull off their blood-spattered patent-leather cavalry boots.

3 A.M.

THE men, led by Colonel Mishich, poured from the Old Konak, surprised to discover a drizzle falling on the parched yard. Bogdanovich and four others remained behind to go through the attic and the cellar once more.

Startled by a sudden gust of wind, Laza Petrovich halted under the marquee. "For God's sake, Colonel," he said to Mishich. "Let me get my cap from the office. Your young men have hair, but mine is thinning as you can see. I'll catch my death if I go bareheaded in this rain."

Mishich gave him a long look. "Are you afraid of dying?"

"Of cold, yes, of a bullet, no—a well-aimed bullet, of course, not a botched job like this." He indicated his bandaged arm.

Captain Ristich tapped a second lieutenant, with hair as thick and unruly as a clown's wig, on the shoulder. "Give your cap to the man. You'd think the army had taught him to take a little rain in his stride. But of course, he never served in the field, since he was assigned to special duty in the queen's bed. And there of course, the weather is always balmy."

"That was an uncalled-for remark, Captain, and in very bad taste," Laza told him, then turned to thank the lieutenant, who had rather unceremoniously plunked his cap on the general's head.

Passing the palace guardhouse, they found Colonel Mashin talking to two civilians, members of the Cabinet in waiting, who had become concerned over the delay of a report on the successful completion of the coup.

"Where are you going?" Mashin asked the officers.

"To the New Konak. To look for them there."

The two civilians pricked up their ears. The young Radical attorney, Ljubomir Zivkovich, asked, "To look for whom?"

Embarrassed, Mashin answered, "The king and queen."

"You don't know where they are?"

"They're not in the Old Konak. Somehow they've slipped out. Just when, we don't know. A footman reported he escorted them to their bedroom shortly after one o'clock, so they couldn't have got far."

The civilians looked incredulous. "You told us everything was progressing according to schedule," Zivkovich reminded Mashin reproachfully.

"They have to be somewhere," Mishich replied nervously. "That old nest has more nooks and crannies than the Catacombs."

"Have you searched it thoroughly?" the other civilian, Genchich, asked.

"We certainly have."

"And what makes you think they are at the New Konak?"

Deflated, Mishich shrugged. "General Petrovich says that's where they must be."

The attorney exchanged a quick glance with his companion. "Well, good luck to you, gentlemen. We'd better report back to our colleagues. Needless to say, their best wishes are with you." After a quick round of handshakes, they started for the gate, appearing to be in a great hurry to leave the field of a still-undecided battle.

The night was starless now, and the rain came down in steady streams. The telltale sound of restlessness rose from the troops who occupied the streets around the Konak.

"Someone's got to address the men and keep them from dispersing," Mashin pointed out.

"And tell them what?" Mishich asked.

"Anything. That the king is dead or left the country. They've heard the explosions; it is dangerous to let them draw their own conclusions."

Mashin looked questioningly at the men around him, waiting for someone to volunteer to address the troops. No one did. He was unable to read their expressions in the dark, but their silence clearly indicated their lethargy and doubt, and he read their thoughts. One hundred and fifty strong, they had invaded the Old Konak, burned and looted it, killed a sergeant of the Palace Guards, but as long as Alexander Obrenovich remained at large, victory eluded them. They had risked their lives to fulfill the ambition of such civilian nonentities as would-be Premier Yovan Avakumovich, the attorney Zivkovich, ex-Minister Genchich and an aging prince residing in sheltered retirement in Geneva. The civilian conspirators had had the foresight to remain in the background and let the uniforms fight their battle. These men, including the prince, would survive to carry on their surreptitious intrigues, while the uniforms would be marched to the gallows.

A young lieutenant, riding bareback on a plump gray horse, galloped in through the gate. On reaching Mashin and the officers, he jumped off smartly and, kicking his heels, performed a stiff salute.

"Lieutenant Milan Marinkovich respectfully requesting permission to report, sir," he shouted in a voice as loud as a trumpet call, his oily-skinned, handsome face glowing with animal pleasure.

"Permission granted," Mashin said limply.

"Sir, I wish to report having personally executed Minister of Defense Milovan Pavlovich and also Home Minister Velya Todorovich."

Mashin looked at him bewilderedly. "You have? But weren't

Captain Yosipovich and Lieutenant what's-his-name assigned to the—" His voice trailed off. The tension and fatigue of the endless night were beginning to cloud his thinking. For a moment, he wasn't even sure why the Home Minister's name had been placed on the death list. The news of the assassinations which an hour earlier he would have greeted with satisfaction became now an added weight to the burdens already on his shoulders.

Flushed with victory, Marinkovich continued, "That's right, sir. Captain Yosipovich and Lieutenant Popovich. But it was like this, sir. When our detachment under the command of the captain reached the Pavlovich house, the minister was standing fully dressed in an upstairs window waiting for us. He must have heard the explosions from the Konak, guessed what was happening and decided to defend himself. Captain Yosipovich ordered the men to open fire, but the minister ducked. He fired his revolver at us and wounded a private. I quickly went around the house, in through the back door and up the stairs. The door to the minister's room was locked. I blasted it open with the dynamite cartridge I'd had the foresight to have on me. Then I shot him. It took him a long time to die, so I had one of the men who followed me upstairs smash his skull with a rifle butt." He halted, waiting proudly, like a retriever bringing in killed game, for a pat of commendation. When none was forthcoming, he continued with somewhat flagging enthusiasm. "As we were leaving the Pavloviches, we saw Lieutenant Popovich's squad surrounding the Todorovich house and the lieutenant go in. After a while he came out and ordered his squad to march off. I went up to him to ask what happened. First he refused to answer; then suddenly he broke down, sobbing. He wasn't able to do it, he said, because when he went in, he found the whole family sitting around the dining-room table, drinking coffee. They, too, knew that something unusual was going on in town; otherwise, they would've been in bed. Recognizing him, the minister rose to greet him, and the wife poured him a cup of coffee and asked him how many lumps of sugar he wanted. He stood for a while, gaping at them, then turned and walked out. I thought someone had to do the job, and it might as well be me. They were still in the dining room when I went in. The minister, his wife, the son and the daughter Lieutenant

Popovich had once been practically engaged to. The minister sat with his back to the door. I shot him twice, and he fell. Captain Yosipovich had followed me in, but his shots missed. One went through the son's sleeve without wounding him. The women screamed, but I don't think they were hurt." He halted, trying to read the faces around him, becoming increasingly alarmed at their indifference. "I rode here on one of their carriage horses because I thought you were anxious to hear the report, sir."

Mashin looked at him wearily. "I'm glad you had your fun. Now get the goddamn horse back to its stable or I'll have you court-martialed for horse stealing when this carnival is over. In case you don't know, Lieutenant, you're supposed to be a Serbian officer and not a bloody Janizary."

Lieutenant Marinkovich reeled as though hit by an unexpected blow. As far as he could tell in the dark, the appearance of the men, their rain-soaked tunics left carelessly unbuttoned over bare chests, their attitude of impotent desperation indicated that the coup had somehow got out of hand. The realization that in case of a final debacle some of the blame would be pinned on him filled him with sudden fury. Short and square, he had a sharp nose and a shock of unruly hair. Flapping his arms and scraping the ground with his spurred boots, he looked like a bantam cock ready to hop on the colonel's head and peck out his eyes.

"You personally gave orders for the executions," he shouted. "I was present when you said that should any of the appointed men fail to carry out or be prevented from carrying out your orders, it was the next man's duty to step into his place. So don't you tell me I acted without authorization!"

It was open mutiny. Mashin's hand went to his holster but dropped when he sensed that the muttering subalterns around him were on Marinkovich's side.

"You don't have to remind me of the orders I gave, Lieutenant." He tried to sound authoritative and in command. "However, let me remind you that I am in charge of this operation and, as commander, consider your tone crass insubordination. This time, though, I am willing to ascribe it to your perturbed state of mind and overlook it. Next time I won't. Dismissed."

He turned to the men surrounding him. "Let's go to the

New Konak, gentlemen. We cannot leave any possibility unexplored, no matter how doubtful."

She stood at the window, peering out into the night. The darkness seemed to have thinned out, or was it only her eyes becoming used to it? A light went on in one of the upstairs rooms of the Russian Legation, only to be extinguished a second later.

"They are awake. They've stayed awake all night, watching this house," she whispered to her husband. "Colonel Grabov and Minister Tcharikoff. I can almost see them, glued to the window, their binoculars trained on us. When they heard the explosions, they must have thought we were killed. Then they started wondering, probably sending a man over to find out what was happening. You said the army was involved. In that case there isn't much hope for us, is there?"

"I didn't mean the whole army. Probably just a few regiments or a battalion or two. That swine Mishich had his accomplices surround the Konak under cover of night. At daybreak they'll have to withdraw. I cannot believe that men like Colonel Nikolich of the Eighth Infantry or Captain Panayotovich of the Palace Guards or Captain Kostich of the Royal Guards would desert us. They'll find a way to get us out of here."

"Panayotovich was on duty last night. And so was Ljuba Kostich. Don't you see? They've either fled or were killed by the rebels. All those loyal to us must be dead. There's no hope, Sasha."

"Yes, there is. If we can hold out till daybreak."

"They'll find us before that."

"They believe we've gotten away; they're scared out of their wits. They'll assume we're in Zimony and about to return at the head of our loyal divisions."

"The trouble is we're not in Zimony, Sasha. We're in this hellhole. How long do you think we can stay here? Hours, days, weeks? Let's suppose we're neither betrayed nor rescued. Just left here, parched and starving to death. How long before we go mad? Before we scream for them to come and massacre us?"

"Hush. Let's not lose our heads."

"Did you hear them, Sasha? The horrible things they shouted? They're mad. They must have slashed every drape to ribbons.

And the bed! If we'd been in that bed, Sasha! What the room must look like! My beautiful room. Of all the rooms in the house the only one I liked. That and the boudoir. Because they were my very own. The others reflected the taste of people who'd lived in them before me. I never liked the salon because of that violet wallpaper. Your mother's choice. That's why I could never stand violets. I never even wore a dress of their color."

"You won't have to look at that paper again, for I am afraid the gentlemen used it for target practice. We'll have the room redone in a color of your choosing."

"Wasn't your mother horrible to us, Sasha? She always said all she wanted was our happiness. Mine and yours. But not our happiness with each other. She was poison. This frightful night. It would never have come to this without her. Serbia would be a peaceful country with your father still alive and king and you the heir, happily married to some nice plump archduchess and the father of six little Obrenoviches. No Russian agents masquerading as icon peddlers in the villages to incite the people against you, no Colonel Mishich, no horde of highwaymen in officers' uniforms rampaging through the Konak."

"And where would the Queen of Serbia be?"

"Who knows? Married to a shopkeeper or a teacher." Or, she thought, walking the streets of Paris. She didn't speak aloud because she knew it would upset him. Despite all their years together, Alexander had never really known her. If he had, he would never have crowned her Queen of Serbia. It wasn't her fault that she had failed. She was not born to be queen. She was a drifter, not a doer. Things happened to her, and she allowed them to happen. She had never planned to marry Svetozar Mashin. He simply proposed, and she accepted him, the only way out of a dead end, her only escape from an alcoholic mother, a brood of hungry siblings, a father in the insane asylum. It seemed she had always been caught in dead ends, like the room she was in now, an iron door the sole exit. But exit to what? Freedom or death? Whichever, it would not be she who opened the door, but someone else. Just as Natalie opened another door for her, leading from another dead end. She, Draga Mashin, had become *dame d'honneur* to a queen, but she'd never applied for the position; it was bestowed upon her, just as later the role of queen had been. Of course, it was a mere tag. Her real position had been doormat. Yet she would have stayed forever with Natalie if she had not been set adrift again. Then Alexander made her his queen. Draga Mashin, Queen of Serbia! What a bizarre idea? Who could blame Czarina Alexandra for refusing to ride in an open carriage with her? Or Kaiser Wilhelm? Or Queen Victoria? Only a person as autocratic and reckless as Sasha could conceive of such an impossible notion. She had never really wanted it. Not in Wiesbaden or Biarritz or Belgrade. Royal mistress was already more than enough. But queen! It was inevitable that she would make a mess of it.

Alexander, pursuing his own train of thought, remarked suddenly, "Mama never loved me."

"But your father did. He loved you very much. You should never have plotted against him. Son against his own father. That was sinful. That's what we are paying for now."

"The attempt failed, didn't it?"

"It was the intent, Sasha. That's what matters. We are guilty, we both are. It makes little difference that Knezevich was a poor shot."

"Now just a minute! When Colonel Taube came to me and asked for my consent to try a second time, didn't I refuse? Didn't I have Knezevich executed publicly and Andjelich in his cell? All that to make amends. All that to set Papa's mind at ease. To dispel the bad feeling between us. I went as far as arresting and trying the Radicals, just to please Papa—"

"They were not involved, and you knew it—"

It was typical of him to ignore the argument. Once he adopted a line of defense, he never wavered from it. "If I had agreed to Colonel Taube's suggestion, we could've been married a year earlier."

"Our marriage. That was what killed your father. We succeeded where Knezevich failed. He loved you and—"

"If he really loved me, he wouldn't have objected to our marriage. Anyway, let's not—" he halted. There was the sound of cabinet and wardrobe doors being opened. "Looters," he whispered. The rustle of paper as the men rummaged in the desk drawers and their comments on the letters they found indicated a search for documents that could be used as incriminating evidence against the royal couple.

"Did you hear that?" Alexander asked after the voices receded in the distance. "They sounded as though they were planning to try us. What a preposterous idea!"

"Better than getting killed," she pointed out. The notion that their lives might not be in imminent danger failed to lift the terrible pressure from her chest. "If they do, they'll charge me with every possible crime under the sky. Murder, embezzlement, whoring. They will have men testify they slept with me and God knows what else. If they do, will you hate me?"

"Never. I—"

Reaching out in the dark, she pressed her face against his silk-clad shoulder. "I know. You've heard all that before but never stopped loving me. I was loved as few women are, and that makes up for all the bad things that lie in store. In every woman's life there are moments when she feels that fate owes her more than what she got. I, too, had such moments, but now, probably because death is so near, only a few rooms away, now—"

"Let's not talk of death," he said. The sudden rough edge to his tone dispelled her mood of passionate tenderness. Couldn't he just once, she asked herself, just once sound like a man and not a precocious adolescent? Perhaps then, she could really love him, the only human being who'd ever been persistently good to her. And not feel like a whore for sleeping with him because he paid her more generously than other men. She crossed to the window. The rain had stopped, and the wind had changed direction, blowing from the east and chasing the clouds like a herd of bolting horses across the sky. The garden below appeared peaceful and deserted. She heard voices coming from the New Konak and the sound of steps from above their heads. It seemed the search was still on in the attic. A light, most likely a kerosene lamp, was burning in a downstairs window, thinning out the darkness at the rear of the building. Suddenly, she spotted a man moving up the path that led from the park gate to the back of the Konak. Straining her eyes, she parted the lace curtain cautiously, pressing her forehead to the glass. As the man approached, she could hear the gravel crackling under his feet and his spurs jingling. He seemed to be in no hurry. At one point he stopped and disappeared behind a bush, perhaps to relieve himself. Or was he trying to reach the Konak unnoticed by the men rampaging in it? Her heart beating wildly, she waited for him to reappear from behind the shrubbery. At last, he was out in the open, slowly—or was it guardedly?—passing the rose garden. Now he was close enough for her eyes to discern the light hue of his tunic, indicating either a cavalry officer or a guardsman. A moment later, as he stepped into the circle lighted by the kerosene lamp, her instinct rather than her eyes recognized him as Captain Ljuba Kostich, commander of the Royal Guards. Heady with excitement, she shouted, "It's Captain Kostich! Sasha! We're saved! Oh, thank God, we're saved!"

Without waiting for an answer from her husband, she threw the window open and leaned out.

"Don't! Don't!" Alexander screamed at her.

"Captain Kostich!" she shouted. "The king is in danger! Save him! Save him! Captain Kostich, for God's sake!—"

Her words broke off in a horrified scream as she watched the man below draw his revolver and take aim. Frantically, she ducked as he fired. The bullet struck the windowframe, ricocheted and skipped along the outside of the building. A second shot rang out, and the bullet whizzed in through the open window, to lodge in the opposite corner below the ceiling. She moved to the side and stood with her back pressed against the wall as if trying to melt into it.

"Is it Kostich?"

"Yes."

"He is one of them," Alexander said quietly.

They waited for more shots, but there were none. Then they heard Kostich hurry to the rear entrance, open and slam the door.

"He's gone to tell them," she said. "Why did I call him? Why?"

"I tried to stop you, but it was too late."

Closing the window, she let down the heavy iron blinds on the outside, realizing the gesture was an unnecessary precaution, for the park remained quiet and deserted.

"Wasn't that insane of me?" she asked wretchedly. "Now we are lost. Forgive me, Sasha."

"Don't reproach yourself. Sooner or later we'd have been found. This just speeds things up, that's all."

She knew he was merely trying to comfort her, for only a few minutes earlier he'd reiterated his firm belief in their escape. She felt deep and sudden compassion for this young man being martyred because of her, a young king who had never reproached her, not even on the threshold of perdition. For the first time in her life with him, she found herself truly admiring him: his courage and the steely integrity of his devotion to her. She dropped to her knees and prayed fervently, begging God to save the life of this poor, betrayed king, offering herself in his stead. She spoke to God as though He were not a nebulous concept in the realm of the perhaps, but a man who stood beside her, bent over a bit in order to hear her better.

Above them the steps in the attic receded in the direction of the stairway. The only other sound was the dim hum of people conversing in the entrance hall, the unchanged volume of muted voices indicating that they were still unaware of Captain Kostich's discovery of the existence of the alcove.

Draga rose from her knees and moved toward Alexander. "How much longer, Sasha?"

"They're in no hurry. Now they know we can't get away."

"They'll kill us."

"No, they won't. If they had found us when they first overran the bedroom, maybe. But since then they've had time to quiet down, to sober up."

"Captain Kostich wanted to kill me. Perhaps it's only me they want. Not you. So let them. Don't try to protect me. Please, please."

He kissed her. "Don't talk nonsense."

"I know you don't believe in God. Still, let us pray together."

"What for?"

"If for nothing else, to ask God's forgiveness for our sins."

She felt his body stiffen. "What sins?" he asked her sternly.

"We have sinned, Sasha. Think of the people we've had jailed, tortured, executed. Because they opposed us."

"I am the king. The highest authority in the land. What would the world come to if people didn't respect authority? Anarchy, that's what it'd come to. When I had men jailed, I did it to protect the freedom of others. To protect lives against lawlessness and—"

She cut him short. "Oh, Sasha, you wanted your own father murdered. Don't tell me God will forgive us for that."

He extricated himself from her embrace. Though unable to see his face in the dark, she knew that there would be on it the expression of haughty invulnerability she knew so well.

"Papa made me king. Then he unmade me, taking charge of the country and me, too. He confused the people. The Serbs have only recently emerged from total oppression. To be loyal to a ruler of their own free will is still something new for them. To have the choice between two rulers is more than they can cope with. Papa should've known better than to put them to such an impossible test. I was merely correcting his error."

The coolly pontifical tone of a political analyst delivered only minutes before a possible confrontation with his mortal enemies grated on her nerves. She wished to scream at him that this was not the opening of a new session of the Skupshtina, but a recess before the tribunal pronounced the death sentence.

He heard them first. Clinging to him, she noticed the changed rhythm of his breathing. Then she, too, heard the wild shouts and drumbeat of feet which came up from the ground floor, approaching through the flight of rooms of the royal apartments. She pressed her face to his chest, finding comfort in the discovery that his heartbeat, fast and loud, was synchronized with hers.

"They're coming," she whispered.

Tightening the hold of his arms around her, Alexander didn't answer.

Apis opened his eyes. He had lain hovering between sleep and unconsciousness ever since Mishich and the group had left for the New Konak. Now he looked around, his gaze clearing.

"Have they found them?" he asked Michael, who was seated at the foot of the couch.

"As far as I know, they haven't."

"What time is it?"

Michael pulled out his watch and looked at it by the light of the lone candle burning on the desk. "Ten to four." He had remained with Apis waiting for the physician.

Fully conscious now, Apis groaned. "Jesus Christ, they've certainly bungled this thing. Where is Mashin?"

"I imagine at the New Konak, wrecking that now."

Apis tried to sit up, but the piercing pain in his chest forced him to fall back. His gaze focused on Captain Miljkovich's body in the far corner of the room. "Yovan! What the hell did the damned fools have to kill him for?" He waited for the pain to subside. "You ought to get out of here before it's too late, Michael. If Alexander has managed to reach the Banjicki camp, the Eighteenth Infantry might be on its way here by now. I cannot move, but you can. Don't just sit here and wait for them to get you."

Since to all appearances, Alexander and Draga had slipped away, Michael could think of no reason for remaining at the Konak except for the leaden fatigue that immobilized him like a straitjacket. The senseless rampage he had just witnessed had left him with a disenchantment he knew he would never lose. How could he ever have believed that the *coup d'état* would be a bloodless affair? Had his long sojourns abroad wiped the atrocities perpetrated by Serbian officers from his memory? Even if he had arrived in Belgrade a pristine innocent, wouldn't the early-morning meeting at the Officers' Club have opened his eyes. Wasn't he, Michael Vassilovich, hiding his hatred for Alexander behind such lofty phrases as *liberté, égalité, fraternité?* Wasn't he, in all truth, another Colonel Mashin plunging a country into a dubious revolution simply to avenge a personal hurt?

Through the open entrance door came the sound of pandemonium erupting in the yard.

"Might be the Eighth Infantry," Apis said with a forced chuckle, only half-joking.

Rising laboriously, Michael said, "I'll see what it is."

"Let me have a cigarette before you go. If it comes to a fight between us and Alexander's men, it might be my last. I won't let them take me alive." With some difficulty, he pulled his revolver from its holster, cocked it and laid it down beside him. Michael lighted a cigarette and pushed it between Apis' parched lips. "Don't do anything foolish, Apis. At least not until I tell you what's happening."

4 A.M.

THE night was thinning to a hazy gray when he stepped from the building. The scene that greeted him reminded him of a Vereshchagin painting, "Soldiers After the Battle." The troops deployed around the Konak had spilled into the yard and were clustered around campfires kept burning despite the drizzle. A group of officers sat under the marquee, getting drunk on wines looted from the royal cellar, engaged in the valiant competition of who could down more wine in less time.

The shouting came from the New Konak. The entire building was ablaze with light, the blackout caused by the explosion evidently confined to the Old Palace. Behind open windows, men were milling about. There was a rush down the stairway, as a group of twenty men stormed across the yard between the two Konaks. They moved at a speed that seemed remarkable after the excesses of the night. Neighing like enraged stallions, they scrambled up the steps to the vestibule, leaped over the drunks who were too surprised to get out of their way. Captain Kostich and a few younger officers were in the lead with the Colonels Mishich and Mashin and a completely exhausted Laza Petrovich bringing up the rear.

"What's happened?" Michael asked Laza.

The general halted, leaning against the doorpost to catch his breath. "Kostich has found them," he said bitterly. "Aren't you pleased?" Then, turning, he trotted after the men.

Michael followed them as they crossed the devastated royal apartment and headed straight for the bedroom. Someone had fetched a kerosene lamp and set it on the dressing table amid the broken perfume bottles and face-cream jars. More and more men streamed into the room, shouting wildly, stumbling over wrecked tables and chairs and becoming entangled in the ripped-off draperies. Their eyes combed the walls for the door

360

that supposedly led to the royal couple's hiding place. Finding none, their cries of triumph gave way to a baffled silence.

"There must be an opening somewhere in the wall," Captain Kostich insisted nervously. "If you go downstairs and look up, you will see that the window from where the queen called is at the very corner of the building in line with this one." He indicated the first of the three windows of the room, all of which faced the park. "There can be no other access to the place but from here."

"Perhaps a trapdoor from the attic," a voice suggested.

"Impossible," Lieutenant Bogdanovich answered. "We've gone over every square meter of the attic floor thoroughly. There is no trapdoor there."

"Get an ax," Mishich shouted. His suggestion was superfluous, as Captain Ristich had had the foresight to send a subaltern to the Konak toolhouse for axes. The man returned with three, distributing them among eagerly reaching hands. A moment later the room reverberated with the sound of ax blows on the silk-covered walls.

Laza Petrovich elbowed his way to Mishich. "For God's sake, Colonel," he said trembling with indignation, "tell them to stop that insane whacking. No need to tear down the house. There *is* a door."

"So you've known it all along?" Mashin replied.

"Yes, I have. But I won't tell you where it is unless you order these maniacs to stop. Haven't they dealt enough destruction to this miserable place already? It looks as if a horde of Tatars had been through it."

Mashin tried to outshout the bedlam. "All right, gentlemen, leave that wall alone." The men, much too absorbed in their wrecking job, continued wielding their axes. Ristich and others had joined them, slashing at the wall with their swords. "Hold it, God damn it!" Mishich bellowed, obviously forgetting that it had been he who had sent for the axes. He turned to Laza. "Where is the bloody door?"

For the first time in his life, Michael felt a deep admiration, even affection for the general. No longer the smart courtier, his white gala uniform smudged and missing a sleeve, his face gaunt with fatigue, its color drained by the loss of blood, he now faced the enemy with dignity and grace, untouched by fear and showing not the slightest inclination toward appeasement.

He pointed. "The door is right there. See the outline? Nevertheless, you won't be able to break it in, because it is an iron door. You could dynamite it, of course, but I'd rather you didn't. If you gentlemen," he addressed the entire group, "give me your word of honor to spare their majesties' lives, I shall ask them to open it for you. I am certain that after this terrible night the king will be ready to abdicate in favor of Prince Peter and give you a chance to achieve your aim without resorting to a criminal act that would reflect badly on the honor of Serbia and her new king."

Looking around, his eyes searched out face after face. The men stared back at him, their expressions ranging from hostile and sullen to well disposed.

"Tell the bastard to quit stalling," Captain Ristich called out to Mashin.

"What are we waiting for?" a voice screeched. "Let's blast the goddamn door."

Angered by Ristich's interference, Mashin pulled himself erect. "Will you gentlemen please calm down. We've come a long way and are at the threshold of victory, so let's be sensible." He turned to Laza. "Yes, I give you my word of honor to spare the king's life."

"And the queen's," Laza said.

"And the queen's. Provided they refrain from provoking us by an unrealistic attitude. Do you agree, Petar?" He asked Colonel Mishich, who answered with a nod. "And you gentlemen?" he addressed the younger men. Wavering between attack and obedience, like circus tigers let into the manege, they answered with murmured yesses. "You have our word," Mashin said. "Now will you tell the king to open up."

There was no doubt in Michael's mind that Mashin sincerely wished to avoid bloodshed. The trials, frustrations and near defeat of the night which had taken their toll on his physical strength had also weakened the intensity of his hatred. After having all but lost the game, he suddenly found himself the winner. This hated woman and her husband had crawled like hunted animals into a hole, hiding there waiting to be flushed. What worse humiliation than that could he mete out to them?

Laza stepped to the section of the wall where, in the light from the kerosene lamp, the outline of the door became visible.

"Your majesties! It's me, Laza. Your Laza. Please, open the door. I am with a group of your officers, who wish to talk to you." When there was no answer, he raised his voice. "Sire! I have their word of honor that no harm shall befall you or her majesty the queen."

"Have they really given you their word of honor, Laza?" the king's voice asked. Alexander had heard the discussion clearly; nevertheless, he insisted that the pledge be repeated.

"Yes, sire, they have. Their word of honor as men and officers."

The key turned twice in the lock, and with a faint creak the door opened. On the threshold, arm in arm, stood the King and Queen of Serbia. Blinking in the lamplight, their eyes strained after the pitch dark of the alcove, they presented a bizarre sight: the king's nakedness, scrawny but potbellied, wrapped in a red silk blouse that barely covered his genitals, and the Queen in a richly embroidered batiste nightgown in front of which she held the singed cloth she had taken from the ironing board. Someone in the back of the room emitted a guffaw that sounded like the snort of a pig. The king drew himself up, his myopic eyes vainly attempting to recognize the men guilty of *lèse majesté*. Draga gazed about, bewildered, a barely audible gasp escaping her lips when she spotted Colonel Mashin among the officers.

Alexander craned his neck above the heads, hoping to catch sight of his pince-nez on the bedside table as his myopia worried him more than his nakedness or the degrading aspects of the confrontation. All he could see were daubs instead of faces bobbing up and down in the yellow light of the kerosene lamp, like a bunch of toy balloons. Screwing up his eyes, he succeeded in sorting out Mishich's face from the balloons.

"What is it you wish, Colonel?" he asked in the clear, steady voice of a ruling monarch.

His tone disconcerted Mishich, who took a deep breath. "We demand your abdication"—there was the hiatus of a split second—"sire," he added.

"Demand? That's an ill-chosen expression, Colonel. Shall I remind you of your loyalty oath? Yes, I might be willing to absolve you from your allegiance to me, but not until you order your drunken comrades to leave my presence."

Mishich blinked nervously. The incredible image of a barefoot Alexander, naked except for a red silk blouse, acting as though he, not Mishich, had the support of twenty cocked guns benumbed him.

"You're in no position to set conditions." Mashin's voice, trembling with excitement, broke in.

Michael, spellbound, watched the scene from the sidelines. Hardly a minute had passed since the couple's emergence from the alcove, yet it seemed to him as though he were witnessing the reenactment of a scene that in reality had happened long before. The two in the doorway couldn't be real people; they had to be actors performing on a stage. Alexander with a paranoic belief in his invulnerability, standing sharply outlined against the darkness of the alcove, his arms defiantly holding the woman, the cynosure of an entire country's hatred, in a demonstrably loving embrace. Yes, he had to be an actor who, after a disappointing performance, still hoped for applause on his exit line.

No such hopes were revealed on Draga's face. No fear, no emotion. She seemed to be in no doubt about what the next minutes would bring. She leaned on Alexander as if he were an execution post.

"I wasn't talking to you," Alexander told Mashin brusquely, then turned to Mishich. "Once again, Colonel, I am appealing to your sense of honor. Will you order these men out of here?"

Though his tone was calm and proper, the words were ill chosen. But he couldn't help it. Michael knew this was the language of a lifetime.

A voice rang out from the end of the room. "Here is honor to you!" and a short, tousled-haired lieutenant, standing legs apart on the rumpled bed, raised his arm and over the heads of the men fired his revolver at Alexander.

"No, no, don't," the queen screamed as the shot hit the king and he staggered. Cradling him in her arms, she held him upright, shielding him with her own body, as a red trickle appeared on his left thigh, looking like a torn frazzle from his shirt. He omitted a low moan but remained standing. In rapid succession the blast of several guns shattered the stunned silence that had followed the first shot. As though trying to throw himself at his attackers, Alexander took a few faltering steps forward, pulling Draga with him, then slumped heavily to the floor. His hand sliding down her erect body as though caressing it for a last time, he grasped hold of the blood-spattered seam of her gown.

She had dropped the ironing cloth when Alexander was first hit, and her body was now exposed through the thin fabric of her nightgown to the leer of twenty drunks.

Leaping forward, Captain Ristich slashed at her with his sword. "You filthy whore." Her gown fell open to expose a long red gash which ran from her left shoulder across her abdomen to the ivory-colored skin of her right thigh. As she raised her arms to ward off the blades flashing at her from all directions, one sword slashed off her left breast. It dropped to the floor, a small red lump soon trampled into a slippery stain on the carpet. Driven wild by the sight of her mutilated but still-alive body, the men fell upon her from all sides, and she collapsed on top of her husband, who writhed in a puddle of his own blood. Despite cuts and the bullet wounds, Alexander was still conscious. Draga, her eyes open and her lips moving, tried to speak to him. When the ring of frenzied attackers became too tight for further swordplay, the boots and spurs went into action, bruising, crushing, kicking.

Trembling with impotent fury, Michael dived into the crazed Laocoon group of slaughter.

"Stop! In the name of God! Stop!" he shouted until a fierce blow on his head, delivered by the butt of a revolver, sent him reeling and a sword slashed through his sleeve, cutting his arm. He ignored both. Desperately determined to save Draga from the horror of being trampled to death, he burrowed his way toward her. Oblivious to the kicking feet, he crawled ahead inch by inch. A man in front of him moved, and through the opening between the bodies he caught a glimpse of her. Despite a deep cut that had disfigured her left cheek and a scalp wound that gushed a river of blood, she was still alive, her eyes open and staring. He shouted her name, and a flicker of recognition seemed to appear in the incredibly green eyes. After a moment, however, he concluded with a sigh of relief that the queen was dead.

It seemed to Michael such cruel irony that she should die

while he was still an arm's length away from her. A moment later a second blow to his head caused him to lose consciousness.

General Laza Petrovich lay dead in the boudoir.

After the first shot, he had thrown himself at Mashin, grabbing the colonel by the shoulders. "Tell them, to stop! You've given your word!"

Mashin stared at him openmouthed as though seeing a ghost; then extricating himself from the general's hold, he dashed to the nearest window, where he spewed a stream of vomit on the flower beds below.

"Leave me alone, damn it," he muttered, wiping his mouth with his handkerchief. "It's too much—too much—" It wasn't clear to Laza what he referred to: the trials of the night or the savagery of his cohorts.

Laza stared numbly at the ring of attackers closing in on the royal couple. He realized that no one was watching him, and if he wanted to save his skin, now was the moment in which to escape. Then he saw Ristich draw his sword and slash at the queen. Seized by an insane fury, he fell on the captain, grabbing him around the waist and wrestling him to the floor. Locked in a murderous embrace, they rolled across the demolished threshold into the boudoir. Taken by surprise, Ristich struggled awkwardly to free himself from his attacker's clutches. Despite his fifty-odd years, Laza Petrovich was still a match for the man twenty years his junior. Pinning him down with his knees, his hands pressed against Ristich's windpipe, he would have choked him to death if Lieutenant Bogdanovich hadn't caught sight of them and rushed to the captain's aid. In the heat of the fight, Laza failed to notice Bogdanovich, looking up only when he felt the cold muzzle of a gun touch the nape of his neck.

"What the—" he started, but the burst of the shot cut him short. His grip tightened, then loosened on Ristich's throat, and he fell forward with a geyser of blood spurting from his mouth. The gush hit the gasping Ristich in the eyes. Blinking the red veil away, he sat up with a groan as Bogdanovich reached down and pulled him to his feet.

"Holy Mother, my good uniform," Ristich complained, wiping at his bespattered tunic. "Why did Colonel Mashin order us to wear our gala uniforms? Is he going to buy me a new one?" he grumbled, forgetting to thank Bogdanovich for saving his life.

In the bedroom, the mass hysteria was beginning to subside. After a few parting kicks, the men backed away from the two lumps of torn flesh that had minutes before been their king and queen. Realizing that the present one was not only their first but probably their last unsupervised visit to the royal apartments, they began a search for souvenirs. One fortunate hunter came upon one hundred thousand dinars, the king's monthly civil list in fresh, crisp bills, which had been delivered only the day before from the treasury; another with equally sharp eyes found the four thousand pounds sterling the queen had facetiously referred to as her escape money. The rings, necklaces and brooches that she had kept in a jewel box on her dressing table were also taken. It was only when Colonel Mashin caught a cadet in the act of slipping a ring off the dead Laza's finger that the looting was stopped.

"I want this man arrested!" Mashin shouted, pointing at the cadet. "Court-martialed! For disgracing the revolution!" He tried to work himself into a righteous rage, but his voice, tired and listless, failed to impress any of the men.

Below, the park began to fill with soldiers. The troops, under control while the night lasted, were out of hand now that the new day dawned. The wildest rumors spread among them, and their officers could offer no explanation since only the men involved in the coup knew the full truth. The ranks had heard the explosions and seen the flames flickering behind the smashed windows of the Old Konak and wondered why they were being kept out of the action. They had been told that they were in the city to defend the king. But where was he and who were the men rampaging through his palace, his friends or his enemies?

Bored and curious, they drifted through the Konak park, the more enterprising ones entering the building, where their voices served to shake Colonel Mashin from the leaden apathy that had immobilized him since the beginning of the assault on the royal couple. Stepping to the window, he leaned out and shouted in a booming voice:

"Alexander Obrenovich is dead! Long live Peter Karageorgevich, King of Serbia!" And again, to make certain he was heard by everyone in the milling crowd: he repeated the stirring cry.

He expected an outbreak of jubilation, but the faces turned up to him wore expressions of doubt, confusion or incomprehension. Only a small fraction had even heard him, the rest appearing too sleepy or disgruntled to pay attention. There was some good-natured horseplay and scuffling among the men; the kicking of a tennis ball soccer-fashion with the goalie planted in the rear entrance door.

"They don't believe it," Captain Ristich said. "They've been fed too many lies during the night."

"Let's prove it to them!" Lieutenant Marinkovich suggested. "Come on, brothers! Let's chuck their majesties out the window. That'll convince the stupid bastards that the colonel wasn't joking."

Mashin gave him a bewildered look. "I don't think we should—"

"The lieutenant is right," Mishich agreed. "We must prove that Alexander is really dead. There are partisans, thousands of his partisans, and by waiting, we might risk a civil war. His death must be proved beyond the shadow of a doubt; otherwise, there will be rumors and whisperings and, at the end, chaos."

Mashin shrugged. "All right. Do as you think best. I still feel it's—" He was about to say that the two bodies presented a sight that wouldn't heap much glory on Serbia's officers' corps, but by then Marinkovich and his comrades had grabbed the inert forms by their feet, arms and hair and were dragging them toward the window. They had great, ribald fun with both corpses, especially that of the queen. Her gown hanging in limp and blood-soaked shreds exposed her body to the aroused men who commented on it amid loud laughter. There was a moment of gruesome perplexity when halfway to the window she moaned. The shock of finding her still alive caused the cadet holding on to her hair to release his grip, and her head hit the floor with a dull thud.

She seemed to writhe as blood bubbled from her mouth. Now a sickly shade of green, the cadet pulled out his gun and pressing its muzzle to her temple, administered the *coup de grâce*, then wheeled and ran from the room.

The shot produced a sobering effect on his comrades as in silence they heaved the body over the sill and tossed it, in one well-coordinated move, out the window, where it flew in a wide arc and landed with a hollow thud on the ground, barely missing the soldiers playing soccer. They stared at the grotesquely spread-eagled female form at their feet, as recognition slowly dawned on them. In contrast with their officers, her savage wounds horrified, rather than elated, them. Politics were the pastime of the educated, for the peasants from the dark hinterlands the kind and queen were abstract images, symbolizing a power only one grade below that of God, the Holy Mother and her Son. To see one of the precious symbols reduced to a lump of mutilated flesh and spilled intestines filled them with a sickening fear.

Another minute later another body landed a few meters away from the queen's, and there was the crack of breaking bones as it hit the ground. His face buried in the trampled-down soil of a flower bed, Alexander's left hand suddenly reached out, to grab a tuft of grass as though he were trying to tear it from its roots. His right hand was now a profusely bleeding stump as, about to be thrown from the window, he had grasped the sill and clung to it with superhuman tenacity. One of the officers—no one would later admit to the deed—severed his fingers with a quick slash of his sword.

Michael opened his eyes and looked around, wondering where he was, then saw the torn canopy and the broken furniture, and his memory cleared. Probing the top of his head, he winced as he touched the wound encrusted with dried blood. At first he thought he had been shot, then, examining it, he remembered the blow and found it to be only a gash. His right sleeve was slashed, and beneath it, the skin superficially scratched.

He staggered to his feet, alone in the room. In the early light of dawn, it seemed incredible to him that the devastation could be the work of a few hours during a single night. In front of the door to the alcove, the pink and white rug revealed a large dark spot, no longer red, but deep brown. There were streaks of the same color leading to the near window. At the window he shrank back in horror. Two naked bodies, horribly mutilated, lay on the ground below, a ring of jostling, gaping, soldiers crowding around them. Beyond the milling, restless mob the park was dotted with picnickers: officers, noncoms and enlisted men, eating and drinking together as though all rank, all class distinction had been swept away.

The quiet of the ravaged room with its blood-spattered walls and strewn debris was in bizarre contrast with the racket coming from below. Michael crossed to the linen storage window which overlooked the front yard, the gate and the wide avenue beyond. A veritable *fête champêtre* seemed to be taking place. Tables and chairs had been set up on the carriageway for civilians and officers who were being served food and beverages— obviously from the royal cellar and kitchen—by an eagerly accommodating palace staff. The same military band that had entertained during the royal couple's last supper played lusty marching songs.

Beyond the gate, the street was filled with people streaming from all directions. The early-rising Belgraders had been stirred from sleep long before dawn. Hearing of the events of the night, they cheered every uniform they saw. An occasional carriageful of officers or a rider on horseback sped through the crowd to carry the news of the successful *coup d'état* to the outskirts of the city. Shouts of "Long live King Peter" occasionally broke through the shouts and laughter.

An attack of nausea drove Michael from the death room. Crossing the boudoir, he almost tripped over Laza Petrovich's body. At sight of the dead man, he realized that whoever had knocked him unconscious had probably saved his life. Nevertheless, he felt no gratitude toward his unknown benefactor, only a twinge of envy for the general who was now beyond pain, guilt or the complexities of honor and dishonor.

In the entrance hall, Naumovich's body lay covered with a damask drapery ripped from its cornice. Michael was surprised to find that area empty as well; then, reaching the vestibule, he understood the reason. The main entrance to the Konak had been locked, no doubt in order to keep out looters and the curious. He turned and started for the stairway, hoping to find the rear exit still open when he was stopped by Apis' voice.

"Hey there—a cigarette—let me have a cigarette!"

Michael found Apis stretched out on the couch in the adjutants' office where he had left him. His wounds bandaged, he was fully conscious. Captain Miljkovich's body had been moved from the room.

"Where have you been?" he asked.

Michael pointed at his bloody head. "Someone decided to give me this souvenir. I must have been out for quite some time." Taking a cigarette from his case, he lighted it and handed it to Apis. "How do you feel?"

"Wretched. And ridiculous for letting a sniper catch me unawares. Me, the great Apis. He wasn't even a good shot. The doctor who bandaged me said that I would be as good as new in six weeks."

"Do you know that the king and queen were dumped out of the window and are lying in the courtyard horribly mauled and naked for everyone to see?"

"Yes, I've heard."

"Good God, she was Queen of Serbia! I wouldn't be surprised if Prince Peter renounced the throne when informed of the details of your glorious *coup d'état*."

"My heart bleeds for all you great patriots who want your revolution served on a silver platter. Revolutionary ideas may be conceived by great humanitarians but then are executed by vandals and sadists, because without vandals and sadists the great concepts hatched in ivory towers would remain dead letters printed in leather-bound books. I'm sure Draga Mashin with her insides hanging out isn't a very pretty sight, but it'll serve as a warning to Prince Peter or whoever follows him to mind his manners. Because there is no stopping now."

"My God, what next?"

"The unification of all Southern Slavs. Yugoslavia. That's next. And anyone who stands in the way must go."

"You're a dreamer, Apis. The monarchy will never tolerate a strong Slav state south of her borders."

"Then the monarchy must go."

"You're mad."

"Don't you remember the Black Prophecy?" Michael gave him a blank look. "The prophecy of the old peasant Mata?"

"Oh, that," Michael said skeptically. "Don't tell me you believe in such nonsense."

"It's hard not to, considering what happened this morning."

Michael was vaguely aware of the story that told of an elderly peasant seen rushing down the main street of Ujitza in 1868, screaming that Michael Obrenovich, the beloved and respected ruling prince of Serbia, was being murdered. To the crowd gathered around him he described long yatagans slashing the prince to death in the woods surrounding distant Belgrade. The police, deciding he was mad, locked him up. The following day, however, an official telegram confirmed the assassination of the prince in the Deer Park near the capital. It had happened at the moment and under the circumstances Mata had described in Ujitza.

At first, the police had suspected the old peasant of being one of the conspirators but in the end accepted him for what he was: a man gifted with extrasensory perception, a visionary. He went on to predict that Prince Michael's successor would father a son by a hated wife and cede the throne voluntarily to this son while still in the prime of his life. The son would marry a woman of the people, who would cause his death before his thirtieth year. After his death another house would reign over Serbia, but not for long as a foreign army would occupy the country. After long years of suffering, a man would lead the fight against the oppressor and unite all Serbs in a great and independent state.

"Yes, the assassination happens to fit the prophecy," Michael admitted. "Alexander did die before his thirtieth year. And there was a connection between his death and his marriage. And Milan did abdicate in the prime of his life. But the rest sounds like wishful thinking. You're twenty-seven, Apis. Don't waste your life chasing dreams. The Habsburgs aren't the Obrenoviches. The monarchy isn't the Old Konak. For the next fifty years our aim should not be conquest, but preservation. Let's pray for a strong, healthy, modern Serbia. Make it part of Europe. And let's not tangle with Austria-Hungary. Let the monarchy forget we exist, so we won't whet its appetite. Because if we do, it might want to swallow us up."

"It remains to be seen who will do the swallowing, my friend. The first to go will be Franz Ferdinand. If he became emperor, he would give Croatia independence from Hungary. The Croats would be free, not needing to join us. But without them, there would be no Yugoslavia. The map of the Balkans would remain unchanged. Full of spots like a dirty tablecloth. Every country a spot of a different color, spilled wine, goulash sauce, sauerkraut. I want it all blue, white and red. Yugoslavian."

"How will you get Franz Ferdinand? Storm Belvedere Castle as you did the Old Konak?"

"We don't have to go to him. He'll come to us. And we'll be ready."

Michael placed his hand on his friend's forehead. "You're running a fever. That explains it. I hope when you're yourself again, you'll look at things more sanely. I had better find Colonel Mashin now. If he has a trace of decency left, he'll have those two unfortunate people picked up and moved inside."

"No!" Apis said vehemently. "Don't look for Mashin. He'll have you shot."

"Mashin? Me? What for?"

"Your note to the queen. It fell into Zivkovich's hands. Whoever delivered it left it with him."

Michael felt a sudden stab of almost physical pain. So that's why the couple had remained in the Konak like animals in a trap waiting to be bludgeoned to death. He closed his eyes, burying his face in his hands to hide his despondency.

"You tried to betray us." Apis' voice seemed far away.

"I wish I had succeeded. I couldn't have lived with myself after this morning if I hadn't tried."

"You won't have to live with anyone if Mashin finds you. Get out of Belgrade, Michael, and stay out till things calm down."

Michael rose. "Why don't *you* shoot me if you think I betrayed you? You wouldn't run any risks. You have a gun, and I don't."

Apis' revolver lay at his side, within easy reach. Picking it up, he held it for a moment as if testing the feel of it, then laid it down again.

"No," he said. "My hand isn't steady enough right now. I might cripple you, and I'd hate that."

Embarrassed, they both laughed, after which Michael bent down, made the sign of the cross on Apis' forehead and kissed him on both cheeks.

"Take care of yourself. And watch out for snipers."

"You, too," Apis called after him.

He found the rear exit open and left the palace unchallenged by the troops holding the beleaguered streets around both Konaks. Beyond their ring, the inner city seemed to be in the grips of carnival fever despite the early hour. Taverns, restaurants and wine shops were open for business with mobs of usually sober Belgraders milling about, laughing, shouting, hailing every uniformed man as if he were a hero returned from a victorious battle.

As he passed the Grand Hotel, usually an island of Western decorum, but now an anthill of frenzied celebrants bringing or seeking information about the last bloody hours, he saw a cluster of people surround a hack in front of the entrance. Looking up, he spotted a woman in a negligee on a balcony, leaning out and waving to the man who had just arrived in the carriage. Michael recognized the woman. She was the wife of the new Premier Avakumovich, and she waved to her husband, the premier, tall and heavyset, sporting a short, dark beard. The crowd greeted him with ear-shattering *zhiveos*. For a moment it seemed as though he were going to be torn to pieces by well-wishers. With some difficulty, he extricated himself and dashed into the hotel lobby. Michael wondered what means of communication had been used to convey the news of Alexander's death since Avakumovich was arriving in Belgrade from Alexinatz, where he had spent the past week, less than an hour after the murders.

Minister Tcharikoff rose from his desk and crossed to the window, where he lifted the binoculars from the sill, training them once again on the Old Konak. In the brightening dawn the row of wrecked windows with their smashed panes and shattered blinds spoke more eloquently of the events of the night then any news report ever could. He knew he would remember this night in vivid detail as long as he lived.

He had been standing behind the French doors that opened on the balcony facing the Old Konak while the shots that killed the sergeant rang out. The explosions, followed by wild firing and shouting, told him that the coup was under way. He heard Draga's desperate cry for help and soon afterward the horrible, animal noises of the assassination.

From the moment of the second explosion that blew out the

bedroom windows, he was able to watch, as though from a box in the theater, the bloody drama unrolling in the light of candles and burning woodwork. He wished he could tear himself away from his observation post, but a morbid fascination held him rooted to the spot. At times, he himself was in danger of being hit by stray bullets. Shots peppered the walls of the legation, one crashing through the upstairs window of his son's room and landing in the wall above the bed. Luckily, he had had the foresight to move his family to rooms facing away from the Konak compound.

A sensitive and honorable man, Tcharikoff was secretly ashamed of the role Russia had played in the overthrow of the Obrenovich dynasty but was unable to prevent it. The presence of Colonel Grabov had demoted him, the official representative of his country, to the role of not so innocent bystander.

He had, for a long time, been troubled by the emergence of men such as the colonel. They were the new breed, ruthless, inhuman and blindly dedicated. In peacetime, when certain advantages for one's country were to be obtained by means of clever diplomacy, these men resorted to torture, kidnappings and assassinations, for the same purpose. What shocked him most, however, was the inhumanity of their methods, the death sentences passed in the cool isolation of offices, to be carried out by remote control. They never stood face to face with their victims because of the unlimited number of executioners at their disposal.

Minister Tcharikoff had never entertained any illusions about the infallibility of his country's executive or judicial branches, but considered past tyrannies gentle and benevolent compared to the system that made the secret service the true ruler of Russia. Secretly he loathed and feared it. These new, faceless men caused him to feel that he was a species doomed to extinction. Every successful plot hatched by the Asian Department undermined the security of his own kind.

He hadn't much cared for King Alexander, but he had sincerely liked Draga, only regretting her displays of bad judgment in certain matters of government, yet appreciating the enormousness of difficulties that only a saint or a genius could have overcome. Although he had entered the Serbian scene long after her marriage, he felt guilt over the treatment she had been accorded by his government—shamelessly exploited, then dropped the moment she ceased to be an asset.

Now, she was humiliated even in death, her savagely mangled body exposed to the curiosity and jeers of men drunk with wine and victory neither of which was rightfully theirs. The morbid horseplay taking place around the two bodies grew louder and more offensive as the gray of dawn thinned to daylight. Despite Colonel Grabov's warning not to interfere, Minister Tcharikoff decided to use the prerogative of his position to order an end to the disgrace.

A light drizzle was falling as he left the legation and hurriedly crossed the park to the spot where the corpses lay. He threw a glance at them, then, nauseated, turned away. He recognized a group of civilians huddled under umbrellas talking to Colonel Mashin, members of the new Cabinet summoned to the Konak to discuss the take-over of the government.

Tcharikoff elbowed his way to them through the crowd of loitering soldiers.

Without deigning to acknowledge the greeting of the civilians, he confronted Mashin. "For heaven's sake, Colonel, have those bodies removed. This is disgraceful! To let them lie there, not only the king, but the queen, too. A woman! She was no Jezebel to have her body trampled upon or her flesh eaten by dogs! She was the Queen of Serbia!"

The civilians eased away in an embarrassed silence, but Mashin drew himself up.

"I've been waiting for instructions from my government."

"Don't make me laugh. At this moment you are the government. Put an end to this ghastly exhibition. Get them inside."

The majordomo was ordered to bring bedsheets from the palace, and the bodies were wrapped in them, carried upstairs and deposited in the billiard room. The small tuft of grass Alexander had clung to when landing on the lawn was still in his hand as no one had had the nerve to force open his stiffened fingers.

It was the decision of a joint conference of the new government and the military leaders to have the victims readied for burial within the shortest possible time. Two pathologists, Dr. Édouard Michel, a Frenchman, and the Greek Dr. Demosthen Nikolajevich were roused from sleep and summoned to the Konak for postmortem examinations.

The two, who in the course of their careers had viewed numerous mutilated and disfigured corpses, reacted with disbelief at the sight that awaited them in the small room opening off the king's study. When they recognized the bodies lying on the two billiard tables under sheets soaked with carbolic acid as the King and Queen of Serbia, they exchanged glances of incredulity.

The presence of Colonel Mashin kept them from making any personal comments. In a deliberately dispassionate tone, Dr. Michel dictated the result of the first cursory examination of the victims to a court stenographer:

"Alexander Obrenovich, twenty-seven, nineteen gunshot wounds, among them one in the heart region, one severing the main artery in the abdomen, one shattering the left eyeball. Five deep gashes inflicted by sweeping sword strokes, fingers of the right hand severed. Back broken, injury occurring when the body was thrown from a second-story window. Draga Obrenovich, née Lunyevitza, thirty-seven, thirty-six gunshot wounds, roughly forty slashes of varied depths, one opening the abdomen, their number difficult to ascertain accurately because of additional bruises and lacerations, face disfigured by cuts, left breast severed and missing."

5 A.M.

AFTER changing to the same civilian suit in which he had arrived the day before, Michael, accompanied by his brother, Voyislav, set out on horseback for the railroad station. He hoped that the trains, at least the international ones, were running again. A boat ride across the Sava to Hungary had always been the preferred escape route for fugitives, but having received no information about the resumption of the crossings after their suspension the night before, he did not wish to waste precious time by going to the pier. Of course, the danger still existed that Mashin might have ordered the station patrolled.

It was not fear for his life alone that had prompted Michael's decision to leave Serbia, but his grief for Draga and his disgust over the savagery of the coup. He wished only to expel its haunting images from his memory and never again to lay eyes on its perpetrators.

On their way, Voyislav, who had spoken to friends at the Radical Party headquarters, reported to Michael on the latest developments. Colonel Nikolich, commandant of the Eighth Infantry, had refused to pledge allegiance to the new king, at which time a detachment of officers had been dispatched to the Banjicki Barracks with orders to execute him. The expedition was only partly successful. In an exchange of shots witnessed by the entire regiment lined up in marching formation, ready to descend upon the city and revenge Alexander's death, the colonel was merely wounded, while two of Mashin's men were killed.

Stunned by the tragic duel, the regiment surrendered without further attempt at resistance.

The brothers avoided the inner city with its crowds, flag-draped houses and military bands playing in the parks and took the back roads to the station. To their consternation, they found all access to it sealed off by troops and a checkpoint set up in front of its entrance. The lieutenant in charge had orders to prevent members of the armed forces, regardless of ranks and service branches, from leaving Belgrade.

At the time of Milan's death, Michael had exchanged his military passport for one that listed his occupation as farmer. It had been a clever move as he now discovered. Dismissing his brother's apprehensions, he decided to risk going through the control. Having taken leave from Voyislav, he boldly handed his passport to the lieutenant. Luckily, the man did not know him. After a cursory glance at the document, he allowed him to pass.

As he had hoped, there was a train scheduled to leave for Vienna, with Zimony its first stop on foreign soil. He joined the long line in front of the ticket window. Because of the slow and thorough passport and customs inspection, travelers usually arrived at the station early.

Five men and a woman were in line ahead of Michael. Much too absorbed in his own problems to be interested in his fellow passengers, at first, he failed to pay any attention to the woman. His destination was Vienna, with no plans beyond that, except for a fervent desire to leave Serbia, possibly for the rest of his life. He had good connections in the West and was hopeful of finding a niche in either Austria or France.

People ahead of him bought their tickets and were moving on when the selling came to a sudden halt. It seemed a quarrel had erupted between the woman passenger and the ticket seller, and it was only now that Michael took a good look at her.

She was tall and solidly broad-beamed, with dark hair, ruddy complexion, very blue eyes and teeth much too white and even not to be dentures. Her heavily accented French revealed her to be British. The man behind the window spoke no language but Serbian, so her tirades in French, broken German and Italian were completely wasted on him. A sizable crowd had gathered to stare at her as if she were a rare animal in a zoo, which—in a way—Michael thought she was. A foreign woman traveling alone in Serbia.

Wearing a tweed suit, sensible shoes and a wide-brimmed straw hat, she wouldn't have elicited a single curious glance in any Western city, but here she was an apparition. She was neither young nor pretty, but frankly middle-aged; still her self-assurance and daring elicited derisive whisperings. There were loud speculations about who she was, where she had come from and what her business in Serbia might be.

An old woman ventured the opinion that it had to be a common practice for English women to travel alone because she had known of another one loosed on Serbia.

"Perhaps they are together," someone suggested.

"Not likely. The other one was here in 1864."

The argument between ticket seller and traveler continued. The delay began to disquiet Michael, and although he knew there would be danger in making himself conspicuous, he offered to interpret for the woman.

"I want to go to Shabats, and the silly man refuses to sell me a ticket," she informed Michael in French. She also introduced herself as Miss Muriel Denham from Salisbury.

The sole railroad connection between Belgrade and Shabats, was through Zimony, which meant changing trains, crossing

DANCE OF THE ASSASSINS

and recrossing the Sava River, as well as the Serbian-Hungarian border. Anyone without ulterior motives would avoid such inconveniences and take the boat to Shabats, was the ticket seller's explanation for refusing to issue her a ticket.

"Oh, I know perfectly well I could go by boat, but it's an hour and a half faster by rail."

By then a sergeant of the station police had joined the altercation. "Ask her whom she wants to visit in Shabats," he told Michael.

"Nobody. I don't know a soul there."

The answer baffled the sergeant. "Why then does she want to go?"

"Because I've never been there," Miss Denham answered cheerfully.

It was too incredible a reason for the sergeant. "Do you think she is crazy?" he asked Michael. "If she is, I'll be forced to deliver her to the State Insane Asylum. Or arrest her as a spy."

Patiently Miss Denham explained that she was traveling through the lands inhabited by Serbs in order to write a book about them. She'd just been to Cetinje, Podgorica and Kolashin in Montenegro, and the following week she was planning to explore Serbia itself.

The mention of Kolashin had an electrifying effect on the sergeant. "Kolashin! That's where I am from! My hometown! I am a Montenegrin! She came all the way from England to see my hometown!"

Like most Montenegrins, he was a big, strapping fellow, looking rather picturesque in his brown uniform with red braiding. He now stared with affectionate admiration at the woman, wanting to know all about her, where she was born, how many brothers and sisters she had, why she had remained single. She answered the questions with admirable goodwill, while the large hand of the station clock moved past the number seven and the line behind her began to grumble. Michael wondered briefly how many more there were in the crowd who had reasons as pressing as his to leave Serbia.

The clerk in charge of passport control became aware of the commotion and rushed up to investigate. He, too, seemed baffled by the presence of Miss Denham and ordered her to follow him to his bureau. As he spoke no foreign language, he ordered Michael to accompany them.

The same questions she had answered before were asked again, only this time not with the bonhomie of the sergeant, but the arrogance of a self-important passport clerk. He, too, suggested that Miss Denham take the boat.

"I wouldn't think of it," the lady replied firmly.

"Why not?"

"Because by now I've come to regard the trip as a sporting event."

The answer stupefied the young man. While precious moments ticked away, he subjected Miss Denham's passport to a most thorough scrutiny, inspecting every stamp, notation and entry in its densely filled pages.

The time of the train's departure grew closer. The long line of passengers waiting to have their papers stamped grew more and more restless. So did Michael.

The phone rang on the wall. The clerk, still busy with Miss Denham, told the police sergeant who had followed them into the bureau, to answer it.

"It's Colonel Mishich. He says he is the new military commander of the city and has a list of people he wants arrested in case they try to leave the country."

"Take down the names, Sergeant," the clerk ordered nervously. "This is the third call I've received. The goddamn train is leaving in a few minutes. I'll have to get these people out of here or they'll miss it."

He handed Miss Denham her passport. "It seems to be in order," he said with evident regret.

"Now will I be issued a ticket to Shabats?"

"If you insist," the young man replied lamely.

"I certainly do!" she cried. With a triumphant "thank you" to the clerk and a wide grin at Michael, she swept from the bureau.

At the phone, the sergeant was jotting down the names being given to him over the line. Michael listened tensely, as he heard his own repeated by the sergeant. By then he had had his passport stamped and was on his way to the platform. Looking back over his shoulder, he saw the clerk trying to make sense of papers handed him by a Jewish family of seven. The wanted list lay beside the telephone where the sergeant had left it.

Unchallenged by the frontier guards patrolling the platform,

Michael boarded a third-class carriage. He thought he would be less conspicuous riding there than in the splendid isolation of a first-class compartment. Leaning back completely exhausted, he wondered if his luck would hold and the train depart before the clerk had time to look carefully at the list.

On a parallel track a train thundered in and came to a halt with screeching wheels and the hiss of escaping steam. It was the same one that had brought him to Belgrade twenty-four hours earlier. He scanned the faces of the new arrivals, recognizing several Karageorgevich partisans among them. Evidently they had been waiting for news of the successful *coup d'état* and boarded the first train for Belgrade. Michael looked at them with a touch of envy, wishing he were like them, able to enjoy the victory without the regicide's irradicable images of horror and ugliness imprinted on his memory.

His fellow third-class passengers settled down on the wooden benches of the coach amid a great deal of noisy chatter. They were mostly workers and peasants. Michael pulled his hat down over his eyes, pretending to sleep, but tuning his ears to their talk.

The main topic of their conversation was Miss Denham and the strange customs and mentality of foreigners. Only after they had exhausted the subject from every angle did they switch to the regicide. They had all heard about it, and several versions were quoted inaccurately. In contrast with the crowds' roisterous attitude on the boulevards, their reaction was one of stoicism. Neither enthusiastic nor sorrowful, they agreed that Draga had "deserved it," condemning Alexander for having allowed a woman to keep him under her thumb. They seemed to entertain no definite feelings about Prince Peter, knowing nothing about him.

"One thing is sure," a man summed up the group's opinion. "He can't be much worse than Alexander."

Michael closed his eyes, and scenes flashed past his mind's eye as though projected from a magic lantern. The bestiality of the murderers, the icy courage of Laza Petrovich, the fantasizing of Apis Dimitriyevich. And superimposed upon them, the wild-stallion kolo of the assassins before the storming of the Konak. It had been a war dance, the kind of ritual practiced by the most primitive tribes of the globe: red Indians, savages of

Africa, aborigines of Australia. Warriors working themselves into a frenzy of courage and hatred. Self-hypnosis which caused a man to become impervious to either pity or pain. How could he ever have believed that after a barbaric prelude such as that kolo these Serbs would perform their parts in the *coup d'état* with the gallantry and restraint of medieval knights?

Shouts suddenly came from the direction of the station exit, followed by the thump of running feet. Looking out the window, Michael saw a detachment of frontier guards led by the passport clerk, approach his carriage. Michael cringed. No doubt the clerk had at last taken a look at the list, found his name on it and was coming to expel him from the train.

Much too exhausted to feel more than slight aggravation, he rose to collect his small traveling case from the net above the seat. Just then the runners thundered past his carriage, and peering after them, he spotted the object of the chase: the indomitable Miss Denham. Bored with the long wait, she had stepped off the train to take a walk on the platform and ventured past the sign written in Serbian NO PASSENGERS PERMITTED BEYOND THIS POINT.

With enough uproar to wake the dead, she was hustled back into her compartment, its door slammed shut and the conductor ordered to lock it and keep it locked until Zimony.

The stationmaster blew his whistle, and the wheels began to turn. Clerk and guards were lined up on the platform, their gaze fixed on Miss Denham, who leaned out the window and waved an enthusiastic farewell to them with her handkerchief. Their eyes followed the train until it rolled onto the Sava bridge; only then did they dare to heave a sigh of relief and return to their posts.

Staring at the frothy waters of the river, Michael wondered if he would have remained on his way to freedom if Miss Denham's appearance hadn't thrown the station personnel into utter confusion. He knew he would always remember her gratefully, not only for having saved him a great deal of unpleasantness, but for adding a bright touch to his unhappy departure with her blessed Anglo-Saxon lunacy of regarding travel in a country where the king and queen had just been slaughtered and their naked bodies thrown from their bedroom window as a "sporting event."

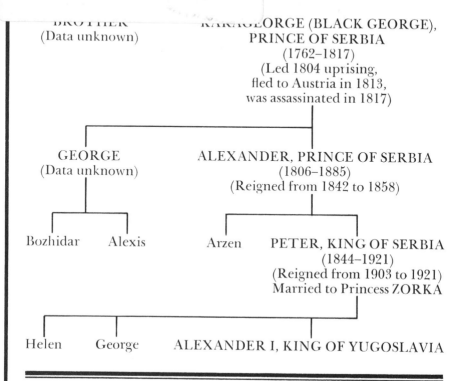

BROTHER
(Data unknown)

KARAGEORGE (BLACK GEORGE),
PRINCE OF SERBIA
(1762–1817)
(Led 1804 uprising,
fled to Austria in 1813,
was assassinated in 1817)

GEORGE
(Data unknown)

ALEXANDER, PRINCE OF SERBIA
(1806–1885)
(Reigned from 1842 to 1858)

Bozhidar   Alexis

Arzen   PETER, KING OF SERBIA
(1844–1921)
(Reigned from 1903 to 1921)
Married to Princess ZORKA

Helen   George   ALEXANDER I, KING OF YUGOSLAVIA

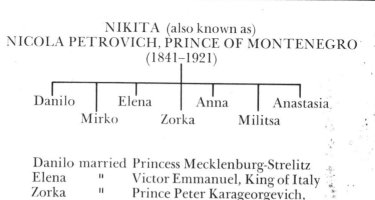

NIKITA (also known as)
NICOLA PETROVICH, PRINCE OF MONTENEGRO
(1841–1921)

Danilo   Elena   Anna   Anastasia
    Mirko   Zorka   Militsa

Danilo married Princess Mecklenburg-Strelitz
Elena   "   Victor Emmanuel, King of Italy
Zorka   "   Prince Peter Karageorgevich,
                later King of Serbia
Anna   "   Prince Francis Joseph Battenberg
Militsa   "   Grand Duke Peter
Anastasia "   Grand Duke Boris(?)